MY ONLY BOY

MY ONLY BOY

ROSA RANKIN-GEE

SCRIBNER

London · New York · Amsterdam/Antwerp · Sydney/Melbourne · Toronto · New Delhi

For Leah,
for her father, David,
and for our daughter, Mara.

'Britain, without volcanoes or Alps or forests, is in general a gentle and domesticated land that seems to be wholly under our control. Yet it is not really controlled. Lie awake at night even in our composed Britain and think how the land about you is changing every hour, as surely as your own body, and as irresistibly.'

JACQUETTA HAWKES, *A Land*

If you were one of very few people in the country who managed not to see the video, this is what you missed.

It starts in a pocket.

With the volume on, the rustling sounds almost like static, air catching in the microphone. And then light appears, a bloom then bust of brightness, as the room swings into view.

We lose the room, catch it, lose it – the camera swerves faster than an eye can – but there's a desk, and chairs, a wall of windows. People. People shouting.

A voice says 'no cameras'; another voice says 'fuck you'.

For a second, it goes dark again, the camera momentarily against the carrier's body.

And then it gets fast. The edges of the image rush. The man who's holding the phone starts to run. We hear the rub of his legs moving, his breath taking off. It sounds like a train picking up speed.

It's a balcony he's heading to. The door to the balcony is open. It was the start of the heatwave and stupidly, even though the air-con was on, the doors to the outside were as open as they could be. The man gets to the balustrade with the phone still in his hand – it clinks clean against the metal.

It might have all gone differently if the chair hadn't been right there. That made it easy. The man's foot hits the seat. The hand holding the

1

phone hits the metal again. As he lifts up one leg then goes for the next, as he clambers over the balustrade, the camera turns to face the sun directly and it's blinding. For a tiny moment, everything goes purely, shining white.

It's unclear if the phone stays in the man's hand, or strays just behind him, but the camera follows as he falls. Moving through the air, the sound the phone captures is almost like an automatic rifle, tt-tt-tt-tt-tt-tt-tt-tt-tt. The fall is longer than you want it to be. The phone lands a second after the man. There's a thud then crack, it goes black, and then light pours back in and readjusts the image.

Somehow the phone doesn't break. Instead, it points up, directly at the building, the nine storeys that took less than three seconds, and the balcony, which, by then, was where we were.

In the video, you can't see our faces, just the shapes of shoulders, heads, then the sound of screaming, quieter than you'd expect.

If you watched it, I was the one at the start who you heard saying 'no cameras'.

I was the most senior person in the room that day, and after everyone on the balcony stopped looking down over the edge and looked around instead, I was the one they all looked at.

It wasn't the first thing to go wrong. There had also been the phone call that morning, and after I'd hung up, how I thought I might lift up off my chair and stay there forever. And beyond that, there was the whole burning world.

No, it had already got bad before then. It's just that it was about to get worse.

PART I

PART I

1

There was an edge in the air, sharp enough to cut. It was the heat, but not just the heat. The whole of London was like a tinderbox. It was a bank holiday, and on the street, drinks had replaced phones in people's hands.

It was so hot you could smell the pavements, and the breeze was like being pummelled by a car exhaust. Bodies had flung themselves to beaches as if by centrifugal force, and all the headlines while we waited for news about the election attempted to blend the two things: *Meltdown Britain*, and a diptych of a man in speedos and a picture of parliament saying *Well Hung*.

Too much was happening. On Wednesday, the man had jumped; yesterday, Thursday, was the election; and today, Friday, we still didn't have a government.

Due to the bank holiday, our offices were closed, but I went in for a directors' meeting that had been called after lunch. Afterwards, I texted my friend Flo to say that I thought I might be having a panic attack in a cage.

A cage??? she replied.

A café

Oh

Are you ok?

I was kind of into the cage, she said later. *At least there's ventilation.*

It was too early for a heatwave. We'd gone from a freezing March to a fever-dream April, as if the sun had observed the turning of the page of the calendar. And I'd forgotten about the dinner at Sean's until the reminder email. *May as well drink while we wait for the locusts,* he'd said. I checked the address again. It was in Notting Hill. I hadn't been to West London for years.

Notting actual hill, I'd responded to the email weeks ago, *in a recession?* This was somewhat tongue in cheek since Sean did things of a highly dubious nature for a big bank. 'Believe me, babe,' he'd responded in a voice note, 'the prices have plummeted,' and he did the sound of a missile falling by whistling through his front teeth.

When I got there, the houses were lovely, ice-cream-coloured. Ex-models in leggings pushed prams or carried flowers, the only people in London not sweating. In contrast, I could feel all the seams of my clothes. The pundits on the news kept saying it was a dark day, but it was a very bright day for a dark day – the clocks had just gone forward, and polished car windows winked back at the still-high sun.

Sean called the dinners a series, The Friday Night Series, TFNS – which he pronounced tifnis, as if it were a venerated institution – but really it was mostly a collection of people with nothing more in common other than wanting to obliterate the week that had passed. The way braincells were smacked made me think of someone doing a break-off in snooker and really splitting all the balls. And I wouldn't have gone – I'd promised myself I wouldn't go back; I'd felt more and more out of place each time – had it not been for everything building.

As I got close to Sean's place, I noticed a man standing outside the front door. I watched him for a minute or so as I walked up the road. He appeared to be rifling through plant pots. Sean had – or claimed to have, because he did seem quite excited about it – a stalker for a while, and I wondered if this was him, though it wasn't really a question you could ask.

'He killed Rosemary,' the man said, when I got to the garden path. This wasn't good. 'Sorry?'

'Rosemary.'

'Who's Rosemary?'

'Rosemary the plant. I didn't know that was possible.' He reached over to pick up a piece. It was crisp brown, crushed. 'Looks like it was roasted with lamb. Though I guess the weather will do that.'

When he stood up, he was very tall. He made an instant shadow. I felt my neck tip. He had longish hair, held up in a rough bun. When he pressed the doorbell, I took another glance and noticed a tiny tattoo to the left of one eye.

I looked at the door number to check I was in the right place, but then the door swung open. It was close to eight and Sean was drunk already, his eyes glazed as a cake. Sean looked at the man, he looked at me. And then he winced. A wince I'd seen so many times in the past few days. 'I thought you wouldn't come!' he said to me. 'Because of—' he pulled his bottom lip taut.

'Sean, I didn't push him . . .' I said.

'Yeesh,' Sean said back, 'stone cold.' Then, as rapidly as it had come, the thought left him and he turned and looked with a kind of goldenness at the tall man. 'It's the prodigy!' he said. So, presumably not a stalker. 'I should alert the paparazzi about both of you. Do you guys know each other?' he asked, once, then twice, his tongue furred with exclamation marks.

'Old friends,' the tall man said. And that was when he looked at me directly for the first time. I looked back at him and for a second, it bounced between us.

We climbed the stairs up to the second-floor flat. At the entrance, there was yellow police tape along the metal carpet trim. My stomach bit into itself thinking of the same tape on the balcony at work two days ago. 'Urgent times call for urgent measures,' Sean said. 'Only joking, Zay bought it instead of a house gift, isn't it ugly? He says this is the line where the politics stops. So none of that,' he fell into a sing-song voice, '*it was all rigged.*' The tall man's eyes flicked at me again.

I realised when we walked inside what must have happened. Recession had contributed to the move, but not in the way Sean had suggested: this was one of Sean's parents' properties. 'Times are tough,' he said. 'The tenants here couldn't afford it anymore and G' – G was Goran, Sean's boyfriend – 'and I realised we were just spunking thousands every month in Haggerston, so needs must. Also, Robbie's sister hasn't had a job since graduating so I got her in to do cocktails. Big mistake,' he said under his breath, 'huge.' There were about a million cracked-open eggs on the counter, the yolks in sloppy, sci-fi-looking piles.

We were handed two sours in oversized martini glasses. 'And just to check,' the tall man said, 'these are vegan?' He looked at the eggs.

The cocktail provider looked back at him, her mouth slightly open. The thing was, he was very good-looking. It was hard not to notice. Something about the frame of bone and brown around blue eyes. Not murderer blue, but light enough. The neatness of his nose. The spade of his jaw.

'It's Pisco,' she said, the 'o' left wide.

'Well anyway,' he said. 'High in protein.' He took a sip. 'It's good. Thank you! Thank you so much. Sorry. I didn't mean to be rude,' he said, when she had gone. He turned back to me. 'That was rude, wasn't it? She's so young. It's just I haven't spoken to anyone all day. Longer than a day. My mouth has kind of forgotten how to move.' He took another sip, and I watched the acid of the lemon, or something not fully liquid, hit the back of his throat.

'What came first,' I asked him, 'the cocktail or the egg?'

He peered into his glass. 'There's actually a whole *yolk* in this one.'

'Well don't show off. Look—' I showed him what I was doing, turning to the side so he could see it in profile. 'Just sip around the edges. You can kind of turn your teeth into a sieve. For the albumen.'

He nodded then tried it. 'Very cold,' he said. 'My first albumen. All ten tracks.' And then we stood silent for a while.

I noticed Sean pointing at me, and the person he was talking to saying 'oh fuck,' before Sean shushed him. It was quite clear I shouldn't have come. I looked away from Sean and his friend, but couldn't really look at the man I was with either, and so I looked around him.

The TV was on, the news playing on mute. One person was watching it, but someone else put their jacket partly over the screen, not to censor it even, but just as if it were a hook. The tall man and I stood near the fireplace, underneath a family portrait which was huge and very confusing, the light falling in all the wrong ways.

'An original Rembrandt,' I said, pointing.

He nodded. 'I think it's one of his best.'

'How do you know Sean?'

'I don't really—'

'Me neither.'

'No, but I really don't. He's a friend of a friend. I'm in town for work and they said I should come by – it was before, all, you know.' He pointed at the TV and worry kicked around inside me again. 'What?' he said. 'Why are you looking at me like that? I am doing the tooth sieve thing. I'm trying, but it's not always easy.' He started to use a nail to pick his teeth.

'We're talking – what am I supposed to do? Shut my eyes?'

'Some of it's frozen.'

I did shut my eyes then. 'Let me know if you walk away,' I said.

I opened my eyes again and asked him if he'd ever tried red wine before. He said no, but he *might* have tried the white kind once: was it very different? I didn't mean to, but I found myself smiling. I could feel the muscles in my face shift into an arrangement they hadn't been used to the past few days. I tamped it down. 'Where is home normally?' I asked him. 'Are you "in town" from like, Greenwich, or something? Because you sound very much like you're English.'

'I am English. But I've been living in New York.'

'The Big Apple.'

'The biggest. It's weird to be here. There were so many journalists on my plane. You could literally hear the tapping.'

I pretended to type. 'T-h-e o-n-c-e g-l-o-r-i-o-u s B-r-i-t-i-s-h E-m-p-i-r-e . . .' I stopped myself. 'Don't they have enough to deal with back home?'

'Course,' he said. 'But new crises always have that little bit of lustre. They can get going on domino effects and the doomsday clock, or whatever. I don't know.' He looked around the room. 'It's different when it's your own country. At the airport, my passport felt so strange in my hand. Like it had a charge to it,' he said. 'Is that weird? Or is it normal? To feel protective? I don't know,' he said again. He had another tattoo on his arm, of the word 'sincerity'. I wanted to ask him if it was ironic. 'Have you ever not lived here for a while?' he said. I nodded. 'Isn't it weird when you come back? I'm saying weird a lot,' he smiled. 'But that brief moment where you can see it all. Before it settles into normal again.'

'It's not all, or always, like this,' I said.

There were other people there, lots of them, but somewhere over the course of the cocktail, we had walked backwards into our own island. Sean, our host, was a gay man who worked in finance. Most of the people in the room seemed to share one or both of these qualities. City boys in tailored shirts with Friday night red cheeks.

'I don't know what I expected but not this,' he said. 'I don't know how we keep . . .' his voice faded.

'Outdoing ourselves?'

'Exactly. And then today – in London anyway, I just would have expected some kind of sombreness. A wake.'

'A wake would be good,' I said. 'Or a sleep. Some kind of hibernation situation.' I looked at him. 'And all today, people were just . . .'

'Lying in the sun,' he said.

Something about him didn't make sense in the room. I kept on wondering why he was here. Whenever they edged close, the other men at the party seemed shy with him too. His height – he had at least a head on everyone else present – allowed him to scan the room and he looked all around it. Serious was maybe the word. Or substantial. I imagined saying that to Flo, and her saying 'Code for fat.' But it wasn't that.

I couldn't work out what he was looking at. When I followed his eyes they didn't seem to have landed on anything interesting. Maybe he was just bored.

On the jacket-covered TV, the headlines scrolled, too small to see. 'What do you think's going to happen?' he said. 'Also, at the door, when Sean looked at you, and his face melted—'

'A master of subtlety.'

'What was that about?' he said. I looked at him again. His eyes were kind when he said that, a tiny bit of crinkly crepe paper at their corners. Up close, they weren't blue actually, but grey, or changing, shot through with green. These threads of it, the way a palm leaf splits and spreads. And he changed too, that's the only way to say it. I kept on thinking of those posters with ridges that morph when you move around them. Double images: tethered, yet easy. Shyness, arrogance.

'It's not a great story. I've had a bad week. A kind of all-time worst

11

week—' I didn't want to talk about that. 'What about you? Why are you a prodigy?'

But then Sean clapped his hands above his head to call us to the table. We meandered in its direction, a slow strategic dance which I imagined was so we could find seats side by side. But then I felt a touch on the back of my head. It was Sean, who swerved me to the top of the table.

'Fuck, babe, tell me everything—' he said. He started to mime a jump, then stopped. 'It was in the news *loads*. Even election week. What happened?' he kept on saying. 'But really?'

Each time I attempted to reply, Sean looked from left to right, like a detectorist scanning for gold on the beach. I did not have the gold that he wanted. And rather than listen to what I was saying, he simply prepared the sentence he wanted to say next: very precise and horrifying details he must have read online. The word 'scrape', and how they'd found a piece of flesh or bone sixteen metres away from where the man landed.

'No Marion?' he said. Marion was a girl I'd been seeing until very recently. I told him it was over. 'Huh,' Sean said, and then he nodded in the direction of the waitress who had been shepherded in to sit on the other side of me, in a chair that didn't fit round the table. 'The egg slayer,' he whispered. 'Bit young but cute, no? Maybe you could cheer yourself up?'

I found myself blinking as if there were acid or smoke in the air. She couldn't have been much older than twenty. I reached for my drink. Sean had ordered food from a caterer and there was overwhelming parmesan in everything, in a way that swerved close to vomit. '*Brief* insider trading moment though,' he said, leaning back from his plate. 'Any idea how this will affect the IPO?'

'The jump or the election?' I said.

'Both. Either.'

'We have a year,' I said. Sean managed enormous portfolios. 'We'll make it work.'

'And the election shitshow. Any intel?'

'Sean, you know I'm not actually in government.'

'Yet!' he said. 'I mean good, you'd have lost your seat! But surely you have fingers in pies? Spies everywhere? No?'

I looked down at his lap, and noticed he was texting, his thumb moving like a saw.

I didn't drink to forget. I drank in a way that felt like someone pulling on the cord of a boat engine: make it start, make it interesting. Before things had ended, Marion had been strict about work emails at the table, so by force of habit, I'd left my phone by the door and couldn't check what was happening.

Sean's boyfriend Goran was on the other side of me. His eyebrows fanned towards each other like cards. When he noticed how frequently I was serving myself, he told me it would get better after the second bottle. 'Why do you think people in my country drink so much?' he said. Goran was Hungarian. 'A government like what's probably coming, forty percent of men are alcoholic. Enjoy,' he said, and he refilled my glass.

I asked him what the tall man I'd arrived with was called, and he said Ed.

It was a nice name, Ed. Kind of solid, like a stump of wood. I found myself looking at him across the table. When pudding was served, three different foil tins pulled floppy-bottomed from the oven, Ed had a bowl of each, and then seconds of one. He hot-crossed each portion into four big bites almost mathematically, then ate them one by one. He had this tidy way of sucking his spoon.

Talking to him had been the one thing that felt nice. Felt like jumping from lily pad to lily pad, a little danger on the leap, a tuck of joy on the landing. Even after everything, we'd stayed above water. This is what I was thinking as he put his napkin on the table, pushed his chair back, then stood up and dusted off his lap to let various crumbs disembark.

I must have been more drunk than I realised because as he got up to go to the bathroom, I looked at his body to see where it went. Nothing about his body pushed at the waist of his jeans. His skin seemed to hold inwards rather than out. Not thin though. Everything about him was broad, I remember thinking. Shoulders broad, neck broad. Even his ears were broad. Lobes that looked like they'd been squashed a little wider, clay between a thumb and a finger. Broad beans. He came by where I was sitting on the way. He asked me if I was having an alright time.

'An alright time,' I repeated. 'Your standards are—'

'Stratospheric.'

Maybe that was it. Time. Something about him did look like he was from another time, and not a recent time, sometime long ago, with swords maybe, or horses. Why would I tell him that? But I did tell him that, and he nodded, not meeting my eye really. 'A time where they didn't have hygiene or septic systems,' he said as he started walking away. 'Good.'

I watched him leave, and felt it happen inside me, autopilot, some kind of analogue recalibration: that things would be paused until he came back.

I went to get my phone. The screen was green with walls of missed calls, messages, tangles of news alerts, a whole papyrus scroll from my boss Daniel, who must have texted at that exact moment too, because his latest suddenly filled my screen. It was a screenshot from an article. The main picture was an aerial shot of the man's body. *This looks like it's taken from OUR balcony, does it not???? Find out who took it*

I swallowed. Or tried to. It seemed to get stuck halfway. Panic wasn't a feeling I was used to. But it came like it had come that morning, heat brushing up and down my body.

It was the way flashbacks rushed in, a terrible flickbook. The cool that had come over me in the seconds after the jump. How I'd gone straight from the balcony to block the boardroom doors and let people out as I needed them. Monitor news, monitor social. Get security, block off the road, keep people away, cover him up, do what you have to. And the ambulance of course. First. I think I did do that first. My voice steady throughout as I told people what to do, like I was ordering coffee.

'Are you going?' I heard Goran saying. I wrenched my mind back into the room. I looked up at Ed and noticed it too: the jacket over his shoulder, and his bag in his arms, like he was carrying a small body.

'Thought I might, yeah,' Ed said. Then he looked at me, and said more quietly, 'I'm finding it hard to be festive anyway.'

Earlier, when we'd been talking, I'd thought his eyes looked like they were used to smiling, those crepe paper edges, but he was not smiling now. 'They've called it,' he said. 'Well it's not called but, the full results are out. And it's – well, obviously, it's not good.' Ed looked around the room again, then back at me. 'Weird to say, but thank you for reminding me that some of it's okay.'

'What's it?'

'England?' He attempted to smile at least. 'No biggy,' he said.

'You're going to go right away?' I asked. It was something about the angle, me sitting, him standing – he looked like he was cut out from another place, a figure moving against a green screen.

I waited for an 'Okay one more then', or 'Okay, one for the road', or 'Okay, because it's all gone wrong', but none of those came.

A little crescent of drunk people had migrated to the sofa seemingly to shout at each other. Guillotine hands chopped emphatically.

Then Ed, by the door, turned back round. 'Hey,' he said to me, 'do you want to come?'

'Come? Where?'

'I don't know, just leave here.'

He didn't seem to care if anyone heard.

I looked at the window in the hallway tight with coats left over from the last of March. It still had the illusion of being bright outside, cuts of pink cloud that seemed to make their own light. I wondered if it would still be hot out there.

'We could walk,' I said.

Full moons, heatwaves. Mad dogs, Englishmen. A feeling that the end was all around us. The least you can do is things you normally wouldn't.

2

I followed Ed down the stairs. 'What's the plan then?' I said. 'Storm parliament?' I tried to make it sound light, but everything felt heavy.

'I don't know why but I keep wanting to say sorry,' he said.

'Did you not vote?'

'I voted. I'm still sorry.'

Something passed between us at the bottom of the stairs. He didn't want to be the one to tell me out loud, or I didn't want him to be the one, as if it would somehow make it his fault. The door, too – it seemed to take on a new meaning. As if, while it stayed shut, and we stayed in the dark of the hallway, it might not have happened yet.

'Could we pause it a little longer?' I said. 'I mean, can I? Just for a few minutes.'

'Okay. If you're sure.' He turned the handle and pushed the door open.

'Brave new world,' I said.

'Weak old world,' he said back.

As we left Sean's building, the sound of the party upstairs poured out of wide-open sash windows. We walked without talking at first, like our silence could make up for their noise.

It was warm enough to be daytime. The jacket in his hand stayed in his hand. His shoulders seemed even bigger in the dark. My head almost had to move to look from one shoulder to the other. I don't remember everything we talked about.

'I've read about this,' I said eventually. 'You can't lead me down a dark alley.'

'Stupid rules. Hey, I'm sorry you had a bad week and then all this came along to crown it.'

He asked me what happened, but I couldn't afford anymore flashbacks rushing in. We'd slowed to a stop. I knew time was running out. I felt hot, but we'd been walking. And so I looked at my phone, the unchecked notifications.

As 22 new parties gain seats, the British two-party system, a force for balance for the past 200 years, dismantled.

I opened the article, started scanning it. 'Unprecedented outcome,' I said, my voice flat. 'Why can't anyone ever precedent anything?'

'I know.'

'And what does it even mean?' Normally I could scan documents at an ungodly speed, but I almost couldn't read. I thought of one of those kids' toys. The words had turned into shapes, and I couldn't find the right holes for them to slip through.

'They'll all be scrambling to get the numbers for a coalition,' Ed said. He pulled up a graphic a friend had sent. 'I mean look at it, it's so split. Labour's asking for a recount – 'cos look at that.' He zoomed in closer.

I flicked to my market app to look at futures and overnight movements. Not a free fall exactly, but a huge tumble.

'That's got to be less than fifteen percent,' he went on. 'And there's a whole bunch of nutters in there. Like we all collectively decided to jump off a cliff.'

I had another flashback to the man jumping, and the ground underneath me really did seem to move, a hand tugging on a tablecloth. The thud, a flinch.

'Are you okay?' he said, like he could see the ground move too.

My mouth was so dry I couldn't even imagine water. I tried to read another article; Ed was looking at his phone too. 'I feel like if we were in a film, we'd be standing in front of a TV shop watching it play out on multiple screens,' he said.

'If we were born in the sixties—' I tried to say, but my voice was barely working.

'Yeah,' he said. 'If only. I mean how bad was the Cuban Missile Crisis *really*?'

We'd paused mid-crossing on a big road. In the traffic island, in the middle, the edges raised like braille, it struck both of us, I think. He looked at me. I looked at him. I looked at his feet. For a second I thought of ballet positions. First, second. Had he stepped closer to me? Should I step back?

It was also that I hadn't said it yet, that I wasn't interested. Not like that. Normally I always said it quickly. My choice to take cards off the table, shape the way the rest of the conversation went. I hadn't done that. I stood still. He did too.

'I have a place I'm staying if you want to, I don't know, watch a disaster film,' he said.

I looked at my wrist even though I wasn't wearing a watch.

'Lars von Trier,' he continued. 'Put some Wagner on and stare into the incoming meteor—'

'Maybe,' I said. 'I'm not sure.'

I could see the tussle in him, back and forth. He hadn't been looking at me when he said it, the sentences just building in the air, and then, as quickly as they came, he undid them. 'Or just a drink,' he said. 'Except I only have water back at the flat, and also – I don't know.' He looked at me and it was like he was trying to work out a maths problem. 'Anyway.'

I remember being aware of my lips, where they were on my face, being aware of his. Wanting to look away. Wanting to run away. Doing neither.

He finished his maths. 'I don't think I should,' he settled on.

I started to understand then. It landed in little drops, the kind that make you look up, the beginning of rain. A girlfriend, of course, or a wife. A guitar string inside me twanged.

'Where are you staying?' I said. 'I won't come, don't worry. You can save the *Tristan and Isolde* for another time.'

'East,' he said, and he arranged his body, east. Mostly, it felt, because he wanted to turn away from me.

'You can do that?'

'By the stars,' he said. 'By the stars, and my phone.' He smiled, and it was a nice smile. A little bit of un-straightness to his bottom teeth. He said he'd drop me off in a car. Then clarified: not a car he'd be driving.

'Don't worry,' I said. 'There aren't going to be riots in the street. Or . . . I don't know. Maybe.'

'Maybe,' he said. 'There should be.'

When the car arrived, it smelled of pine and chilled air. As it took us away from Notting Hill, or Bayswater, which is roughly where we'd walked to by then, we saw no riots.

We passed a man living in a play tent for kids. There was a swastika on a nearby wall, but it was old, and maybe backwards. We looked for signs that other people had noticed, that it mattered. But the world doesn't stop. It's all always happening all together, all at once.

In the car, the radio played Darondo 'Didn't I', before it changed to the news, before – even quicker – it changed to techno. I kept thinking: how does it all exist at once?

Something sat between us in the middle seat of the car, a new awkwardness maybe. Ed smoothed out his palms like they were pieces of paper. I looked again at the tiny tattoo by his eye. It was of a 'J'. I remember thinking, there are still questions I can ask him. We can stay talking.

I asked him to talk to me about something else that wasn't the election, and he told me he loved being driven by his dad as a kid. The way if you sit side by side with someone you can talk about anything. 'I don't even think we talked about much,' he said, 'but we had the best chance of it, if you know what I mean? You're allowed to be silent, and just look.'

Mostly we were silent and just looked.

We slid by swoops of Georgian terraces and the Union Jack colours of chicken shops. When we slowed at a set of traffic lights, I thought a woman on a bench was hyperventilating but she was just eating a pastry out of a brown paper bag with her eyes closed.

I had grown up in London but I felt such a distance to it now. Everything was repeated and repeated and repeated. Highlighted hair and cheeks, and jewellery shifting from gold to silver back to gold again, the crowds outside pubs, and the sound of it, the same on every corner, like stock footage. Men in going-out shirts and Boohoo ads, and the way that everyone kept saying 'so you're back now', like I would never leave again.

Ed looked out of the window like his eyes were eating. He spun a ring on his finger with his thumb. It wasn't on his ring finger, but maybe he'd moved it. These were only notes of thoughts. Quiet ones, keys half-pressed on the piano.

And then I noticed something on his cheek and thought it must be raining. The way rain can come in the heat. But I looked up, his eyes were wet too.

'Sorry,' he said, wiping them away quickly with his sleeve. 'I think it's – it's all the times I've been here before. How fast it's all gone. Or goes,' he corrected. 'Or jet lag—'

'Or societal breakdown—'

'Or that. But you know, that's old news.' He reached for a bottle of water in the door pocket. 'My dad was a crier. These big sobs. Like a human bagpipe.' He tried to laugh.

Ed's hand was on the seat between us. He stretched out his fingers. I knew that feeling, what was happening inside his hands. The desire to let it out, the desire to escape. I put my hand not on top of his but near to it. He moved his hand closer to mine, and then I did the same. We didn't hold our whole hands. Just a few fingers.

'It's so stupid,' Ed said, looking out the window again. 'You know that clocks don't stop. Rationally, you know that, we all do, but—'

'You want people to stop too . . .' I said. I thought about work: what it would look like now. Everything I'd have to do. 'But they can't.'

South of where we were, people did lie down in front of parliament. Broke through barriers because the roads around it were closed. Maybe. Though that might have been the next night, or the one after. A lot of things happened.

'But I guess London is London,' I said. 'Just like New York is New York. You turn a corner and it all disappears.'

At some point, the crossroads near my house came into view. The car speaker told us we were approaching our destination.

'I'm not here for long,' Ed said. 'After all that. If you want to. I'd like to see you again.'

3

In bed, the room did soft circles, back-and-forth half-pipes.

My brain did circles too, a paintbrush moving against a wall. The thought of Marion rushed in. Marion who'd been there 'til a week ago. She'd played the piano so perfectly, so delicately, that a neighbour had once waited outside our door until she was finished, then knocked to find out what the music was. I took a deep breath as if making space in my lungs would make me feel something about losing her. But as I held it, other things flooded in instead. I imagined rain coming in through the open window of the boardroom and hitting the long table. The sound of the man's body landing, how it landed in the base of my belly too. The call before it all happened that morning. Everything.

My circles traced around for something good to settle on, in the same way that my hand traced around the bed looking for my phone. I fell asleep before I got to either.

4

The next day, Saturday, I was late for lunch at Flo's house. But she was later. As in, still not awake when I got there.

Her face when she got to the door. Pillow welts that looked like whip marks. 'Why did we say so *early* though?' she said. She was wearing one of her muumuus.

'Flo, it's one p.m.—'

'Anyway, it's good you're here, I was just having the most terrible dream about you.'

I looked at her standing in the doorway. Flo had something Rossetti-ish about her. Her hair wasn't red, but there was a mass of it, a tumble, and her mouth had such a strong shape that when she wore lipstick she looked, from a distance, like she must have gone over the lines.

'What dream?'

'Oh, just anxiety dreams because you've been through so much? I don't know, my brain's just transformed it.'

We walked into her living room. The low bamboo table in the centre was strewn with bottles that suggested the end of the cupboard: Amarula, Tia Maria, Plantation Rum.

24

'People over?' I said.

'People,' she said, 'person.'

She was sleeping with her PhD supervisor. He had the air of being almost middle-attractive in his university website photos but only because they were very old. 'He's not as good-looking as that in real life,' she'd told me, and I looked at her out of the corner of my eye. He had a wife, of course, and he had three teenage children, of course, and obviously – obviously – he came to Flo's house so he could be a teenager himself.

She called him The Professor. TP for short. I told her people used that for toilet paper but it hadn't put her off.

'It's all very self-aware, you know?' she'd say. 'We joke about it.' ('Ah,' she'd also said once, 'good old self-awareness. A smart casual jacket we put on the shoulders of shit.')

'There are nice men out there now,' I said. Ed from the night before flicked into my mind. 'Normal and nice and not even ...' what was the word? 'horrible.' I wondered whether I'd have shown her a picture if I'd had one. I wondered if they'd be good together.

'I heard!' she said. 'Three of them apparently. Have to go at them with a bow and arrow.' She held her phone up like a mirror, then typed in her passcode instead. 'Doesn't recognise me. The shame of it. The shame of everything. Can you believe it? Also, sorry about Marion,' she reached over and gave my hand a light, tender scratch. 'I know she was truly the textbook definition of a rebound, but she really did have amazing legs.'

'Amazing legs,' I agreed. The type of legs people would say are 'up to here', then touch their shoulder.

'And crucially, she wasn't Bonnie.' She did a dad thumbs up: good job. 'For which I will always be grateful—'

Bonnie. The call from Bonnie. But I couldn't talk about Bonnie right now.

Flo knocked some books and a bra onto the floor to make space for us on the sofa. There was something comforting about it, the way she did it with her foot. I wondered occasionally if I had something in common with TP, in that I liked to come to her house for the time-travel back to a world arrested in the chaos of our twenties, particularly when my own life was so different now.

'It'll be okay,' I said. I flicked a tiny piece of old bread off the seat before I sat down. 'The Marion stuff.'

I told Flo it was hard to make myself feel anything. After the jump, someone from work had sent the team a supposedly inspirational affirmation saying there might be a gap between experience and feeling. It made me think of the gap in double glazing, everything insulated and harder to reach.

Flo gave me a hug then and the smell of her took me in a million different directions. 'Did he stay over?' I asked.

'No,' she said. 'Not all of it.' We sat as we always sat, opposite ends of the sofa, but legs entangled in the middle. 'But this is where it all played out.'

'Where what played out?' I arched my back to lift myself off the cushions.

'Last night! Viewing party, booing party. Then it got "real"' she did the speech marks, 'and he said he should "be with his family."' The speech marks got more extreme. 'His wife and his kids were texting. Is it wrong to say I felt something each time a new thing happened? When they were like, *never in British history have we seen results like this.* Like, there's a thrill in it building even if it's awful? He was holding my hand really tight like I was experiencing *history* with him.' She half laughed.

'And he'd know,' I said.

'What? Oh, 'cos he's elderly. Anyway, I hate it all. That voting slip was like the ravings of a madman. Did you understand it? It was like, *two* fucking pages. And even I didn't really get the whole first then second then third thing. It's fucked. I'm swearing a lot which is a further sign of my being stupid.'

'It's all fucked,' I said. 'I think a man even tried to invite me back to his last night.'

'What? Are you okay? Honestly, yesterday was disgusting.' She blew out. 'At least it takes the heat off your stuff. I mean, does it even?'

She hadn't seen me since the man had jumped. She did the obligatory wince, and I felt the familiar washing machine start to spin behind my belly button. Slow, splashy. That thump where it hit the bottom. 'It's not "my stuff"' I said. 'Things like that, there are always complex issues happening in the background.' That was a sentence I'd tried to tell myself anyway. 'It's not like it was my fault.'

'No but you were there.'

'I was there.'

I looked away from her. She was sitting on my shirt. I tried to pull it out from under her without her realising. Her vape hung out of her mouth as she looked at her phone. 'Why the fuck isn't there any *actual* news? Why is it just random people we know making statements like they're the diplomatic service of a nation state? We don't even fully know what's happening yet ...'

She was always able to look at six screens at once, even on her phone. '*In tucked-away rooms, policies are no doubt being horse-traded,*' she read from an article. '*Who knows what reciprocal concessions and nothing-to-lose bargaining is happening behind closed doors.* Whoopee yet again.' She exhaled upwards in a way that made me think of a train. 'Can you explain it to me? Like I'm an idiot.'

'*Like* you're an idiot?' I said.

'But you won't have to work with them?'

'Flo, obviously—' I said. I stopped. I felt the panic start to begin its laps inside me again.

I said we should be outside. But she said it was too hot and that the sun would age us. She looked around the room, and I could tell she was looking for signs from last night, like there would be a clue that would answer a question. 'Sometimes I wonder if I love him,' she said. 'TP. I fucking hope I don't. But sometimes I feel this ... trick in my chest like I do. Do you know what I mean?'

I nodded.

'Sometimes I feel a desire to say it, but what I think I really mean is I'm happy,' Flo said. 'Sometimes I think that's what love is. I love you, by which I mean these crisps are delicious and the weather is nice and I've had a sip of beer and I'm happy, you know?'

'What if you're crying and begging someone not to leave you?' My brain flicked back to Marion a week ago. A pinch came, or perhaps I made it.

'Well. That's like saying I'm *not* happy.'

'Okay.'

'Or I'm scared. It just means *you affect me.*'

'I thought you said it was crisps and weather,' I said. 'This is your PhD thesis, right?'

I was trying to be normal, but the panic kept coming in surges. Suddenly it was sharp behind the bridge of my nose, the desire to cry. 'Do you think there's any chance it might be okay?' I said.

'It was all a dream,' she said. 'I used to read *Word Up* magazine.'

'Seriously though. What are we going to do?'

'We?' she said. 'You're the one in trouble.'

'But in general—' I looked at her.

'Same thing we do every day, Pinky,' she said. 'Shout into the internet.'

5

When I got home, I said hello to the air even though I didn't need to.

Marion hadn't been there very long. We'd only been going out since October, but because she'd had a tricky roommate situation, she'd moved in quicker than either of us thought was a good idea. And in that moment, when things had started to get bad at work, there was something homely about her. She'd shopped for a whole week in advance, lit candles. She'd made me get a Christmas tree. I'd found it almost unbearably hot to watch her cook or clean. I'd tell her it turned me on, and she'd move her underwear to the side so I could see everything, then tell me I needed therapy.

Speaking of therapy, early the next morning, a text came through on my personal number: *Hey Ellen!* (That was not my name) *I'm here whenever you want to talk :)*

As a response to the jump, at our directors' meeting on Friday, our Head of People had announced a collaboration with a digital therapy start-up. Everyone who was in the office that day was eligible for three hours' credit, and those who were in 'the room where it happened' would have twice that.

The Ellen message followed a call from an unknown number,

which obviously no one would pick up. Then a second message came through offering fifteen percent off a de-stress massage, subtitled *tantalising*.

Other flashes from Friday's meeting stuttered into my mind. My waves of nausea in the lift on the way up, imagining the same journey downwards much faster. The way Daniel still looked entirely unaffected: drinking coffee from a transparent plastic water bottle meant for exercise that steamed up like a shower. 'All great leaps forward have costs,' he'd said. 'But in the scheme of things, we must see that those costs are pixel small.' Right after it had happened, it might have been exactly what I'd hoped he would say, but it was the way he pressed his finger and thumb to make the pixel now, so hard both fingertips lost blood. He tilted the conversation to the election.

'Whoever, *whatever* it turns out to be,' he'd said, 'we make it fucking work. Your policy team ...' It was me he looked at. 'Your little Westminster goal hangers. All that shit. We just make it work. We all know what year it is.' As ever, the room was compelled to nod. 'IPO year. Runway to IPO. This is it. This is fucking it.' Bolded, italicised, underlined. 'The British public can vote in a bunch of flying dwarves for all I care. Eyes on the prize,' he said, and looked at me again.

How was that only two days ago? Back in my kitchen, there was still dirt on the shelf from where Marion had taken away kitchen plants.

A message broke the reverie. Not one message. Many. A series of messages from my father.

Not a good day today. Many reasons but mum. Love, dad.

She would still love to see you though she is saying. Love, dad.

When you come if could bring oranges for her and also flowers, that would make her happy love dad.

It was Sunday. I'd forgotten I was supposed to go and see them. My mum was ill. It was one of the reasons I had come home from Lisbon, where I'd been living, though home was not really where I had gone. Was not really where I wanted to be.

Of course! I wrote back. I sent a flotilla of hearts.

When I look back at messages to my parents from that time, they're hard to bear. It was the contrast to who I was everywhere else in my life. My stoniness at work – all through the beginning of my career, I'd challenge myself to see how few words I could use in an email; now, if direct reports sent long emails full of brackets and caveats, I'd simply reply 'try again' – and then myself-self, or at least my old self, with Flo. With my parents, however, I had this new garish expansiveness, shiny as sweets, anything to keep spirits high. I'm sure spirits were not what they wanted from me, but they were all I brought.

Often, when they spoke about my mum's illness, I could not hear anything. I would ask them to repeat what they had said, even if it was simple. When a question came up later – and you, Elle, which route do you think sounds better? – they would have to start everything again. I couldn't remember the name of medicines. I couldn't look at her sometimes, even when she seemed fine.

Also I have to talk to you about something. Sensitive. Sorry Love dad

The last bit of the origami of dread folded into place.

I got dressed. Questions about my life, too. There would be questions about my life. And I knew what would happen. It would all play out in the opening seconds when I got there.

They could often detect things that weren't there. Colds that never came. Worries that didn't exist until they said them into being.

I would go. I wouldn't. I played both scenarios until it was long past the time I should have left.

Dad, I wrote, *I'm so sorry. I got to the train station.* I was sitting in my house. *My boss called. Big emergency. You know what the week was like – a nightmare.*

Ok . . . we're watching the news . . .

31

Sunday sitting, love dad.

And at the same time, Flo texted too. *Are you watching this?*

The way news unfolded now, it made me think of market traders with walls of screens. I had my phone, I was being sent things. The flashing red dots of live news, breaking and breaking and breaking.

A coalition – roaming, ranging, but mostly hard to the right – had managed to get the numbers. They'd called themselves the Alliance for Britain. It was there in black and white, oddly solid to see it printed so fast, on a cheap-looking podium. I tried to scan faces to see if I recognised anyone, but I didn't. Not a single face.

A section was playing called 'Meet the Kingmakers', and with very little preparation time, it attempted to introduce some of the new MPs.

All these single issue fuckfaces, Flo texted.

The voting form had looked more like a list of ideas. *End Austerity, Save Pettiford NHS Trust!, Student Loans Should Be Illegal.* Things like that. But those weren't the ideas on the screen now.

Already, there was footage emerging of far-right salutes, because, well, of course.

LOVE how they don't even deny it anymore, Flo wrote.

Remember when they used to be like, it's a deep fake!

Don't mind me, I was only dancing!

O the glory days . . .

The Alliance had rallied around a woman called Michaela Liddle, a fringe player until very recently.

She's quite fit?? Flo texted, a constant livestream.

Is she??

She was Northern. Made a joke, frequently it turned out, that her accent got stronger with every mile further north she drove up the M1. She was 41 but she looked younger. I googled her; scanned through a barely-there, bubbling-up-in-real-time Wikipedia page.

'Recently, we've had a lot of showboats up here,' she said in her acceptance speech. It was Leeds, her accent. She played with the lethargy of it, these slow forward rolls. 'Grandstanders. Boasters. Blaggers. Not to forget the dullards,' she smiled briefly, then cut it like an engine. 'But now it's time for hard work.'

My thumb did its automatic flick to check the FTSE. The market seemed to be holding its breath.

In the questions – she only took three – someone asked her about small boats.

'Small boats,' she said. 'Retro. It's big boats I worry about. People have been calling it an invasion. *Scary.*' She paused. 'Have they never seen one? This – right now – this is the calm before the storm. And what do you do before a storm?' She looked up at the camera and let the viewer answer the sentence.

On a stage, the Alliance stood together and all raised their hands up. They roared.

I can smell their breath through the TV, Flo texted.

I opened a bottle of wine I'd intended to keep. What was the point of keeping anything? And then an unknown number flicked its green ribbon onto my screen.

Hi, it's Ed, it said.

From the end of the world

A piece of string in my stomach pulled tight.

I feel I've lost the power to say anything interesting.

Not that I ever had it

A stupid question, but how are you doing?

I thought of us on the traffic island, cars rushing on either side. The speed around us, the quiet where we were. The way my brain had told me, like it was getting the numbers wrong and making a miscalculation, you will remember this.

But what could I say to him? There was so much to say that it shrunk to nothing.

6

In the car to work, the driver took corners sharply. Pinball angles. He had a talk radio show on and some guy who'd called in was so brimming over with pride, the host said, 'Don't explode, mate – I can almost hear your skin getting tighter.'

The driver and I sat in silence. I scanned the news. They'd changed the formatting of the page. It was almost all black. I refreshed my emails. A new millefeuille rattled in, layer after layer of absolute shit.

Crisis comms

PR on JD incident URGENT

New gov – war room today

Protestors outside RIGHT now

WHERE THE FUCK IS ELLE

The driver turned the steering wheel so hard it was like he was playing a game where you got more points the quicker you did it. We got into streets I knew. I sat forward so I couldn't feel my heartbeat against the seat. Then, in the vase-shaped gap between the two front seats, I saw the office building.

Tall, metal, it slapped back the sun. The protest was worse than the pictures I'd been sent so far, either unaffected by the weekend's news or bigger because of it. There were three tents, one more like a small gazebo. Someone was pouring coffee or tea into polystyrene cups. There were signs everywhere. Blood, hands.

Then, 'I just remembered . . . ' I found myself saying. A sensation that defined my younger years: being suddenly afraid on the street. How I would look at my watch as if I were late to justify running. 'Can I change the address?'

'I got jobs—' the driver said. He tapped on the screen of his phone with his fingernail.

'Just somewhere close.'

He pulled nearer to the office as he did the U-turn. In red paint, poured rather that painted, they'd put the shape of a body on the street.

I got the driver to take me to Oxford Street. I don't know why, maybe it reminded me of weekends as a teenager. When I got out of the car, even in the early morning, the sun was a punch. The smell of chips, new trainers, stalled buses, plywood windows. I was in front of a shop called Tennerland, and I could almost feel the static coming off the clothes inside. For the first time since childhood, I thought of spontaneous combustion.

It was 9.15 a.m. now. People would be arriving at the office. I'd tried to push it down, aside, away, at bay all weekend, but it rushed in now and wouldn't stop coming. It was how I'd barely paused, like I always barely paused. And all the other things you don't see in the video. How, after I'd broken the news to Daniel, after I'd spoken to the police, I couldn't breathe properly when I got back to my desk. Up-down, up-down, like I'd run up stairs, but I was just sitting still. A kid on my team had come to my office door. She'd teetered on the threshold.

'What's happening on social?' I'd asked her, as she took a step in.

'There are pictures—' she'd said. 'There's a video.' And then she leaned forward and vomited. The sudden smell of acid, heat. I'd tried to clean it up with junk mail leaflets and it slid off the paper.

But it was after she left that it really happened. It was when I watched the video she'd told me about and saw what everyone else had seen. That was when something had finally broken.

And then, right there on Oxford Street, I was no longer in my body. I was a camera moving in circles around me.

I sent a message to work, but it took longer than it should have because my hands were shaking.

In shortly. Dealing with something urgent – five attempts on that word as I couldn't get my thumb to hit the T.

I kept on seeing the red body on the street. It flickered: paint, then the man himself, then paint, then the man.

The panic might come in waves. That was another message the text therapist had sent. *Remember waves pass, remember to breathe in between them.*

Ed came into my mind. I don't know why that happened. I opened his message. I could feel my heart beat in the tips of my fingers now.

Hi, I wrote.

It didn't make sense to do it.

Sorry for not replying before
It would be great to meet

He wrote back right away.

Oh hi! For a moment I thought you'd given
me the flirt divert number . . .

What about now? I wrote.

Don't you have a job you hate?

I do, I said.
Are you free?

7

He suggested we meet at the British Museum. I wondered if I was having a breakdown, except there wasn't much to wonder about. I had never missed work before.

The café, when I got there, was bigger than I remembered; echo-y as soon as I stepped inside. I saw Ed from behind. From the way his head was moving it looked like he was reading. I stopped for a moment. I wanted to prepare something to say. I also had the profound sensation of wanting to turn around and leave.

'Strange day to choose this place,' I said.

'Oh, I don't know,' he replied. He half stood up to say hello, but the table got in the way. 'Just thought I would revel in my heritage. See everything our great ancestors stole.' He smiled but he looked like he hadn't slept. 'Mainly, I just thought there would be air-con ...'

'Ah. So that's why the security was crazy.' On my way from Oxford Street, a national alert had made a chorus of phones blare out in people's pockets. A red exclamation mark; the risk of social unrest had been put up to its highest level. There had been full bag searches to get into the museum, even after airport-style security.

At first I found I couldn't look at him straight on. A fear that I had remembered him wrong. That he would be different at midday with the clarity of sun, even if the sun was outside. That I would like him, that I wouldn't. It's hard when you've got on with someone before. Something to lose, something like that.

'I was glad to get your message,' he said. 'I wondered if you'd reply. I don't know.' He looked at me. 'I was confused about whether to write.'

'What is this?' I started. 'Some kind of radical honesty thing?' But then I heard my phone start to ring, and I felt in my pocket to silence it.

'No. Just.' He shrugged. 'I did think about it.'

He looked worried, a bounce between his eyebrows. Maybe he was nervous. Maybe it was just the situation. He was wearing a baseball cap, the brim bent a little in a V. His hair had dried like he'd been swimming in the sea. My eyes surfed over him. I wondered if he thought I looked the same, or different, or if he wasn't even thinking about anything like that at all. That double image again, a change whenever I shifted in my seat: maybe he was awful? Maybe whatever I liked, I'd got wrong. Words suddenly crowded in like passengers trying to board a full train: straight, white, male, arrogance.

'Was it the first time you'd ever been with a woman that didn't pounce on you?' I said.

'No,' he said, 'far from that.'

It struck me how absurd it all was then, to be sitting with a stranger, today of all days. The protest outside work, the changing of the guard at Westminster. 'I don't even know what it is you really do,' I said. 'Apart from being a prodigy.' My lips shaped it sharply, partly because my phone wouldn't stop buzzing.

'I'm a writer actually,' he said.

'Why actually?'

'What do you mean?'

'I don't know. It sounds a bit like, can you believe it?'

I could see it in his face, confusion at a simple thing: you were nice to me last time. And I saw it going wrong. Something I knew could happen: my capacity to ruin things, once a tiny ruining had begun.

'Well I don't mean it like that.'

'Only writer I've ever seen with a face tattoo,' I said. I tried to make that softer. 'Who's J?' I asked. 'J for JK Rowling?'

'Who else?' he said. 'No, J for someone I loved.' The silence wasn't long, but it stretched. 'Are you okay?'

'I walked out of work to meet someone I barely know. I'm—' I said. But I looked at him and stopped. 'How long do you have?'

'Well evidently I'm unemployed,' he said. 'And always looking for material.'

It was the way he looked at me, the openness of his face. 'My mum's ill,' I told him.

'How ill?'

'Ill-ill. So bad-bad. Oh, and I broke up with someone.'

'How long ago?'

How long ago had Marion left? 'A week ago. Ten days?' It seemed like so much longer. 'But there was another one, a bigger one, before that—'

'I'm so sorry,' he said. They're easy words to say, but it really did sound like he meant them. It felt like a knife, the tip of the blade, down the back of my spine, someone being kind to me.

'It's okay,' I said. 'And it's not even that. It's also stuff that's been happening at work. Sean's face when he saw me at the door—'

'Well at least the world hasn't gone to shit . . .' he said.

'At least that.'

'My friends in New York are all sending me condolence messages. Or like, Welcome to the Club. Here to support you too, brother,' he said. 'What am I supposed to say? Thanks?' He stopped. 'And actually, I think I do know why I messaged you.' He paused again and allowed himself to think. I watched it happen. So few people did that. 'Something about being bound together by the moment? Is there a phrase for that? Probably in Finnish or something. You want some?' he asked, pointing down at his plate. 'It's almost nice, almost horrible.'

He offered me his fork. I took a bite of his cake. My phone started to vibrate again and it went on for so long this time that whoever it was must have been calling me twice in a row.

'And it's not just the air-con,' he said. 'There's something comforting about knowing how long time has gone on for. That it's not just *this*, now—'

'Thanks,' I said. I moved my leg so I could feel my phone less.

'Not you,' he said. 'Just what we were saying in the taxi. How life just continues.' He looked around us, then pointed, proof: the shrieks of groups of school kids in miniature high-vis jackets.

'I'm doing my bit,' I said. 'I'm in the British Museum on a Monday.'

'Rosie the Riveter,' he said. 'Where should you be?'

Each time I thought about work, it was like my stomach was a mine, and someone was taking a chisel to it. 'We haven't expanded into the US yet, so perhaps you've been spared the word Gigr?' I said. I hoped he had. Slightly safer than the current situation, I cherry-picked him through the villain origin story. How it had started as a platform where entertainers – musicians, comedians – could sign up to fill a spot at an event. 'The amazing thing was,' I said, 'they got to work for free.'

'For free!'

'Exposure. And the beautiful twist, of course, was that Gigr got paid. They had these cheesy names then: GigrWatt if you wanted to do it more than once a week. Gigglr if you just wanted to do it occasionally.'

'And what now?' he said.

'Our tagline is "make work work".' I looked at the café staff. They probably worked through Gigr now. Maybe even the museum attendants did. 'We're everywhere.'

After we'd finished his bad cake, we wandered through the Enlightenment room, other rooms too. I tried to focus – the dogs on Greek vases the colour of eggs; ringlets rendered immaculately in stone – but every few minutes my phone would buzz into me again. I pointed at a couple ahead of us and said that when I was young, that was what I imagined dates would be like.

'And what were they actually?' Ed said.

'Underage discos and oversized tongues.'

'What an image,' he said. 'All mine took place in Costa.'

He put his arm out for me and I linked mine in his, and I noticed it more than I thought I would, the place where our bodies were touching.

I asked him what he wrote about when we left the building. We were hovering on the steps outside and they were so hot I could feel the stone through the heels of my shoes. New groups of kids were arriving in caterpillar formations. This group had caps on with flaps at the back to cover their necks.

'I don't know. So far,' he said. 'Mostly things about young, um ... people?'

He looked distracted suddenly. I noticed his tallness in a different way.

'And how do you do that when we're old?'

'Imagination,' he said. 'Just really work the cogs. I wrote it – my book, I have a book coming out – when I was young. I worry about that actually. Listen,' he said. 'I don't know if it's weirder if I say it or I don't say? But I'll say it because there do seem to be a lot about. I think they made a mistake, or over-ordered or got a deal, I don't know but, yeah.' He was speaking fast. 'That's mine,' he said. 'Me.' He pointed, then did something between a wink and a wince, one eye shrinking to a star.

His finger guided my eyes to a big billboard poster on the street facing the museum. The glue gave it a gleam.

The book was called *Love Songs*. It said that huge, and then it said his name, Ed L Jakobs, which seemed to have so many angles in it, that it looked, I thought in that moment, almost like a faraway outline of a city.

Biggest of all, the billboard said:

The great gay novelist of our times has arrived.

A tiny forcefield thrummed upon my skin. The back of my neck. My fingertips.

'You're joking—' I said.

'Joking because?'

'Look at it! It's a billboard! And it doesn't look like you made it yourself.'

'I tried,' he said. 'They wouldn't let me.'

My face felt like a mask, or more: I was aware of some kind of gap between me and it. 'It's such a great cover.'

'It's true. I do not hate it.'

On the poster, two male bodies pressed against each other. A cigarette in one of their hands; you could make out the beginning of undone jeans. All of it caught bright in a Wolfgang Tillmans flash.

'What's the L for?' I said. Then I saw he was looking at his phone. '—Sorry, it's okay,' I finished. 'I have to go too.'

'No, I just wanted something to do with my hands. It's so big! It's awkward! I'm surprised no one's defaced it yet—'

'I could get on your shoulders if you like?' I said. 'I'm sure I could find a sharpie somewhere, colour in some teeth—'

'Thank you.'

'It's funny,' I said then. 'I wouldn't have guessed.'

'Guessed what?'

'The great gay novelist of our time,' I said.

'What do you mean?'

'I don't know. No visual indicators.'

'My pin badge came off in the wash,' he said. 'Now we've all got to hide from the cops. They'll probably ban the posters soon, burn the books ...'

Wash was the word. Something was washing over me anyway. The way things he'd said had played in my head. The light rush of butterflies, a steel brush against a drum, as I walked into the café.

'Sorry I didn't say,' he said. 'Particularly when—'

'When what? Sorry I didn't ask!'

'When there was a moment?' His face couldn't make up its mind.

'Was there? I don't know.'

'It's totally fine. Completely fine of course,' I said a second time. 'Anyway, it's amazing, the poster.' I looked down at my phone. When I saw Daniel himself had just called me, I said I had to leave. Then: 'Also, it's not just you,' I said.

'What?'

'It's not just you. Me too.' It was strange how I felt it in that particular instant. Like his gayness filled the air around us, felt bigger than mine, probably just because he was bigger. 'The break-up I mentioned. That was a girl. A woman.'

'Oh, okay,' he said. His face did a little Rubik's cube move. 'And why didn't *you* say before?' he asked me.

'It didn't come up,' I said. 'And then I didn't want to cramp your moment. Your big coming out.'

'But before,' he said.

'What was I supposed to do?'

'A megaphone and a sandwich board,' he said. 'At the very least.'

He looked at me. 'I haven't always been that regular in befriending lesbians.'

'Very original of you.'

'I know,' he said. 'Throwback.'

'Anyway, no point now. They'll probably ban surrogacy in the next ten minutes too.'

He laughed at that. We were standing in direct sunlight. It was either find shade to stay longer, or leave. I needed to leave. My phone lit up with Daniel's name again.

Five missed calls. Now six. Reality. I pointed in the direction of the tube.

'Hey—' Ed called after me, as my walk turned into a run.

'What?'

'Are you normally the boy one or the girl one?' He looked very serious for a second, then broke into a stupid, bomb-like smile.

As I made my way to work, the feelings passed like strobe lighting, moving beams.

8

When I got back to the office, there was a new effigy made from boxy, insulated food delivery bags blocking the door. A couple of security guards – stab-vests over suits, coiled cables coming from earpieces – were talking to the protestors and laughing, but tightened up, straightened their backs, as I brought out my key fob.

'Do you guys need anything?' I asked. 'Bottles of water? It's hot.' But they all knew exactly who I was and just looked at me.

Before the crisis had deepened, it would give me comfort to get to the office before everyone else, as if time, for me alone, expanded. No matter what I got done in those morning hours, knowing they would exist allowed me to sleep the night before.

I knew all the cleaners. An older Portuguese couple who seemed to have nothing but bad luck, and a Syrian man called Adnan, who'd been a surgeon in a previous life. Every single day he would offer me a different operation, and every single day, I'd reply: 'lobotomy'.

My desk was made of a textured metal that always felt cool. In the early morning, I'd often run my hands over it as if it were a freshly made bed. I had a PA and an EA by then. After years of climbing up a sheer cliff-face with my fingertips raw and bleeding, it had felt like

I'd finally hit a plateau, and there was a great view. Or *a* view anyway. I'd get cheery notifications from my pension app. *This month £600 has been topped up by 300 thanks to Gigr. That's the equivalent of 112½ beach-side margaritas! Cheers!*

It was supposedly one of those 'fun' offices, in a way that would have once meant Foosball, but now meant food. An open plan chef's kitchen, a huge island. At 7 a.m., fruit in a crate of ice would be delivered, a basket of whole fruits, and next to it – as if a 'before and after' demonstration of civilisation – the same fruit prepared into slices and cubes. There was a seed bar, which had spurred a hundred sperm bank jokes, and a fridge full of new drinks from other start-ups. CBD things, and some kind of fizzy coffee that tasted like Thames river-water had been put through a Sodastream.

The building was close to a huge roundabout, and throughout the office, there was an air filtration system that they put scents into. They often featured the fragrance profile in the weekly newsletter, which was written in a chirpy and almost indecipherable way by one of the youngest employees in the office. *STOP YA DOOM SCROLLIN: READ THIS.* Last week was sage and salt. 'The smell,' Adnan had said the Wednesday morning just before the man jumped. His accent sounded Italian to me, in the lilt and pauses. He pulled a face and did a wave in front of his face. 'The smell is very bad.'

This was the thing. It wasn't just the jump. There had been a spate of deaths by then.

There were deaths before I joined the team – deaths and critical accidents: heavy rain, bad grip, drivers forced to go too fast – but the week I started was the first time we'd ever had two deaths in a single day.

That second death was the problem. Five hours into his shift, the guy had fallen asleep at the wheel and burst through the window of a Boots. He'd nearly crashed into a woman pushing a double-wide pram with twins in it. And it wasn't just that. He hadn't died on impact. He'd staggered around like a zombie before collapsing, and people had taken their phones out.

After the incident, I'd looked at his time tracker. He'd worked forty hours in three days: not the worst. But then it emerged he was a policeman and he'd worked eight hours each day doing that too. That meant eight hours *not* working over three days.

The family requested the numbers, then sent them to the press.

SLEEP COMA POLICEMAN'S GRUELLING FINAL HOURS ON GIGR.

WALKING DEAD: WELCOME TO APOCALYPSE LONDON

There were lots of semantic fields for the subs to play with. There were photos everywhere. Opinion pieces about how many of our public servants weren't able to do their work because of 'para-sites' like Gigr. It emerged that a record sixty-two percent of hospital workers now had a second job, and Gigr was the most common moonlight option of choice. A bill was proposed which had us firmly in its sight. 'Zero Left Behind' would take into account all work done, not just done for us, to make sure that overtime stayed in legal limits.

And the whole time, the deaths wouldn't stop. In the months that followed the Boots incident, with more and more people joining the platform, we'd had a death every four weeks, then every three weeks, then every two. I'd always hear about them first from someone very junior who'd got the call. Their arms would look too weak to push open my door, and after that, it fell to me and my team to talk to the press.

We'd attempted to win back some favour. Built a community club for Gigr workers in Soho, where they could use the internet, charge phones, cool down or heat up, talk to someone. There were lots of signs about talking to someone, and a neon sign above their fruit bar – Tesco fruit in their case, the signs of a long journey by boat very visible – that said 'healthy mind, healthy body'. ('Healthy profitz' someone had scratched in next to it.)

But it was undeniable: when someone plotted the deaths on a graph, it looked like a rocket taking off. That was why, on the Wednesday, we'd let three of the union people into the office for a discussion about the crisis, a discussion they wanted to stream live. Something I'd said 'no' to from the start.

It was only five minutes into the meeting, when the man stood up, and as everyone knows, instead of filming the meeting, he filmed himself jumping from the balcony.

Right away, it brought back the zombie memes. Even in election week, politicians were filming long statements, and making the ZLB Bill a big part of their platform.

I walked through the building back to my desk. *Act normal, be normal* – I tried to get it to hit my bloodstream.

I turned on my computer, took a single breath, then: 'Where the fuck were you?' Daniel said from my doorway. 'Are you joking? MIA *this* morning?' He was theoretically handsome. He should have been, but his nostrils flared in a way that made me think of the poison-spitting dinosaur in *Jurassic Park*. 'It's not FB, is it?' That was a phrase he often used. 'He's on FB': fucking burnout.

'Daniel,' I said. 'Not in that tone. It's me so whatever, but other people, you can't do that. Not at the moment.'

He was known in the industry for being hard work. But he'd told me he liked it when I was 'honest' to him – that it was bracing, like 'getting in that bullshit British sea'.

'Well I need to fucking know,' he said. 'Where were you today?'

'It's personal.'

'How's it personal? It affects me, it's not like asking if you're on your period.'

48

'Daniel, are you serious? I don't have burnout and I'm working. I'm on it. I've been on it.'

He got closer. 'You better be – this is serious.' He looked for a place to sit down. 'You took the chair away again.'

At other companies I'd worked for, the CEO had felt untouchable, a bride at a wedding, but Daniel always seemed to be in fifteen places at once, and it seemed like most of those places were my office. 'Like I said, I have work to do.'

'Well you work for me! You're a director. You're the fucking *Comms* Director. This whole thing – that's you. You can't go swanning off like you're in some royal park.'

He had every right to be angry. If someone on my team had skipped class, I'd have made their position swiftly untenable. I kept my face still. 'Yes I work for you,' I said. 'And no, I wasn't swanning off.'

Until recently, I had never been scared of him. He'd seemed like such a caricature, I had often felt myself becoming 2D too, and all of the blows and comebacks just felt slapstick.

'Fortunately,' he said, 'the main Bill bitch has lost her seat.'

'To a maniac—'

'Don't even—' he said. He gave me a look like, come on, it's just you and me here. 'You know this whole election thing is good air cover for the jump. Anyway, she's in the bin. Which is good. But we still have to be clever!' He scratched his nose and I wondered if he'd taken something. 'We need to make it okay for the new government not to pursue the ZLB.'

'I get that. I'm on it.'

'They'll see that as an easy win, eighty percent of people want it, yadda yadda, but it's fucking shortsighted. I know communists like you will want to come out storming.' He paused, leaving a hopeful little break where I might correct him. 'But we have to keep them sweet, keep them on side.'

'Daniel, you don't have to go all red scare. I work *here*. I'm hardly Lenin. I'm just saying there are eight new MPs who were previously on extremist watchlists—'

'Who fucking cares? The ZLB Bill sunk our IPO projections by forty percent.' He went at his nose again. 'It has to stay dead. We need to come out blazing, but at the state of *things*. Not the actual *state*-state.' His body looked like he was leaving, but then he turned back: 'Also, you heard we nailed the jumper?'

'He has a name, Daniel.'

'We found a Gofundme. Terminal illness!' he said. It wasn't a grin, but his teeth were bared. 'He was dying anyway. Nothing to lose. And guess what – he didn't even work here! It was *his son*.' He whispered it in a soap opera away. 'Look, it's very sad etcetera etcetera, but between you and me it was a scam. So I say we leak the *context*—' He was talking 'quietly', but it was still so loud.

'Daniel, no. The plan stays the same. We donate to a mental health charity. We continue what we're doing in the mental health space.'

'Anyway, it's still the zombie guy who's the death of me. I say we shift some of the blame of recent shit onto the heat. It's normal! People weren't sleeping in the heat. Aren't sleeping. Aren't there studies? People go nutso?'

'That teacher a few weeks ago, he clocked thirty-four hours in two days on the app. Same with the anaesthesiologist. Plus they had normal jobs. That's zero sleep regardless of heat.'

'Okay, perfect,' he said, nodding. Then: 'Sounds good. Take it straight to the *Mail*.'

'That's not what I'm saying.'

'Look, I'm nice, I'm nice.' His hands went up. Palms, peace.

'But?'

'Find a fucking angle.'

*

Later, when he messaged me again about this angle, he wrote it 'angel'. Then put 'lol', with the angel emoji.

I felt sick after he left. It wasn't great when he had a point. I did briefly wonder if he could kill someone. With his bare hands too, not just his app. I could imagine him looking into it, using a normal private browser.

The air-con created a coolness that congregated on my forearms. *Angle/angel*, I wrote on a bit of paper and underlined it.

I found the notes on one of last week's deaths. A junior anaesthesiologist by trade, she worked in between her shifts for us. That one was suicide, after she'd got a dosage badly wrong for the second time. I looked up her Gigr profile. On the days before she died, she'd toggled between driving, retail and cleaning in a restaurant. This is what had made Gigr skyrocket: it became a shift marketplace. It allowed anyone to buy an hour of your time. I looked at her record of short jobs all across London. Two nights before she died, she'd rejected the extension of one job, and because, in the list of reasons, she'd put 'none of the above', we docked her ten percent of the work she'd already done.

We're cunts, I wrote after that.

I looked through the orders in the courier section. Lemsip and paracetamol was in one.

Delivered medicine, I noted. *Line of service play?*

I replied to Daniel's message about the angel.

Separately what's the budget? I asked.

For?

Family, kids, charity, damage control

Which of our shituations? Lol

Don't you always say death's the easy one?

Get out of jail

I'd made the mistake once of telling him that death, though

horrible, brought with it a buffer: a set way of speaking; a legal excuse for not saying much ... *Very concerned, working closely with the police and authorities. Due to the sensitive nature, we can't talk about it as the police investigate* ... Time automatically bought with things like coroner reports.

I didn't reply. Daniel is typing ... then nothing. Daniel is typing ... then nothing.

I don't know – 50k?

100 tops

Ok

But wrap it right

Can't become an every time thing

We'll be broke in 5 seconds lol! And remember I'm saving up for my bullet proof vest haha

He stayed online, waiting for me to reply, I could feel it.

Also, don't you have a benchmark on this?

The job was never meant to be about fighting fires. The job was instead to be a Cassandra, to forecast catastrophe. *You don't retroactively change headlines; you prevent them in the first place.* That was a line I'd said in my interview, two years ago now.

Like every job I'd had, my first month was spent plotting out worst-case scenarios – what if there's a strike? What if the office has widespread asbestos? What if the CEO's a paedophile? – both from my own brain, and from all the people who worked there. The best intel was always from Customer Service Reps, the clever ones. They could often spot things years out. And then you start planning. You write and write. The handbook for disaster builds. Answers for Radio 4 become ready.

The job, by its nature, was also to hold the anxiety for everyone else, particularly those up high. To see risks everywhere. To point them out. To make plans. So that other people could say, *what are you worrying about, that's ridiculous!*, their own fear leaving their body for a moment, all the while letting you prepare.

And the job was to be steel. To be what Flo called 'the cum bucket for all man's worry' – and it was all men, everyone with real power was a man at least – while appearing entirely unfazed. To be the person everyone came to when something went wrong. And to find excitement in it somewhere, a thumb rolling the stone of a lighter, enough to keep a flame burning harder and brighter than anyone else's until it was all over.

'So it's basically kind mummy and domme matron, all in one?' Flo had also said, when I tried to explain it to her once. She'd ask me how I could be so calm. Being airdropped into huge press conferences or parliamentary boards or police interviews without a second to prepare. In my shoes, she'd say, she'd collapse into a puddle of tears and lie there waiting for death.

'You wouldn't,' I'd reply.

'I would.'

'No,' I'd say. 'You'd just do what you have to do.'

But she'd still look horrified, and so I couldn't tell her how it actually was. Or how it had been. How sometimes when the stress was at its most extreme, I would go into a cubicle in the bathroom and find myself laughing.

Nervous laughter? I could imagine her saying.

But it wasn't that. It was closer to disbelief. Or glee. Not glee, but sometimes it was that I had known the moment would come. Or it was that I had tricked the system and my own body. I'm still here, I'd think, I'm still alive. I'm doing this. And I know what to do.

I imagined her face dropping. *A villain's cackle? Like, muahahahaha?*

In truth, at first, it had always been closer to that. The company was a body. I could feel its heart beating. I could wear it like a suit and make it move with me. And at first I could step outside it – step in, step out, be a robot whenever I needed to be – until it was too late to notice that our central nervous systems had fused.

I looked at the paper in front of me. *Angel/Angle*, and next to it: *we're cunts*.

But it was worth it. It had to be worth it. Didn't it? I stood to make a lot of money. The timing worked out. I'd just received some '30 under 30' thing, even though I wasn't, and after everything had collapsed with Bonnie and I'd come back from Lisbon, a recruiter called George got in touch. He had Lego-man hair and said *exactly* all the time, pushing at it like it was a door. He got me a package that seemed so good I was sure he'd made mistakes on it. 'Exactly,' he said, when I asked him if he had.

It was a risk, but if I could pull it off, the pay-off could be huge. There were levers and KPIs and cliffs, but if I stayed for four years, I would vest a number of shares that in current projections – if the IPO went ahead, and went well – would be worth just north of three million pounds.

'Three fucking million!' Flo had said the night I signed the contract. 'It's amazing! Because you know what it's like. It's like getting the inheritance that all the fuckers we went to university with will get. It's like tricking your way into being equal! I love it,' she'd said. 'Very chic.'

She was like me. We both changed our voices when we got to university. I'd found it embarrassing. It being me, but also, that it was what the situation demanded. And that I knew which voice to do already, and it arrived so whole, like I'd been studying it my entire life.

'Chic, but currently fictional,' I'd said to Flo. I told her how none of the numbers were real. It could equally amount to nothing. People talk about Monopoly money, but it wasn't even that. Because even if that was a game and the money was shrunken and on pastel paper, you could still touch it. All my theoretical money, all that was literally just plucked from the air.

We'd gone to Noble Rot and both worn nice clothes. Laughter, and the sound of people biting into things in the candlelight, made me think my life could be full of things that were good. Flo made so many jokes about the Château Lafite you could get a sip of for £47 that I had two sips waiting for us when she came back from the loo.

'I will be frugal after this,' I said.

'Fuck that! No.' She almost spat out her sip. 'As a yoga teacher once said to me, do not squander your one life.'

The annual salary wasn't the best but it wasn't the worst. 'Eyes on the prize,' George had said, just like Daniel kept on saying about the IPO, and a signing bonus had gone directly into renewing my parents' lease. I knew they wouldn't accept the money, so I had to pay it secretly but say that I'd called the council and found a loophole. It was only £4,000 now, I told them, not the £37,000 they had been asked for, and my main memory of that moment – when I went over to tell them the news – was my mum chastising my dad. She could have guessed it was because he'd done the forms wrong.

I'd brought champagne in my bag because I thought I might tell them what I'd done if it felt right – if it somehow all unfolded and felt celebratory and right that night – but it was hot in my bag when I left.

'Hey, I got a new job,' I'd said to my dad as we stood in the door.

'Who are you fleecing this time?' he'd said, but not un-proudly. Everybody knew it was good to have a job right now.

'They're fleecing *me*,' I said back. 'These are the best years of my life.'

All this to say, that was why I stayed. And, of course, all around us, London was on the steady downhill slide of a recession.

On harder evenings, I would look at the document that outlined all my stock options and do maths on my phone, and then again, on paper, with a pen, to make it feel more solid. I would shut my eyes and imagine the payment coming through. All the numbers. All the zeros after them.

This was my plan: I would say it had been like winning the lottery, and that it was all of ours. I would pay off my mum's student debt. I would buy them a different house that didn't flood. I would pay whatever she needed to go private for healthcare, even if I had to trick her again to do it. And with whatever was left after tax, alongside the other money I'd put aside over the last ten years, I would have a proper down payment for something of my own.

'I feel your dream is the dream of a different time,' Flo had said, that contract-signing night. 'Like you're cosplaying the fifties or the nineties or something. A thirty-five-year-long mortgage! The whole thing will have burned down.'

'I know,' I said. Then: 'Just to check. Which thing? The house itself or the world?'

'Both. Isn't it so stupid?' Which I nodded at, even though again, 'it' meant me.

I did not think she was wrong. I thought so often, about the things I did, that I did them because my younger self wanted them, or my parents wanted them before that, or maybe even my ancestors. But for years, I imagined it – getting a house – as being like gravity. Or like a switch. That when I landed or hit it, suddenly I would feel safe.

Or less eternal than that, that all of the shit I'd done, all the yeses I'd said – so many yeses that no had all but disappeared – would have all been worth it.

I thought of the three Cs of crisis management. Concern, Control, Commitment.

And then I looked at my phone.

I clicked away from the thread with Daniel and found myself flicking over to my last message to Ed.

I do. Are you free?

It felt like a different person had written them. Who was she? And what did she want?

9

Towards the end of the day, Daniel had changed his tune. I wondered what he'd taken, because he kept on clapping with new resolution, and at one point I even saw him slap or high-five a wall in a way that seemed to be a demonstration of the fact he'd had an idea. He said that with everything that had been going on, we all needed to blow off steam, but that it was best not to go to our usual pub because of optics. 'Faisal, you do it,' he said to this young man I'd never seen without a cap on. 'Go out and get boatloads.' There was a back way, Daniel said, an exit through an assault course of bins: he was to use that.

'Isn't this what the government did during lockdown?' I heard. It was someone I'd never seen before – a girl, or rather a woman who was young enough to be called a girl. Our eyes met with a bang. 'The old-old government,' she said. She looked down. 'May they rest in peace.'

At the start of Gigr, Daniel used to man a G&T bar on Fridays. 'Let's crack open the Kool-Aid!' he'd always say, and I was never sure if he understood the reference. 'Thirty min countdown to fun!' he shouted now.

It used to be at these drinks – underpinned with a pseudo-religious vibe, always endless references to family – that Daniel would give out his weekly 'Gi-had' awards for people who had sacrificed more than most for the business that week. The stories were always awful – four days at the office without going home; sitting through an investor meeting with an upset stomach and not moving from the seat until the deal was signed – and people would always clap and whoop. (For years, I had clapped and whooped too. A symptom of a collective madness despite knowing of at least two early miscarriages, where people had bled in the toilet, and then gone back to their desk.)

'My people,' I said to my team after Daniel's countdown. They all sat close to my door. 'Come to my office for a second—'

They sloped their way in. There were fifteen now – the team had been steadily growing.

'Idiotic question, I know,' I started, 'but—' Tone. The question was always tone. How to get it right. How to modulate it so it didn't feel erratic, psychopathic, being their boss, being friendly. I thought about the orders I'd given them a few days before. 'How are you all doing?'

There was silence and then a couple of yeahs. To my surprise, the woman or girl I hadn't seen before followed the team into my office. She leaned against the wall.

I looked at them all. I was in a position of leadership. That was another thing to consider. There was the jump, yes, but surely I should say something about the election?

'It can feel,' I said, 'that a lot of bad things happen at once—' I looked up and they were all looking down. 'So I guess it comes down to self-care,' I said. 'I know, very embarrassing. But whatever you need, we can provide it. Don't worry about forms or jumping through hoops. Just put it on an expense invoice and I'll approve it.' I paused. For a comms team, they were always so quiet. 'I don't know what people do. Spas? Therapy? Daniel would kill me but whatever. Take a couple of days off if you need.'

'What about if you weren't there on the day itself?' a voice that wasn't mine finally said. It was the new girl. Her shoulders stayed leaning against the white of the wall. And that was when I looked at her properly. Her boxer braids, her bandeau top. On her skin, the heatwave had turned to something gentler. 'If the trauma's just kind of . . . ambient?' she said.

'You picked a great week to start. Well, welcome,' I said. There were a few laughs, weak ones.

'It's okay,' she said. 'I'm taking lots of notes.' Her eyes flicked up at me again. 'For my exposé.' I was unsure what to do with my face. 'Don't worry,' she said. Then: 'I really can't afford not to have a job at the moment . . .'

'Good,' I said. 'Those are the words we love to hear.' Another few laughs, even more strained this time. Their faces – I scanned across them. Did they like me? Were they scared of me? Worse, were they sorry for me?

'Do you want to have a quick catch up?' I asked her when the time came for everyone to leave the room. 'Not really a catch up since we've never spoken in person before.'

'We have spoken,' she said. 'Over at the other building. You were in the lift saying "Graham, you're a fucking idiot" to your phone.'

'Oh,' I said, 'do you know Graham?'

'I was on his team,' she said. I remembered, vaguely, approving a transfer. 'As well as stupid, he's also very racist. That's all going in my report too.'

I looked at her. She was a curious combination of things, closed and bold. Her pupils caught the light from so far away. I asked her why they moved her to me from Graham.

'Golden Graham. I challenged his authority, they said. It wasn't appropriate for an intern apparently.'

It could have been annoying; it should have been. But there was this gentle coolness in how she pushed it. 'How old are you?' I said. I didn't mean to. A reflex left over from childhood.

'I'm pretty sure you're not allowed to ask that. But I'm twenty-three.'

The two junior members of staff came back with heavy bags. We heard the clink of bottles hitting the floor. When I told her she should partake, she turned around to leave and her back was almost bare. Levis tight at the hip, the label the same colour as her skin. Her top like a strap across her back. My eyes rolled up and down her. It was a question of geometry almost – how was that body possible?

I rubbed my eyes, chastising them for misbehaving, and stayed at my desk until Daniel sent someone to get me. I wandered over to the guys from New Markets, these barrow-boy types, who very sweetly had a book club together.

'What's it this month?' I asked.

'*World War Z*,' one said. They had a private supply of IPAs on their table, and they were making a circle around it. 'Zombies.' He cracked another beer, then had to chase it with his lips as foam exploded out. 'A-fucking-gain.'

My team was on one side of the room, talking in quite an animated way now I wasn't there. And then I looked the other way, through to the board room. There was a new safety lock on the balcony door, red with a cable you had to cut, and something about it made me think of an artery or umbilical cord.

I felt it in my spine. The marrow cooled. I had to get out of there.

As I walked home, I didn't know if it was the weather or me, but rushes of heat kept coming, and I knew they shouldn't have come, because it was dark by then.

Since the man had jumped, or since watching the video, whatever it was that that had unlocked, I kept seeing it again. And then my body would shake. It felt like the back of me and the front of me were pulsing. Back and forth, vibrating, but I couldn't tell what they were doing, whether they were threatening to meet and touch and stick together, or to break clean apart. I would forget to breathe.

As I walked, it felt like the distance between me and the floor had changed. I was more sensitive to the world, like my skin wasn't there, or at least there was less of it. Sounds felt louder. Anyone shouting found their way into my bones, and there seemed to be so much madness everywhere, more than ever before, and fewer Bluetooth headphones to explain it. Just then, a woman wearing a broken motorbike helmet ran by me. Normal enough until I looked at her feet and saw she was wearing flip-flops.

I was supposed to hold it all and be okay. That was the job: to hold it all and be okay. But it had been creeping up, and getting worse, anxiety. It was getting worse for everyone. Everyone kept talking about 'my anxiety', like it was a pet. And how could it not? It hadn't been like this before. Not all of it bad. Not love, and work, and family, and the world. Not for me, anyway. There'd always been a good part before. Somewhere safe to land, even if it was just a short break to refuel.

And now, this new feeling, the invisible shake.

Home, I thought, just get home. As if the door, when I shut it behind me, would be the thing that made it stop.

When I got there, the fridge was full of things Marion had bought that were now long dead. There was a bottle of wine. Comfort in the single bottle, the solid glass, un-stretchable edges of it.

As ever: numbers. I'd try to calm down with numbers. I opened my document, opened my spreadsheet. I'd made various scenarios, so I could change one number and see how all others changed too. It felt like playing with an abacus, and when the abacus felt strong and unbreakable, that could buy me some relief.

On the radio, someone was saying that something was scandalous, regressive. 'Shocking,' he said. 'We should all be shocked.'

My phone skeetered on the table. It was my dad.

Her big Appointment tomorrow. Dad

Pls don't forget. Dad

His usual love was missing. There was also a link from Flo: 'Chaos in Commons after Heated Clash'.

Fuck me it's embarrassing, she said.

Day fucking one!

'Member suspended after

calling out homophobic slur'

I mean, faggot! Of all things

I thought about what Daniel had said. Come out blazing, but at the state of things, not the state-state.

I looked at my laptop. For now, I had the numbers. I had little else.

10

When it came to stamping out any return of the ZLB Bill, Daniel had told me we needed a 'final solution' by Friday.

From the car window, on the way to work, I saw sad men wearing overhead headphones like black rainbows. A teenage girl in a faded Duff Beer cap, ankles flexing like wrists out of baggy jeans. On one stretch of road, I watched two men with hammers attack moped locks in the bright light of the morning.

Texts from Flo punctuated the days with odd studs. Half nostalgic:

You know what I forgot
about til yesterday?
Chocolate body paint!

Or

Remember when people used to text TB.
Text back! Tuberculosis!

And half about what was happening in the news:

All these fucking podcast people,
'It's not in the national psyche to be fascists'.

READ THE ROOM, FUCKO
It's like waking up with the world's worst
hangover and it's not just paranoia
you've found a body in the bed
(A dead one), she clarified.

It was one morning that week that Ed texted to invite me to his book launch. He sent a picture of the invitation too, and I zoomed into all the corners of the image, not because it was visually complex, but because I wanted to see everything. It was in a bookshop in East London. It said to RSVP to Joan at his publisher.

Joan of Ed, I replied.

I'll tell her yes.

Ofed, he wrote back.

Under his eye 👁

I sat there with my phone in my hands. I didn't want the conversation to end.

At first I thought it said book lunch, I replied.

I was excited

We could have lunch?
Big fan of lunch
Definitely one of my top 3 meals of the day.

It's just I've made the very grown-up
decision of attending work recently

What about Sunday?

This Sunday?

Sunday was so soon. A flash of excitement drop-shifted to worry. What would we talk about?

Okay

Excellent
Your enthusiasm is electric

It was though. Or was it? Some kind of energy, anyway, made a path inside me; cut its way through the thicket that had grown up.

Normally at work I was a machine, but since the jump and the election, it felt like operating in mist so thick it was solid. Sometimes I would forget I was on a call until someone said my name for a second time, or a third.

But in the strange little rush of energy that came, perhaps, from Ed, I sent flowers to my mum, and promised I would visit this weekend. And, as if they were bound together, as if I could control one element of my life and others would follow suit, I started writing the statement.

I was thirteen when it began. Studying the news when my parents watched it after dinner. The stories were irrelevant; it was the language I'd listen to. I'd transcribe speeches sometimes, pause a video and try to predict the next word before it came. The phrases, the flips, the builds then shifts. When the TV was live, sometimes I'd look behind me at my parents with a lack of generosity only a teenager can muster. I was a kid, I was ambitious, and they had no power in the world. *Control the narrative*, I had written next to my keyboard in my teenage bedroom – I didn't even hide it when people came over – *and you control everything*.

I picked my angle/angel for the statement, a second's beat, and then relief. Just like it had done a thousand times, it came out in a single burst. Like I knew the notes, like music.

11

On the train to my parents' house, it was a sticky 28 degrees which felt double that. Teenage boys had their T-shirts in their back pockets, and across from me, a man read a bible and circled things in biro, and I wondered what terrible things he'd done or was trying not to do.

I picked up yesterday's paper from an empty seat. Inside was a profile of the new PM, with the headline *LIDDLE BRITAIN*. Infographics charted her astronomical rise. She wasn't a household name before becoming leader, but the machine was working now, and her face was everywhere.

My eyes scanned over the bullet points. Soundbites that had gone viral. She was the one who had said 'Britain deserves better than boring'; fans had made T-shirts. The fact that, years ago, she'd walked in her university fashion show. *Agent Provocateur*, a caption read. I sent a photo to Flo.

TP sent me this too, she replied,
saying Big Clit Energy.
Why is he so old?
It's true tho

Finally got a Sanna Marin,
and she's a hitler youth

I know

What even are her policies though?
I feel like all the articles are either like
Liddle STUNS in Zara dress, or like
evil witch will be the death of us all

My parents' house was like a third person in their relationship; they'd got every bit of timing with it wrong. A mortgage when rates were twelve percent. Some scheme where they'd only half bought it, where it cost them tens of thousands more than it ever should have. And worst of all, it was in Stanford-le-Hope. It was meant to be their seaside move, but you still had to drive to get to the beach. That said, it was lower than the sea level, so 'the sea came to you', the joke went.

Even though they had been there for eight years now, their home was still a new home, and they wanted me to ask how it was. My dad would always answer the same thing – fine apart from the local men who met for curries and beers and to complain about their wives and Albanians each Thursday, and the fact that the postcode didn't work for deliveries.

There were sentences I said about my parents that made them cartoons. How my mum was fired for secretly teaching socialism at the school where they both worked. How they lived in a three-bed pebbledash semi, and my dad had been trying to take the pebbledash off for years by himself with a spade.

What was I trying to say when I said these things? What was I trying to apologise for? Why was it so much harder and bigger to say the real things?

My mum was funny. Could make a whole room laugh if she was tuned into the right channel of herself. An unexpected dryness that would make people cough before the laugh came. She had an arcane set of rules and standards which she judged everyone by, that she denied existed, yet whose presence was defined in absolute terms whenever you strayed up against one. For years I tried to work out the inner logic, so I could predict them, but I'd always failed.

She would look at me with love, and then, the only word I can think of was suspicion. I probably looked the same way back. I think what we were suspicious of was the power we had to hurt each other. Mothers and daughters, she would say, as if this were an outside force that we ourselves had nothing to do with.

It inched up as I walked from the station. I started looking for danger. Awkward kerbs, unsteady paving stones. Sometimes when I thought about them – when I thought about their financial things, or one of them running for a bus and slipping over – something happened in my chest. I would shrink away from the sides, like how, if you were to touch the head of a snail, it would quickly disappear into itself. I thought of them and shrunk.

'She's here!' I heard my dad shout as I rang the bell. The door opened like he'd been waiting behind it.

'Were you lurking?'

'Been here since the crack of dawn,' he said, 'just peering through the letterbox. She's here!' he shouted again, impossible though it was that my mum hadn't heard the first time. He reached for the flowers, but I wanted to keep them with me.

They'd moved everything to one floor. They said they loved it. I hated their new bathroom. The builder had insisted on handles by the bath, handles everywhere. You don't need it yet, I'd said. This was before my mum got ill. Well, they'd said. We're thinking of you. We never want to be a b-word.

I walked into their bedroom. In the alcove where the dining table had been, my mum had had a custom reading chair made for her.

You look happy, you look well, they were only words we put on top to make things more understandable – she could look at me and see everything.

I didn't want to look at her though, because I was scared of what I would see. I looked past her, through her, across her. Fast so it didn't seem noticeable, although it was definitely noticeable. And as if it were only seeing things that made them real. Her skin thinner, her hair less.

'Sorry,' I said as I passed her the flowers. 'They look like they come from a service station. Everything had something lime green in it. I think they put dye in the water. Don't try to smell them. They don't smell of anything.' A string of sentences I had prepared as I walked from the station.

'More leaf than flower . . .' she said.

'That's what I said. It was the best I could do though.' I felt her climb up my throat: me at fourteen.

'I like them,' she said. 'Sweetheart—' Her hand reached for me.

Strange how you could be shy with someone when you had once been inside their body.

'You feel cold?' she said. 'Late nights?'

'I'm fine,' I said. 'How are you?'

'Well,' she said. Hesitation, not an adjective. 'I still have a pulse.' The skin on her hands was like tissue paper. Softer than that; it terrified me.

'Has he been looking after you?' I said. I can only imagine the bounce of it, the face I might have pulled, jovial. I remember thinking at the time: *because I am young, or at least not old, I haven't been around a lot of death yet, so I have to copy other voices.* Whatever it was, I didn't feel like myself.

'It makes him happy when you're here,' she said. 'He shouts at the radio when he's happy. Men are nice to be around.'

'I'm sure,' I said. A small, tight sound.

'How's Marianne?' she said, her voice turning crisp.

'Marion,' I said. 'She's Swedish.'

'Mari*on* then.'

'She – oh it's—' I looked at her looking at the bad flowers I'd brought. 'We – I suppose we're taking some time.'

She nodded. All she did was nod.

'You don't have to look quite so happy about it,' I said. I said it medium-strength. I could still have stopped then.

'It seemed . . . it didn't seem. I don't know.'

Why did she look so tired? I knew why she looked tired. But why did she insist on letting me know that I made her so extra tired? 'Please don't,' I said.

She took a breath in, and it felt like she wanted me to hear the sound of her lungs. It wasn't a good sound.

'Are you enjoying it?' I said about the book that was beside her, one I'd recommended, but the air had broken.

'I just worry,' she said. 'I mean. When do you think you'll ever—'

She didn't even finish her sentence. 'Please don't,' I said. 'Because it's possible not to—'

'What?'

'Can't you *nearly* say it but just stop yourself?' I said. 'Please.'

At that moment, my dad came in with sandwiches. He'd made patterns with them on the plate. His face was bright but dulled as soon as he saw us.

'She called her Marianne again,' I said, 'and also we broke up.'

'Sorry, kid,' my dad said.

'Anyway, whatever. There are obviously more important things going on. I brought you the paper. I almost wanted to cry on the train—'

'You can't cry,' my mum said. It was how declarative she was. It shrunk the space for movement.

'It's a turn of phrase,' I said. 'But okay then. That's that cleared up.'

'We've been alive longer than you. It's all happened before. It's often not as extreme as you think—'

'You've seen the thirty day plan? Aren't you supposed to be radical? Greenham Common gang over here …'

'You can't let things affect you so much.'

'It's fine to let things affect you,' I said. Honestly, I didn't think that was true. I would have fought her side if we'd swapped positions. But positions had been taken. 'It's worse to pretend everything's normal.'

'It's just if I'm … leaving,' she said. 'I need to know you're okay.' That might have sounded like a nice thing to say. But it wasn't.

'What's that face for?' I said to her.

'She's ill—' my dad said.

'That's not the face,' I said.

'It's just that nothing seems to … stick,' she said.

'Stick?' I said.

'In your life, I mean.'

'In my life? Life is such a big word. I've never quit a job. I have good jobs—'

'Not your work,' she said.

'I would have done anything for Bonnie.'

'Well Bonnie, she was a—' She started to shake her head.

'It's nice outside,' my dad tried, 'we could sit in the garden.'

'You're not a child anymore,' my mum said.

'I couldn't be more aware I'm not a child—'

'You're shouting,' she said, and then she just started to cough and cough. 'Tell her to stop,' she said to my dad.

'I didn't do anything,' I said. But it was true. It didn't look good, her holding her chest like that.

She put her hand up like she was drowning. My dad crossed the room in a way he hadn't done since I was a kid. A speed I wasn't used to. Hard steps, his shoulders swelling. 'You can't do this,' he said. 'You can't come here, if you're going to make her upset.'

'Fine,' I said. The flowers in a vase with no water in it. The sandwiches on a side table. He'd put salad all round the edge.

'You can't upset her,' he said. 'She can't afford it.'

'Shall I just go then?' I said. Neither of them said anything. 'I'm an adult – you want me to storm out like a—'

And then I did. My heart was pounding when I left. As I shut the door behind me, it felt like I'd swallowed my tongue. This thickness all through my throat.

I took the train back. Perhaps it was the heat, perhaps it was just me again, but it shook on its tracks. Rocks and squeaks that didn't seem normal. I walked home from the station. A door was left out on the street that had been kicked in – these deep, wood-crunching welts. I looked at people sitting in pubs. I thought how easy it would be to step off the street and find a seat at a bar and stay there until everything, everything, all of it was over. It was Saturday night, and everyone in England was drinking.

When I got home, I didn't want it to be the place I went, but even more than numbers, it was still the only place I knew that really worked. It was still Bonnie. Always Bonnie.

I'd think about how we slept. We had slept so knitted together in the night. I would kiss her, and she would nod afterwards, still asleep. Her body was hot in a way that made me think of technology – dry and hot at the same time. Smooth, metal. But completely a person. It didn't make sense.

When we'd first met, her name would run like a ribbon through my head. I'd play it like music. When my hands were cold I would think of the soft bits of her inner leg that were always warm. When I was worried in crowded places about a man with a sports holdall,

I would think about her lips instead. I'll die like that, I'd think, with her lips in my head. I always had her to go to.

I'd never had them all come together before. The liking, the loving, the ways that days would disappear. I made her come so hard once that she broke my nose. I was doing circles, circles with my tongue, and her pelvis erupted forward so hard there was a click. She broke the bone in two places. I remember feeling this pride afterwards, a rocket taking off in my chest. 'Did you tell your friends?' I asked her, as she led me down the stairs because I couldn't see with all the tissues in front of my face. It hurt when I laughed, but I didn't care, I was so in love.

My mum's face at the thought of Bonnie suddenly ripped through my head. All the things my parents had said years before. Or didn't say, because the rules seemed so clear they didn't even need to say them out loud.

'But what does it *mean*?' That was their regular refrain back then, all of us misunderstanding each other. It was painted on their faces: the ways it could unfold into disaster. 'Will you ... cut your hair?' my mum had said.

'No,' I replied. 'I thought I'd let it grow 'til eventually it trailed on the floor behind me ...'

'I just mean. Will you have a life that is normal? Not normal. Good.' Will you succeed? she meant. Will you find love?

'I'm seeing someone,' I reminded them, 'this is why I'm telling you.' It wasn't Bonnie, it was the only older woman I'd ever been with. My mum struggled to swallow even when I deducted a decade from her age. 'But does this ... woman have a job, a house?' my mum asked. 'Yes, she has a job,' I'd replied. 'And a big house actually. She had a family before. She has kids.'

'Well perhaps that would have been the right order of doing things,' my mum said.

There was a word that came up in French: *assumer*. After the mother of three, a French girl young enough to be her daughter. She could have been a model if she wasn't 5'2". 'How are your family finding it?' I asked her. Again, this was a long time ago. *'Bof,'* she said, which I didn't know French people actually said. *'Mais ça va, parce que je l'assume.'* But it's okay because ... what? She looked it up for me. There wasn't really a word for it in English. Was it 'accept'? Was it 'own'? It seemed to be its own thing. She had a job, she was successful – there it was, success again – so there was nothing in her life for them to *méprise*. We looked up that word too. 'Scorn,' she said. She said it scowern. Then she said a word more clearly: despise.

All this was another time. It was crazy to me: how could so close a time be so different a time? I'd find myself shaking my head when I thought of it. At my very first job, when eventually, I did mention a girlfriend one lunchtime, the two older women performed uncomfortable like they were in the running for Oscars. I saw one look at my hands to check my nails. They asked for the bill.

It was too much in a lifetime, and less than a lifetime, twenty years, for how quickly it changed, and how many times. For it to have been like that, then all at once, it felt imperative for me to bring it up in all pitches. 'Drop the L-bomb,' Daniel used to say when I first started.

'Oh what, give us ten million in funding because I'm a lesbian?'

'Exactly. You're homophobic if you don't.' He'd smile at me. 'You're my diversity double-trouble. Oooh that could be a good one. Triple threat. Slap more make-up on. Make you look a little Arab. That's hot! Lipstick lesbian in a burqa. Come on—'

'I've got an idea,' I'd said. 'I'll break your legs and put you in a wheelchair if you like?'

He'd burst out laughing, and affected a few steps of a dramatic limp. You could see it in the dance of his cheeks – he loved this shit. Loved that I would take it. Loved that I would give it back. And then it had changed again. Almost overnight, he'd become obsessed with woke-tanking, his own coinage.

'Don't woke us into oblivion!' he kept saying to me now. 'I don't even mean the government backlash, I mean the *people* backlash. Newsflash! Sense of humours are back! We don't have to be pussies anymore. Speaking of, you *are* a woman, right? A real one?' And he'd wink at me.

But anyway. Bonnie. The rare times panic had come before all this, she had been the most reliable way to make it fade, but now – what happened now? How had it all happened in the same week – the jump, the election, and before the election, after the jump, the morning she'd called me.

To meet my news – the fact I was in the news – with her own news: an email she sent through for me to open, live, while she was on the line.

My eyes couldn't make it out at first. Black, white, an upside-down rainbow, some kind of Rorschach drawing.

'You see it?' she said.

I didn't say anything.

'Him, or her,' she said then. 'Not it.'

'Oh,' I'd said. 'Oh.'

I looked away. I looked back. There was its head, the white sweep of its nose. How would legs that tiny, just lines really, carry a head like that, but there was its head.

The sun had cut through the gap in the curtain like a sword – it sliced pure heat across my cheek.

12

Ed and I decided to meet at Broadway Market. On weekends it was like Noah's Ark, all the animals walking two by two. Why would you go to a butcher, unless you specifically needed meat? Yet so many people seemed to be in there on dates.

Here? Ed texted.

I'm just in the Portuguese soap shop

He was emerging when I got there. 'Cleaner now?' I asked.

He tapped a soap-shaped bulge in his pocket. 'Or am I just pleased to see you?' he said, then looked faintly embarrassed. 'It's very expensive. I don't use it, of course. I just place it artfully by a sink and hope a guest never has the audacity.'

'My kind of host.'

'Joking. It's for my mum.'

A razor ran through my belly thinking of the day before.

'Hi,' he said, and I said: 'How are you?' We gave each other a hug that was more of a knock.

'Oh, you know,' he said. 'It was the worst of times, it was the worst of times.'

He couldn't find his sunglasses and occasionally held a book up to

77

shield his face from the light. When we got to one of the cafés along the canal, as if by magic, a table appeared in the perfect half-sun right in front of us, crumbs left behind on it from the people who'd just left. I felt a little trill of luck then, like I'd created the table myself. The few times I had seen Ed, it always felt like borrowed time, like life had expanded in a little curve to the left.

'I looked up your company,' he said.

Another razor through my belly. Less sharp, but longer this time.

'You did?' I said. 'Let me guess. You want a job, right? They all come crawling in the end ...'

He put out his hands like a bowl: please sir.

'We're always saying it's for creative people,' I said. 'So they can top up! Pursue their passion!'

'Is that ever true?'

'There was one person. Made an album with 500 quid we gave him. We made a film about it with a much bigger budget. Poor guy had to put Gigr *on* the album artwork.' Ed made his eyes big. 'How are your posters going?' I asked him. 'Still no defacings?'

'A friend sent one. Love Schlongs. But I kind of liked that.'

'The sequel,' I said. 'How are you feeling about it? It's so soon—' It was coming out in a week.

'Not soon! Don't say soon. The word soon is banned. It's just kind of ... un-processable? You do something entirely alone. The writing, I mean. And then people can say whatever they like about you in a national newspaper. And that's if you're lucky.' A fly kept landing on his wrist like he had a trace of sugar on it. His wrists were more delicate than the rest of his arms. A dip, a vein, a curve. 'Anyway, thank you for suggesting this,' he said. 'So I can depress you.'

'You suggested it.'

'Well for saying yes then. It's nice. We're kind of old to make friends.' He'd found his sunglasses at the bottom of his backpack, and put them on, a slight wonk stemming from the nose bit, so I couldn't see his eyes. 'I don't know – you just ...'

'What?

'Kept popping up in my head.'

'It's the little chip I inserted,' I said.

'I think – I was thinking you might remind me of my sister?'

Oh, I remember thinking. 'But we don't look alike?' I said.

'She didn't look like me. But looks aside, just ... spirit? She's—' he said, and then he said, 'She was—' He took a breath in and it looked like it hit something sharp. 'I hate the shift in the tense, I hate it. She was different to you. I mean who knows how she'd have turned out.' His jaw clenched, the structure came to the surface. 'She was eighteen. One of those terrible freak things that – happen. Because of course they happen. A holiday with friends. After A-levels.'

That hot-cold feeling of realisation. I hated hearing about people dying. Why was everyone always dying? I wished he wasn't tipping back on his chair.

I asked him what had happened.

'Some midnight swim, cliff jump stupid thing. Rocks in the water. She could have missed it by an inch. But isn't that anything, I guess.'

'I'm so sorry,' I said. I moved to touch his arm but he'd tipped back even further.

'And you're not her. I'm not saying you're her. Obviously. It's not that. She was beautiful, and you're beautiful, of course.' His eyes flashed up at me then looked away again. His voice was tipping around like his chair. 'Anyway, I shouldn't have brought it up.' He paused. 'Do you want to see a picture? Just I've said it now.' He took out his phone. 'It's not your face. It's timing. Something. Maybe? She was so smart.'

He flicked around, then put his phone down on the table. He was in the picture too. It looked nearly a decade old, Ed's hair shorter. Their arms were around each other, and she was tall, and her legs looked like they'd suddenly shot up, like the bones were fresh, and her hair was long, the same colour as mine, but with a touch of strawberry to it.

'She's gorgeous,' I said.

'Yeah. My older brother's terrible. We had the same childhood, a fine childhood, and who knows what monsters he voted for just now. Told my mum it was her fault for letting Anna go to Portugal. Made a donation in her name to some youth alcohol prevention charity. Like actually fuck you, I wish it had been you, you know. She was born in 2005! *2005.* A fucking space odyssey number.' He shook his head.

'Grief makes people mad.'

'Yeah, and don't judge, but I fucking judge.' He took a breath. 'Do you have siblings?'

'Only child,' I said. 'Lonely child. No, I like it ... And after years of therapy I can finally share—'

He reached to take a sip of my glass of wine, and I said, 'Don't you dare.'

'Have you ever known a death?' he said then. He looked worried, anticipating what my answer might be, then embarrassed at the roundabout way he'd said it.

My whole life, particularly my job, was so frequently tennis. Hitting shots back as quickly as I could, never letting anything land, my body doing it without me even asking. I was going say something to diffuse it, a queue of jokes appeared to me. But the thing about Ed was, he knew how to play, and also when to put the racquet down. I wasn't used to it. 'I mean, my mum now,' I said, 'being who-knows-how close to it. But I don't want to equate it with what you're saying.'

'You've had your heart broken though?' he said. 'Not in the box-of-chocolates way, in the actual pain in your chest, people like die from it way?'

It never failed to amaze me, how the brain did it. How whole stories could rush in in a second.

I had proposed to Bonnie as a joke, and it was meant to be a joke, then in my mouth, or as it left my mouth, it became intensely serious. I'd never been more serious about anything in my life, I realised. Down on one knee, I wanted to cry. 'It started out as a joke, but I'm serious,' I said. I felt soundwaves or heatwaves – this beaming thing – coming out of my chest.

'You are joking,' Bonnie had said. Not said, she told me.

'I'm not.' I took her hand and put it to my chest, and it felt like my heart was coming out to meet it.

'What do you think?' I said. 'I love you.'

'It sounds dangerous in there,' she said. She meant my heart.

At first it had been okay.

'Is that a yes?' I said.

'Of course,' she said.

'Is of course a yes?'

'Yes.'

I kept on asking her to say it again, her yes. The thrill that came with commitment. 'As you aways say,' she said – neither happy nor sad about it, just fact – 'commitment makes you wet.'

Later, I discovered there was no shortage of people she told about how tormenting those weeks afterwards were for her. I was working with someone once who recounted an engagement horror story – a girl who'd been secretly sick every day until she called it off – and eventually I worked out that it had come from Bonnie. Her ways of saying things were stamped all through the story like a watermark.

'I don't know if the love way is the same as death,' I said to Ed.

He said he'd read an article about it. 'Medically it's not far off.'

'Then yeah,' I said. 'Crushed to pieces.'

We ordered rare steak that came sliced and tumbled with beetroot that also bled, and horseradish. We ordered a second drink, and then a third. The combination of things was right. It somehow turned to something close to happiness in my bloodstream. I started to levitate above it: my parents, the pressures of work, what Ed had said about his sister, Bonnie.

The blossom had arrived and died early that year – pink turned into cream crisp almost overnight in the heatwave around the election – but for some reason, maybe cooled by the close canal, the tree above us was still a picture of April. It kept dusting our table with pink confetti. Also my shoulders, my hair.

'In a different life, we look like we just got married,' Ed said.

We ate, we talked, people looked at us and I saw them do their little wonder about whether we were together. Strange, but I didn't want them to think definitely no.

'What does the great gay novelist mean?' I asked him eventually.

'I didn't come up with that—'

'Yeah but how do you earn the title?'

'Top shagger,' he said. He took a deep draw of the iced coffee he'd ordered.

'The Grindr King,' I said. I asked him what his type was.

'I don't have a type because we're not twelve.'

'The last three guys you slept with then—'

'Are you accusing me of sex before marriage?' he said. He shut one eye as if performing thinking. His cheeks had a little bit of pink in them, right on the crest. 'Since I've been here, there's one guy I've seen a couple of times,' he said. 'I don't want to make you jealous, but he is . . .' he shut his eyes, 'an influencer.'

'Oh wow.'

'Yeah, big time.'

'How big?'

'Too big.'

'Let me see him.'

'I can't show you his pictures. I can't. He is sweet in real life, but it's like a time portal to 2018 or something.'

Our heads pooled together to look at his screen. The man's teeth were very white. In many of the photos he didn't have a top on, his abs as pronounced as the underside of an egg carton. In one of the older photos, he was having an elaborate picnic spread in front of the Eiffel Tower. The caption said La Dolce Vita.

'He has so many different pairs of sunglasses,' I said.

'He's not like that in person,' Ed said. 'He's quite shy actually. Last night he wanted to text for a bit even when we were in the same room.'

'How old is he?' I asked, and Ed's shoulders raised up in a shrug.

We paid the bill, our cards sword-fighting at the machine. I asked him what he was doing that evening. 'Another date with the influencer?' I said. Again, I felt a strong sensation of not wanting to leave. Ed had a feather on his T-shirt and I wanted to pluck, or blow, it off.

'The influenza,' he said. '1918 edition. I did say I'd see him again, yeah.'

'Two days in a row?' I replied. 'Wow.'

He looked at me. His forehead seemed to flicker a tiny bit, but I might have imagined it. 'So I better prepare the space in my attic where I keep my dead bodies,' he said.

'I was thinking we should have saved some confetti . . .'

The feather on Ed's T-shirt moved of its own accord in the wind. It fell in a sycamore spin. The goodbye seemed to go a little faster after that.

13

I was sad after I left, but I told myself there could be many reasons for that. I walked in the sun, reading a thinly thought-through piece about why the S&P 500 was so turbulent, and I squinted so much that when I got home, I had new lines. I'd kept wanting the walk to be longer and longer.

On the plus side, the draft statement I'd sent to Daniel had 'nailed it'.

That's what you call a fucking statement! he'd texted me. *OK helmet on, we're going out fighting!*

Then, when I didn't reply, *we ride at dawn!!!*

He'd emailed too.

Statement is good. Becky in press cc'ed. Thinks she can get us an intvw tomorrow.

Let's get on TPs.

The other TP of my life – talking points.

Another message came through. What now? I thought. But the name that appeared was Ed's.

Hey, later, it said.

It turns out I'm meeting my social
media star right by your house

Or where I think your house is?
If you weren't doing a decoy mission in that uber
I thought back to that moment. The late-night world playing like a film out of each of our car windows.

Not lying for once
La Dalsta Vita

No worries if not, or you're not there,
but any chance I could pop by for a quick chat before?
just quickly
A breeze blew through me.

Sure

clear things up?
you can say no
Clear what things? Say no to what?

it's fine, I wrote,
i'm here all night

Specific address?
Or I can just walk through
the streets bellowing your name
It's kind of soonish

I told him the address and after that, I found myself wandering around the house, imagining everything through his eyes. All my appliances in the kitchen, which Flo called 'my technologies'. ('May as well have stacks of cash on the counter,' she'd also said.) I checked my bed was made, smelled my pillowcase, then felt stupid for doing that. I felt a little sick too, sherbet on the stomach.

I looked up Ed's route, if he was coming from where he was staying. It seemed too quick. Perhaps it wouldn't be too late to text him and tell him not to come. I had talking points to do. I had so much to do. Then the doorbell rang, a sharp drilling sound. When I opened the door I saw his back. He turned round. He had a bottle of wine in his hand.

He said he liked my place. He was diligent at pointing out things for compliments: a print, some flowers, the Greek key detailing on a fireguard. He said those things, I said some others. All of our sentences were full sentences. Like we were in a play. Like we were passing them between us. I put the bottle he'd bought against my wrist, said it wasn't cold enough yet, and put it in the freezer.

'We could always drink it with ice.' He looked a little itchy in his body. 'It's nice, but not too nice for ice.' Then: 'So basically here's what I was thinking,' he said, right out, water bursting from a dam, as I was putting in the corkscrew. I focused on the stamp on the cork, tried to read it even though I knew it was German. 'We get on,' he said after that. 'Obviously I like you,' he said. 'You make me laugh. I just got a bit worried. Because – do you want me to help you with that?'

'No, I can do it.'

'Something about it feels confusing,' he said. 'You know?' He left a small pause but it wasn't long enough for me to feel forced to say anything. 'Or maybe you don't know? Confusing is the only word I can get to.' I knew he was looking at me, but I couldn't look at him yet. I just kept opening the bottle, incredibly slowly. 'So I suppose I just wanted to make sure that this is just friendship for you,' he said. 'Because it is, right?'

I wished I could put the bottle, even if it wasn't that cold, against my cheek. Embarrassment felt sharp. He'd come all the way to my house to check I didn't have a crush on him.

Ed looked like he was having a conversation with himself almost, doing both sides. The way his body was moving back and forth too, like he was driving a car in an arcade. 'I just wanted to check it was cool with you,' he said. 'I mean, cool is such a dumb word, and why wouldn't it be cool? I just wanted to check stuff was cool with us, and normal.' He looked relieved to have found that word. 'Normal's what I want.'

'Ed, yes, it's fine. I'm a lesbian, remember?'

'Right, of course.' He nodded diligently, a kid in school. 'I just didn't know if you were bi or something.'

'I'm not. Are you?'

'No,' he said. 'Not at all. No. Okay, cool. That's good. Just it would have been a mess.'

'What time is this guy expecting you?'

He looked relieved then, like he had all the time in the world. I understood the relief. I'd felt something close to it too. But someone else's relief. Why did that feel so awful?

The wine tasted like licking the wrist of someone who had just applied perfume. Ed seemed to know a lot about wine or at least it was him who turned the label to face him and said he really liked the maker. He'd brought round some Comté too and you could taste the crystals of salt in it.

I asked him if he was secretly rich, and he nodded again like he was taking the question seriously. 'No,' he said. 'When my dad died, he left me money. But I didn't spend it.'

'You didn't spend it,' I repeated. 'So you have it.'

'I don't have it, per se,' he said. *Per se*, I thought. 'It's not a lot and it's locked away. I don't understand it. But it has given me some liberty,' he said. 'Knowing it was there.'

He told me his mum was very normal. His favourite word again. He said that her boyfriend had a gardening business called Lawn Order. Then he stood up and he walked around. He looked at my books. It seemed like the collection had shrunk, and the only ones he pointed out, I hadn't read.

We talked about other things too. The types of fish that were still sustainable for some reason. And what had got us into this mess in the first place, the broader country mess. He said he'd been taking Boris bikes and whenever he got to the end of the journey and put the bike back, he kicked it.

'You don't want to keep an influential man waiting ...' I said eventually.

When Ed said goodbye to me, he kissed me on the middle of my cheek. After he left, I sat at the table with the remaining third of the bottle, which I finished in tiny glassfuls, each sip tasting thicker and sweeter and less cold than the one before.

I did the talking points, organised a 7 a.m. rendezvous at the office the next day, and then, because the encounter with Ed kept feeling like this huge, confusing pinch, I decided to lean into masochism.

Forget Bonnie. I had no choice but to forget Bonnie now. But what about Marion? It occurred to me in a tidal wave that I had been an idiot. Why hadn't I tried to fix things with Marion? Marion had been nice, Marion had liked me, she smelled good, even the middle of her back smelled good. Sometimes, when we were fucking, I'd shut my eyes and truly not be able to work out what was happening to my body, whether it was hand or thumb or tongue or eight people or a machine or who even knew.

I scrolled down to find her name, weeks ago away, and looked back at her last message after the breakup. She'd said I was dead, not even dead to her, just dead. But I could text her something simple. I could ask her how she was. Hello from the underworld, something like that.

I was just about to when the doorbell rang again.

14

I opened the door. It was dark out there. It must have been eleven or twelve by that point. And then I noticed the arm, the face. Ed's face.

His forearm was up high leaning on the doorway, and when he saw how much taller he was than me, I saw him look at his hand, then move it.

It's hard to explain what I felt. It's not that I expected him, but I didn't feel shock. There seemed to be some correctness to it; the way that, when a boomerang leaves your hand, there's some sense or instinct, or hope, it might come back.

'I don't know how to do this,' Ed said. He stepped away. 'As a guy, do you even go to a door?'

'Have you come back to tell me I'm your friend again?'

'I went on my date.'

'I know you went on your date.'

'His name is Rory by the way.'

'Did he text you that from the table?'

'What? No, I was saying his name's Rory.'

'Okay.'

'And what did I do? Keep doing?'

'I don't know, Ed.'

'I talked about you. A lot. I talked about you. Fucking weird.'

He was drunk. He kept on standing on one foot, then the other. I could think of a thousand worlds where I would hate this, but I seemed to be in the one world where I didn't.

'Shall I get wine?' he said. 'I can go to get wine—'

'Just come inside.'

'Is this friendship,' he said, 'for me. For you?'

'You already asked that,' I said. 'Have water.'

'I need some water,' he said. Again, hard to explain. It wasn't a drunkenness that knocked things over, it was much quieter and softer than that. He seemed peeled open.

'Come sit down,' I said.

'I just don't know what to do. What the adult thing to do is.'

'I don't think adults ever know what to do.'

'When I was with Rory what I thought was—' He looked up and around for me. 'Maybe we just look at each other and think about what it is that we want,' he said. 'You and me, I mean.'

'Did you say that?'

'To who?'

'To Rory.'

'No, I was just thinking it in my head.'

'Okay.'

'Just to look at each other and see. Whether it's in that way. Not just to spend time. Is that stupid? It's so stupid. Maybe I'm completely wrong about all this.' He looked at me, and I did have to say something this time.

'No—' I started.

'So I *am* wrong?'

'No, I mean I don't think you're wrong.'

90

'What do you think?' That back-and-forth body again. 'Should we do that? I can also go.'

It surprised me how obvious it felt. I didn't want him to go.

'I had a couple of drinks by the way,' Ed said.

'I guessed.'

'I've drunk with you, but I don't normally drink so much – I've felt shy or—'

'It's okay,' I said.

'It is okay, I feel better now I said it.' He took a big swig of the water. 'I know it's stupid,' he said. 'Unless you want to do it … then it's a great idea.' His smile was stupid. He knew it was stupid.

Stupid, too, the way I'd tried, and even then I tried again, to look for things that were feminine. Was it that his hair was long, not even that long, but could be? Was it a gentleness I wasn't used to, in men I'd known? His tears in the taxi. Was it just that I knew he was attractive? Because he was, objectively. He would be, to anyone.

Whatever the reason was, I'd put him into the wrong place in my body. With other men, years and years ago, the happiness had always come when they left. When I had days ahead, days I'd bought, before I saw them again. But Ed – I had felt it every time, that thing, I think, that wanting someone is: I wanted to be where he was, I wanted him to be where I was.

The kitchen seemed so full of hard lines. I wanted to go somewhere softer. I told him that if he was serious, we should go to the bedroom.

When he got there, he sat down on the duvet. 'Do you want me to then?' he said. I didn't say no or yes. Then he took off his T-shirt, his arms criss-crossing over his body. There were one or two more tattoos: a planet, a line of text on the side of his ribcage.

I looked at him on my bed. Should you do things that scare you? Or should you listen to fear? It had always confused me. I stood up.

I turned to face him, my bare feet on my rug. I remember looking down at my toes and wondering how long ago that nail varnish was from. The underside of my hair at the back of my neck was still wet from the bath. 'Do you mean actually, like?' I touched the button of my shirt. 'It's ridiculous, we're not kids—'

'I know we're not kids,' he said.

Ed folded the T-shirt he'd taken off. The ridges on his chest when he sat back down, like a bar of white chocolate. As I took off my shirt too, I could see him keeping his eyes on my face, then doing these quick looks lower, but always returning to my face.

My legs were tight together, ankles hard. I opened them slightly. I was wearing a bra that was slightly see-through.

I wondered if there was a point where one of us would say stop, but neither of us did. The trousers I was wearing were loose, for the heat. They dropped to the floor as soon as I undid the button. I don't know you, I kept thinking, but somehow I know you.

I tried to imagine pulling down his black boxers. Tried to imagine what the skin there would be like. Tried to imagine him getting hard in my hand. Some stoic thing. Draft it before it happens.

For those first moments though, I tried to push my mind between my own legs, but no matter what I did, I could only think about what he thought of me. I was aware of everything about my body that was least like what he was used to.

'How you doing?' I asked him.

'I'm okay.'

He shifted on the bed. The shape of his underwear started to change. It made a kind of leaning tower of Pisa within the cotton.

'It's straight, really,' he said.

I didn't make a joke. I nodded.

At first, like I said, it was Ed I was trying to read. It was him I was worrying about. His feeling I was trying to judge. Because it's not just their arms, not just their bodies. It's their everything we're taught is stronger.

A new sobriety came over him. A soberness. Perhaps they're the same thing.

'If you were a man I'd know what to do,' he said.

'If you were a woman, I'd feel the same.'

'Even though I know it's all invented,' he said. 'Will you come?' He moved over on the bed. My bed. But suddenly it felt different.

I lay down next to him. I'm trying to think back into the feeling. When does nervousness meet excitement, when is it just nervousness? We lay on our sides facing each other. His body from the side, any body from the side – the way they make landscapes.

'I mean, I do know *what* to do,' he said. 'Theoretically. I've seen films.'

'Is that right?'

'When I don't cover my eyes for the rude bits.'

He smiled, then swallowed it. We hadn't kissed yet. I'd thought it many times: how it was impossible to look at both of someone's eyes at once. How it was strange you always had to pick one, or look between them, from one to the other, a slow bounce. He looked at my lips like he was tracing them, I saw the pupils, in tiny flickers, follow their shape.

It wouldn't always be that way – it hadn't been for me earlier, even minutes before, and later, there were so many ways we slipped out of balance – but in that exact moment, it felt perfectly equal.

I tipped my head back and kissed his forehead. It was warm and brought me closer to his hair, which smelled like head. A nice head.

'I haven't kissed a girl since I was sixteen,' he said.

I could smell alcohol on his breath, but that too wasn't bad. I kept on looking for something to shrink everything, or to make me shrink, for the turn to happen, but it still wasn't coming.

'I'm pretty good at it,' I said.

'I'm sure.'

It's not just that you can't look at both eyes at once; it's hard to focus on someone when your faces are that close. I caught glimpses. I wanted to lean back, see all of him.

'You do it here, right?' he said. He kissed the lower part of my cheek.

'You start there,' I said.

'Then here.' He kissed the corner of my mouth. 'Or that's what I heard.'

His lips stayed against my skin. I felt him breathe. I waited to flinch. I waited for disappointment, an awful thing to say, but then I realised I wasn't breathing. Or, no I was, but the breath had to try so hard to get to the base of me.

'Close,' I said.

Still, for one final moment, my brain played paper fortune-teller: you want to feel good if it's happening, but what does it mean if it does feel good? You want it to feel good for him, because it's happening, but what does it mean if it doesn't?

I don't know what I expected my body to do when I touched his. For the first seconds of the kiss, the back-and-forth came with me everywhere. My eyes shut and then they opened – it's Ed, it's him, stay with him, is this? is he? – and then it happened: hands on each other's skin now, no gap between us, I waited for my body to take over and it did.

Our bodies were tight together; our underwear soon bundled at our feet. I remember various things. The wingspan of his hand, wider than an octave, how far away I'd feel a thumb from a little finger on my back. The cool of his ring. The knock of his chest. His penis, the way it said 'I'm here'. Our mouths open, Ed pushed his finger inside me, two, then one again, and not for long. 'It's hot,' he said. 'Actual heat.' My legs, the way they found their way around parts of his body. The way I could feel his heart beating, beating so hard it was almost punching me.

Afterwards, not that we went anywhere particularly far, I crawled onto him like I was crawling onto a rock. He tilted around on the bed until my head was comfortable on him.

The feeling came all at once. I wanted him to like me. I couldn't even work out what I felt yet, but I wanted him to like me. I wanted him to think I was clever. I wanted him to think I was a nice girl, or woman, or whatever it was that I was by then. I wanted him to think I was good.

It was his breathing I noticed then. He was barely doing it at all.

'I just worry it's the wrong way,' he said. At first, I wondered if he meant the ceiling.

'What do you mean?'

'I don't know,' he said. 'Just the wrong thing. Now. The wrong time.'

'Yeah,' I said. Everything had been in the air, thrown high, high up there, and now it was all crystallising.

'Like people who march for guns. Protest abortion. Are against—' he said. He stopped. 'Maybe. I just worry.'

I looked round the room, round his body. Male nipples were so small. His were almost the same colour as his skin.

I saw us in bed from above. Him big, me small. Yet another man and woman. We lay there still, separate, backs to the bed, chest to the sky. And then, I didn't see it, but I felt it, he curled up in a ball next to me.

'Fuck,' he said, quietly, like he'd forgotten something.

'What?'

For a second it was silent.

'We should sleep now,' he said, 'I have to sleep.'

*

That next morning, Ed left early. Early even for me. He said something about already being late. I was half-asleep. I quarter-watched him get dressed. His eyes looked very open. He pulled on his trainers, straightened the tongue, and patted his pockets for his wallet. I thought he might lean down and kiss me, because there are things that you do to soften endings, blur edges. Then I saw his hand: it looked like he was going to touch my head but he touched the bed instead. He looked at me. I saw it again in his face, his eyes, in the way they moved: a problem, and one that had not been solved. I pretended I was still asleep because I still thought he'd turn back. But he turned away and he left.

15

Daniel and I sat in the green room of the TV studio. I hadn't had time to bring in Fred, our unassuming-looking, Rottweiler-like mock interviewer, but I'd pummelled Daniel as best I could.

'BBC would have been better,' Daniel said. 'Sorry *new* BBC. NBBC. New makes things sound ancient, doesn't it? But this is okay. This is okay.'

It was a morning show, and the hosts were a polished couple whose outfits always chimed colour-wise. They had five children, each of whom regularly featured in sections about new kids' toys and what was happening in the world squashed into simple, Play-Doh shapes for 'younger minds'.

'*Up + At 'Em Britain*. Who the fuck came up with that? It's like a tongue-twister,' Daniel said. 'Anyway, the tone you hit on the statement is killer. There'll be a little resistance I'm sure, but honestly, people are going to eat it up.'

What I had said in the statement was along the lines of this:

That really, all we were doing at Gigr, was attempting to uphold the country during an unending cost of living crisis. Doing something that previous governments, by their own admission, couldn't do. As requested by Daniel, we'd thrown a couple of fallen MPs (namely the aforementioned 'Bill bitch') under the bus, and thrown in some stats too. Over the past year, wages had gone down fifteen percent in real terms – twenty-five percent in some sectors. What were people supposed to do? What did it tell you if a police inspector, nineteen years into the job, had no choice but to work in the evenings? People were always asking for jobs for British people: and we were doing that, weren't we? More than anyone else was anyway.

What had happened at Gigr was only symptomatic of deeper problems, ones that we were working to solve. *We are a nation of workers,* I'd written. *Moonlighting is stigmatised, but surely we could all acknowledge it's just people looking for hope in the dark.*

It was five minutes until Daniel was on. 'You know the lines?' I asked him.

'I know the lines. And your A, B, C thing,' Acknowledge, Bridge, Comment. 'I know it all.'

Up close, the make-up they'd put on him – it wasn't that it was starting to crack, not yet, it was just that his face was flawless, made of velour or something, rather than skin.

'Thanks for insisting on the clear mascara this time,' he said. 'When they did black I looked like I was on a fast-track to HRT!' I looked at him. 'What?'

'Just ... don't,' I said.

'Oh I fucking know the drill,' he said. '*Behave.* Though these guys are definitely a bit "hands off our kids" aren't they? They'd lap it up.'

The camera might add ten pounds, but I'd discovered many times, watching Daniel on screen, that it also had the power to subtract just the right amount of uncontrolled energy. To bring it to an almost perfect notch just above base level. Daniel came on, introduced as a controversial figure. The audience made an ominous sound in between an ooh and boo, a sound they obviously enjoyed.

It would always play out the same way. It was remarkable how quickly it happened. It was the cut of his suit. It was his hands in his pockets and the way they came out, palms up like open cups, like he had nothing to hide. It was the way he nodded when challenged, like he was hearing every word. It was the way he said: 'Good question.' '*Great* question.' The hosts softened to him like he'd put something in their water. I watched it play out through the monitor. The colour hadn't been graded; it would be sleeker when it went out into the world. But he said the lines I had given him word for word, and I found myself nodding too. That purr that comes in a chest, the feeling of something going right. The lines worked, they landed. Daniel's caricature sharpened into a photograph. Sometimes he could be so good at what he did it was terrifying.

That afternoon, after the show had gone out, after journalists had had time to file, Daniel came into my office again to read one of the articles out loud.

'"Gigr merely reflects the *grim reality* of contemporary Britain." See!' he said. 'This is great!' He carried on reading. '"Where would Britain be without its polyfiller?" That's good! It's good, right? Was that us?'

'I didn't say polyfiller,' I said.

He carried on reading: '"The entrepreneurs",' – he'd started to read it like poetry, line breaks, flicks of the page – '"that step in to plug the government's leaky, creaky gaps are more vital than ever before" . . .' He looked quite moved. 'Good work,' he said, still shaking his head.

He took a step away from me. I thought he was leaving the room and then he turned back.

'Listen,' he said. 'I know Westminster's a shit show at the moment, and your policy weirdos are all scrambling to get a new lay of the land. But I need you on it hard.'

'I always am,' I said.

'I'll make it worth your while. If you're ready to go there – go there I'll make you a VP.' He leaned back while standing, looked at me. 'Hey, come on. That's sexy, right? Throw a few extra points in the package?' Punchy of him with the door open: talking about shares was verboten. 'But I need you to get tight with them. Whatever shit they're coming out with, I'll need you to suck it up. The IPO's nearly on our doorstep now—'

'I know.'

'The new gov's whole thing's deregulation, isn't it?' he said. 'We need to hold them to it, angle grinder.' And he pushed his fist into his hand.

16

At home, my bed was still unmade from the night before and the sheets had tangled into a weird, howling mouth.

Ed. Each time he'd burst into my head through the day, I'd pushed him away. The skills of a childhood hypochondriac. *Later. Worry about it later.*

I looked to see if he had left anything behind. He hadn't. I checked my phone again to see if he had written. He still hadn't. I felt a strong sensation that he should say something first. Internalised rules from over twenty years ago.

I tried to work it out, how it picked around inside me. A needle, knitting, knotting, nicking.

I didn't want to tell Flo. I could imagine what she would say. *Two weeks in with the new government and conversion therapy is off to a cracking start!* But I wanted to talk about it with someone, and that someone was him. I thought about things that I might write, and in the end, when it got late, and there was still no word, I settled for the simplest thing. *It was good to see you,* I wrote.

I put my phone away, to allow myself not to read a reply too quickly, then picked it back up: I was too old for that.

Ha, yes! he'd written.
Thanks for having me!
Sorry I left so early
Hectic week coming up with the
book as you can imagine

I put the back of my hand against my cheek, I could feel it had gone red.

Of course, I said.

He was online momentarily, then blinked out, an open sign being turned off.

See you soon, I said.

I waited for him to say something more. I willed it to happen.

I waited that night, then the next day too. Then the day after that, but nothing. The ticks by the last messages I'd sent him stayed ghostly grey.

And so, when the day rolled round, I couldn't work out what was weirder: to go to Ed's book launch, or not to, so I asked Flo to come with me.

Fuck no, she'd said.
What book? I hate book launches

A friend's
What friend?
What do you need a friend for, we're not lonely!

Where are you?
In my bed alone lol

It was the first day the entire Jubilee line stopped working and they had no idea what had caused it. Flo sent me a picture from her local stop. A message board which said 'Jubilee down because ... Life is broken', with the Nintendo 'game over' sign in outsized pixels next to it. I ordered her a car.

The bookshop was orange and it didn't have a name, it just said 'books!' There was a gaggle of people outside, smoking. 'Your usual not-your-usual bookshop crowd,' Flo said as we approached, then 'air-con', as we stepped inside, emphasis on con, like it was a scam. 'That's a second forest of trees razed to the ground.'

The feeling of entering a room where you know no one. The air-conditioning in concert with fans made a mousetrap game designed to move the cool air in a square. I wanted to see Ed but I didn't want to look for him. I didn't need to be worried for him though; the room was already full.

'I got us the biggest ones,' Flo said, handing me a glass of wine. 'I eyed them from the side. Which one's your friend?'

The word friend sounded too loud. 'Let's go outside,' I said. 'It's hot.'

'It's hotter out there!'

'Well then let's go outside because I hate people.'

'Fair enough.'

As we stepped outside the door, we went a different way to the smokers.

'Why are you being—' Flo started.

'I'm not.'

'Well you're definitely being something.'

'It's nothing,' I said. But she wasn't wrong; the whole way we walked over I couldn't find the right path into anything I wanted to say. 'We,' I said. 'Me and this guy – who's gay – just had a moment.'

'What kind of moment? Oh no.' She looked like she'd smelled something bad. 'Is he one of those edgelord gay men—'

'No.'

'Like rude like Milo Yannapo-whatever-his-name-was?' she said.

'No,' I said. I stopped. I was trying to think how to say it correctly. 'We—'

'What? You look awful.'

'That's just my face! Anyway, it doesn't matter.'

'Don't go with *doesn't matter*. Don't make me desperate to know.'

'We just kind of – whatever – ended up in bed together. I don't know—'

'What? What kind of bed?'

'My bed.'

'But in what way?'

And then I saw him, walking down the street towards us. He was with a girl shorter than him, younger than him, she had a bag of ice in her arms, cuddled like an infant. Ed had a similar bag on his shoulder and one on his head.

'Truly fuck off,' Flo said, and I told her to be quiet. I prepared my face in a smile. Not a smile, but at least not *not* a smile. The other smokers went towards Ed. Hugs, 'the man himself', something about Vanilla Ice.

When he got to us, he said 'hi' to me, but looked more quickly at Flo.

'Luckiest guy in London . . .' she said. We all looked at each other. 'The ice!' she said.

'This is my friend Flo,' I said.

'Hi Friend Flo,' Ed said.

'You should go put it down,' I said. 'Give the people what they want.'

He smiled. There was melted ice-water dripping down his forehead. 'Congratulations,' Flo said as he went in to a chorus of voices getting louder as they saw him.

'Fuckoff,' she said again, one word. 'What kind of bed?'

'I don't fucking know. I don't want to talk about it. We get on. And there was something? Something I don't— And he went on a date, but then he came back to my house. And it – I didn't even – I've been trying to work it out—'

'You're not speaking properly. It's like you hate the English language.'

'But it's like who cares? Just feels old for experimenting.' The word experimenting – the length of it, how it just kept on going – sounded so ridiculous we both laughed. 'I don't understand it at all. Except really though.' It felt like pedalling a bike, but with no resistance at all. Whenever I tried to land, my feet kept falling through the floor.

'Well, I think they *do* have a word for it ... I never know how to pronounce it but I believe it's—' She took a long pause, and tried to get her mouth into the right position '—bee-sexual ? ... bye-sexualé?'

'It's not that. I mean in the way that everyone is. But he isn't. And I'm not. I was about to say "I aren't".'

'Well,' she said. 'I don't know. Maybe it's the age.'

'The age like my age?'

'No! I mean, yes, but also the, like, *epoch*. I mean "who cares" as you said. All the kids are doing it.'

'You don't know the kids.'

'I know what they're doing! Or were doing. I did my month-long subscription to *Teen Vogue* years ago or whatever that was.' Her glass was empty. 'But wait, it was consensual?'

'Consensual, yes. Of course yes. Just ... yeah. He came over and. Yeah.' I asked her if we could move away from the other people.

'If you're going to give lyrical descriptions like that,' she said. 'Don't want the writers to be jealous ... And just to check, you came really hard, of course—'

'Can we just talk about it at dinner?'

Inside, people were starting to gather. We stayed by the door. There was some laughter up at the front. Ed's editor made a speech, called herself the Ed-itor, did the classic start light then swerve to 'in all seriousness' thing. Ed touched his chest. I couldn't work out whether he liked her or not.

Ed was charming in what he said. That studies show that people who are grateful lived longer, and that he was due to outlive that

106

man in Japan, or was it a woman in France now, due to how much gratitude he felt.

Then he read. He had to stop a couple of lines in, and ask for water. He stretched out his mouth in the same way he'd done when I first met him. Something else I'd noticed that night too and saw again, or rather heard: the gentleness to Ed's voice, how it was soft yet carried without him shouting. There was a little shake in his hands at first – ever so slightly, the square of his book shook – and then he found his breath and settled.

At first I found myself conscious of how I would look to him if he looked up and looked at me. Or how the face I had when I listened would look to other people. Then his sentences pulled me in. In the beginning, I couldn't work out if it was just his voice, the way he read them, because you can trick people like that, but his sentences – I don't know how to say it, but they each had this shape. Feather-light and heavy at the same time, like the weight had been calibrated perfectly. They worked in his mouth, and later, on the page, and you felt, if you held them in your hand, let them rest on a finger, they would balance. Then these surprises, these little jabs.

'Anyway, thank you for coming,' he said at the end. 'Don't feel obliged to buy the book, though please do. I didn't even read the best bit!' he said. 'Honestly. Page 57 is really good. And it's downhill from there. But seriously—' that same swerve, it always felt like a plane landing, '—us gay people need all the help we can get at the moment.' There were some claps, woos, and also boos, but not for him. 'So yeah, here's to gay books.'

Someone in the crowd, who swayed like one of those inflatable tube men, shouted, 'Keep the cocks coming!' and people laughed, and then the noise of talking started back up, and the swarm started at the till, and for those who already had books in their hands, around Ed.

'I've changed my mind,' Flo said. 'I may well take a copy, he's alright your b—'

'Seriously stop it—'

'What?' she said. 'Bum boy is rude now?', pretending to look shocked.

I bought two copies of the book. They felt heavy in my hand. We stood for a short while, the queue around Ed only growing.

'You look – what's that fashionable word?' Flo said. 'Disassociated. Can we get a pizza?'

'Do I say bye?' I looked around, but there were a million people there.

'Ugh, shit,' Flo said, skirting a brown mass on the pavement. 'That one looked like pâté. It really is *Decline and Fall* these days.' As we walked, two kids came up to us and asked for change for their bus ride home, and then, seeing that we had given them something, another woman came up and asked for money too. 'Do you notice that more and more people asking for money look like normal people?' Flo said.

'They are normal people.'

'I know, but you used to look up and notice right away, like . . . your shoes have no laces. But now it's just – you are a very hot man who I would date . . . And might date! How's a fiver? Not that I have one.' One of the many things I loved about Flo was that she could embark on these long monologues and I found peace in them. 'Anyway, I'm going to have two pizzas. Maybe three. If you're paying. I mean it's shit like that—' she pointed at a doorway of a gentrification-grey house with a stained-glass transom window. 'Everyone knows people are fucking starving, do you really think your neon purple Mindful Chef box is going to sit on your doorstep for six hours? Please. Also, oh my god, in the car I was reading this piece about how the plan is – wait for it – respectability politics for now. Lull us into a false sense of security.' She screwed up her face in a playground mime for stupid. 'Love how MPs calling each other faggots in parliament is respectable these days—'

From behind us I heard a 'hey'.

I wondered for a second if it was the kids again, but it wasn't a child's voice, and I knew the voice.

'Oh hi,' Flo said.

'Can I . . . ' Ed said, about me.

'Can you what? Oh yeah, sure. Sorry—' Flo turned away and started looking at a tree.

I walked back towards him, just a few steps.

'You're leaving—' he said to me.

'Sorry. She was hungry. She's like a child.'

'I hope I didn't make you leave?' he said. He looked worried, but he also looked frustrated. That line appearing then disappearing between his eyebrows. 'I know it's weird,' he said. He looked at me like he wanted me to say it. 'And I was the one who asked, and came over, it's all me. My fault.' Did he want me to say it wasn't? 'I've felt very complicated. It's just, it's not – it's not . . .' he looked at the ground then. 'And, like, my publishers are there, and my friends—'

'Right,' I said.

'I know it's stupid, I'm sorry.'

It was like there was an invisible barrier in front of him, or one of those lines that attached astronauts to space stations. He couldn't come any further.

'It's okay,' I said.

'I'm sorry,' he said again. 'I am sorry. I am. I have to go back now.'

18

All through dinner, there was a chew in my stomach.

'What's wrong?' Flo said. 'You aren't eating your madly expensive sourdough pizza. Don't you remember when pizzas were around the ten-pound mark. Margarita at least. Wasn't it nine quid? When we were adults, I mean. Twenty-five-pound margaritas feel like a hate crime.' She dipped her crust into a small vial of aioli. 'Anyway, thank you, it's delicious.'

The bottoms of our pizzas were burned, and the bitterness of that mixed with the sour of the sourdough.

'I thought it was nice of him to come and find you and say good-bye,' she said. 'Was it?'

'What? To say sorry, and no?'

I hoped that was it. The sharpness of the feeling. The simple trick of someone pulling close, then pulling away.

'But in what world do you want him to say *yes*?' she said. 'Can you tell me what actually happened? I thought it was a joke at first.'

I tried to explain. How we'd met the night after the election, how we'd walked.

'You walked and ... what?' she said. 'You walked into a whole different plane of the universe?'

'That's what I'm saying, I don't know. But it happened to both of us. I think. I don't know. Emotions aren't typically my *forté* ...'

'And you don't think he's pretending? Like those men who say they're infertile, but actually have fifteen kids.'

'The book launch would have been quite an elaborate ruse.'

'And you wanted it? That's what I'm trying to understand? Because I know you and you don't fancy men. *I'm* what happens when you fancy men. TP wears a buffed-leather bomber jacket.' She puffed out her mouth like a balloon. 'And I've been there, remember. For that sad little thing called your life.'

I nodded. My life. Increasingly, I was starting to lose my sense of it.

'I always remember what you said about girls,' she said. 'How it was like stars.' Her hands became the sky.

'Not stars ...'

'Come brother, for I have tasted stars.'

'Not stars,' I said again. But it was stars.

When it first happened to me, in a club, later than it should have been, when the first girl I kissed fell into me against a wall and it seemed she couldn't stop, suddenly I wasn't a camera looking at me anymore, there was a camera in me and I was deep inside the world. I'd lost my keys that night. My phone. My bag, my coat. I dream-walked out of the club and forgot everything. Even when I woke up I could not make myself care. My stomach flipped and rolled, flipped and rolled.

'Also, didn't he say he was based in New York ...' she said. 'As well as the minor hurdle of him being gay. When's he going back?'

'Soon I guess.' I didn't know. 'But you know what I mean though. Imagine if you suddenly met a woman.'

'I'd be overjoyed! I went on a date the other night and the guy's dandruff got on *top* of the brim of his cap.'

111

'But it's different,' I said. How to say it? 'To go back, not forward.'

'Seriously,' she said. 'Don't come out here.' She dotted a licked finger over crust crumbs. 'And anyway, he's wrong. '

'What?'

'Apparently it's not gratitude anymore.'

'What?'

'That keeps you alive longer. There was a study,' she said. She reached over for a slice of my pizza and did a little grin. 'It's spite.'

19

The day of Ed's book launch was the start of the proper heatwave. The brief cool since the week after the election was like jumping hard on a trampoline to make yourself go even higher. What followed was a full month of no-cloud sun, and each day the heat ratcheted up. *Global WOW-ing,* one paper called it, rays radiating from the 'O'.

It was a heat you felt in your eyes. It burned bright right through to the back of the retina. Mascara melted. Parks were bare, burned to a bleached close shave.

A video went viral of birds falling from the sky somewhere in Pakistan. Flo sent me an infographic of organs failing after heatstroke. *State of the nation,* she wrote. *Pathetic fallacy is so GCSE English but truly!!*

It was too hot to put a laptop on your lap. *Not only has the world got hotter,* she continued, *but we have to operate our whole lives with metal things. My hot little phone in my hot little hand. My laptop like a fucking George Foreman grill under my wrists*

I kept on getting words wrong, weird mistakes, but often the same kind of glitch, a computer misfiring. It felt like that when the flashes came too. Short jump cuts in a film – the man's phone hitting the metal of the banister on the balcony, his knee knocking into it soon afterwards. A shock of disorientation too, because the scale of what I was seeing kept changing too. I'd suddenly get a close-up.

I'd finally had one of the calls with the obligatory therapist by then. Her voice was so stilted I wondered if she was AI. 'Are you real?' I asked. 'Are you having problems differentiating between what's real and what isn't?' she replied.

I'd said I wouldn't be able to come, but I took a midnight taxi nearly five hours to Devon to make it to a distant aunt's eightieth birthday. Since waiting lists had swelled, my mum had to pause treatments, so there was a small inlet of her feeling well. Also, she was one of those English people the sun is good for, and by the miracle of separate rooms in a large hotel, over two full days, we managed to keep the arguments at bay. The sea was warm in a way that felt bodily. There were tents on the beach, which made it look more like a desert than something by the sea. 'Lesbos,' my dad had said, and then quite sweetly smiled at me.

Work ramped up like the heat. I went on trips to Paris, Lisbon, Amsterdam, Munich – all interchangeable; bored-looking men waiting at airports with my name on an iPad – the first of many outreach 'moments', all part of our pre-IPO personality building.

The teams in the new territories were all unreasonably young, eager enough to still be at school. If I took them out for a cocktail after our debrief sessions – up our 'cool credentials', that was another element Daniel had asked for – they would often ask, frowns concentrated, about everything that was happening in the UK. I was curious why they cared. A lot of their countries were just as bad.

'Because of the health of the company,' one young guy from Holland explained. Moments earlier he'd said he'd heard no one in London wore watches anymore, or covered their wrists when they did, to avoid being stabbed. 'So I'm worried,' he said. Others nodded. I looked at them and tried to find irony in what he was saying.

'It'll be fine,' I replied, 'you know how it is. Capitalism *über alles* . . .' I tried to bring them with me – it was all knowing, wasn't it? – but they simply looked reassured, in a genuine way, and nodded.

Back at home, paradoxically, given the heat she had enjoyed, my mum got pneumonia. Heavy phlegm into handkerchiefs, a flickering heartbeat, a tan that turned yellow. For a few weeks, she couldn't really speak, because it made her cough these long terrible empty-thick coughs, so mostly, when I diverted a car from the airport and visited her, we sat in silence, which was more gentle than it had been and also desperately sad.

Once, after seeing her, when I got to my front door, Flo was waiting on the doorstep. 'I lost my key,' she said. 'I know when you're MIA you forget to eat.' Then, 'Had to.' She held up the Gigr-stamped paper bag full of food. 'No choice. You raptors have killed off the competition.'

We bundled through my hallway. I told her about the work trips; about visiting my mum. How I'd also spent days holed up at Parliament.

'A gunpowder plot?' she said, crossing her fingers on both hands.

'I wish. It's a fucking disaster. No one knows who anyone *is*, let alone who's doing what.' Prior to the election, apart from the ZLB Bill, my team had been in strong shape over at Whitehall. We'd co-sponsored two All Party Political Groups, and hosted regular parliamentary drinks on topics like 'the future of work'. But now, any lay of the land and allies we'd had had been decimated. And so I had to send my policy team out to try to hunt down people outside advisory committees, like a bunch of groupies in ill-fitting suits.

'Potstickers,' Flo said, pulling out some dumplings, but another thing stuck when she pulled them out of the bag. Three leaflets, in a clump. *IMMIGRATION RAIDS: KNOW YOUR RIGHTS.*

Over the past few weeks, the coalition had been united in

theatrically reinvestigating 'dodgy' asylum claims, through a new task force they'd instructed to be 'less nice than ICE'. In response, leaflets like these ones had been littered all through the city. I looked at one now. *You do not have to answer any questions. You do not have to let them in. Try to leave if you are not under arrest.*

'In the actual bag? They can't do that—' I went to take a picture.

'Elle, fuck *actually* off,' she said, blocking my camera.

'But it's so unprofessional—'

She lightly wrestled my phone off me and put it away on the table. 'Did you see that other thing too today?'

'War stuff?'

'Gay as a cause for asylum stuff. Apparently they're taking it *back* off the ones that had it. Past five years. Isn't that mental? There goes half your dating pool.'

I was about to reach for the leaflets to take another look, but she slid them towards her and then crushed them into her pocket. She did a conversational dogleg and told me that her own situation had got decidedly worse. 'TP said he needs the summer with his family to ob- serve their annual holiday thing. Corfu, I think. But then. Then.' The muscles in her neck tightened. 'Then he said he wants to *be* with me.'

'Why are you pulling that face?'

'He got on his knees to say it,' she said. I looked at her. 'No, no, both knees. Worse. Pleading. I don't know. Maybe he's changed his mind anyway. Hopefully. We were both a little high. A lottle.'

'What do you talk about?' I asked her.

'What does anyone talk about? I feel bad. It feels good, but I feel bad? His wife teaches the disabled. She is in every way an excellent woman. She's not even ugly. Beautiful in fact.'

'I can't one hundred percent say I understand it,' I said.

'If you must know, I love to watch him sleep.'

She said it was the only time in her life when she felt completely at peace, and I remember how she said it because it broke my heart later. I looked at her. We'd known each other for eighteen years by then: a whole adult.

'You're at peace now,' I said. 'Not in a dead way.'

'Yes and no. With him it's like peace plus. Like business class peace, you know?'

Her eyes kept flashing at something, and when I looked to see what it was, it was Ed's book on the table. She asked me if I'd read it yet. 'No,' I said. 'But you can use it as a coaster if you like.'

'That's aggressive,' she said. She started nodding in her I-got-you way.

'What?'

'I can tell you want to talk about it. Why else would you have left it directly at eye-line?'

'I didn't know you were coming.'

I flipped it over which made it worse, his photo smiling out from the back instead. I flipped it back. Both were pointless. I didn't need the book out; I kept finding reasons to think of him everywhere. He kept walking into my head like all the doors and windows were open. In the weird subsidised café at Parliament. In a bad Munich cocktail bar that relied far too heavily on dry ice. There was no reason to think of him; I thought of him.

'It just keeps on circulating,' I said, trying to keep my voice even.

'Because he pulled away! That's just how it works. That's what maths is. Personally, I need to perfect my technique ... But anyway, anyway, it's not about him, or you. Both of you are irrelevant.'

'Maybe,' I said. It wasn't easy to express it. The slippery feeling all of it gave me. 'I just don't want it to, like, *lift a lid on something deeper.*' I doused it in irony. 'Discover I'm some repressed heterosexual or something.'

'God forbid.'

'I don't have time—' I meant it as a joke but when it came out I realised there was a touch of panic in my voice.

'So, like I said, you're one percent bi or something, so what? It can be *our little secret.*'

'But I'm not.'

'Why do you keep saying that?' she said. She looked at me like I was a painting she wasn't sure about. 'What's in it for you? Does it make it less interesting or something? Isn't it, I don't know, bi-phobic?'

'Honestly, don't,' I said. 'Bi-phobic.' I rolled my eyes.

'Oh what, because once when we were at university that guy asked, "Would you prefer to have a son who was gay or a son who had no legs?" And everyone said no legs.'

'They did say that.'

'So you yourself could never be phobic of anything? Idiot.'

'Just bi is . . .' I said. I shook my head. 'It's nothing.'

'Dicing with death,' she said then, doing quick, choppy kung-fu arms, 'who's going to cancel her?'

She was in a silly mood. So what was I supposed to say? That rather than nothing, maybe it was something and that something, if it was even there, felt too big. My brain kept stacking piles in both directions, and the piles were a mess, papers everywhere.

Sometimes, nearly always, gayness was the only thing that made sense to me – I truly couldn't believe that anyone could have any other inclination; that heterosexuality was anywhere close to as powerful could seem so implausible to me I often found myself thinking of Flo's crushes as tiny toy versions – and then sometimes I couldn't understand it at all. I'd look at two women getting married in white dresses and think, *how strange.* ('Only when they're ugly,' Flo had said when I told her this once.)

'Your phone,' Flo said, interrupting my head-on brain collision. From across the table, she'd sent me a short clip from *Trainspotting,* the colour of everything watered down as if physical proof of how old we were.

The world is changing; music is changing; drugs are changing; even men and women are changing. One thousand years from now there will be no guys and no girls, just wankers. Sounds great to me.

I looked over at her and she gave me a thumbs up.

20

After she left, I moved Ed's book from the table and put it on a shelf. The spine was skin-coloured, almost eerily his skin colour when I'd seen it. It was true what I'd told her: I still hadn't read it yet. I'd read the reviews. Sometimes, I'd look to see if a new one had appeared. And despite everything that had happened, I found myself defensive when I read one review which described the sex scenes as 'somehow breathless despite all the heavy breathing'.

Occasionally I allowed myself to search for him specifically rather than the book's title, and whenever I did that, I deleted my history afterwards, because it caused a jolt in my stomach to search for something else and see his name come up.

I'd always look at the results in the last week. I felt a strong desire to know where he was. He'd had a series of photos taken for *The Times* and every other piece syndicated them. So it looked like he was permanently next to a giant yellow recycling bin, permanently doing a goofy, clever smile, permanently in that second London heatwave in May.

On my phone at work, while I was waiting for meetings, I tried to work it out. To get into the edges of it. To try to understand. His face. There it was in the palm of my hand. *Go on then,* I'd think. *Kiss him.*

And I might feel peace at feeling nothing, but then a memory might catch me and a feeling would come: a roll down my body. I tried to remember his voice – at first I could recall a few pairs of words, a flicker of an American accent, a tilt towards a's on o's, but soon that was gone. I couldn't turn it into words he might say to me, the way I had with other people.

Still. It snagged inside me, a burr catching. I tried to tell myself that it was perhaps because it was a smaller worry than my other ones, or that it was a moot point anyway: over before it started.

'It doesn't feel good because he can't, isn't able to.' That was another thing Flo had said when she was talking about how it was all 'psychology 101'. 'But he's gay – what do you expect? It's not your "fault". It's nothing even to do with you ...'

'I keep on thinking about a river,' I told her eventually. That was the only bit of truth I got to that day.

I told her it made me think of all the little shoots that had gone off. It wasn't that I didn't like where the river had taken me, and yet, it felt strange to imagine other little tributaries I might have taken. 'Maybe! Not even definitely,' I said. 'But was the river I took thinner than it needed to be?'

The river analogy annoyed her. 'But couldn't that be anything?' she'd said. 'Career, where you live? It's just one decision leading to another. Surely it's just called *moving through life*.'

But didn't she see that that was terrifying? And even if it wasn't about the past, and only the future – it was simply that it could change. That something so solid could change like that. I could understand how it could – should – be a happy thing. Life bigger rather than smaller, more rather than less. Options, openness. And who would care? But I tormented myself thinking of the waste of it. The waste of being brave and making space, only to maybe return to the nowhere, everywhere, where everyone else was. *You're back now.* Like you'd never leave again.

So it was hard to understand – the pull both ways. The desire to see his face, his name, and just as strong, a sensation in reverse: that I did not want to go there. I did not want to be called there. Particularly by someone who wasn't even calling.

On the other side of the city, Ed is finding somewhere quiet to take a call. He hates the phone. Imagines people bored at the end of the line. Imagines eyes wandering, hands doodling. Thinks about the way his voice changes, how everyone's does, how it always makes the distance swell. Also, London never used to be this hot. New York was different – buffeting, relentless – but with the relief of dipping into shops for quick, bright baths of cold air, and the breeze of the subway, like standing up front on a boat. He finds a doorstep to perch on.

He prepares for the call with a smile, tries to make it reach his eyes, wishes he had water. He hasn't always been this anxious, but it whirs now, a blender.

Earlier in the day, he read an article called 'Body Politic: Loss over a Lifetime'. It plotted out the future impact on British bodies based on the first sixty days of the current government and the trajectory continuing. It tried to take into account a range of factors – new policies put in place: the thinning out of welfare payments, the stripping of services. More nebulous things: the stress of your rights being debated, higher addiction, higher suicides, things like that. It was interactive, and you could move bits around. 'Good for engagement!' he'd imagined the commissioning editor saying. The piece ended with a calculator where you could input your age and sexuality and race and education level and various things, and it would assess how your life expectancy had changed. Ed's isn't the worst, but when he does it for friends, it's seven, eight, nine years they're losing. A decade.

Someone wanders past him selling a digital download of the *Big Issue*. 'Would you like to buy a big shoe?' is what it sounds like in the woman's voice. 'No thank you,' he says. He smiles at her, in a way that fades into: please go away.

His phone lights up right on time. He lets it ring twice. Does his smile again. 'Matey,' he says as he picks up, that old sound on his tongue, 'it's been a million years.'

'More than that!' The voice on the phone is cool, expansive. British too, but posher than Ed's. 'Last time we spoke, it was a different ... what do we say these days? Era?'

'It was, it was.'

'How's London Burning? Warming your hands on the flames?'

'Scalding,' Ed said, 'in every sense of the word.'

They have known each other for – what – ten years now? Not regular friends, but seasonal check-ins. Both aliens in New York. The man on the other end of the line, Teddy, Ted, Winn – a man of many monikers – is only a couple of years older, but always paid for dinners. Subtly, of course. A check signed for on the way back from taking a call outside. Get me a beer afterwards, he'd always say, but the beer never happened. What do I give you? Ed had often thought. An ex had asked if they'd ever slept together – 'hands on cocks in college *surely*' was how he'd said it. Not at all, Ed said, and it was true. In any case, Teddy was straight, whatever that meant.

There was a flicker of appreciation Ed saw occasionally, but it wasn't that Teddy wanted him, it was just that he liked people who were interesting. He remembered a conversation they'd had once about Florence. 'The Italians,' Teddy had said, 'I mean they're *broadly-speaking* racist, sure. They don't want newly-arrived Black bodies,' he over-enunciated the b's, 'sleeping in the shade outside transit hubs *but,*' Ed had shrunk as Teddy said all this, hoping that no one in the restaurant saw or heard, 'they *are* always open to a good story. Less rigid in that way than the Brits. As long as you have something to say or you're writing a book,' he'd pointed at Ed then, 'or you sing for your supper in some way, the Medicis will entertain you.'

And so, after this, Ed had made sure, each time they ate together and Teddy paid, that he kept on singing. This is why the call is hard. Better warm up the vocal strings. 'I—' he says now, '—had a question. A favour to ask you. Your house . . .'

'My house,' Teddy repeats. 'Ah, that little thing.'

'Big thing,' Ed says. Flatter him. 'I just wondered what's happening with it while you're away? I remember your sister was there for a while. But I saw she's in Paris now, so I—'

'You're staying in London?' Teddy says.

'Just for a bit, for the book.' Make it sound solid, thought-through. 'And for the start of the next one.' But don't make it sound too long.

'I'm waiting for them – the magic words—'

Ed hates stuff like this. When Teddy patronises, dangles.

'What do you mean magic words? Like, please? I'm very happy to say please . . .'

'Patron of the arts! Will I get a little shout out at the fag-end of your next masterpiece?'

'If you *want* to be in the fag-end,' Ed says, a little archly.

Teddy laughs. 'I'll check with Sof, but in theory that could work.'

Teddy says something about how Ed might resuscitate some dead plants for him, might also coordinate with some contractors about a finicky ground source heat pump. There's quite a long little to-do list. 'We're coming home in a few months, you see,' Teddy says then. 'To whatever's left of it.'

'The house when I'm done with it, or the country?' Ed asks.

'Both. I didn't want to rush back right away. Thought I'd let the chips fall first.'

'Well,' Ed says, 'currently they're cold and on the floor and people are treading them into the pavement.' He feels a wave of depression. 'I forgot you were a fan of chaos.'

'Not chaos itself . . .' A pause, in which Ed can hear a smile. 'Just opportunity for order. Anyway, as I said, I'm sure you'll be welcome to keep the beds warm for us, ' Teddy says. An explosion of horns beep their way into the call. 'But be sure to change the sheets,' he finishes.

Thank fuck, Ed thinks, when the call is done. He hates asking for things – but two months, maybe three, of somewhere free, somewhere nice, to stay and write in London, that's something. It's a guilt he feels, growing and dispersed, a lot of it, most of it, for other people. The faith they've placed in him, the meals they've paid for. He wants meaning to come from it.

He imagines it being like gravity. That when he does it, when he does enough of it, and does it well, suddenly he'll feel sturdier on the surface of the world. And that all of it, all of the favours he's asked for, and lines and moments he's taken and transformed, will have all, all of it, been worth it.

He moves to a café. He has a book he's been trying to read for the past few days – it's supposed to be good, he knows he's not *supposed* to care about plot – but at the moment, with everything how it is, he needs a clear thread to follow.

He tries another page, then checks his messages again. They're slowing down already, the quick little hits he got from people sharing pictures of *Love Songs*, the short notes they sent after reading it. 'Reading it' – fifty percent of the time, maybe less, they're actually reading it, he guesses.

Often, at least once a day, he finds himself scrolling down past newer messages to a single name, and clicking on it. Scrolling up to the beginning of the conversation, then scrolling through, each time with a different motive: make it nothing, make it something.

Bronze hair. Bronze, brunette? But blonde in it too, the way men didn't do. An expensive haircut, the way it just skimmed her shoulders. An expensive shirt, the way it hit her wrists. A sharpness in her eyes, the way they were delineated, high definition. The edges tipped up, he found that beautiful. He could see the way they pierced through things. Faster than everyone else that night; X-ray vision. He remembers looking at one of her ears the night he met her, her hair tucked behind it, gold studs in an Orion's belt up to a cuff, and the ear itself, the hard folds of it, the curlicue. *That leads into your head*, he'd thought. Baffling how it happened again and again, the simplest, most basic thoughts appearing like major discoveries when he saw her.

How do you make sense of it, the way two bodies sometimes react to each other? A moment that returns to him in swerves: standing on a traffic island, lit by streetlights, he'd looked at her and noticed her heartbeat through her shirt. The material had moved. Just a fraction, and you'd have to be staring, so he'd realised, then, he must have been standing closer than he thought. He'd stepped away, but when he stepped back, feeling his body move of its own accord, there'd been a flick, flicker, electric. A misfiring maybe, he'd thought it must be, but when they'd stepped forward together, it was undeniable.

Her body, all of it, when he had seen it later. The side of her breasts, the underside of her breasts, who knew?, a magnet to the palm of his hand, like there was a teenage boy living inside him he'd had no idea was there before. Not a teenage boy who wanted that anyway. The slight bow to her legs when her ankles were together, brackets without a sentence or a space between them.

After the first night they met, when she was rattling around in his head, he tried to think of her in an unidealised way, to *My Funny*

Valentine her, or something like that. He roamed around the images he remembered. One of her eyes, the white of it had a blush, like she'd pushed at it too hard. And there was a light cloud under each eye too, unslept. But who had slept normally that week? He liked that he could see it on her.

Her lipstick disappeared with food, and left lipliner, and when you looked at it like that, her bottom lip might be a little fuller on one side, like a hill might look turned upside down, soft asymmetries.

A tiny scar on her chin that held its line when she laughed. A laugh he wanted to win, because that was the other thing: the angles of everything, the angles of her hair, her suit, the angles that she looked at things, it all came together, geodesic. Armour. He wanted to find a way in.

He clicks out of their chat, and scrolls up to another. Rory, the influencer with all the sunglasses.

Hey how's it going, Ed says.

The freedom, in this particular case, of not caring what he writes.

That article this morning. Even when he did the calculation for himself – all the things he knows about himself, levelled at him a million times before: white, male, master's degree, brought up by two parents, no disabilities, stands to inherit a house, all of this – the calculator shows that based on the projection of current policies, he loses two years. Three. Cry me a river, he thinks, but still, a light coating of sickness sticks to his stomach.

He crosses the sweltering city. When Rory opens the door, Ed asks, 'are we here alone?' And even before he gets a yes, his hand reaches down, the curve of Rory's cock strapped back by a metal zip. A magnet his palm's more used to. It fills his hand.

'You didn't call me—' It's nearly all Rory says.

'It's better when we don't speak,' Ed says. 'I've been thinking about fucking you all day.'

Not strictly true, but it feels right in that second.

They kiss, a skirmish between teeth, mouths hot and open, and then Ed gets rid of Rory's face, turns him to the wall of the corridor instead. Rory's hands help Ed's pull down his trousers, then he puts his hands up on the wall again. Leans into it. Knows the angle he wants to be at, but moves when Ed tilts him.

'Good?'

'Yeah.'

It starts not slow, but measured, then goes straight to deep. Deep, deep, deepness, almost as a destination. New tilt, full hilt. It knocks a sound out from the pit of Rory's lungs. The wall where Rory's mouth is will be wet, is already wet, from his lips, from the way he's breathing. Ed thinks of another piece he read that morning, about wet-bulb temperature. Heat, humidity, how you can reach a point where sweat can't cool you down. The sweat between them makes it hard to grip, the way a car can slip, but he doesn't need to hold on for long. He comes like it's coming from his coccyx, likes it's come from his backbone. Bone. Bone, bone, bone, until every last drop of it has left him.

~

21

Daniel came to my office to check how the trips to Europe had gone. 'Did you find the fucker in France making those posts with fifteen fonts and tell them we have a little thing called a brand book?'

'I did.'

'And how is local compliance looking?'

'Good. Every other business and trade department in Europe is easier to work with than ours. A key starting point being that they, y'know, actually exist ...'

'What do you mean *exist*?' he said. I watched him lift one arm subtly but also not that subtly to check if he had sweat patches. 'Whenever I want you, someone says you've fucked off to parliament for a meeting. Who are you meeting? Ghosts?'

I told him it was changing every week. And that with the opposition scrambling too, it could feel impossible to get stuff done.

'But we need stuff done,' he said.

'I'm aware. You pushed for us to leave the trade alliance. That means forging all new connections.'

'So make it happen. I'm serious.' He checked his other armpit. 'Don't make me regret the VP thing.'

Not long after he'd left, I heard the words 'are you busy?' A head ventured round the parapet of my door. It was the girl with the bandeau top who'd started the week the man had jumped. I'd checked on her file. Safer to look at words on a screen rather than look at her in person. She was on our lowest salary grade, one that skirted a single penny above minimum wage. Today, she was wearing a thin black cotton top that showed the beam of her collarbone. Her name, I'd discovered, was Luisa.

'Not un-busy,' I said. At work I operated my face as if I were wearing glasses – something balancing on my nose, justification for distraction. 'Just catching up on something. Urgent?'

'It's really urgent.' She came in, shut the door behind her, then bowed her head as if respectfully at a funeral. 'It's about "Operation Valve Release".'

'The party?' I said. I let my eyes flash up.

She nodded. 'Yes. The party. Anyway, just grab me whenever.' She held the edge of the door on her way out. 'I could tell you were busy. Shutting your eyes a lot.'

My team at work kept growing. Before all of this had happened, it was a funding year – our series D en route to our IPO – and as they kept on reminding us, we needed to see 'significant year-on-year growth in every arena'. Day after day new people arrived at my desk, and said 'I'm with you'. I'd barely remember their final interview, but I'd soon know them from their mounting personal problems.

There was a copy guy with toothpick legs and caviar-ish eyes, whose dad had ALS. A girl who was very depressed unless she saw an animal of some kind, at which point she would step out of her personality like it was a loose pair of dungarees. I refrained from calling them kids, though it did feel like an assembly sometimes.

Due to the tide turning in our favour after the statement, and positive meetings with our new investor group, Daniel had sent an all-office telling the senior management group to organise a 'state-sponsored' night out. This was Operation Valve Release. I'd been given a token budget of £3000 to boost morale and 'welcome the newbies'.

At Luisa's prompting, I asked the team what they wanted to do at our Monday meeting. There were a few pubs – pub, pub, pub – landing like soft bullets. There was a Laser Quest request. A Kew Gardens from a blowhard. Another rapid fire of pub pub pub. And then there was Luisa.

'Romford,' she said. 'The dogs.' She put a crisp in her mouth. She would eat, I realised, almost constantly. Like a steam train, she told me at some point later, gotta constantly throw coal in the engine.

'What?' I said. And she repeated it, still not looking up from her computer. She tended to continue working while I spoke, in a way that blurred rude and diligent. 'My vote is the dogs in Romford,' she said, sucking the salt off her finger. Then she did look up and without her pupils landing on anything else, they landed on me. 'Dog racing. Romford's a shithole! But it's a fun way to blow company money. Anyway, just an idea.'

Afterwards, her name appeared in a direct message.

Laser quest sounds like a good one
Love to be in a small dark place,
breathing heavily, when we're due a new pandemic.

You mean this?

I sent a link.

Where they used to race cheetahs in 1964?
What do you have against cheetahs?

Luisa had clearly read the vibe right, because the little poll thing we did made it win by a country mile. People voted with emojis that danced too, in double approval.

you win, I said.

I created a powerful lobbying group, she replied. *Get ready for my Union ...*

22

We arrived in Romford in a convoy of cars. There was an enormous plasticised banner – ropes hanging it up from eye hooks – which said 'Ruff N ready, but back in action!'

'Brace yourselves for the canine puns,' Luisa said, leading the group, or rather, everyone holding back so she could go first. 'They were shut for about five years, but what with the government removing all restrictions, except for our hallowed right to protest, they opened back up a couple of weeks ago ...'

Looking around, you could still see the dust, on top of metal barriers painted lapis lazuli. I gave everyone four tokens each for the bar, and £150 to bet with as they saw fit. 'Avoid number twelve,' Luisa said about one dog, who had leopard markings on his hind legs. 'Looks busted.'

It was extraordinary in there. The floodlights, the trains rushing by. The smoothed-down sand, the fresh islands of it poured onto any spilled blood. The dogs with their high-arched backs and matchstick legs. The cages they exploded from. The up-and-down hammer attack of their run. The '50s suburban houses in a ring around us. If you held your camera up to take a picture you saw the ripple of strobe lighting.

Two hours, and twice as many drinks in, I asked Luisa, our resident expert, about the commentators: 'Is that their actual voice? The speed and the nasalness? Or does the tannoy kind of transmogrify it?'

'Transmogrify,' she repeated. 'Would you say you're a transmogrification exclusive radical feminist?'

It was busy, but Luisa seemed to be standing a little closer to me than she needed to, or I was to her. But neither of us were moving. I watched her watch the race. The way her torso lifted to follow the furthest side of the track. I was going to say something but she put her hand up.

'Shit,' she said.

'Which one's yours?'

'Six.' Her eyes stayed rock solid on it. 'My first dud.'

In front of us, an old man filled in a crossword with a short, hollow betting pen that looked more like a birthday cake candle. 'How much is left in the pot?' Luisa said. There was something so distinctive about her voice; it was like she threw it almost. It ducked and weaved through the noise around us.

I flared the notes in my pocket. 'Five hundred quid?' I said. 'Give or take.'

'Take?' she said. She looked at me. 'Shall I double it for you?'

As she waited for me to make a decision, she put her arms up to stretch the way people do on long haul planes. I'd realised, when I watched her through the glass at work sometimes, that she had impeccable posture. She wore loose parachute pants and tight tank tops, exactly the clothes I'd worn as a teenager. Maybe that was why it was sometimes hard to stop looking.

'Give me ten minutes,' she said.

And I gave it to her – the time and the money. I wanted to watch her, see how she did it. But she skirted through the crowds, her body ducking and weaving too, and disappeared.

Dutifully, I talked to the others. They felt markedly boring in comparison. I wondered what Luisa was betting on. I wanted her to come back. When she did, she handed back the envelope, and it was twice as thick.

'I took commission,' she said. 'A little bonus.' One of her eyes closed as if a very bright light was shining in her face.

'Wow,' I said. There was a chunk of money between my fingers. It felt like a thin book.

'Not me,' she said. 'My dad.'

'Is he here?'

'No—'

'You brought your dad on a school trip?'

'No, no. But, yeah. My dad was a gambling man.'

We sat back down next to each other on metal benches that made the sound of a lock being rattled. My suit trousers next to the satin of her basketball shorts. The wine at our feet.

'I'm funny with you,' she said. She'd had a few glasses already, and the confidence of the glass ahead, the glass in her hand, shined like a ruby. 'For some reason . . . and believe me, I do not understand it, I want you to like me.'

'Well obviously,' I said. 'I have the keys to the palace.'

'No, like you-you. As a "person".' She made the quote marks heavy. I looked at her and she didn't look away. She had a cigarette in her mouth and she asked one of the girls in front of us to find her a lighter. The girl received the request like a gift.

'Where did you get your confidence from?' I asked her.

'It was reduced. Someone else had returned it. It's all bashed around if you look closely.'

Not sure I'm allowed to do that, I thought. Then: *don't say it.* 'Not sure I'm allowed to do that,' I said.

Someone else, some girl from marketing, someone who was a much more suitable peer for Luisa, came over to join the conversation, and so I made excuses and left. I went to the bathroom, which was unspeakable. I stayed away from the group for a bit. Looked at the history of dog racing (nothing good), read the news (incomparably worse).

'What are you doing?' It was Luisa.

'Oh you know me,' I said. 'Out here sending a little fax.'

She nodded. 'I've seen your computer screen,' she said. 'You do know you can bookmark tabs? You don't have to have the whole internet open at once.'

I looked at her. 'That pound shop confidence again,' I said.

'What's your deal?' she asked me.

'Is that ... code?'

'No. Just. I don't know. Let's say it's representation in the workplace. Representation at a time we need it the most,' she said, in her go-to faux-sincerity. 'Let's just say maybe one time I saw you on an app. Can I say that? I hate the word app. They should make a better word. This was a while ago. But yeah – and maybe I'm wrong, or maybe it was wishful thinking,' wishful thinking, that was the thing that ran around my head later, 'but I'm pretty sure it was in the girl looking for girl section.'

'I don't know if—'

'What if I want a mentor,' she said. 'At a time like this. In the workplace I mean.'

'Right—' I said.

'You're obviously someone who knows what they're doing.' She leaned on that. 'Anyway,' she said. 'Just a thought ...' There was a pint glass in her hand now, empty. 'Far too much,' she said, looking at her hand like it had been making its own decisions. The ruby of confidence showed its flush on her neck now – a creeping collar. 'I gotta run,' she said, and she grabbed a bag I hadn't realised was at her feet, and disappeared.

23

My flight the next morning was at an ungodly hour. I was headed to Egypt, because Daniel said it was an unmissable opportunity. Due to the level of state surveillance, the tech team set me up with a blanked phone and two different VPNs.

'There's one rival app there, but it's a total shit salad,' Daniel had said. 'We'll get it, it's cheap, then we'll just whip everything over onto our platform. Ya basta. Just need to curry some good favour.' He went on. The way he spoke had too many flavours. 'It's a no brainer to suck them up before the IPO. Inroads in MENA. Show we have global scope, and what we've done so far is just the beginning yadda yadda yadda. Kairos will be there as acquisitions manager – down in the weeds stuff – but I want you there to keep things smiling. We don't want a hostile takeover; we want everybody happy. So be nice.'

'Are we going to keep the local team then?' I asked him. 'If I'm going to be all pally-pally.'

'Yeah sure,' he said. 'For a couple of months at least.'

My flight was from London City. There was never an airport more full of men. 'Any excuse to leave at the moment,' I heard one guy say in the queue. All the way through security there were posters advertising tax breaks in Portugal or healthcare in Malta. We were easy marks.

I had never been to Egypt before. I had slept with someone from there once, but that was it. I'd forgotten her name, but she'd had a piercing on the back of her neck and nowhere else; a small, cold surprise.

At Sharm El Sheikh airport, I took out cash that came out hot and smelled like sick, then took a taxi. It was half Las Vegas, and half hundreds of years ago, and I looked at it and thought: *this is what is ahead of us in England*. Such was the desperation for jobs that people waited on the streets with signs in their hands. I'd have to text Daniel, he'd be thrilled.

Four teenage boys whipped past sharing the same motorbike. The lanes of traffic careened so close together the faces in the windows might as well be sitting with you in the same car. Eventually the taxi pulled off onto a dirt track that led to a compound. The name of the hotel was a conjunction of other hotel names. I can't remember exactly now but the Grand Plaza Continental, or the Inter Elysium Hiltown. Something like that. The shared Gigr PA was a very fat and handsome guy called Bev. 'Got you a banger,' he'd said, about the hotel. 'Well not a banger, but it's very expensive. Reviews aren't FAB, but ignore the one with the picture of the welcome platter of decomposing grapes – there are new owners and they're doing *loads* of outreach. A whole cultural programme. Plus the room is fifty-six metres squared, ie. bigger than my flat, so please don't be a biotch about it.'

There were palm trees, both plastic and not. The marble was real, the leather was fake. There were almost as many staff as guests. At the buffet, a young boy walked past with a plate heaped with cucumber rings. And Bev was right; my room was enormous. Copper hangers in a sky-high wardrobe clanged like church bells.

After a day in the hotel basement – it always stunned me, how conference rooms looked exactly the same, the world over: white-boards and fabric sheath covers for metal chairs – a day that was largely non-combative, because, in all honesty, they seemed desperate to be bought, we emerged up into a cordoned-off section of the lounge.

I was talking to a man whose hair was matte in a way that suggested it would soon thin. He wasn't the founder of the app we were attempting to subsume, but he was the lead acquisition manager on their side, and he was wearing so much aftershave he left a contrail each time he reached for a canapé. He kept on saying our countries were friends now.

'The government's a lot better these days,' he said.

'Yours?' I asked.

'No, you,' he said.

Anyway, I was talking to him, and then . . . it doesn't make sense to say it, because then and still now, it will always feel imagined rather than real.

Through the wall, which was carved wood, with glass set in the gaps, I saw a face I knew.

I waited for him to turn away and pretend he hadn't seen me, but he didn't. He just stood there looking, working it out, and though there were people between us, and there was glass between us, and time and space between us, I saw things work across his face and I saw him swallow and I saw him smile and he lifted his hand to wave and I did not look away and neither did he.

PART II

PART II

1

I held a finger up, one moment, and he nodded. But I found it impossible to enter back into the conversation I'd been in.

'You have a friend?' the man I'd been talking to said.

'Do you mind if I come right back?'

Ed was standing by the door. He was wearing a grey T-shirt.

'I've got too comfortable,' he said. He looked down at the shining white hotel slippers on his feet.

'I'm just in a meeting,' I started, 'but this—'

'It's crazy,' he said. 'It's totally crazy.' It's hard to describe how his face looked. When I think back to that moment now, because I can still see it now, I think of that old screensaver with stars – an endless unfolding.

'I'm here for work,' I said, my arm reaching back to the conversation I'd come from.

'Go back,' he said. 'To your meeting. I'll wait. I'll wait right here. I won't go anywhere, I promise.'

He did wait right there. When I came out of the meeting an hour later, he was sitting on a Chesterton-style leather sofa, all pucks and buttons. 'It's not just you,' he said. He was wearing shorts. 'By now, I *can't* get up. If I do, I'll need a skin graft.'

'They just put out cheeses,' I told him.

'In Egypt?' he said. 'What kind?'

'These kind of roulade ones. Fruit, nuts and herbs in them.'

'Quite a lot going on,' he said.

I asked him why he was here, and he said he was doing a residency at the hotel.

'A residency? You've moved in?'

'A writing residency. A different writer comes each month and we leave, I don't know, what's the word in their brochure? ... a *legacy*,' he said, making his lips tense to show his teeth. 'What about you?'

'Something in the realm of layer after layer of corruption ...'

I saw his eyes trace the edges of me. My arms, my shoulders, then back to my face.

'I know you have the weird cheese,' he said, 'but if you want dinner?'

'I could have dinner.'

'Great.' I saw his toe nudge against the inside of his slipper.

'Big fan of dinner,' I said. 'Definitely one of my top three meals of the day.'

2

The same music played wherever you were in the hotel complex. Covers of three decades' worth of hits all brought into the same voice, cadence and time signature. 'Can't Help Falling in Love' played on a sax accompanied me from the hallways, into the lift and out into the lobby.

At eight p.m. Ed was waiting in reception, standing, not even looking at his phone. I remember him breaking into a smile when he saw me. He had changed. His clothes, I mean. Not a suit, but smart. 'This is mad,' he said again. 'Can I—?' He hugged me.

I had meant to feel angry, or rather, at some earlier point, before I'd gone down, I remember saying to myself 'he hurt you, don't forget that'. On my way down, I felt it in my shoulders, muscles closing in on bones, but the truth was, as soon as I was with him, I forgot.

He asked me if I minded if we left the compound. We walked out of the hotel past security, proper gunmen who guarded the door.

'Do you have good news?' I asked him.

'What? No—'

'You seem like a man who's had good news,' I said.

It was how he walked – someone who wanted to walk even faster

147

than they were, intentionally slowing themselves down. 'Not good news, no. Honestly, I'm just happy to see you,' he said. 'I would be a tiny bit happy to see anyone, but I'm so glad it's you.'

I wondered if he'd had a drink, but I couldn't smell anything on him.

'I'd been wanting to write to you, or call you,' he said.

'Don't *call* me—'

'But I didn't know what to say. And then you just appeared. Which is kind of. I don't know. Like Mary Magdalene on a piece of toast or something.'

Above us, birds flew like bullets, wings back.

'Fuck, I'm so glad to be out of there.' He looked up for cameras in the palm trees. 'You arrived in daylight, right? A construction site in a desert, and suddenly: boom. We got grass, baby!'

It wasn't just his walk; I could tell he wanted to talk. The residency had been a wash, he told me: he'd barely written a thing. The blank page he'd been looking forward to had become some mad person on the tube. 'You know when you're studiously avoiding their eye? And before I came here, I felt like one of those toy cars, all revved up and ready to go.'

'That's a lot of metaphors,' I said.

'Still got it,' he said, false-happily. He was tanned. A considerably different colour from when I'd last seen him. 'But what about you? What are you doing here?'

'Exploitation?' I said. 'It's complicated. We need to expand to new markets. Fast growth ahead of the IPO, and they have some black holes in their regulation that make it ...' I did a chef's kiss.

He hailed a car, dusty dents in its roof, and it took us to a main drag. 'Drink before dinner?' he said. We were standing outside a bar which had a sign in the window: BEAR WINE GIN SOLD :) 'Two bears coming right up. It's funny getting booze here,' he said as he pushed open the door. 'It's like, excuse me, do you sell ethanol? *No?!* Well, then we're not interested.'

He pulled up close to the bar, like he was tucking himself in. At first we both drank slowly. I remember thinking: if we go for it, let him go first. He kept looking at me like I was a figment of his imagination, like if he looked hard enough he might be able to see through me.

A little later, when my eyes flicked at my phone, it was a mess of messages and emails. I checked my diary to make sure I wasn't missing a call and he saw the candy-cane cage of all the highlighted strips.

'You're such a proper person,' he said.

'Maybe. Mostly.' I told him that whenever I was in another place or time zone, everything seemed so much less urgent. 'Like I'm seeing it through a window then another window.'

He said that when he was in New York all of England had been like that for him. Watching it start to warp and break from America. That he kept this neat distance, a moat the size of an ocean.

I didn't say, you weren't the best at replying to messages even in the same time zone. 'It's not like America's better,' I said.

'I mean, obviously. But it wasn't my responsibility. It wasn't *in* me. And coming back when I did. That's why meeting you caught me – it was like. In amidst all the shit. An England I could love? Not love.' He shook his head. 'But does that make sense?'

I picked up his drink. 'What the hell is in this?'

'I mean it! That's what I think the reason is. Was. Is.' A rocking chair.

'England? I have Scottish heritage. Look at these freckles. I'm not even English, so you can put your St George away—'

He pretended to wave a small flag in a sad back-and-forth. 'I know it doesn't make sense,' he looked at me. 'But it was that night, don't you think? When we met.'

*

We moved on for dinner at an Italian restaurant on the water. We paid a kid to go out and pick up wine for us. I asked Ed what going back to New York had been like. A citronella candle between us was not working, and I reached down to scratch my ankle.

'I've been in London,' he said. And it was like someone hit a small gong in me. He'd been there the whole time. 'I did go back to New York,' he said quickly, 'but for a week or two. Then I returned.' He looked at me. I looked back at him. I imagined, madly, and all bundled into a single split second, that he would say some huge, stupid thing like he had come back because of me.

'The publisher has "hopes" for the book,' he said. He did a little pad round the word with irony. 'Which means hope for prizes. And there's a couple I have to be resident in the UK for. They also said I had to "establish myself on the literary scene".'

'And the prize for air quotes goes to—' I said.

'No, I know! Saying that feels like toxic gas being released in my chest. Chemical attack or something. But anyway, all of which means spending more time in London? Like more than fifty percent of the year. So I thought I'd start. Sorry, it's a bizarre thing to say out loud.'

'It's okay,' I said. I wanted so much to look unaffected. 'It's the tag-line of Chat magazine.'

'What?'

'Or it was. Life exclamation mark, death exclamation mark, prizes exclamation mark. All equal weighting.'

'What more is there?' he said. And there it was again, his ease. Even if it was something he found difficult to talk about. The puzzle piece he needed was so often the first one he reached for. I asked him where he was living.

'At a friend's. That bit's lucky. But I've been looking for places for when I have to leave. It's—'

'Wild.'

'Everything's three times more expensive than when I last lived in London, and eight times worse. I went to one place,' he said, 'in Surrey Quays. The guy was playing *Come Dine with Me* in the background the whole time, but also, genuinely, I think he was secretly keeping a seagull there.'

'What?'

'The smell,' he said. 'And a rustling sound.'

He asked me how I found my flat and it hit another note inside me: that he had come there, that he had been in London, and still not come back.

'My ex was an estate agent. Friends of hers. I'm pretty sure it was a scam. I'm pretty sure *I* was scammed.'

'Miracles happen,' he said. 'You agreed to come for dinner with me. Anything's possible. I too may get the chance to live with a seagull in Surrey.'

'Surrey Quays.'

'Either one will do,' he said. 'Wanted: one female roommate. Non-smoker, non-ugly.'

'Non seagull,' I added.

After dinner, we walked through the night market. Legs of cows hung mummified in sheets. Sweet potatoes roasted in small handmade ovens with the welding drips still visible. Above the bright bulbs shining on crates of fresh fruit, satellite dishes made a retro future. 'It's nice to be somewhere real,' Ed said. 'The hotel is really un-real.' Then, noticing the repetition: 'Real, real, real.'

When we got back to the unreal hotel, Ed asked what floor my room was on. He asked what my room was like.

'I think they're all the same,' I said.

'Do you want to come to mine? Or me to yours? Just to check? Just to chat.' I thought of his toe nervously pushing at his slippers earlier – the way he said it had the same energy.

'Haven't we done this before?' I said.

When we got into his room, the lights were dimmed, and the bed sheets were folded open.

'It's a turndown service,' he said. 'I didn't do it! Or ask for it.'

I saw briefly in his face exactly what he would have looked like as a boy. An eagerness collapsing into a frown. 'I've been wanting to say. I've been thinking about it all night. What I did was—' he changed tack, '—it wasn't . . .'

'I think actually it was very normal,' I said. 'Doesn't that happen like a thousand times every minute across the world?'

'Probably. That makes it worse though. So here's what I think,' he said. 'It didn't seem right at dinner.'

I asked him if he had notes, and he said, yes, he had jotted down some things in his phone. 'I thought it would be an answer,' he said, 'and it wasn't an answer, it was still a question. And not just one, loads of them.' It was already unclear what he was saying and his face, if anything, made it even more so. 'And sometimes I'm not good at that. I just want to look away and do the things I know. I know this is stupid.'

'It's not stupid—'

'And like, the opposite of the point of life—'

'Again, it's all so normal.'

I looked around his room. A stack of books by the bed. A face moisturiser, which I couldn't help but think was sweet.

'The first night I met you,' he said, 'I didn't have a model for it so I didn't know how to be. It would feel natural, so I'd follow it,' he made a path with his hand, 'and then I'd kind of choke. Not in my throat, an engine choking. And when I left you that morning, I choked.'

'Choking's not great—'

'Also it feels crazy to me that this is a thing,' he said. 'Like it's what-ever year it is. It's fine. It's fine. It's fine. But it's not about the world. It's about me.'

'It is about the world too. You said that your publishers—'

'I hate that I said that. What did I even mean? What the fuck does Eloise in marketing care? They're all so straight. "Three years with this one" on their Instagram, you know. I don't want that.'

'I didn't even take that badly. I kind of got it. All those posters. It would be quite a big ...' What was the word?

'Product recall,' he said.

'And it's not even that,' I said. 'It's that I hate it too. Like, I hate this story. And it's not even a story, but whatever's happening. Happened.'

He looked at me.

'The *Kids are Alright* thing,' I said. '*Kissing Jessica Stein*. The lesbian ends up with a guy. The trope of, like, hitting a certain age and being like, bam, biology, is that you?' I shook my head. 'I'm not saying this is that. It isn't. But it's just – not what I want at all. I remember this girl I knew. A lesbian, like *definitely* a lesbian. All through our twen-ties she wore a fucking monocle! And then she just like ... married a man.' Did I sound angry? I didn't mean to sound angry, but they had been things I had been thinking and wanting to say for more than a month. 'The pictures were just there. Her and this guy. Like – there it is. And it's her thing, fine fine. But it doesn't feel good. And then with everything in the news. And being here, which is ...' I faded. 'Did you get the email on the way from the airline? If you have any rainbow, LGBT – I can't even remember the word they used now, but like mementos? miscellanea? – you may be denied boarding.'

'I know,' he said. 'It's so fucked up.' I looked at his tattoo, the sin-cerity one, the hairs over it and through it, in a way that meant it was just part of him now. 'And I get it,' he said. 'I do. Class traitors.'

'I kind of forgot that. And I was focusing on you, and what you felt. Or didn't feel. And I also think—' I stopped.

'What do you think?'

I laughed then. 'I think about if my parents could hear us talk, and they'd be like: why do these people say everything? Stop – showing – vulnerability.' I made my voice metallic.

'And I think about the kids too,' Ed said, 'and they'd be shocked. Why do these boomers worry about everything? So fucking stodgy.'

'Pretty sure we're millennial still—'

'Yeah,' he nodded. 'But they're right. Sometimes I'm like, life can't only be talking—'

'It's a lot of talking.'

'But it's doing things too.'

'And what do you want to do?' I said.

'I don't know. There are lots of things I want to say – more fucking talking – but as a man to a woman it's complicated. Sometimes I'm like, fuck it, whatever, this is not a big deal, and other times it feels huge. I was on Tottenham Court Road the other day,' he said. He stopped. 'Before I got here. Before I saw you again. But you came into my head. And I had this profound feeling like . . .' He wasn't just looking round the room for how to say it; he was feeling for it in his hands too. 'Like every single person I can see – and all of the eight or nine billion that I *can't* see – came from this. Something like this. It's the most normal, basic-ass thing you can do. So why does it feel so . . .' The end of the sentence collapsed.

'I don't know if talking about it helps. But if we're saying things.'

'Please,' he said. It felt like we'd crested, like things were moving downhill now.

'I imagined so many things last time,' I said. 'About what it had been like for you. If you'd hated it. I didn't even entertain liked. Not after you disappeared – and you know it's funny. But it's the second

154

time I felt it. I also felt it with straight girls. Wondered all the things they might be missing. Missing with me. Like everything I had wouldn't be enough.'

He nodded. We were sitting next to each other on his bed, and I could feel the space between us exactly, like I'd be able to draw the shape of the air on a piece of paper.

'It felt worse with you,' I said. 'At least girls had girls' bodies so they weren't shocked by them. I don't know what I'm saying.'

'I think I do.'

'What's that thing they say on reality TV shows?' I said.

'They say a lot of things.'

'"In my head". That they feel "in their head". I feel in my head.'

'That's okay. I don't want you out of your head. Can I just tell you something then? Maybe it's important. Maybe it isn't.' He leaned over me to turn the light up a little, like it would make it easier for me to hear, and he left the hand he needed for balance next to my leg. 'I just want you to know that last time, I thought about you afterwards. I don't mean that as some . . . gift. But I kept on thinking about how your legs were different. I kept on thinking about the shape. I kept on looking at you. What I could remember. It was like looking at an alien—'

'Is this supposed to help?'

'Wait, I want to explain. Like, society knows it to be good. Women's bodies equals good. And I knew it in this distant theoretical way. I get it. Posters, boobs, bikini. I thought about it and it wasn't that, it was a whole new thing. Or no, it was both. Like all the historical hotness of women and then you – new – who I knew' – he said this bit like he was walking down steps – 'who I wanted to – it's confusing. After twenty years of men.'

Twenty, I thought. Twenty. Of course it felt hard. Still: 'I don't want to be confusing,' I said. 'I want to be simple. When you thought of me what happened?'

His hand was hot next to my leg, or my leg was hot next to his hand. Either way, his hand was still there.

'Do you mean ... what like?' He looked down. 'I got hard. But I never made myself come. It felt wrong to, after everything. After I'd disappeared like that. But I'd lie there or wake up and look at your body in my head.'

'You didn't take a photograph?'

'I didn't take a photograph. But I'd lie there and wonder what the fuck was happening,' he took his hand away, 'and think I might explode.'

I wondered how it would happen. Because that part I knew by then, that it would. But how would it work? With girls, I'd been the one to stand tall, to tip, to push.

'I haven't even asked,' I said. 'Are you a top or a bottom?' I stopped myself from smiling. 'I don't know how to drive this thing.'

I looked at him, this thing, and he looked at me.

'It's just body,' he said.

It's just body, it ran through my head, a back-and-forth river, calming me on each curve. *It's just body.*

3

That first night, or the second night I guess, we took it easy. I think of cats playing, I think of teenagers again. I think of looking to find the desire, and finding it, and finding it. I think of how hours had passed in ways that didn't line up with how I'd ever experienced time before.

When I woke up deep into the night, our bodies were still touching. I wondered if Ed was dreaming. His face was still, then would move. Hotel sheets always stayed so cool. I looked for worry, in the same way that I looked for desire, but that first night, I couldn't find any. I kept my foot against the base of his and fell back asleep.

Then, in the morning, before he said anything else, he asked me to stay. I didn't know if he meant for breakfast, or longer. I said I couldn't, then couldn't think of a reason why not. In theory anyway, it was a weekend. 'Not to be gay or anything,' he said, 'but I have this feeling like if you leave it will disappear.'

Ed in bed in the morning. The dimples in his back I didn't know men got. He ordered breakfast to the room, and it came on a tray the size of a magic carpet. When I said I'd stay, at least for a bit, he kept smiling for no reason. 'You know halloumi,' he said, 'how it squeaks in your cheeks? It's like that.' He played with it.

'Why do you keep laughing though?' I said. 'Is this a trick?'

'Not a trick—'

'Have you been given a ten dollar dare to take me to a dance?'

'Ten dollars?' he said. 'In this economy? I just feel surprised and I . . .' his voice dropped to a deep movie trailer voice, 'I didn't think anything could surprise me anymore.' He spooned some scrambled egg onto a soldier of toast that cantilevered out of his hand. 'Do you feel strange or normal?'

I thought about it. I looked at my body as if it would tell me. 'Both things at once, I think.' I bit into watermelon, almost too firm, unripe at its edges, which reminded me of gums.

'Me too,' he said.

We finished our breakfast. In the bathroom, loud enough for me to hear it too, he listened to the news on his phone. A new royal baby had been born that morning. 'A-fucking-nother one,' Ed said. 'Benefit thieves.' I looked at his fingers as he held a mug with one hand. I looked at his penis as he came back into the room. It was darker than the rest of his skin.

'It's less scary than I thought,' I said.

'Excuse me?' he said, feigning offence.

I looked at it again. 'It's kind of like a bat.'

'Jesus—'

'Not in a bad way! Just how it hangs.'

He started laughing. 'Fucking hell.' He turned to put his towel away. This small island of hair at the base of his back, rather than the top, where I'd have imagined it would be.

'Honestly though,' I said, as he got back under the covers, 'the first time I nearly slept with a man – with anyone – I was twenty.' I told him I'd been avoiding it because I genuinely didn't know how I was going to react to seeing his dick. 'I genuinely wondered if I would scream? Put someone in therapy for years.'

'Twenty! And did you?' He had the face of someone getting comfortable in pyjamas. 'Scream, I mean?'

'I did not. Stuffed the sheet in my mouth of course. No. It felt – it sounds wrong to say it – but it felt—' I gagged, 'at the *time*, like being saved.'

'Not being saved!'

'No, but I did feel grateful to him. Like, thank you for making it okay. If I can't do what I want to do, and have to do this, you've made it okay. He was such a good person.'

Twenty years. Well, fifteen. But strange to think about that for myself. A tenderness, a distance, a sadness, what are you meant to feel?

'What happened to him?' Ed asked.

'He's married obviously. Three kids. I raise my orange juice glass to him.'

Ed cheersed with me. 'Matt Ryder,' he said. 'For me. If we're doing this.'

'What a name!'

'What a fucking bod. Fell in love with him at my local park. He had a pitbull and maybe the first vape I'd ever seen. Big cloud of smoke around him like he was doing shisha.'

'Badman.'

'The baddest. He was a drug dealer. Had a person *murdered*, he told me later. Actual murder, and I was like: brilliant. I was seventeen. I started buying drugs! I gave them to friends.'

'How did you know he was gay?'

'Oh there was something about him. Fur hood. But in a kind of LL Cool J rather than J Lo way? Honestly, he was the business.'

Ed had invited Matt Ryder back to his house. Matt Ryder had invited Matt Ryder's friends to Ed's house. 'My mum used to do life classes,' Ed said. 'There was this huge painting of a woman she was

so proud of. Matt Ryder thought it would be a wonderful place to ...
extinguish a joint. I still kissed him. I think I kissed him. I woke up
at three in the morning. They were all gone. The house was demol-
ished. How the fuck do you even smash the glass in an oven? She
came home, and it all poured out of my mouth. How could it get
worse? Or just ...' He thought about it. 'I had to make my mum worry,
rather than angry. I said I was gay and I didn't know how to handle
it. Liberal arty parents you know.'

'What did they say?'

'Oh, she was furious. People who are supposed to be great about
it are the worst. The fucking worst. All these gay friends. Two *god-
fathers* who are gay. And they all got in this little intervention and
suggested therapy! Said it was obviously because my dad had died.
All this – shit. I found her ...' he said. It wasn't the first time I saw
this: Ed's eyes like he was watching a film of it. 'I found her crying
in her room.'

'Your mum?'

'At the foot of the bed, crying like someone had died. I asked her
what was wrong and she just said—' he stopped. His shoulders
moved. 'She said she didn't want me to have a hard life.'

I looked at him. 'That old classic,' I said. 'Personally, I thought I'd
just have to wait. That I could maybe be with women when my parents were dead? I don't know. The shape of it's all wrong.'

'Required you to be a very old lesbian.' He tried to smile again but
I could still see the story about his mum on him. 'What was the plan?'
he said. 'Shack up with a dude 'til then?' He put his finger in his mug
to scoop up the last of the foam.

'I had a couple of ideas. Really good ones. The first one was to
become an actor. Which would, you know, require acting. But I figured at least once or twice I would get a role where I could kiss a girl.
But it would be acting! Not gay: *acting*. But we'd get to practise. And

I'd find it difficult of course, so I'd need a lot of practice. I thought that would be cool.'

'The West End's longest running lesbian tragicomedy—' He made his hands the bright lights.

'Precisely. Make it good. Keep it running. Get a kiss every god-damn night!' I said. 'The other plan was prison.'

'Nice,' he said. 'Traditional. Hey, will you stay?' he said again. Desperate's not the word. But he knew that risk was there. 'Not just today? Will you change your flight? I'd pay for it—'

'Danger,' I said. 'We're moving into Richard Gere territory.' But I wanted to. I looked in my body; I looked again. I wanted to.

4

I was supposed to leave just before midnight that evening. I texted Bev to ask for the change.

Done, he said.

No doubt found yourself a princess Jasmine lol

Just be careful

Bail not covered!

Strange to think, instead, that I felt like I was breaking laws doing what I did.

When I went down on Ed that afternoon, my head was full of old words for it. I shut my eyes and they appeared. His skin was soft, and smelled soft, like it had been washed with fabric conditioner. Globe, dome, round, the skin moving loose around hardness, then the surprise of it hitting the back of my throat. I was there, I wasn't there; I could imagine what would feel good. And I was aware of everything: the awareness that comes over you when you're walking on a new street at night.

He only opened his eyes when he was going to come. 'It might be too much,' he said, his breath short, 'it's a lot.'

'Is it?' I said. 'Go on.' Afterwards, he let his head fall back like he wanted to serve his Adam's apple on a tray. I looked up at him. Questions appeared alongside the words. Could he tell my mouth was not a man's mouth? Women's mouths, my mouth, were they different? What did he want?

'Come up,' he said afterwards. 'Please come.' All these comes, some of it still in my mouth.

At first, I found it easiest when his penis was outside me. When I could choose how wide my mouth would open, or how it moved through my hand. The first time he was inside me, afterwards, we lay on our side. I lay in front of him, he lay behind me. For a while neither of us said anything. My brain flicked everything over, a slide show in an old projector. In the simplest sense, I had liked it. There were many moments where I thought 'I like this', and it had surprised me, and hadn't, but also: anticipation of pain, that wasn't something I was used to. The concentration on his face, the concentration in his torso, trying to go slowly, so much so the tension made him shake. 'Is it okay?' he kept asking. Maybe he was looking at me, but I was looking down. A sharper pain than I expected right at the start, but fear made everything smaller.

Turned away from him, afterwards, I felt sure I would cry. Not because of sadness, just because of scale. Whenever anything had been inside me before I had felt dislodged. The hugeness of another person being inside your body deeper than you can go yourself.

'Are you okay?' he said. He could feel the way the muscles in my stomach held tense.

'It's been a long time,' I said. 'Not in a bad way. I'm not sad. It's just a lot. Are you okay?'

I thought of all the different things he must be used to.

'It's so interesting,' he said. 'I know that sounds terrible.'

Earlier with the condom, he had handed it to me. My pause, we both tried to work out all the reasons I might be pausing. 'I'm not—' he started. 'Also, not that I need to be, but I'm on PrEP—'

'Not that,' I said. I handed it back to him: it was better if he did it. 'More practice,' I said.

Now, afterwards, he did sound lighter than me. 'I found it just kind of wild,' he said. 'That sounds so thin, but I mean it world-big.' His thumb made a circle on my forearm. 'I kept thinking, woah.'

I wasn't sure if it was true or if he was just being kind to me, because there's an obligation to be nice to someone whose body you've been inside.

All of it happens at once, and all of it's true at once. I liked him, I liked his body, I liked kissing him, I wanted to touch him. And sometimes, pleasure could feel un-holdably big. Still, as I lay there after the first time he'd been inside me, I also thought this: he had done it nicely, I had wanted him there, I had pulled him closer to me, and still, feeling the shape of where he'd been, I thought of all of the times in the world when the woman hadn't wanted that.

'I'm just more used to being the person who does that,' I said. What I meant was, I can imagine being you more than I can imagine being me.

I asked Ed what he was used to, and he said he wasn't used to anything. It was always different. 'If you sleep with one person for a long time, you make a language,' he said, 'you know what to say, you know how it works. You can speak quickly. Bing, bang, bosh.'

But I wanted specifics. I wanted to know the beats of it, the exact order. I wanted to know if normally, he would talk with men, if they faced each other, if it was hard or soft, if their eyes were open. If they came inside each other, or on skin. I told him I always found it funny that we see people in the world and we know their handwriting, and so much about them, but you never know what they're like in bed.

'Unless you sleep with them,' he said.

'It's just oddly buttoned-up for an open world.'

'Not asking people if they're into pegging . . . It's hardly Victorians covering up table legs,' he said.

'But there are whole parts of your experience – maybe – that I wouldn't know about—'

He asked me what I wanted to know.

'Like how much,' I said, '*rumours aside*, how much more is there with gay men than the straight population?'

'More what? Also, rumours? Don't you have gay friends?'

'Yeah, but. I don't get them to put marks on a calendar.'

'Oh,' he said. 'You're missing a trick.'

'Tell me something then.'

'Like what?'

'You're smiling and I can see you looking all over my face thinking what can she take. Her poor little lady ears.'

He was shaking his head. 'It's a lot of things. Life is varied. It's not just some gay conveyor belt where everyone has a set-piece experience.'

'Wait . . .' I said. 'Gay men are . . . individuals too?'

'I'm trying to think about what's different. Because when it comes to love, people are just people are just people. But I guess you get used to being in rooms only full of men. And if a girl is there, a woman, you know it will be different.'

'And these people. They're your friends? Is it app stuff? I realise I sound like a Facebook mum.'

'Friends, not friends, naked, not naked. Mostly not naked.' He was smiling in his chewy way, new dimples appearing in his cheeks. 'You're just together, and it's nice to be together, and it's just a reflection of the world outside – there are people who are happy and people who aren't happy. It's the same as normal life, just in someone's house.' He put his hand over my belly, fingers wide like he was holding a basketball. 'I feel like you want me to say something shocking. Like eight dicks coming at me like spears and one in my ear or something. But there's, like, music, and it's chill.' He was looking at me to see when he'd said enough, this light searching. 'I don't know, I think of one thing. This one time, a bunch of us had gone in a convoy of Ubers to New Jersey. And I just remember feeling like I was on a beach in winter. As in, it was winter at the time but I felt like I was on a beach. You're in someone's flat but you're wearing boxers or shorts, and it's just like warm. And there are boys and it's nice.'

'Boys plural. Are we talking hanging out, or like ... group activities?'

'Sometimes,' he said. 'I don't know – lots of guys hate that. I think of so many of my friends who would be like, good old Ed, leaning into the stereotype. But I want to be honest about both directions. I've also been an old married man, long-term monogamous, tons of times. Or, like, three times,' he laughed.

'Actually married?'

'Not actually married. But "well behaved" as society sees it. One of the good guys,' he patted his chest. 'But sometimes, for me – I like more rather than less.'

I told him I'd only had a threesome once, but it was weirdly sleepy. 'I think I came too quickly,' I said. My legs were over his body. 'Rookie error.'

'I don't know,' he said. 'I get the sleepy thing. With men in particular people always think it's Pumpsville Tennessee. But it's not that. Or always that. Not for me, anyway.' He said, in his book, some of them were other people's stories. 'The kind of Party and Play whole weekend bit. The guy who gets fired by someone who's fucked him the previous day? That was a guy called Crew. I changed him a bit. Crew actually has one arm. I gave him two in the book.'

'Generous.'

'And the apps. I don't know. The few periods I've done that, it's just a river of humanity running past, and you can make of it what you want. You can tell who's been there for a million years, and will stay there for a million years. I think you can kind of surf around the black hole.'

'Any hole's a goal.'

'Well not some of them. The things I've seen,' he said, a soldier in the trenches. He looked at me. 'And now I'm looking at you.'

'Finally got there,' I said. 'The bottom of the barrel.'

He shook his head and said it again: 'I can't stop thinking it. It's mad that you're here. Here, and here. Right here with me.'

Later that night, the sound from the entertainment faded into the sound of drunk people making their way to bed. We fell asleep with our mouths together, not kissing exactly, more like fish. I remember thinking: do you think any other two humans have slept this close? I remember thinking: I've asked myself this every single time.

5

While we were in Egypt, Ed said twice, or maybe more than that, that it was 'time outside of time', which sounded like the tagline for something, but was maybe also true. I also thought, *if this is outside time, what will happen later, inside time?*

It wasn't a very long time we had, only one extra full day really. We barely left the bedroom, bar a few short excursions. We ate at the buffet. Grill chefs with tall white hats. Sauces that had been sitting for a long time. The unexpectedly udder-y taste of long-life milk. In the evening, we had cocktails. One was called Love Maker, the other Ocean Emotion. At the beach bar, we ordered pomegranate juices which came blended with the seeds in, and beers in cups made of such thin plastic they felt like embryonic sacks in our hands. All of the strangeness of the resort aside, the sand was so perfect I wondered if they'd imported it, and the water looked like drinking water, filled with fish so bright they seemed lit within as they swam up to the dock. Ed read his book, and I read mine, our hands holding like a hammock between our sun loungers.

He told me that when his friends, two guys in a couple, had come here, they'd pushed their beds together at night, then separated them each morning before the cleaner came.

'What's the penalty?' I said.

'Oh, death,' Ed said. 'The big boy. My agency—' he started. He looked around to make sure no one on the beach could hear. He told me that the hotel had requested a different author, but that guy broke his leg, so he became the consolation prize. 'I should have guessed when they edited my bio. And then my agent called me. The new stuff, she said, do you ...? Is it? Her face must have been white, I could literally hear it. She asked if I had an encrypted hard drive.'

'Hot,' I said.

'Then called back again to say: Don't take any copies of *Love Songs*, of course.' He was good at doing the voice; a tense Emma Thompson slipped from him easily. 'Tell them we have stock issues. Just ... well *you're* a writer. *Euphemise.*' Ed crushed his beer vial. 'It would be illicit material *and* promotion of homosexuality, apparently.' He sat up. 'You know, it's embarrassing, but part of me thought – maybe they knew. Or someone did. I mean they must have seen the reviews. My website. So I thought maybe it was some kind of, you know, *effort*. That someone would meet me and there'd be a secret handshake—'

'A secret handshake!'

'Not like that. Just that I'd be representing in a tricky place. In my brief fantasy I was like, I'll give some teenage boy *hope*. That was not what happened.'

'What happened?'

'You know when people win an Oscar and they say they're humbled. *That* isn't humbling. This was humbling.'

He told me that as part of the residency, he was supposed to do a reading and two workshops for the guests. But the day after he arrived, they had a guy who was definitely undercover security find him and say this: we're not going to send you home, but you are free from all your engagements.

'Why?' I asked.

'Why do you think why? Oh and he told me not to go near children.' Ed shook sand off his feet. 'Anyway. All this shit. Probably be the same in England by the time we get home,' he said.

Between us, above the perfect beach, our held hands swung.

6

I took the last flight back to London that evening. The plane was nearly empty, which made it feel somehow more unfeasible that it should be up in the air. Thin plastic seats, slight as deck chairs, which would surely stack like deck chairs too, if something bad happened. I was sat next to a man who could only wheeze due to an emphysema that had collapsed his cheeks too – he had a permanently deflated look.

There are brief moments where we see everything. I saw everything. The website of the world loading that fraction slower, as if it had to find all the images on the page afresh. The roundness of a Pringles tube. Frost like tiny spiders on the airplane window. A single row of seats which still had ashtrays in the armrests.

Nearly everyone on the plane slept in the same neck-tipped-back-mouth-open way that made it look like they'd been drugged. I watched the one non-sleeping man take the chewing gum from his mouth and use it to stick his phone to the seat in front of him, so it stopped flopping forward onto his tray.

We landed in London at night, the city spread like fresh spilled lava, the river a dark ripple. At Heathrow, the queues got longer and longer. The monitors for the video – *following new immigration and tourism rules, please have proof of funds ready alongside your pass-port* – were slightly out of sync so it sounded like two kids playing the repetition game. When I got to the front, only three of twelve machines were working and the border guard told me to knock my passport on the side before I went through.

'Why?' I asked.

'Activates the chip or something. I don't know. Cheapest bits of rubbish—' his voice faded.

Slow was okay though. I wanted time.

How do you keep the feeling in your hands? I had the sensation I wanted to keep it. That it was interesting, and that it would be to me in the future too, and yet I couldn't put my hands or mind around the shape of it.

Ed had texted while I was in the air, a good boy now.

I let them come to me, the things that we had done. The strangeness of utter normalness. How else to explain it?

Because, in every combination, hadn't it always been so? A glow. That everyone could fuck. That you could fuck anyone. That everyone was naked underneath their clothes. That all the made-up boundaries could suddenly be broken.

7

The next morning, Daniel asked me how the trip had been.

I told him I'd never been anywhere so morally bankrupt, and he said he presumed it had gone well then. 'It will fill a hole,' he said, and the way he said hole, even if he didn't mean it to, sounded disgusting. He was being weird though. These curtailed paces around the room.

'I just don't get it,' he said.

'Get what?'

'What in-roads are you making? With the government. As far as I can see, you've basically been gone.' It burst out of him; he spat as he said it.

'I was in Egypt,' I said. 'You *wanted* me in Egypt, and I stayed on a single extra day. A weekend day.' I was reminded of the article I'd found one of the times I'd googled Daniel: that he had been forced to step down as CEO at the last two companies he'd founded.

'But before that. I don't know. I'm just concerned. I met someone-who-knew-someone-who-knew-someone at a dinner and they asked me over to Whitehall for a meeting. That's not my job. That's your job! I don't want my hands on shit like this!'

'Hands on shit like what?'

'Over at parliament, have you been speaking to people really junior? I know their business folk are a mess, but they were clear with *me* about what they wanted.'

He was right again. I'd been grasping, but I still hadn't gripped it. A tightness seized my chest. 'Who did you meet with?' I said.

'That one Liddle put in to satisfy the Nazis or whatever. Silly Sally or whatever they're calling her.'

'Dizzy Izzy,' I said. What was I doing extending trips to stay in bed?

'She's trying to throw her weight around. They want impact, they want it fast, and obviously *we* want to fly under the radar.'

'Right.'

'So obviously they want some backscratching thing. Business working with the broader country aim. In *concert*, was the word she used.'

'Okay, but what does she actually want?'

He checked the door was shut. 'They want us to make sure everyone on the platform is fucking legal. Make them upload a passport type thing.' Currently, on the app, all anyone had to do was tick a box saying they had the right to work in the country. 'Well fuck if I'm doing that.'

'Okay, good,' I replied.

'We'd lose half the cheapest ones!'

'What?'

'It's . . .' He looked at me. 'Fuck off, Elle, you know this.'

'No, of course.'

What he meant was this: the questions we asked potential employees fed an algorithm. Your level of English, your ethnicity, your country of origin, your education level, how many dependants you had. People who the algorithm flagged as 'more likely to be in need'– of which, people who were flagged as potentially undocumented certainly fit the bill – were fed jobs for almost half the going rate.

'We need to find something else to give them,' he said. 'Something good.'

'A visit from a sharpshooter,' I said. 'A bullet between the eyes.'

'Honestly, what the fuck? You're being nice to them when you see them, right? I've told you a million times! No more bullshit. You need to be finding ways to the top. The top-top, not small fry. That's your job,' he said. He put his hands up like binoculars. 'Don't make me say it.'

I saw Luisa ahead of me in the kitchen. I flickered between wanting to say something, and wanting to pretend I couldn't see her, when someone came in shouting 'Counsellor's here!' as if a food delivery had arrived. The text therapy had been so badly reviewed, a few different therapists now came by the office, and anyone who had been there on the balcony day had to do mandatory twenty-minute slots for the following however-many weeks.

'Don't try this one,' Luisa said to me, holding out a green can she'd taken from the fridge. 'Tastes like the end of all happiness. You didn't say you were going to Egypt,' she said then, and in my head, I finished her sentence: when we were sitting so close to each other at that dog race.

'I'll never be the same again,' I replied. 'Hey, about the other night . . .' It was right to clear the air.

Her strap had fallen off her shoulder and she brought it back up. 'Oh, don't. I was drunk, and being—' she started. 'Overly curious.' Normally, she was so breezy. I'd never seen her shy before. She looked down. 'Sorry if it was a lot,' she said.

I hadn't meant to make her apologise, but she said it and I let her.

8

I avoided seeing Flo that week, because I didn't want to tell her about Ed, and I didn't want to have seen her and not said anything.

He was back from Egypt too now, minus precisely fifty words written, he said, and we agreed to meet not far from my house, in a storm that was announced after we'd both set off. I got a weather alert warning – winds of 120mph, red weather advisory, risk to life.

Normally, I liked wind. I could find the anarchy of it funny. Men trying to keep baggy short legs down in a kind of anti-Marilyn; the way people had to hold onto hats as though they were in a musical and about to break into dance. But that year, I had started to be un-nerved. It was how quickly it could come, and how much bigger it seemed than it had before, the volume turned on full blast for all of it.

The clouds made it look like London was flanked by mountains, and when I got to the meeting point, Ed was cowering in a doorway, hunched a little bit, as if lowering his centre of gravity would make it less likely for him to fly up in the air. 'Beautiful day,' he said.

As I stepped into the doorway where he was standing, I stepped into silence. I wondered how we'd greet each other, but then, maybe as a joke, he shook my hand. 'Weather's crazy, isn't it? I know that's dumb. But the fact you can't escape it.' He kept his eyes focused on the street.

'I've heard you can go inside.'

'No but like . . . it's just so big! And it's everywhere,' he said.

'I hope all this stuff is going into your new book,' I said. I looked at him. Ed with his tan in stormy England.

'No, I just think that with climate change, they're always leading with the heat—' he said. 'Don't lead with that! Lead with the rain! Lead with the wind! With hailstones. Hello,' he said then. He was still holding my hand and he squeezed it, then pushed his fingers into the gaps between mine, a lattice.

In a brief lull, the trees drunkenly swaying, we braved it. We were heading to the cinema. The film had something to do with space. We arrived when it had already begun. The iced air, the cold seats, the way the acoustics seemed to make things bounce and disappear. At the concessions stand, Ed had bought everything. Hotdogs and nachos for both of us. Sweets, drinks, popcorn, which his hand rummaged around in. 'Snacks!' he'd said as we sat down.

The cinema could often make my lack of sleep catch up with me, but I felt incredibly awake. I thought about my eyes adjusting in the dark. I thought of fighters with night vision. I thought of their breath, the sound of feet in the forest. I thought of helmets slipping off. I thought of my whole life. I barely watched the film.

Ed's foot shifted and our knees touched. Then his bounced away. And then he put it back. It was all so hard to work out. With Bonnie, we'd always sit at the back if we went to the cinema. She'd turned me on so much in the middle of a film once – a 'no' I knew meant 'yes' – that I'd slipped to my knees after she took my hand and showed me that she'd shrugged off her shorts.

I heard Ed start to shift in his seat. 'I'm sorry about this,' he whispered in my ear. I turned to face him. 'It's so bad,' he said.

I nodded. His face stayed where it was, and then he turned it slightly. He stayed still for a while. I wondered if he was smelling my hair.

'Why are we being funny?' I whispered.

'I don't know.'

'I feel weirdly—' Aware of everything? Self-conscious? Scared?

He said it for me. 'Not scared but—'

I nodded.

'I know,' he said. 'Me too.'

He'd finished the popcorn. He handed me his drink, and for a fraction of a second I felt sure he was going to leave. But then he coughed, and stretched up and put his arm around my shoulder.

'Is that better?' he said.

'You're an idiot. Yes.'

Afterwards, outside, our eyes shrinking in the sharp beams of streetlights, the white light made everything look slightly unnatural.

'I want to kiss you,' he said, 'but I don't want to force you to do anything you don't want to. I don't know the rules outside Egypt—'

'No forcing,' I said. 'Now there's an offer that doesn't come along often.'

'Just you said you were—'

'Scared,' I said it myself this time. 'Maybe.'

It's true. I was nervous in a different way before. Simple fears. What if our bodies didn't let us? If they had once, but wouldn't again.

There are things you can't make up. Before, with men, with so few men, but still: I could never get it to reach my body. And then the opposite. With Bonnie, with Marion, with a list of girls, it could shock me, the sudden rush of it. Zero gravity, the speed of light, a waterfall, all of it suddenly inside me.

'I know, rationally, that being afraid of something doesn't

178

necessarily mean it's wrong,' I said. What was it about his face? The
star after star thing, the openness. It wasn't just that I wanted to tell
him the truth, it was that I felt I could. 'At work, it's in my job descrip-
tion to be constantly . . .' I looked for the word. 'On fire. In the right
sense. As in, never actually burning. But recently, when I'm not there,
I've realised I'm afraid all the time.'

He nodded.

'Funny but,' I said. 'I see myself dying all the time.'

'Oh—'

'Or other people. I see it constantly. I'll just – it's like my body keeps
walking but I'm where I once stood. And I see myself, from where I
was, just collapse to the floor. Or it could be you. You might leave on
a train. And I'd suddenly see you just—'

I kept on saying just.

'That doesn't sound fun,' he said.

'So it's everywhere is what I mean. The fear. I don't know how to
unpick the ones I don't need, and listen to the ones I do.'

'Is it better for you if it scares me too and I tell you, or if I pretend
I'm fine?'

'I don't know.'

'Well I'm scared too, and I'm also not. I'm sorry about the things
you see.' He stepped back and took in my face. 'From my professional
opinion, as a person who isn't even a doctor of philosophy, you look
very healthy to me.'

'Well that's good. What are you looking at?'

He took my hands. 'Fingernails,' he said. 'Checking for iron.'

'What else?'

'Eyes,' he said. He looked into mine.

'Looking for?'

'A soul.'

'Very good.'

He was still holding my hands. 'Palm lines,' he said then.

'Oh now we're really getting medical—'

'A long life,' he said. I looked away and he said: 'Look at it. Look at them.' They looked like the italic *M* in the name of a café my family used to go to when I was a kid.

'No soul,' I said, 'but a long life.'

'I'm sorry for all the things that scare you. I don't want to be one of them.'

If I was about to cry, I did not want him to see it. I made a croaking sound, a little false death, and fell against him, but from close together, letting him catch me. I put my face against his chest, finding a gap in his jacket, the bristle of wool not unlike fine stubble.

I don't remember how I got from his chest, to us kissing, but we were, and our mouths were warm, and I felt safe and in trouble, and then we went home.

9

In the morning, I left early for work. Gigr gave us small, weight-calibrated personal safes to keep our laptops in – one for work, one for home – and Ed was impressed by that, me tapping in the code to let it out. Also, my suit.

'It's very hot,' he said, making a show of his eyes running over the lines of my tailoring. 'I thought people in start-ups had to wear baggy jeans and condom hats.'

'I can tell you don't work in an office.'

'And I can tell you're good at what you do. It's the way you don't really talk about it.'

I told him – another evasion – I was still at the Fisher Price stage of capitalism, clunky-chunky plastic till. 'Still,' he said. 'Ka-*ching*.'

Ed stayed in bed, sitting up, the duvet huddled like a slumped cloud around his lower back, and I left him a note on the table downstairs telling him not to break anything. He texted me when I was halfway through the journey.

This is going to sound weird, but I feel like I'm always waiting for something to happen

I looked out of the car window. Yesterday's wind had blown over

every dustbin, and the pavements were carpeted with rubbish. It was
so sunny though, that the colours of crisp packets and empty cups
still looked beautiful.

But when I'm with you
it feels like life is happening
I felt it in my cheeks, my mouth start to smile.
Even if it's in a subtle way!

Thanks

Still here, he texted.
Still here, he texted again the next hour.

Contribute to my rent then

Not going anywhere.
Still here

Creep

Not a creep
You're smiling. I can see you
through your office window

10

Flo had texted me too. I'd cancelled on her twice by then, and she guessed something was up. *And you seem cheerful!* she wrote. *It's unfair! You can't only darken my door when you're a dead weight. To confirm, just not Bonnie?*

Not Bonnie, I replied.

She came to meet me after work and I'd rushed the last few calls to get to her at a reasonable time. I was still late though, and she was a little standoffish, though trying to make light of it. 'I feel very myself in this outfit,' she said.

It was a colder day than it had been in ages, a sudden retraction, like someone pulling back a syringe, and she was wearing cowboy boots and cropped jeans, a huge tweed jacket and a Mets cap she'd found on the street on the way here. 'Very new though,' she said, 'so not sure if it belonged to someone? It was, I admit, on a table.'

'Was someone sitting there?'

She shrugged with her mouth. The outfit shouldn't have worked but it semi-did. Still, it crossed my mind what work people would say if they saw me with her. Sometimes, when she came to meet me near work, she'd ask if I needed to do a silent decompression walk round the block. 'Who are you going to be today?' she'd say. 'You-you or work you?' But I was starting to lose track of which me was true.

I asked her how TP was.

'Well, the whole "end of family" family holiday isn't over yet,' she said. 'And I can tell, now he's said it, about wanting to be with me, that he now isn't sure what he wants, and I can tell' – she had all these things she could tell – 'he's looking at me as if it's my idea. These suspicious eyes where he's like: look what you've done to my children. Also the sex has been vile.'

'Call it quits,' I said. 'Move to Brazil.'

'No, no, unfortunately I'm so into it.' She walked like someone who wasn't fully adult yet. A mix and match of strides, with these glidey ice skater moves threaded in and out of them.

'So what are you going to do?' I asked her. It was easier when it was this way round.

'About my Old Age Pensioner? Or about graduating with a humanities PhD in a recession unlike any other? Why? Are you offering to sponsor me? Anyway,' she said, momentarily flipping her cap backwards. 'What have you been doing? *Who* have you been doing that's not seeing me?'

'Work,' I said. 'More trips. Egypt. Continued pressure to befriend the cretins in Whitehall ...'

I couldn't really look at her, but she was looking at me. 'You've always been a terrible actor.'

'I'm not acting.'

'I can see there's something hiding in your mouth.'

'Come find it,' I said, and I opened up.

'Ew,' she said. 'Your tongue has toothmarks around the edge.' Then: '*Whose?*'

I knew her face. In an instant, I saw it change from fun! to 'there's something you're not telling me'. I considered my options and then, finally, I told her I'd run into Ed again.

'Oh god,' she said. 'You mean you generated some encounter? A sting operation—'

'No, it was ...'

'Don't say fate.'

I told her what had happened. She was quiet for a while. I flipped my phone like a beer mat, still nothing.

'I feel – I don't know what I feel,' she said. 'Like, I want to be supportive? But it's very confusing for someone as intelligent as me.'

'Weren't you the one who said it wasn't a big deal?' I said. I stopped. 'We're just two people,' I said, which sounded right, but wasn't exactly what I felt about it.

'Two big gaylords though,' she replied. 'It's like you said. If it were the other way round – if I'd fallen in love with a woman – you'd obviously have to be all *positive*. What was that thing Sean said for ages when he came back from Greece? Yassas kween. But I can't be like, yay you've shaken off the shackles of your homosexuality ... *And* taken another one down with you. Particularly not at the moment.'

'The moment hasn't got anything to do with it,' I said. But it was true. I kept on thinking of that incident where a politician's wife said to him, after a speech he'd made, 'Darling, all the wrong people are clapping.' 'And anyway, what am I supposed to do? I don't want to be all hand-wringy. Like, I'm a *lesbian*, but I met a *man* and I don't know what to do about it because of my *community* and sense of self. It's so—'

'You don't have a community,' Flo said. She'd opened a bag of popcorn and ate the kernels from her palm, the way a horse eats. 'Or a sense of self. Oh my god, when I told AJ last time—'

AJ was Flo's friend from primary school, and also a lesbian, and so I'd always felt an array of rivalries. Before I'd come out, Flo had invited me to everything she did with AJ and had invited AJ to everything she did with me, a way of saying: *look, it's possible.* 'I don't see why I have to do it like *that*,' I'd always said to Flo back then; Flo who was, at that point, the only person I'd told. All AJ's friends I'd met fit so neatly into types, it was easier to tell Flo how trapped they looked rather than talk about how trapped I was. 'Can't I just be me?' I'd say. Flo would play a tiny violin in the sky and then say 'And how's that working out for you?'

'Why the fuck did you tell AJ?' I said now.

'Because it was *gossip*,' she said. 'All she said was "Well I hope she's disappointed in herself."' She started to laugh.

'How open-minded . . .'

'*Fondly*,' Flo went on. 'She likes you. Always has. She didn't say it meanly. Also she does a great impression of you after you finally got laid.' She paused for a second, then said, in an amplified version of my voice: 'So I don't do the socialising part, I do the actually fucking part. I don't *quite* think that makes me less gay?' I didn't react. 'Oh come on! You were such a dick about it.' She reached for my shoulder. 'The texts are funny, look. Her theory's that it's connected to your penchant for turning straight girls.'

She searched for 'JWT Turner', apparently a nickname.

JWT Turner strikes again! Except she's gone up a level. Pass go and collect 200 dollars.

Ffs it's like she's trying to find the final boss . . .

I scrolled. None of it was too bad and some of it was quite funny, but there was something about overhearing a conversation about you that you were not intended to be a part of. She must have watched my face falling.

'It's all good,' she said, taking her phone back. 'I think her feeling was basically, cool, great, just don't, like, bring him to a pride parade. Not that you'd ever go to one.'

'He's allowed at Pride,' I said. 'He is gay – like gay-gay.'

'Just like Bonnie was straight-straight . . .' she said. She shook her head. 'See? Extraordinary. The eternal pursuit of points . . .'

11

Ed was staying on Camberwell Grove, the angle of the road sweeping upwards as if it had been fine-tuned for beauty. When I got to the address, there were nine, or twelve, windows, all delicately redone sash, and only one doorbell for all of it.

'What the hell is this?' I asked him as he opened the door.

'Not mine is what it is,' he said. 'Oh and it's worse than you think.' He was only a third of the way down the corridor by the end of the next sentence. 'He's pretty much our age. Older, but not mad old.' From the corridor you could see through glass doors, which were approximately a tennis court away, to the garden. 'It's a little bit architects-drawing-of-a-nice-house . . .' Ed said.

I felt a twinge: was this huge house where he'd been the whole time? 'Make sure to tell them that in your after-stay feedback.'

'Look,' he said, 'the fridge shames you!' He pressed a button with a snowflake on it and text ran across the LCD saying 'room temperature water is better for hydration.' 'I will admit: better for hydration, less good for flavour. It tastes like the inside of a tap mixed with blood? But it's good for you!'

'Ice cold please,' I said. 'Fuck the fridge.'

At first, some kind of tectonic gap always re-formed between us when we were apart. The toothbrush and underwear that I had brought in my bag suddenly felt presumptuous. I wanted to touch him, close the gap, I think I did, but at the start, it could feel like there was lava underfoot. 'You tricked me into feeling sorry for you with that sob story about the seagull, and now look at you,' I said.

'It's this guy. Old friend. Brit in New York too. He's an interesting—'

'Immensely rich—'

'An interesting, immensely rich guy I know.'

I looked around the room. Potentially Matisse or Magritte's signature, I always got them confused, on a pencil drawing that didn't look like a print. 'He must be a crude oil dealer or something.'

'Not crude oil. Very against oil actually. Extraordinary family. His dad was one of those intellectual, semi-politician conservative types who actually *liked* culture. Can you imagine? But there are all these books. It's so funny.' He kept on saying funny. 'There are so many notes. To Howie love Popkins, or whatever, and it's Steinbeck.'

'You shake your head when you talk about him.'

'Well he's kind of bonkers.'

'Oh great, another bonkers man with large amounts of money.'

Ed looked all over my face. 'You don't have to worry about that with me,' he said. Then: 'The having money part.' He winked. He kissed near my mouth, and then near my temple. The tectonic gap narrowed but never fully closed.

Ed's friend was coming home next month, and so, Ed told me he'd taken to saying goodbye to things. 'Goodbye nice Crittall doors. Goodbye hot water tap. Stuff like that.'

'Surely you'll be able to find another hot water tap,' I said.

'But this one does boiling water. For tea.'

'Why does he want to come back now? Right when we're finally ahead for the first time in our life.'

'I don't know – but he did say something about from a shit show cometh an opportunity.'

'Did he say cometh?'

'He did, unfortunately, say cometh.'

Ed told me his friend did lobbying, that he was frequently in DC when they both lived in New York. I asked him what issues and what side, and Ed said he didn't really know.

'Ed, that's the kind of thing you ask!'

'Do *you* ask at work? And, what? Be dethroned from the palace! No way! I'm bringing back "don't ask don't tell". Just for the moment.'

He had three different pans on the stove, and was shaking one rather than stirring it, a hand movement I was about to comment on, when his phone started to ring. I scooted it over the table to him like an ice hockey puck.

He mouthed that it was his agent, and aligned his shoulders in a more proper way. 'She can't *see* you,' I said.

'Can I take it?' he asked, and he picked up, toggling into a bright voice.

There were some niceties, or, as it always was now, *not* niceties. 'It's awful, isn't it?' he said. 'Yeah, I saw the email and it's really good you're doing that.'

Inspired by something long done in Canada, certain companies, of which Gigr was decidedly not one, had started putting a note at the bottom of their email signatures saying they acknowledged they were working at a time of increased injustice and that they stood against the climate encouraged by the new government. Ed rolled his eyes at me: sorry this is taking so long.

I heard her say 'but about the book' and 'dream run' and something about having really been able to 'capitalise on the times', then he replied, 'yeah, it's been good!', then a second later, 'thank you', as if he'd forgotten it and had to reopen the bag to stuff it in. 'One sec,' he said, and he bundled into the other room.

He had these things he said about it. That you had to take both the good and bad with a pinch of salt, because it was random. That the way the reviews had unfolded, from luminous to spectacular to necessary to urgent, almost like a chocolate fountain or something, was because no one really trusted their own opinions so just looked at what others had said before them. That prizes were a crap shoot. But that he was coming at it from the easy way, because it had gone well, perhaps because a lot of people felt guilty at the moment.

'Sorry about that,' he said when he came back.

'Are you kidding? Daniel literally calls me at three a.m.'

Ed was in a strange mood after the call. 'It was good,' he said. 'I mean sales . . . sales are . . . it's literary fiction. It means it sells nothing. But the publisher seems okay. They've been asking about what's next. Which is good. Which is better than, please for the love of god don't ever do this again.'

'You look worried—'

'I thought I'd get a break.' His hand scratched at his torso, looking for a break, too, between his ribs.

'I thought you said you finished editing it two years ago?'

'Ouch – I mean. I just thought it would be enough for a while. Particularly with the reviews.'

'Now he says they're good . . .'

Of the twelve, apart from the line about breathless sex, there was only a single other sentence that was somewhat less than complimentary. Something about a 'gauche approach to bodily fluids'. Ed said 'gauche approach' so many times after that. Even that night, when he served pasta and the tomato sauce left a blood splatter on the plate, 'Some would call it a gauche approach,' he'd said.

'No, they're good. Apart from their obsession with the sex in it, it's been good. But it's – she kept saying "what's next?" "what's next?" And "how did you get on in Egypt?" as if it was exciting to ask that. And then she was like, you can do anything, anything at *all*, but it *has* to speak to the fans.' He carried a hot pot over to the table with his sleeves over his fingers to protect his hand.

'Who are the fans?' I said. 'Not in a mean way.'

'Literally about three I know of,' he said. 'But you know what they mean.'

'Well, here I am,' I said.

'Here you are.' He put his hand on the back of his neck like it was hot and his hand was a cold towel. 'But it's everyone in publishing. I had a drink with my editor the other week and floated a couple of ideas. I had a nutty one I was into set in the late Viking era and she listened, nodding, while I went through all these warring tribes,' he half laughed. 'And then she said: "But they're gay, right?"' He paused. 'I brought up their other concerns. Namely, you know, *staying alive*. She looked at me and said, "But it would be more *you* to make them gay." Followed by this knowing "Gay people *have* existed throughout time, you know ..."'

'They've *what*?' I said. 'And let me guess. She's straight with sixteen children?'

'Course. It just makes me feel anxious. With my agent just now, I told her I have something I'm excited about, and it just ... isn't true. I don't have anything. Fuck, I'm going to be sick—'

'I've broken you already,' I said.

'It would be great if you could slap me,' he said. 'Hard.' He was starting to laugh now. His head homed its way into my hands, and he said, 'Please, just a little one.'

I swooshed at him, and then just touched three fingers against his cheek. 'Domestic violence against men,' I said. 'That's your material.'

The Beatles were playing on an elaborate speaker system buried in the walls and ceiling, and Ed turned it down for the beginning of 'You Never Give Me Your Money' because he said it always made him want to cry. With his back to me, I kissed his back, his neck, the back of his neck, until he turned back around.

Later, the question I was always asked – and I'm sure he was asked too, if he told people about me – was, in that moment, did you want it? Did you feel it? Did you want it the same way? I see people's eyes as they say it, and they want something clear, for it to be one way or the other.

I found my way to a different part of myself, a part that liked hardness not softness, biggerness not smallness. Too obvious but true. Too obvious but true too, that it was like tuning into a different part of the radio. And the notes and the lyrics of the song, where to put my hands, how to move, presented themselves to me, because the world's played it your whole life.

That didn't make it clearer. Close-ups could. The way it could feel like opening something. Not a present, but the underside of his arms, the sides of his neck, these long lengths of body I followed up, then back down. Sometimes, when our faces were eye to eye, it would be almost too much, and one or the other of us would break away. What do you want the answer to be?

That night, in bed – an enormous bed, for the first time in my life I wasn't aware of the edge – I asked him what he thought his friends would say. Flo's messages with AJ rushed through my mind.

'I don't have friends,' he said. 'Joking but. No one can say anything can they? Legally. I'll record it on my GoPro.' He kissed my head, and left his lips there.

'Free speech!' I said weakly. 'Anyway, they'll think it.'

We were both quiet for a second. Our bodies were touching in as many places as was possible but I could feel him shift around for a new one. 'It makes more sense – most sense – when I don't think about anyone else,' he said. 'Also I don't think boys "announce" things as much as girls.'

'You're not a different species.'

'You know what I mean though.' We were both silent, and I don't think I moved but he said, 'Hey – what happened? You just closed like a shell.'

'Nothing,' I said. 'Thinking.' I had often found it hard to say exactly what I meant, in situations like that. But with Ed, particularly at the beginning, I would find the words, and not just any words, the ones I actually wanted to say, coming out of my mouth. 'My head keeps saying you're going to do it again.'

'Do what again?'

'I keep thinking, how will this end?'

'It's the beginning, why are you thinking about the end?'

'At the beginning I think about the end, and at the end I think about the beginning.'

'Do you ever just enjoy it?'

I thought about it.

'Melancholic-aholic,' he said. He found my hand under the sheets and held it. 'I don't know. There could be a million reasons why this doesn't work. For both of us.'

'I know that. I'm not saying that.'

'But I'm not going to disappear,' he said. 'I'm really not. And isn't the beauty of this – whatever it is – that we can do it our own way? Could try to.'

In those first moments, we could find our way back to each other so easily.

'I'll message everyone I know right now if you like,' he said. 'Do that broadcast thing. Hire a skywriter. Ed 4 El. E L. Because you pay by the letter you know.'

'I bet they'll make a spelling mistake,' I said. But saying it all out loud had helped it leave my body for a moment.

'Is that what's happening then?' he said. 'Are we doing this?'

'What's this?'

'I don't know – gritting our teeth and bearing it.'

'What's this and what's it?'

'I like you,' he said. 'I do. Begrudgingly.'

There was a tiny stretch of dry skin on the left of his face. You're just a normal person, I remember thinking. You're different from anyone I've ever met and also a normal person all at once. It summoned waves inside me.

'I'll think about it,' I said.

12

I had successfully avoided talking to Ed about my work. When Flo asked to meet him, it occurred to me that it might come up, but I knew I couldn't ignore it forever and so after another bludgeoning week at the office that bulldozed through a weekend and deep into the next, we met on Hampstead Heath.

Finally! she'd texted. *Shall we go to the ladies pond*
Leave Ed to peer in through the bushes?

Ed and I turned up together. Ed and Flo both bee-lined straight for each other.

'Friend Flo,' he said.

'What's Ed short for, anyway?' she said as she gave him a hug. 'Edstopher?'

It was the day after the unsuccessful knife attack on the gay bar in Farringdon, and Ed told us a story about his book. How a month ago, he'd done an event near Brighton of all places, and after the bookshop had put a display of his book in the window, the tills were down by forty percent. 'Someone also threw black paint across the windows. Probably just kids but, like, *Brighton*. It changes like that.' He clicked his wide fingers.

'Like I was saying to Elle, it's a good time to get out,' Flo said. She pointed at the two of us.

'What? Oh, right,' Ed said. 'Yeah. My beard.'

'Soul patch,' I said. I was feeling quiet.

'But anyway, for the government to decline to comment,' he said.

'On your relationship?' Flo said.

'No, on the the knife thing.'

'What are they going to say? Good job! It's the thought that counts, just try harder next time.' She pulled a face. 'I never get why these nutjobs always step up attacks when they *have* power. I mean I do get it technically. *Emboldening* or whatever, but ... yeah. Hot civil disobedience summer,' she said, making a face. A squirrel bobbed by us with its dandelion tail. 'Meanwhile we just sit in a park having a picnic—'

I thought about a text she'd sent me in the early days: *We will fight them on the beaches ... with irony!*

'Are you having to cozy up to them still?' she said and when no one spoke, I realised it was me she was talking to. I looked at Ed, saw his eyes trained on me too. Then he looked away.

'It's not *cozying up*,' I said.

'Well. Whatever. Getting them "on side". Being a "collabo".'

She was joking. Was she joking? Ed looked up at me again.

'Yeah, I have to keep my job, and half the jobs in the country afloat in this sea of shit,' I said.

'Yum,' she said. 'Vivid. Sorry. Let's talk about something else. Don't want to upset you.' She touched my arm. 'My friend, the Vichy government. *Anyway*, it is exciting to be with a man. The scent of Davidoff Cool Water bracing the air—' She breathed in deeply. 'What's it your mum always says?'

I tried to let the little spike of cortisol that had come leave my body. 'Oh you spend time with *men* too, do you?' I did my mum's voice, glad we were on safer ground. 'Like they're rare gold.'

Ed asked Flo if she was gay too, and she said she was straight enough for it to be embarrassing. 'The last straight person in Britain I think she called me once,' she said. 'And now look at her.'

The afternoon melted away, each of us taking a turn to get a new bottle of wine from the closest shop. I felt proud of Flo. Proud of both of them. Proud, I mean, that they were connected to me. It painted these flashes of warmth up and down my body.

They shared a quality, this way of having no walls. A freedom, an unbound spring. The opposite of how I could be. Flo touched Ed's facial hair to feel its thickness. For a brief moment, it felt like we had no clothes, no skin. Like life from another time. Like we were young still. Kids playing in a park.

It was my first full day off since Egypt. We walked from Hampstead to Soho for late-night Chinese food, a journey that felt all downhill. In Soho Square, there was a vigil or a protest, a gathering anyway, for last night's attack. A big group of Evangelicals were counter-protesting, as well as a shirtless lone ranger with five or six placards made from flattened shoeboxes.

'Good timing from the Christians,' Flo said as we walked past. 'Really biblical.' She gave them the finger, the childish one where you mechanically wind it up with your other hand.

I didn't care about the Christians or the man with walls of cardboard. It was the teenagers I cared about. The group on the other side of the square, mostly boys, but some girls too, laughing and shouting from time to time, then laughing more.

'They're just reactionary,' Ed said, when he saw how I looked at them. 'They're teenagers. They're meant to react.'

At the restaurant, the chicken was so deep-fried, my teeth registered it as bone. Our conversation slowed down. Beer couldn't make its way through the sauce. 'Goodbye young lovers,' Flo said when we parted ways.

I took out my phone to call us a car, but Ed wanted to take the night bus as a trip down memory lane. We made our way to a seat on the top deck. The bus drove off before we sat down. That feeling of swinging through a jungle, the whole of the chatty London night around us.

'I like her,' Ed said. 'She's not sure about me in a way that I respect.'

'Why?' I said. 'Are you not sure about yourself either?'

It was when I looked out of the window that the cortisol fizz came back. But it wasn't Ed I was worried about, or Flo, or even work this time. I kept on thinking of the edges of the square. The flattened cardboard, the teenagers. How quickly it could swing back.

Memory lane of a different kind. It came – a flicker, seismology, that needle, something buried, but never far – all the times I'd been afraid. The times I'd turned a corner then gone back, to see if the girl I'd kissed and left was okay. The amount of times one of us had said 'not here'.

Even if I was bad at community, that was something we all shared. When Flo had told me AJ was organising solidarity club nights in protest of the government, I'd said something along the lines of 'and jelly shots will do it, right?', but at least she was doing something. And what was I doing? This.

'The protests,' I said as the hydraulics of the bus hissed at a stop. 'I don't have to say the things. You know them.'

'Yeah,' Ed said. 'I know some things.'

He put his arm around me. A wall the world decided it understood. Suddenly it felt so heavy it was crushing. It wasn't Ed's fault, rationally I knew that, and so I tried to make myself soften. I thought about our arms around other people, other people's arms around us, but somehow it only made it worse. It was always the thing I'd found most unbearable: the ways that loving someone had put them in danger rather than made them safe.

13

At work, Daniel was angry. It radiated. 'The weekend was awful,' he said.

'Why?' I asked him. 'What did you do?'

'What did *I* do?' He looked at me, like *head in the clouds*. 'I'm just saying the protests, riots. They were getting so big and out of control, the government knocked out all the fucking phone signal.'

'The gay one?' I said. 'I saw it, it was tiny.'

'No, not that one. Some cost of living thing bashed into some stop the deportations stop all the wars thing and it started to get hairy. I don't mind them tamping it down. But they were fucking rough with it! Took out half of zone one,' he said. 'Don't dare talk about *boundaries* at the weekend. It totally fucked up the app. That was basically all of retail and F&B out—'

'No, I know,' I said. 'I was following it of course.'

'We need to step in and suggest something else ... Who's your best contact inside at the moment?'

Panic again: it came like a claw. 'I've had a lot on my plate with other territories, with keeping marketing on track here—'

'And? You're supposed to have ten plates spinning. We have

twenty-four-hour trackers on all our guys, right? Can't we say we'll identify anyone who's protesting and put them on the subs bench, or dock their pay?

'Our guys aren't protesting. They're working—'

'Everyone has something they care about though, don't they? The gov might press the wrong buttons and suddenly our lot will want to bear arms – well we can stop them! That would have an impact, everyone needs cash at the moment.'

'Daniel, that's—'

'Come on, it's a good idea!'

'It's dystopian.'

He put his hands up and waved his fingers. '*Scary*. Get with the programme.'

14

It had been so long since I saw my parents that my dad had once again removed his love from his messages. I asked Flo if she'd join me for a visit – a technique we'd employed previously to reduce the likelihood of an argument. She agreed to come: her last free day, she said, before PhD prison.

'It's funny how it changes,' she said. 'How it's cool to bring your friend to family things and then it's weird. Things like Christmas I mean.'

'Lucky it's only September.'

'Hey, what tone should I take with your mum, by the way?' she said as our train pulled out of the station. 'Tone's not the word, but do I be normal? It's not – it isn't goodbye, right?'

'Anything you do will be fine because you aren't me. Also,' I said, 'don't mention Ed.'

The plan was that we would take them out for the day. Something I'd been promising for over a year, but had cancelled so many times by then.

'Anyway, this is the end of everything,' Flo had said on the train.

'Freedom!' she said in a Braveheart voice. 'Then off to the concentration camp for me.' She touched the window.

'Stanford-le-Hope. What a way to go.'

Flo was so nice about the house. From Edmonton to *this*, she said, what a win. They took her into every room. On the way there, Flo made these jokes – I can't wait to see their faces *light up* when they see me – but the truth was, they did light up. She was loose in her limbs and happy, and I wanted to mirror it, but I felt my back get tighter.

The four of us in their tiny car. The seals had gone around each window and my dad would always say it was his re-wilding effort, that there were species of algae in here you wouldn't find anywhere else.

'Lots of posters for the Alliance,' Flo noticed out loud. She was good at keeping talking, and not in the way that I did it. It seemed more real. I tried to send emails with my phone beside my leg so no one could see the light.

'Prime flag-shagger territory,' my dad said from the driver's seat, with that voice he had when he knew a word for something. 'Coast people fear invasion. Though why anyone would want to come *here* these days . . .'

The drive wasn't long. We were the girls in the back. My dad kept calling us girls. Girls, do you see that? There's the castle! Look, girls! Later on the train Flo said 'it's so contextual who we *are*. I wish context worked for the skin. Young again 'cos your dad called us girls.'

They liked a beach called Bell Wharf, in Leigh-on-Sea, because it was tiny, so it didn't make you feel obliged to walk, but the boats made it feel like somewhere in France, and there was a pub they liked.

The late-September Indian summer was tropical. In the heat, pints lost their cool within minutes. My mum had wine with ice, which shrunk, too, like glaciers. At one point, she wandered down to the sand and sat with her face in the light, her eyes tight shut, like the sun could be collected, like she was gathering it.

It should have been me who walked over to her, but it was Flo. That was when my dad took my hand. He stroked one of my fingers with his and I wondered if he was thinking how my hands were no longer a child's hands, when he said, 'We . . .' then stopped. 'I've never asked. I wouldn't ask.' He looked like he was standing on something sharp. 'I don't know how to ask—'

'You can ask anything,' I said to him. A corkscrew turning, a winch upwards.

'It's our pensions,' he said. 'They're not a lot, but they'd always been enough. Nothing crazy, but to – live.' He nodded and I nodded too. 'The thing is. The ones they gave us, the ones we got, they're not ad-justed for inflation. Which means there's a gap. And it's been getting bigger.' He looked around to make sure no one else could hear. He was trying to speak so carefully. 'Quite big now. Difficult.' I remem-bered his message months ago, about something sensitive. 'I wouldn't ask. I'd never ask,' he said again, 'I've tried for a long time not to.'

'Dad, it's nothing,' I said. I always said this when I paid for dinner when we went out. 'I have too much for just me.'

'But you shouldn't have to—'

'I want to. I didn't sell my soul to the devil for me and me alone. And I heard this rumour,' I said. I leaned in a little.

'What?' he said, worried.

'That you and that woman over there had *something* to do with me being born.'

They were walking back now, Flo and my mum.

'And you're sure?' he said. It was just over two thousand pounds a month they needed.

'Positive.'

'There they are!' my dad said then. When birds are wet they shake out their feathers so they are light enough to fly again – the way he'd brightened up now reminded me of that.

Flo was from the Midlands, so it played okay when she sat back at the table and said, quite loudly, 'Shall we sophisticated city folk do a vox-pop of the real people of Britain?'

'Like I was saying, hardline country round here,' my dad said. 'Even Liddle's a little soft for them. The Thursday night lads are always—' He did the yapping symbol with his hand. He was drinking lemonade now, and it looked both cute and heartbreaking in his cup. 'They're obsessed with fair share. *We've had our fair share.* Used to be migrants. But now they want their fair share of *stuff.* With all the food shortages we should get different rations. British people should get different rations they mean. They *love* a ration book!' His cheerfulness now. 'The idea of one. Brings back the war.'

'What you said earlier,' Flo said. 'About coast people fearing invasion. That's the scary thing about this shithole.' She finished her drink then mine. 'The country, I mean. Islands are all coast.'

We had avoided an argument. In that way it was a success. When I hugged them both, I let myself do it so tightly. 'Thank you,' my dad said into my ear. 'It'll change everything,' he said when we were pulling apart.

'Your mum was very quiet,' Flo said on the train back. 'She didn't even tell you which of your clothes she didn't like.'

'I know.' I thought about her on the beach, collecting sun. How much did she get? What was she using it for? Where was she planning to take it? I thought of my dad, the way he'd nervously made a hotdog of his thumbs inside his fingers when he asked me about the money, and how much his hands were sweating. His lemonade. My mum with skin so thin if she wore a watch it would cut her. It was all shrinking.

I looked out of the window at fields that should have been green left to bake. Across the ocean, Canadian wildfires had knocked out a lot of the global wheat supply, and the papers were sharing recipes of cornbread and rye bread and other breads as if that would be enough of a solution.

'Do you think they *will* do rations?' Flo asked me, when we said goodbye to each other at the station. 'Sweet little book, Made in China like our passports?'

'No idea.' More and more emails had stacked up while we were at the beach. I was suddenly desperate to get home.

'Also, do you miss pussy?' Flo asked me.

'Sorry, what?' The way her mind hopscotched.

'You can see mine if you want. I mean, not *here*—'

'I'm okay, thanks.'

'I just find it sad. What was that website you wanted to make?' She started to laugh.

'Flo, I was twenty-five, that was a joke—'

'The tasting notes thing—'

'Pussy sommelier.'

'It's perfect.'

'Fine, I'll make it my next start-up,' I said.

'But you don't taste it anymore! You'll have lost your edge. How's your sexy intern by the way? The one you said you needed blinkers for.'

Luisa. I'd been keeping her at bay.

I had no time to reply. 'Oh my god, look at him,' Flo said, pointing at this crow walking past a bin with a limp. 'Look at his swagger. Literally if he was an inch taller I'd date him.'

15

Weeks ticked by, in a continuing blaze of battering heat that made no sense for the season, and Ed and I saw each other most evenings, however late I left work, swapping his AC for my fan, and back again.

The week of the election, and the days that followed, stayed clear and full in my head for a long time afterwards. But other things, it's harder to recall in the exact order. The state visits from world leaders that were as well-oiled as they'd always been. The crunchy handshakes, the sustained smiles. Occasional 'comments' from France and Spain, always subtle enough to be interpreted in infinite ways. And new friendships, always referred to as friendships – gleaming photoshoots and lavish diplomatic gifts – with people who'd formerly been our adversaries. And how all these things wove in and out of the updates my mum had from meetings with new doctors, or the days such newly shameful things happened at work I felt I should leave, but I always looked at the numbers and thought about the slow and slowing way my parents walked to their car, and the money my dad had asked me for, and what I wanted for myself, and always came back the next day.

The date when Ed's rich friend would be back to reclaim his house edged closer, and that was when Ed's room search started in earnest. I looked over his shoulder as he scrolled through listings on his laptop. 'Why do they always say "benefits from laminate flooring"?' I said. 'That is not a benefit. Also, why are you looking in Streatham?'

'My friend says the yummy mummies, or whatever the word is these days – they call it Saint Reatham.'

'I don't care,' I said. 'I won't go there.'

'It's just hard,' he said. He kissed my nose, then let his teeth out and bit the tip of it. 'It's only three or four more months here.' I didn't mean for my face to change, but of course it did. He held me back a little. 'I'm joking, or at least,' he said. 'I don't really know. We haven't talked about it . . .'

'Is we – you and me? Or you and someone else?'

'You and me,' he said. 'Dickhead.' He reached for me again, put his thumb through one of my belt loops and stroked my skin with his free fingers. 'We can chat about it. I'd like to.'

'Chat,' I said.

'Life, death, prizes,' he said, 'all equal weighting.' But that was when I noticed the other tab open and saw the word Gigr. Not just one: four tabs with the word Gigr.

I looked at him. 'Are you running my licence?'

'Forget a woman,' he said, 'I can't believe I'm sleeping with some-one who works at Gigr—' He tried to smile.

'Fair,' I said. But was it? 'Maybe I'd feel a little differently if I had something locked away somewhere—'

'Hey . . .'

'If my mum wasn't ill—'

'Hey,' he said again. 'I'm joking. I get it.'

'Do you?'

'Yes,' he said. He closed the tabs, one by one, making a bullet sound like he was shooting them at a gun range. 'If I really thought you were a heartless, ruthless—' he started.

'Stop it.'

'Okay. But I do get it. I do. Anyway, it might be too much. Or not right. But, I was thinking, if you wanted a lodger ...'

'Ed, you're not a lodger—'

'But you're saving for a house, right? That's the whole point of it. If I paid half your rent that would buy a nice sink or something?'

'A tile ...'

'A Delft though! I don't know – maybe it's a bad idea.'

I looked at him and his laptop which he had accidentally bought in a size too small. It made him look like a giant crowding a tiny keyboard and I felt a surge of affection for him. Even with his tabs. I kissed his head. It smelled, in a nice way, of waxy potatoes.

'Moving in quickly,' I said. 'It's incredibly lesbian of you.'

'Cultural appropriation,' he said, looking faintly proud.

16

Flo had said many times that she believed it happened chemically. That exes could somehow, wherever they were in the universe, smell when you were happy.

Bonnie wrote to me. She was in town from Lisbon – actually, she lived in Cascais now, which she'd once said was like a Costa del Sol for white-collar criminals – and wanted to have lunch. The obvious thing was not to go. But I was never not going to go. I told myself it would be cleansing. A smudge stick, an exorcism.

As I walked there, I thought about how my friend Seb called them 'anti-dates'. Because of how you hoped they would go badly. And because of how you hoped they might fix something. I found a way to make it work in my head.

She'd dyed her hair pink, the pale kind, a translucence to it, the colour of Himalayan salt. She must have had eyelash extensions too, because they seemed to go on forever, Bambi painted black around the blue. The blue, the blue, and her eyes rolling back when she came: a shock rushed through my belly.

Her shoulders were sleek, the scooped dips around the clavicle. She was the only person on the street who looked cool in the heat.

And then there it was, perfect, tight, high, like a little scooter helmet under her dress.

'Hello,' she said.

A banana boat rushed back and forth through my own belly. You have a baby in there, a whole baby, I thought, and I just have a banana boat in mine.

'You look so well,' I said. She was tanned, had freckles in a neat bridge across her nose. 'And that – that's amazing.' I could barely look at it, the way we try not to look directly at the sun. 'It looks so . . . real?'

'I know,' she said.

I gave it a tiny fake little tap with my fist and made a knock-knock sound with my mouth. 'Totally hollow, right?' I said. 'You use it for shoplifting?'

We walked through the café, her ahead of me, and I found myself looking for things she might bump into, people who might walk into her. My hands were ready. I imagined pushing an inter-loper over.

'What brings you here?'

'I came to see you,' she said.

'Ha.'

'No, I did.'

'Well,' I said. I looked at both sides of the menu, unable to really understand any of the words. 'How do you feel? Have you been sick? Are you excited? Do you have names? Is it a—'

'Elle, it's just me.'

'Yes, it's you,' I said.

'It's me, it's you, it's us, we can be us.'

The waiter came over that moment. She told him we hadn't looked yet.

'Fine,' I said, when the waiter left, I sat back in my chair, 'how ya doin', you big old bitch?'

She laughed then. 'I am a big old bitch. Six months.'

My mind did maths, but not her maths of when it happened; our maths. Our lives felt out of balance. All of this life inside her, and my mum. Life leaving me.

When the waitress asked if we had any allergies, and I said, 'not today, thank you', Bonnie said: 'Dad jokes. You'd be a good dad.'

We talked about work. She said she'd looked me up on the Gigr website and saw I was a big shot now. We talked about people we'd both known in Lisbon. 'Amelia says she can't come back to the country or she'll be arrested,' she told me. 'For *posts* or whatever,' her voice skipped with a little laugh, 'it's all *very* dramatic—'

Whenever she wasn't talking her lips moved in these tiny ways you'd only notice if you were really looking. Additional subtitles – these little cues and clues. I couldn't stop looking.

She asked me if I had a new girlfriend, and I took the way out the question offered me and said no. I gave Bonnie the more cooked eggs. I paid for the bill.

'Would you walk with me?' she said, when we got to the restaurant door.

'It was like a poison,' I told Flo later.

''Tis the season,' she said. 'Novichok again?'

'No,' I said, 'the *Tempest* one, or *Midsummer Night's Dream*.'

Bonnie and I hadn't even been with each other for an hour. In that second, I felt that I'd walk with her anywhere.

With Bonnie by my side, the road felt alive with danger. Cars seemed designed to knock over pregnant women, zebra crossings seemed like an invitation to a nightmare. I wanted to put my hands above her head to protect her from the sun. People crowded into the shaded side of the road. On the bench opposite ours in the park, the shadow of leaves on a woman's arm looked like a sleeve of tattoos.

'Didn't we always say,' Bonnie said, 'no matter what happens to us, that one day we'd find each other again?'

It was true. But it had always felt small. We'd have an affair. Something sordid, hidden.

'I've been thinking that what we had was so good,' she said. 'You helped me so much with my work too. Supported me.'

I had written listing after listing for her. I wrote tricky emails. Before I'd accepted the first job that had taken over my life, I'd even taken pictures sometimes, and done a few visits.

'We also, yeah—' she said.

I knew what yeah was. A combustibility between us. I nodded.

'A lot of good things. So many good things, don't you think? I think as you get older, these things get clearer.'

'Fuck, Bon,' I said.

'What?'

'Is this like the bit in Bridget Jones where Hugh Grant says the thing about her, and her skirt? If he can't make it with her, he can't make it with anyone?'

'Does Bridget say no?'

'She says no.'

'Then it's not that bit,' she said. She looked at my eyes. She looked at my lips. She looked at my eyes again. It was so slow and obvious I found my body mirroring her.

'In the simplest way,' she said, 'I just miss you. And everything that's happened – how quickly it happens – it's a dose of perspective.'

What did I want? In a way, it didn't matter what me today wanted; there was a chorus of me's from before, me's from so many years. All of them wanted her.

'I don't ask it lightly – I know it would take a lot for you to trust me again. It's just it was so much time,' she said. 'And I kind of feel like if *we* started again, all of that time would start again? Does that make sense?'

'I think your hormones are making you crazy,' I said. Something was making me crazy too.

'Good point. Also, women love it when you say that.'

I wondered what it would be like to sleep with her pregnant. Would I put my hands on her belly? Would her legs open less? Would she taste different? It ripped through me again, the thought of her face as she came.

'How's your nose doing?' she said. 'Any recent injuries?'

'She's doing okay,' I said. Her hand came towards me and she lightly touched the tip of my nose with her finger.

'We had it so good,' she said. The same finger was back on her belly now. 'I think we could have everything.'

17

'This is paint-by-numbers,' Flo said when I told her. I called her as I walked back to the office. 'Now she's suddenly a lesbian? And to complete the typecasting she's stepped up her evil-ness?'

'Why is it evil if she's realised she loves me?'

'And spoiler alert, if she's finally gay she's going to die at the end of the book. Or you will. Fucking Bonnie,' I could hear her shaking her head. 'Bonnie all banged up.'

'She's not in jail.'

'She should be in jail.'

'Hey, that's the mother of my child you're talking about.'

'Please don't. Don't even joke.' She said it like if she were with me, she'd have squeezed my hand until I saw my skin change colour. 'It's not the life you want. With Bonnie very specifically I mean. You said that yourself. She had you on a tightrope. You said you could never have been happy in the end.'

I told her Bonnie had said I should make a decision by Monday.

'Oh fuck off. It's Saturday. And what about Ed?'

Ed. I'd stayed in the park after Bonnie left. I must have looked mad, looked like the other people who were mad, because I just sat there, thinking. Having conversations in my head then realising my mouth was moving.

'I know. I do know. But remember those months when he—'

'When he understandably freaked out and ultimately came back?'

'Was discovered hiding in a hotel.'

'Still. He's a picture of reliability in comparison to her. Elle, you found emails. You read them all.'

'Not emails, it was that dumb chat thing—'

'Whatever! *I* still remember some of it word for word and it wasn't even about me.'

It was true. I'd heard the lines for a long time. They sat in my head. Waited for me when I looked in the mirror. They were from a chat she was still logged into on one of my browser windows.

No doubt with Andrew it will be MUCH easier, Bonnie's friend, Reuben, had written. It would take a while for the older messages to load sometimes, and the whirling loading circle felt like an eye watching me. Andrew, of course, was the man Bonnie had left me for. A generic English guy who also went to her expensive gym in Lisbon. Bonnie said that nothing had happened with him until everything was done and dusted with us, but after I found out they were together, so many things slotted into place. A new passcode on her phone (she'd said she was organising something for my birthday; a birthday our relationship did not last until, not even close). A long scratch on her back she'd said was from a protruding nail on a construction site.

The baby thing I mean, Reuben continued.

Totally, Bonnie wrote back, *and it's just . . . a purity between two people*

Bonnie would often add ellipses into messages when she wanted to come across as meaningful. She said she didn't want to have to add a third person. Not a random one. They all had god complexes, she wrote, or were crossing state lines to jizz in any cup that would have them. *As IF they really went to Harvard, you know? It's just . . . when*

216

you love someone you want to make a child with *them*, she wrote, *not an unknown entity. When you love someone you want to fuck ... you know ... *them* and let life come if it possibly ... could ?*

Reuben: *Let life come, let Andy come lol*

Bonnie: *not that it couldn't ...* Those dots again, a touch of piousness floating off the sans-serif, *be complicated for straight people too. But when you're into someone, you do kind of want to see your faces together?*

My throat finished shrinking to a knot then, and for about an hour, I couldn't swallow.

They were all the things I'd admitted to her I found difficult. Things I'd told her when we felt close enough that my body couldn't believe we'd ever not be touching. I'd simply spoken them into reality.

'It wasn't nice to see,' I said to Flo, 'But I get it. And something about me and Bonnie. It's beyond that.'

'Please tell me you're not doing some dumb thing where you meet on a bridge to say yes. Please don't say yes, Elle.'

'I don't get it,' I said to her after that. 'Are you jealous? Why did you always hate her so much?'

When Flo came to stay with us in Lisbon, the two of them assessed each other like cats. They'd look at each other across the room, planning attacks. 'But what is it, the spell,' Flo would ask. 'Seriously, what is it? I see she's conventionally attractive—'

'Famously an awful thing to be.'

'But the power she has is disproportionate!'

'Because she's objectively a bad person,' she said now.

'Day one you didn't like her. And I think it was because I did. Because I liked her so much.'

Flo's recurrent accusation on those tricky trips to Lisbon: that I had been drugged or blackmailed. The way I served love on a platter. Kept it stocked, kept refilling it, kept it high, like I was the only one responsible.

The thing that Flo didn't understand – still couldn't understand – was that it felt like I had already won. Winning was that it was possible. That I could be with someone like Bonnie. A girl, a woman.

Any first love feels like a swelling. Like waves are crashing on either side of you. But this had something else in it too. It was that we could do it, she and I, and that we were. There was no other way to say it: it had felt like a walkway appearing into the sky.

18

I asked Ed to come over for breakfast without asking him to stay the night before. I hadn't made up my mind exactly, but I would tell him. Talk to him about it. That would be the fair, adult thing to do. Though why did adult feel like such a special add-on when I'd been one for so long? And also maybe novichok was right because a whole half of me, more than that, didn't want to do it. I went out and bought croissants and a pastry spiral that curlicued cheese and marmite, and left the bag it came in oil-sodden.

It was when I pushed the front door open – my hands welted in swirls from heavy bags – that the message came through from Bonnie. I thought there was another day to go. But it just said this:

I think after long hard thinking, that it's easiest and makes more sense if I try again with Andy.

I hope, as I have always hoped, that we can remain friends. B x

A sea rushed through my body. *I think after long hard thinking.* She can't have even re-read that email once. I read it again, taking in each word.

At the bottom, it said 'Sent from my iPhone'.

219

19

I did tell Ed. Not about the email, but that I had seen her and that it had – the way I described it was like a cat following one of those mouse toys. It had thrown me around a bit. I could see him swallow his croissant more heavily, or at least I wanted to see that. Nothing else about the vibration of his body changed though.

'I get it,' he said. 'Honouring the part of you that would have wanted that. I don't mind if you talk about her. Or see her. As long as she's ugly—'

'Hideous.'

'Or that you felt fucked up about it. I mean, I do have the first letter of a man's name tattooed to my face.'

He seemed so unfazed by it I wondered if I could or should have said more. I remembered the way he'd said it about the tattoo. Someone he loved. It had felt like it was made of brass, all polished. 'What was his name?'

'Jonny? I think I talk about him all the time, in a way that I probably edit out the talking.' He reached for his glass of water.

'Is this New York guy?'

'Upstate now.'

I asked how they met. 'Paris,' he said. Again I saw him re-watch it in real time. He puffed out his T-shirt to eject croissant crumbs. 'He was sitting at some zinc bar, eating sardines. One of those cool guys, you know. Cool guys, then. Baseball cap, earring, Caesar cut long before George Osborne killed that. Impeccable interior design taste,' he started to laugh. 'No, but you'd like him I think.'

'I'm sure I would.'

'All those words I used to describe him are terrible, but it was wild falling in love with him. Felt like a Phoenix song. By which I probably mean I was listening to Phoenix songs on repeat at the time. But all of them, they burst through my chest. They still do sometimes. It's like a gun.'

'Does he know you have that thing?' I pointed at his face.

It came, a cut of jealousy, that too-sharp feeling I'd felt so often with Bonnie. Would he ever get a tattoo for me?

'Believe it or not,' Ed said, 'he got one too. Granted not on his face. His neck. We were in Crete. They were cheap. All this to say, I get why that happened.'

'She's wrong for me, and it wouldn't have been right,' I said. I made it sound so easy. 'I know what you mean about the gun through the chest. All those big classic love songs. They made sense to me for the first time.'

'Shall we just call it one all?' he said. 'Though I know they're not equal.'

'One all,' I repeated. I reached for his hand; a hand shake.

'I also think we could stop the game here,' he said.

A week or so later, I found out from a mutual friend that the day Bonnie asked me for lunch, she'd had a fight with Andy – Andy, who, it turned out, had been in London the whole time with her – because he wouldn't hand over fifty percent equity in the place they were – or rather, pretty much he alone was – buying.

'She did say you seemed really well and looked good and were successful,' the friend told me. 'She did *actually* consider it.' She said this like it was high praise.

'Right,' I said.

'She had to be realistic. Not just think about herself. Think about the kid too.'

'Right,' I said again. I kept on saying right.

'Portugal's safe for now, but think about the worry! Think about the hassle.'

Apparently, Bonnie had sent her email to me just after Andy conceded on the equity side of things.

They did not feel connected, though I am sure my parents' armchair psychology business of two would have had a field day. 'When does your rich friend get back exactly?' I asked Ed. And I told him – until he found a place of his own anyway – he could stay with me.

20

It was pretty much as fast as that: Ed moved in. The first night, he cooked me dinner, and the house smelled of hot spices and sugar when I came back from work.

I took a bath and he brought me a gin and tonic. Flo called and said she was going silently mad and asked if I'd come over and watch a bad film. 'I'll let you send emails,' she said, 'I know you do it anyway.'

I told her I'd love to but couldn't. 'Ed is cooking katsu.' I made it clear with my voice that I was rolling my eyes. 'He's singing in the kitchen.'

'It's like he's conducting military campaigns to make you like men. Is he a paid operative?'

'Probably,' I said.

'Did your mother do the paying?'

'So how many cats went into this?' I said as I walked into the kitchen.

'One, but he had nine lives so I really had to go at it hard—'

'I hope it's the one that shits in the garden.'

'Oh, now.' He gave the brown sauce a stir. 'Please don't swear.'

Ed in my kitchen. Tall and analogue in front of all my

ridiculous appliances. He told me that as a writer-slash-freelancer-slash-freeloader, he'd been conditioned to be a good guest. 'Leave only footprints in the sand,' he said.

He spun the plate as he put it in front of me in a professional way that suggested he had once been a waiter. Little slices of pink pickled ginger, cut thin as skin. We drank a Japanese beer that dipped for the finish line just over five percent. Each sip had a bit more push than usual. It felt nice to be pushed like that.

The first night felt like a sleepover, his still-packed suitcases in one corner, but a whole toiletry bag in the bathroom now. He called it a dopp kit.

'Have you ever . . .' I thought about how to say it as we brushed our teeth, 'been domestic before?'

'No . . .' he said. 'But I would always do my business in a tiny little neat pile in the corner of the room . . .'

'I mean, did you live with "Jonny"?' It so happened to coincide with the moment I needed to spit out my toothpaste. 'If that even is his name.'

'It better be. And yes I did.'

'Would you prefer for me to leave my dirty boxers on *this* bit of floor, or on *this* bit?' he asked me later. He said he'd get a cool sign about always leaving the toilet seat down. He said my bed frame was nice, but wouldn't I like one that looked like a red race car? I remember laughing a lot.

'The marital bed,' Ed said as we folded into it. All these words found their way to us – marital bed, his'n'hers – all spritzed with the freeing feeling that they were automatically subverted.

We lay there, pillows at our backs. 'It's giving Grandpa and Grandma Joe in *Charlie in the Chocolate Factory*,' Ed said. 'Hey, do you remember Section 28?'

'I don't think that was in the film version . . .'

'No, but I was reading about it for *my* hateful book. And the policy line is so – mental. You couldn't talk about the acceptability of homo-sexuality as a pretended family relationship.' He said the words like he'd knitted them – all these syllables. 'Pretended. In a nice way, I'm just like, *this* feels fully silly. Us in bed. Way more pretend.'

'Great,' I said.

'Not you and me specifically. Just the whole shebang of it.'

21

It was only by late October that the highest beats of heat finally started to fade. The bleach of the sun less and less strong in the sky, but the colours at the end of the day extraordinary, as if saying goodbye.

Ed was still stuck with his book, or whatever it was he was writing, but there were days he said he could feel pleasure in that. 'Another day in the trenches,' he'd say, as he slid his laptop into his backpack. Or 'I'm going out!', his bag on like a schoolboy's, then duck: stealth mode. 'Cover me.'

The seeming freedom of his job. The suffocating hardness of mine. When I told him I likely wouldn't be back 'til eleven most nights he said 'The real you', and I had to say it back, 'The real me.'

'What about the weekend?' he said. 'I could take you away?'

'Week-*end*?' I said, like I wasn't sure how to say it. 'It's not like the app stops ...'

'That's okay,' he said. 'I can work too.'

It was Ramsgate he took me to. Crescents smiling into the sea, boats. The first morning, we sat on benches, facing the water. Other people were there too with takeaway coffee cups, all tilted towards the sun, in a way that made me think of old photographs of eclipses.

Ed brought his notebook and he held his pen like he was drawing. I remember him reaching for me without looking at me, to check I was there, or like touching me was filling up his ink.

'Why is our life not this?' he said, and I liked the way he said it: our life.

What I'd felt before about being with him, that it let life expand in a curve to the left. When I was with him, it really could feel like that; a brief shot at being a person again.

'I mean it,' he said. 'When life's so short, why wouldn't you do this always?'

'It wouldn't be this though. It would rain.'

'No you're right. Glad you mention that, because it's never rained in London or New York, has it?'

He was right though: maybe you could. With someone else, you could. Split the risk of it.

Even that late in the year, we still got sunburn. Funny V's and sleeves. A reason to be tender. Sunlight hit the sea like slow motion rain in a graphic novel, bouncing individual specks. A vendor let go of a crowd of helium balloons and they stormed off like sperm.

We could see France from the cliffs, a shifting wafer of grey on the horizon. It had temporarily shut its south-western land border, so they could process a backlog, and Ed recounted an article he'd read: diseases were rushing through the camps at Irun. Giardia, Legionella, typhoid. All the plagues of the bible, he said.

All through town, there were posters about reporting small boats if you saw them. In a stylised Second World War way, the figures on the boats like an opposing army. 'I'm going to call about each yacht in the harbour individually. Take up their time,' Ed said. We were watching the sun set. 'It's so hard to get the scale of it,' he said after that.

'What?' For a second I thought he really was drawing this time, trying to get perspective on the boat masts. But later when I looked at the notebook, the only thing he'd written down was something I'd said.

'Life,' he said.

'Not that old thing again.'

'Sometimes I just want the simplest life. Simple simple simple. And then I want everything huge. I just feel desperate not to waste it,' he said.

An image pushed into my head: nearly dying once. Somewhere prosaic, where death shouldn't have been close, but it had rained and rained and not stopped raining. And as we drove – this was Bonnie and me – occasionally at first, reparably at first, the car started to lift. The road we were on was long and ran alongside a river. Again the car started to lift, then started to drift. The rain trampled on the ceiling of the car so hard and fast that it was almost a single noise. And single thoughts came too, calmly at first.

We can't die here. It's Connecticut.

How could rain, each drop of it so small, do this?

We will die here. We are going to die.

Then, strange, the other thing: pity. Pity that Bonnie would only have me, who she didn't fully love, who recently, once more, she'd proved she didn't love, to die with. An indignity, somehow.

'If a meteor were to strike us right now,' I started. I tried to make it taste like something fun. 'Would it add to your sadness that I was the person you died with?'

He looked at me. 'I forget,' he said. 'Do you have first aid training?'

'It's a meteor. We're toast.'

'It would be an honour to be with you.' He stayed looking at me. 'How could it not?'

22

The clocks went back. It was a shock in the evening, darkness with the number four involved, but it was the mornings I noticed, waking an hour and one minute before my alarm.

I had the same feeling I had before – if I did certain things before the day officially started, they counted less. As Daniel requested, when a minor figure I'd finally had a bilat with at Whitehall said it couldn't hurt, I authorised the tracking of Gigr workers near protest sites. I managed to make them add a pop-up – *you are now entering a protest zone, turn around* – but I still felt sick when I did it.

And I who did my thesis on George Orwell, I wanted to text Flo, but it stayed in my drafts. Instead I briefed Ollie in Ops, and told him the messaging should be around their own protection. 'The protests have been violent etcetera. Stuff like that.'

'Course,' he said, 'we'll get the leaders of the sub-communities on side. That's the best way to stop the rest kicking up a fuss.' It wasn't just the algorithm that divided up the workers; we did it too. Ops grouped them into unofficial battalions by nationality or language, and every sub-community had their ringleader. A guy called José was currently very influential among the Brazilians; Naz was currently king of the Bangladeshis. 'Cameron over there's infiltrated the Polish WhatsApp,' he said. 'Absolute joke. He runs it through translate whenever he wants to know what's happening on the DL. Apparently they've got some big beef with the Pakistanis! Shall we turn on their body cams for the body slams? Go viral? Now *that's* content—' he said as I was walking away.

I was late to meet Ed's mum.

'Well that was one of the weirder conversations I've had in my life,' Ed had said a few nights earlier. 'She asked me if this was ..."you know".'

'Sorry?'

'You know ... *you know*, she kept saying,' he said. I still looked blank. 'The thing that's in her paper every single day of the week?' He paused. 'She asked me if you were born a woman. Also asked me if I was planning on doing it too. Like ...' He opened his hands like he was freeing balloons, and the balloons were her final fragments of sanity.

'Well, are you?' I said.

'Super progressive though. She still wants to have lunch. So she can ask her *questions*. Edward,' he did her voice, straightening his back, making it look like he had glasses on his nose, '"What *is* non-binary? Sorry, what *are* non-binary?" She knows some of the words but not how to use them or what they mean. But it's the same with everything. I've heard her use the word screenshot to describe pretty much anything to do with technology.'

'You did tell her I'm just a lesbian?' I said.

'Just?!' In a continuation of his am-dram, he took my hands and kissed my fingers. 'You're so much more, mon amour.'

That morning, I'd asked him what look I should do. 'Do you want a pretty girlfriend? Or a cool one?' I said, like a waitress going through a menu. 'Or something kind of androgynous to, y'know, bridge the change?'

I'd tried to say it breezily but it gave me a crunched-up feeling in my stomach. A feeling of performance, a reminder that through our lives there was barely a moment we weren't performing. Play-acting. That was another word that kept on appearing in my head, like it was in the ether, or the crossword that day.

Performing girlfriend for a boy was different to performing girl-friend for a girl. I could imagine winter more: cream jumpers and scarves, a bundled-up face poking out of cashmere. That worked for everyone. On a still warm day, there were more ways to get it wrong.

In the end I just wore black. Not a suit for once; something that followed the shape of my body. I wore lipstick, I wore earrings. I smiled so much afterwards my cheeks had a dull ache, as if I'd been blowing up balloons.

When girls took me home, I always wanted to show parents that I could protect their daughter. That I was serious but not too serious and tall and could earn money and would protect their daughter. With Ed, social maths told me to show that he could protect me, and that I would look after him. Feed him. Stroke him. I felt my body going backwards; I reversed everything I did at work. I wanted to be sweet, and there were lots of sentences that I stopped before they got to my throat.

Sometime later, one evening at her house in Surrey, Sandra – his mum's name was Sandra – asked if we wanted to stay the night. I looked at Ed and I couldn't read him quick enough but Sandra's face was so easy to read it felt painful. 'I made up the bed, just in case,' she said. We watched TV, or they did, as I looked at a shitty pitch, and over time, Ed's body graduated downwards in stages until he was sleeping on my lap. Sandra kept on looking over. But she looked happy when she did.

I felt I could rub a thumb over his forehead. Not even could, should. I could lean down and kiss him if I wanted to. I placed my hand so his head didn't fall in an unfortunate position and make his neck crick. It creaked around inside me: a touch of happiness, a touch of feeling sick.

With girls, with their parents anyway, it had been so much more difficult to show I loved them. It wasn't a gentle touch; it was the sign of a seductress. What the parents had imagined all along. And so, attempting to be serious, tall, capable, neutral – neutered – I didn't touch them at all.

Anyway, that first meeting, at an Italian restaurant where Sandra seemed sure that sauce would get on her cream linen suit, at first she tried not to look at me too closely. Her mascara was navy. She had done her hair.

'Ah, so—' she'd said, when we were both sitting in front of her. Then looked worried.

'Very exciting,' Ed had replied. 'You don't have to dob her in when she goes to the bathroom.'

'Edward, I personally wouldn't!' She looked at me. 'I wouldn't!'

'Just call the *Daily Mail* later—' he said.

'You *know* I'm very against the backlash,' she said.

'I'm kidding!' He reached for her arm.

Before the drinks came, and through the starter, she was still waiting for the trick to come. That I was just a friend. That there were cameras somewhere. That we were waiting for her to say something wrong.

She asked me what I did. I told her I worked at Gigr. 'But don't worry, I'm trying to dismantle it from the inside,' I said.

'No, it's good!' she said. 'Provider!' And that was when tomato sauce finally did fall on her jacket. 'Bring home the bacon! Very modern.' She looked at Ed. I saw it more and more, I think. Parents' desperation for their children not to hate them.

He dipped his napkin in his fizzy water and used it to clean the stain. He ordered a second bottle of wine that we were all grateful for.

'Can you?' he asked me.

'Course! We don't breathalyse HQ yet, thank god.' I smiled again.

The first glass into the second bottle – she kept on saying 'Ed, stop!' but keeping her glass intentionally tipped for him to pour – she said she had a coat she thought would look beautiful on me. When we left there was something else of hers she wanted to give me, but I can't remember what now.

'That wasn't so bad,' Ed said as he walked me back to the office. 'She didn't even demand to see your genitalia.'

'Don't say genitalia. I feel like – I liked it. She was sweet. She's sweet.'

I was smiling. Still smiling. But I also felt profoundly sad. My nose, I could feel it bouncing around. 'I've been avoiding my parents because it's hard there anyway. I know I make it funny when I tell it. But it isn't always funny. I already can't bear it.' I was speaking fast. We were nearly at the door to the office and I wanted to say it all before the drawbridge went back up. 'Their whatever-it-is-that-they'll-feel. I shut my eyes and see glee.'

'Fuck 'em,' he said. 'I'll be a dick.'

'They won't care. You have one.'

The office loomed over us like Mordor. Box breathing, wasn't that what you were supposed to do? But I was so bad at it. Holding the out-breath always made me think of air-locked cabins in sunken sailboats. It was all just building and building again. Our relationship too. The people it made happy, the people it made sad – the inescapability in both directions.

In the end, for my parents, Ed hired a car, which completed the whole laughable postcard of it. The clap of handshakes – this was with my dad – that turned into a long-held hug. The way we sat in the room, the four of us, more of a mirror now.

They bubbled up inside me, things my parents said when I first told them about Bonnie. It wasn't just the unspoken rules about the rest of my life being right. They'd had theories too. Theories they settled on together. Pride, or something else, making their eyes dewy. For their subtlety. For their sensitivity.

Here was one of them: it was because it was easier. Because I'd known girls, because I was used to being with them, that in a way it was like staying at school, a way of never becoming an adult.

I looked at them then. I kept on looking. It was hard to compute the lack of understanding. How was this easier? The things I'd thought about on the night bus with Ed. All of the people joking that they can fuck it out of you. All of the people who say it's a waste. The places you go to as sisters. The places you can't go to at all. And what if that place became here?

Box breathing turned into imaginary boxing, round after round in my head. And even if I felt allowed to touch Ed, this time my hands stayed by my side.

It wasn't cold, but my mum had four jumpers on, the competing necklines tight against her tendons. And in fairness to her, it wasn't as black and white as that. The hardness she'd had with all my partners rose to the surface with Ed too. Questions Ed said most often came up with neighbours on long train rides. So do you make money from that, do you? But in a different tone: in what ways will my daughter have to pay for this thing you want to do?

While they were talking, my dad pulled me into the kitchen. 'What you're doing for us, it's been amazing,' he said. 'Amazing, truly amazing, just amazing—' his head shaking, and I knew then, on the second amazing or the third, that it wasn't enough. 'What they can give her under normal plans on the NHS, the standard ones ... it's ... it's not working.'

'Just tell me whatever it is you guys need,' I said.

'I'm watching her disappear,' he said, and his voice disappeared too.

'When you said the illness was bad-bad,' Ed said on the way home. 'What sort of bad?'

I told him about the conversation with my dad. I told him I was going to help them do a bit more in the system here. I told him about the brochure my dad had printed out for me, about more targeted treatment in the Netherlands. I told him the prices for non-Dutch people were astronomical now.

'I was listening to something about that,' he said. He took one hand off the wheel to touch my leg for a second. 'It's for seawalls, things like that?'

'A levy for the levee. Yeah.'

He pulled into the car rental place. 'I'm so sorry,' he said. 'I thought they were lovely by the way. Completely.'

'Lovely,' I repeated. We sat in the parked car. The feeling of being still in something made for movement. 'They worked their whole life,' I said. 'I mean everyone works their whole life. But service, it was a life of proper service. In comparison to the absolute shit I do.'

Back in Edmonton, whenever we'd gone into town, people would cross cafés, cross streets, leave the till where they were paying at the supermarket and walk to them, my parents. Like they couldn't miss it, like they were famous. These people might be twenty-five, or thirty now, but they would still call my parents 'miss' or 'sir'. And they would tell them what had happened in their life, about the children they had had; they'd take out their phone, and show a picture and say *look,* or talk about the job they were trying to get, the flat they were buying, and say thank you. And when things had gone wrong, they'd say those things too. It's been bad miss, they'd say. My dad wasn't the best at names, had ways around it, 'my favourite student' or 'an all-time legend', but Mum never forgot a single name, never once. She'd remember siblings, ill parents, all of it.

Back in the car Ed's hand was still on my knee. 'But you do it for them though,' he said, 'right?'

23

A tent village had appeared outside Westminster and when it was destroyed, when they threw the tents into the back of a rubbish truck that hydraulically crushed everything that entered it, the papers ran with a picture of the one geodesic dome: *Glampers evicted: meet the DEFINITION of champagne socialists.*

A bunch of kids – *blessed are the children*, as Flo regularly texted me – were missing school. Fridays for the climate, Wednesdays were NMN – No More Nazis. The police – always helmeted, like astronauts or bugs – were so heavy-handed the papers got into stuff like *Baton Britain* and *Wild, Wild Westminster*. One girl had to do her exams orally from some youth detention centre because both her wrists had been broken when she was arrested.

Daniel had decided to 'escape the climate' and work from Bali from a bit. This meant early-morning calls from his shaky connection in a tented eco-community, and fondness for a new phrase, 'on you'. Perhaps he was saying it to everybody, but it did feel like pretty much everything was 'on me'. For example:

Daniel: *Is the gov stuff back on track? Are they happy we've been keeping our guys away from the protests? That's on you.*

Me: *Well, they've been a little busy revoking people's citizenships.*
Daniel: *Har har har*
He was silent for a moment then:
Daniel: *I'm not joking. We're 5 months out now. We need to get through all the FCA regulatory stuff – I don't want Anything that makes that tricky.*

In big ways and small ways, everything was breaking. There was a mortgage boycott, and rather than negotiate, the response to the pro-testors was punitive. Foreclosure signs up neon orange and red across London streets, which always made Ed say, 'Welcome to America.' One of the big water companies collapsed. We got new temporary coolers at the office, but dehydration ripped through the rest of the workers until the taps across a third of London were back running. At the supermarket, there were handwritten signs on the door: *no milk, no salad's, no egg's, no tomato's!!* And with what they did have, there seemed to be security tags on everything, especially meat, these big grey plastic things that had to be taken off at the till.

We felt, or I felt – I could feel when I was with Ed – a different winter. It wrapped around us. I was still temporarily immune to all of it. Not immune, but it was like what I'd said to Ed about time zones: I saw it all through a window then another window. The fizz of pressure from work, the deep, deep hole that was getting deeper all around us. How quickly it settled into normal, to walk past an Apple Store with smashed and boarded-up windows into the calm of a bookshop.

At an event for his book in Dulwich, the room was full of men. Men who spanned boys to elderly, all different shades of gay. I'd wanted to surprise Ed, but the car journey across London was interminable and Daniel's eyes had bored into me when I left the office at six. I slipped in just after the event had started, and stood at the side, towards the back.

Ed read a passage I hadn't heard him do before. It was about an older man swimming in an icy lake, upstate and alone, in spring. In the middle of the lake, the man floats on his back, and as he loses sensation in his toes and fingers, and soon his legs and shoulders, his whole life comes to him. An old love who went with him to the hospital when his dad was dying, who fed his father with a small spoon. A male nurse. And what it answered inside him, four men in a room, all looking after each other.

During the questions at the end, I knew most of Ed's go-to answers by then. The nearly inevitable, particularly from people who had only read reviews: How do you write sex scenes? *Lots of practice.* What's your next project? *A mental breakdown.* How do you write about love like that? *I'm an unapologetic romantic,* and he held his arm with the sincerity tattoo up.

The last question came from the back. I turned to look who had said it. Medium height, shoulders broad as a sail. 'This is a very complex literary question,' the guy said, 'but it's the one we all want to know. Do you have a boyfriend?' The room filled with laughter. But neither the man nor Ed laughed. Ed's eyes stayed firmly at the back of the room.

'My PR team have asked me to remain silent on that front,' he said. I wondered if his eyes would flick at me. I almost didn't want to look to check. The room went silent. Then he smiled. 'Only joking. No PR team,' he said. 'And, no – no. No boyfriend.'

Something inside me pulled tighter as everyone else relaxed, the silence scrunching up like used wrapping paper. 'On that note,' the bookshop owner said, anticipating the ring of the till, 'we'll move onto the signing.'

I slipped out of the shop.

> *I'll leave you to your adoring fans,* I texted.
> *I'm just at the pub*
> *Pick up your secret sidebitch later*

I saw the way he walked in. Looking for someone angry, then relieved I didn't look too mad. Something no doubt due to two glasses of wine I'd thrown back in very quick succession. I raised my hand to order another. He looked at me. 'Not here?' I said. 'Right. Of course. Too public for a public figure—'

'I'm not a public figure. And I'm sorry, that must have been shitty. But it's work—'

'Look, I get work.' There was a contact-lens-sized amount of wine in my glass. I finished it.

'Publishing is desperate to be on, you know, the right side at the moment,' he said. 'Which is good. Better than the opposite. But they've built me up as this thing, this thing I am, but like, I'm getting all these emails – Our LGBTQ family of writers, we support you! – what am I supposed to do?' He kept looking at the door of the pub. 'Sorry lads, I'm with a chick now?' He looked like he was changing his mind about the drink, his eyes scanned bottles. 'They see it in this backwards way, like ... I don't know. I told my editor I'd heard this interesting story. Or thought of it. I can't remember how I said it. But something about a gay man and a lesbian.'

'No way,' I said, flatly. 'Never in a million years.'

'Mm,' he said. 'After what she said last time about the Vikings I was like, these ones are gay, don't worry. Both of them.'

'Buy one, get one free,' I said. 'What did she say?'

'She said it was *very imaginative.*' Perhaps it was the comedown after the event, but there was a touch of manic-ness to how he was talking. 'But obviously she worried it was slightly regressive, from a gender and/or sexuality perspective. Not sure she knows the difference.

And yeah, she was like – I'm just a little concerned it could imply gay people could dot dot dot *change* . . . Rather than it being what it should be, that anyone should be able to be together with anyone, because why not? Because why put limits anywhere?' I wondered who he was trying to convince, whether it was me, or her, or himself.

I nodded. 'I see your problem,' I said. 'You're too ahead of your time.'

'It's just something for me to work out.' He opened the door for me. 'I will. But do you know what I mean? With so much of myself in the world, I also want to be able to have a private life. Our life.'

I thought back to his other occasional hesitations. How when we ran into someone he knew on the street, he might introduce me by name alone, rather than our relationship. All the things I'd felt started to grow in me too; helixes of worry that twisted into one and finished each other's sentences.

But still, still, something washed over all of it. At first something did. You can put it down to chemicals, you can try to understand it. But something just happens. The body fills in all the gaps with something good.

Love, limerence. The balance of that word. Like travelling over low waves. Once or twice, I looked it up again – limerence, meaning; limerence, science – something I'd first done when it happened with Bonnie. Something comforting in knowing it's just chemicals firing.

'You're so funny,' Ed said one evening. 'When you're watching something you turn your head to one side.'

'Do I?' I said. He did an impression: a little cock to the left. 'Slight deafness,' I said. 'I think. This ear's better. So I angle it.'

'Whenever you do it,' he said, 'at first, I always think you're looking at me. I hope!' he added.

'Says the person who's doing all the watching.'

'But when you love someone don't you do that?' he said.

'When you what?'

'When you live in their house and eat their food, I mean,' he said. He'd stood up. 'When you love them.'

That's how it was said.

'Of course it's true I'm always looking at you,' he said. 'Trying to work out all the things that make you up.'

'Love,' I said. I tipped my head to the side again for him.

'But isn't that what it is? Trying to see a person. Wanting to. Never being bored. Your foot,' he said. 'You're always tapping the side of it. And your hair is different at the nape of your neck. Maybe because it's hot there.'

'Love,' I said again, teasing him a little, because he couldn't look at me by then.

'I'm getting a glass of water,' he said.

Film paused, when he came back, I was standing too. In the almost dark, he pulled me into him.

His thumbs on my lower back. The width of his hands. The rock of his chest, I tapped my head into it. Unused to it, still, to be the smaller one. I felt what it must have been like for shorter girls with me. His hands on my back, then moving down, broad like a bench I could have sat on. I backed into the wall, my fingers trying to find something to grip onto and finding nothing.

For a while, pleasure still made ground for us to walk on. Even as the days shrunk to nothing, even as England shrunk with them, for a while I could think of him and find sun.

~

Ed's godfather says it's not a members' club, that it's a library, and it's true: there are books everywhere.

Ed remembers coming for lunch as a boy here. The first time, it was his twelfth birthday and his dad had written a letter giving him permission. He remembers the envelope being cut open at the front desk with what looked like a sword, and being terrified that the letter inside would be ruined and therefore the lunch. Then relief, a rush: a fuss was made. *In six years, will you be considering a membership, sir? Shall we give you a tour of the premises, sir? Have you thought about what professional path you might embark upon, sir?*

After lunch, or was it before – his memory plays it both ways – a half glass of port, presented by a waiter in a simultaneously secretive yet elaborate flourish.

He had felt a crush of happiness, pure child, but something adult coming through too. The way he had noticed, differently from how he noticed at school: it is all men here. Men not boys. The thrill and fear, the impossible-feeling jump: that he would become one. And the different ways to be. He still has postcard snapshots from that lunch. A finger reaching down to straighten a sock. A broad hand with a signet ring reaching round to cusp the back of another man's neck. A broadsheet pointing into a tall man's lap.

Twenty-three years later, early December, it's Ed's birthday again. 'Permission slip all in order?' his godfather asks.

'Forged it perfectly,' Ed replies. He leans down to kiss his cheek. 'Joe,' he says, and the name feels as round as the world in his mouth.

His father's dorm-mate at university, and the one writer Ed had known growing up – an alive, glittery feeling rippling through him whenever he knew Joe was coming for dinner, or joining them, as he did once, on holiday. The recipient of Ed's childhood stories, mini manuscripts stapled together, always finishing with a whole page for an underlined and cursive *The End*. And the pains Joe took to reply, writing letters that took boyhood Ed far more seriously than Joe needed to.

Joe with his blue eyes and thick hair and slightly tufted-forward ears that had made half of gay London fall in love with him in certain decades. 'Don't forget New York,' he'd say, 'or Paris.' Joe with his short stories which had won fan letters from across the world. Joe with his light Yorkshire accent and never-quite-right clothes, even when he made all that money.

In front of each other now, their height difference has reversed. When Joe puts his arm up to get the waiter's attention, it looks like two different bellies are competing underneath his shirt. He has not tried to stay young but it's all still there in his face: infinitely lovable.

On the childhood holiday, Ed could barely keep his eyes off them, Joe and the friend he'd brought. This was in the gulf of Florida: the sand like crushed sugar, rumours of sharks. Not content with looking at them in the water, or on the beach, or at lunch, or at dinner, Ed had gone into their room once in the morning – he was only seven – to find them both reading. 'What's going on here then?' he'd said, slightly officiously, and both men had laughed so hard they'd cried.

Joe who Ed had dedicated his book to.

'Look, it's the new me,' Joe says, about Ed, when he sees him.

'Never,' Ed says back.

'By all accounts, you've taken the baton and run with it. Franco,' Joe puts his hand up to his own face. Franco is Joe's boyfriend. 'Floods of tears. Floods of them! You should have seen him. Like one of those rainfall showers. And he didn't even know you as a kid.' Joe does look proud, but also like he's not fully sure he's allowed to be. 'I'm beginning to think I can sell off your juvenilia to fund my care home ...'

'You're *years* off a care home,' Ed says. It isn't true, but Joe will somehow always be the age when they first met, in shorts, on a bodyboard, flying through waves, a kid at forty. A knot appears in Ed's stomach when he says, 'Did you get a chance to take a look too?'

'I'm halfway through. But not because it's not good. I do think it's good.' Joe stops. '*Nearly* as good as your story about the elephant and giraffe that collude to break out of the zoo ...' He smiles. Ed is desperate for him to say more. 'I just find it—' Joe takes a handful of the air. 'The generations. Our different generations.'

In Joe – it's too much for one man to represent, Ed knows this – Ed's always found a repository of history. What it was like in the '50s, in the '60s. These flashes of culture. How they used to euphemise a gay man in Hollywood: 'He's *very* good at dialogue.'

'It's reminding me of what it was like to feel young,' Joe says. 'For the first time I found that painful, for it to be so far away.'

The library which is not a library serves them quiche and salad. It's not good, it's not bad. It's the same as it's been for forty years, the menu specifying a champagne vinaigrette. The conversation marauds around both their lives, and the lives of people who aren't around anymore.

'Can I ask you something?' Ed asks eventually. It's part of the reason he wanted to see Joe. 'Women – a woman. Did you ever?'

'What do you mean?' Joe casts it wide like a net. 'Oh. At seventeen or eighteen, yes. *De rigueur.* In Paris, I was even engaged to one briefly,' Joe says.

'And did you – what did you feel?' Ed asks.

Joe says she was a marvellous woman.

'But were you intimate? Sorry.' For everything they've discussed, they've never spoken about sex before. Ed's read every word Joe's ever written, so he knows, as the world knows, he's no prude, but the words that exist in Joe's books, words that fill Ed's head sometimes, they've never been in the air between them. 'Or was it an arrangement? Did she know? Maybe she was a lesbian – I—'

'We did, then we didn't. She knew certain things, about me. And then. The balance tipped. Why?' Joe's mouth no longer opens wide enough to take the whole salad leaf.

'Why?' Ed repeats, and he wonders it too, why has he started? 'Why? Because I met one.'

'Ah,' Joe says. 'Awfully common. Fifty-two percent of the world now. And even here these days ...' Joe looks around for one of these mythical creatures.

'I just wanted to know if it had happened to you. Or people you know. Knew.'

Ed imagined this going differently. Joe's eyes had always landed on him so easily. It was easy for them together, and now Joe is seemingly still looking round the room for a woman, or for Ed to be saying something else. There's a hope that it's all still in Ed's head.

'An experiment?' Joe says. 'I suppose your generation has done away with sex, with gender, with all of it, with gayness – old-fashioned.' Joe dabs his lips with a white napkin just in time for old-fashioned. The faster Joe speaks, the more the conversation is shrinking.

'Perhaps. Not really. But it isn't that. Joe,' Ed says then, 'come on. You were the one who stood side-by-side with my mum after I came out; *Very important to keep your options open.*'

'We've spoken about this. I had to disprove any "bad influence".' His eyes flash to the ceiling. 'A ridiculous situation—'

'And now, what? Keep your options shut?'

It is a second of silence. Ed sees it flicker, or imagines it: a mirage coming in and out of sight. Everything they'd shared. Everything Ed had been privy to, everything he'd sucked up with a straw.

'But you're what?' Joe says 'In love? In ... cognito?'

'It's a shock for me too.'

'Is the shock the point of it?' Joe says it gently, follows the question like a path.

'No – I just wanted advice.'

'Advice from an old queen.' All their different words. 'I'm sure she's a lovely girl.'

'She is ...'

'An artist? Are you going to tell me it's "the mind you've gone for"?'

'The mind's part of it. She's actually not an artist.'

Ed's actually again. None of it is stuff Ed would have imagined saying. *Meet my girlfriend, she works high up in corporate hell.* Maybe there would be ways for it to be okay. 'She's a lesbian. Or was, or—'

Joe laughs. 'Sometimes I think your generation is *very* confused. Listen, it's not that I don't like women. I think they're the best of us. I would have just guessed you'd have done this *first*. That tends to be the tradition.'

They have come here, to the members' club which isn't a members' club, for many birthdays. Joe's, Ed's, perhaps three or four birthdays each. Every single time since Ed's twelfth, they have had the same port. But this time, Joe says he shouldn't. Age, he says, but he won't stop Ed.

'I would like to get lunch,' Ed says, 'you've got so many lunches.'

'Please let me,' Joe says. 'To celebrate. Everything you've achieved. The book. Next time. There will be many more.'

Afterwards, they stand in the street. Ed wants to be able to walk with Joe, but Joe with the way his legs are now, something about veins that need to be cleared, is getting a taxi. When Joe opens the door, Ed wants to get in the car with him. He doesn't want it to end, not like this.

'I don't want it to be ... ' Ed says, holding the door open.

'Oh, Ed, young man,' Joe says. 'It's nothing. A small thing.'

'But something,' Ed says.

'Tiny,' Joe says. 'Just one less thing in common.'

When Ed had imagined it going differently, he envisioned the list of names Joe would tell him of other men it had happened to. He'd imagined them laughing. Imagined another shared thing, maybe even more bonding in its niche-ness.

A swell of anger. If that part of Ed's life means that much to Joe, why hasn't he finished the book? The fight continues in his head. Joe had looked at him like the past twenty years of his life had evaporated. *If you change who you are, whether forever or for a moment,* he wants to say to Joe, *it doesn't cancel out who you were before. Surely.* Surely.

Ed doesn't want to cry on the street. He wants to keep shouting in silence. He wants to make his own list: every man he's slept with, every man he's loved. He wants to say does this not count then, does that not? Ed had watched it in Joe's face, the various routes to un-derstanding – Ed was a trickster now, pretending somehow, playing a game, trying to provoke. Or that Ed had been a trickster for the past twenty years, pretending somehow, playing a game, trying to provoke.

'What do you want me to do?' Ed says it out loud. He's in Soho. Prove myself by telling you about the guy I followed home from right here? Give you a list of the books I read and *cities I visited* because a guy I had a crush on mentioned them in passing? 'Do you want to see a fucking blue plaque?'

Next to him, a sparrow pecks at old vomit.

A text arrives from Elle. Sometimes just seeing her name can make a small tornado inside him; it lifts light things into its centre. But it doesn't work its magic now, the anger's drowning. Why should love in any combination make people uncomfortable? What gives them the right? But then what about him, himself? When he thinks about it directly – when he stares directly into the sun – he knows what they mean, he can feel it too.

It's true what he told her. It makes most sense when they're alone.

~

24

The stuck-ness of January hit. It rained so much the curbs disappeared, and there were puddles deep enough to cover headlights. Fake bricks washed off the sand-coloured *Help to Buys,* and bins would occasionally log-flume down roads that didn't even have a slope to them.

My parents' house flooded, and the water pooled over their carpet, the fibres underneath it swelling, swaying, like a sea creature.

'But you have insurance?' I asked my dad on the phone. My mum had gone to stay with a friend because the floodwater had backed-up sewage in it too, and she had no immune system, and it was impossible to heat now.

'It's Act of God stuff,' my dad said. 'They never pay with Act of God stuff.'

'But do you have insurance?' The water was the colour of builders' tea. He'd sent a picture. Later it got a green tinge to it.

'Yes,' he said. 'We did.'

'Dad—'

'It got too much—' he said, until I understood.

*

Two restaurants near us closed down, dry January, or 'die January' as one called it, being the final straw. Inflation was back up over ten percent again, but it felt exponential. Applications to Gigr had never been higher. We used to give our people bonuses for referrals, but now we had a waiting list.

'Is it just me,' Ed said, 'or does Daniel call you every other hour, all through the evening, at the moment?'

Daniel and I had just had a minor skirmish on the phone.

'I heard about that fucking call-out on the rider GCs—' he'd shouted as soon as I picked up. '"*If you're Black, avoid central today,*"' he quoted. 'If you're Black? What, anyone who's Black? Who said that, fucking fire them!'

'It wasn't a threat, it was a warning, they're looking out for each other—'

'I get that, but are they actually *doing* it? If you're Black avoid central today,' he repeated with a sense of incredulity. 'That sounds like laziness to me!'

'We took away the report abuse button,' I said. I had to say we. Daniel didn't like it when I said you.

'Well, we couldn't handle all of it! They were smashing that hate crime button like it was the morphine thing in hospital. More-more-more—'

'Daniel.'

'And it's little stuff! A fucking name here and there, who cares? I worked in a pub, I got shit about my ears, it's how we *talk to each other in this country.*'

'No one was ripping a turban off your head ...'

'I could have *done* with a turban, strap these bad boys down—' He stopped. 'So what? You take a bit of shit when you're different, it's called *the price of admission.* And if they don't like it, well – take what I'm about to do as a metaphor,' he said, and he hung up.

'It's just a huge amount of money on the line,' I said to Ed after the call. 'For him. For me.' And I need it, I thought. I'd managed to get my parents back onto an insurance plan, but it was another thousand pounds a month, and that was on top of other things I was paying for. 'I don't know if I'll have another shot at a lot ...'

'What do you mean?' Ed said. 'I thought the work you do was easy for you.'

'It's not easy.'

And what could he really know about easy or hard? I'd leave most mornings before he was out of bed. The levitation I'd felt through the first few months together, the way time went out the window, that was starting to falter. My face could feel back against the ground sometimes, and the ground was gravel, and the ground was moving. 'If I'm going to make it happen, it has to be now. I don't know if I can do it again.' And as if by clockwork, Daniel's name appeared again on my screen.

You could feel it in the air – or lack of it – at the office, that we had entered the calendar year that the IPO would happen. 120 days to go – it was marked out on a giant whiteboard now, and being ticked off, like a prison calendar.

And Ed was in a similar countdown too. Four months to go, and nothing to show for it, he'd say on a daily basis. What had started as funny – frequent references to the character in *The Full Monty* who wore a suit and pretended he was going to work, but was actually just going to the Job Centre – had melted into the flatness of someone who was hungry and had no way of getting full. 'I'm scared I've lost it,' he'd say. 'If I ever even had it.' He'd had lunch with his godfather, also a writer, and come back with eyes ringed with red. 'I'm guessing *not* helpful?' I said, and he'd said he felt even worse. He'd chewed his cuticles to the point where I saw blood smear on his teeth.

I'd been alive long enough by then – I knew how depression

worked. And yet, on days where there seemed to be no break in it, I couldn't shake the fact that if I were enough, he would be happy.

'Every day I wake up and my stomach's ... carbonated,' he said one morning. 'Just like – I don't know what the fuck I'm doing.' I looked at him. 'With the book, I mean.'

I asked if he wanted to show me what he had. 'But what?' he said. 'There's literally nothing.' When I told him he should write a love story, he said there needed to be more happening.

'What's more happening than love?' I asked him, and I felt a little nudge in my chest – it seemed sad if love wasn't enough.

'Sorry. I'm just out of sorts,' he said, his winter skin cool against white sheets. 'Out of everything.'

That was the day – I think it might have even been Blue Monday exactly – that we got the invitation to Teddy's for dinner.

'Who?' I said. On my phone, I looked at my calendar, looked for proof I wouldn't be able to come.

'My interesting, immensely rich friend,' Ed said.

And then I remembered: the owner of the house on Camberwell Grove where Ed had lived for that first stretch in London. 'The lobbying one?'

'Yeah,' he said. 'I was actually thinking he could be useful to you? With work. From what I've gleaned, he's re-entered the system high up. I don't know. All the pressure Daniel puts on you. But also, just in general,' he said. 'You know the apocalypse game?'

Ed liked to give me scenarios. Someone with a virus that was *highly contagious* and *ninety-eight percent fatal* was landing *right this moment* at Luton. ('Not Luton,' I said. 'The virus won't stand a chance.') Or a *nuclear bomb* is going to *strike Manhattan* in *two hours* and you've got to get off the island.

'Oh I know the apocalypse game.'

'It's always useful to throw in a rich person,' he said. 'Someone who might have access to a private jet.'

On Camberwell Grove, at the door, I remembered the first time I went to see Ed at the house. The mad naivety at the start of things. How you think you know someone purely because you don't know them at all.

'We do have a problem though,' I said, 'I can't call a grown man Teddy ...'

'Not like bear,' Ed whispered, 'like old money. Like Roosevelt—'

The door opened.

'Eddyboy!' the man standing there said. He was younger than I expected. 'And here she is – the woman who's broken a thousand hearts.' He smelled good. It filled the air. Cassis, perhaps, musk. In the cold air on the steps, warmth from within emanated from behind him. He pushed his sleeves up, and something about the colour and the tautness of the skin suggested recent exercise. 'Come through,' he said. His arms were expansive. 'Well! You know where to go.'

Teddy's wife was American. She had a very erect back. Shiny hair, Nordic blonde, a low bun, small gold earrings, invisible make-up, one of those tall, thin bodies. 'Our house-sitter,' she said to Ed.

'Always regret not claiming squatter's rights,' he said, kissing her cheek. 'If they still exist.'

'Since it's Wednesday, champagne,' the wife said. She handed the bottle to Teddy to open.

'It's so nice to meet you,' I said as we did our cheers. 'Your house is beautiful. Ed says we get to pick one item to take home from each room.'

'I like her already,' Teddy said.

I did the only thing that tended to work with men like this: I was faintly rude to him. Over the start of proceedings – the champagne and the ruffled waves of charcuterie – Teddy said a few times that he liked me. And it was the third one, when he was about to say it again, but didn't, when I thought: *perhaps I have reached neutral status with this man.*

They were curious to observe. Everyone who came to Ed's book launch had looked like friends, aesthetically compatible; Teddy seemed more sibling-like, or rather Ed seemed to relate to him as a younger brother would.

Teddy was outwardly friendly, but there was something colder underneath. I thought of those metal soaps that cooks use to get rid of the smell of garlic. I was thinking about how I'd say it to Ed afterwards: he seemed to have multiple personalities, close proximity but different angles. You could get caught on the edge, but just when you thought you'd tripped, he picked you up.

He asked Ed about the book, and really listened to the answer, which was all the things I'd heard so many times by then. 'And the new one?'

'Strongly considering burning my passport and moving to Mexico,' Ed said.

'Don't all struggling writers end up writing novels about struggling writers? If it ain't broke—'

'I saw a rave for the last one,' the wife said, coming back into the room with a new bottle. '*Telegraph*, I think. Headline: "*A World without Women* ..."' That was one other line that Ed had taken umbrage at, though by all measures it was true. 'Tonight must be quite a revelation with *two* of us here—'

'Ha, yes,' Ed said.

With the exercise and a ginger concoction he was swigging from, I presumed Teddy was on some kind of health kick, but in the middle of talking he suddenly said, 'I think my blood sugar's low,' and opened a giant packet of crisps on the counter. 'Truffle flavoured,' he said. 'Vile. The au pair gets them.' He offered them round like a hellmouth, then finished the packet.

Their slight variations of poshness overlapped, interweaved. Still, it was nice to have made it through the rain to somewhere other than work or home, and game-face and game-voice on, I had not yet, so far, been caught out.

Teddy poured with a heavy hand – we'd already had three bottles between the four of us. When I went to the bathroom, I'd drunk enough on a relatively empty stomach to have the sensation of being on a very large boat in calm waters. Their expensive toilet had an in-built bidet function which aimed with immense precision, and I was just about to similarly spray one of the wife's perfumes on my wrist before realising it was a terrible, instantly incriminating idea, when I sensed a presence by the door. I looked up at adult height, then let my eyes fall. A serious-looking blonde child with hair as white as her skin. Three? Four?

'Hello,' I said. 'Do you … speak?'

'This is my house,' she said.

'I know your mum and dad. We're having dinner downstairs.'

'What's your name?'

'I'm Elle,' I told her. I reached my hand out to shake hers, but when she held her blanket tighter, I turned it into a wave. 'Aren't you sup-posed to be in bed?'

'I was sleeping,' she said.

How to engage with someone else's child and not seem weird? 'Shall I get your mum or dad so they can put you back to bed?'

'No, you,' she said, and she took my hand. Hers was a bit sticky, like she'd been sucking it, cold from that, and hot at the same time. 'Here.' She led me to her room.

'It's pretty,' I said.

She looked at me. Would she be one of those strange children who revealed parents' secrets like a blunt object?

'Lovely room,' I said. 'Cool books.' Even though she was decidedly under five, I was embarrassed to have said cool.

'Bye bye,' she said then, once she got under the covers.

As I approached the table, I could hear Teddy saying, 'well we need her!' Then to me: 'Come back, we need you.'

'Your daughter's very sweet—' I said.

'It's very boring,' the wife said. 'Class.' In her accent, it was a cliff with a sheer face, sliding downwards. I felt the same slide downwards in me.

'Has she escaped bed?' Teddy said, signalling he might stand, but giving up halfway, as I said, 'she's asleep again now', and he said, voice louder, for her to hear: 'We're going to take any children who are awake at this time to PRISON.'

'They were saying,' the wife went on, 'well, were just *confirming* that cliché that, while you're supposed to deny it, anyone in England can identify anyone else's class as soon as they speak.'

I wanted to keep my mouth shut, but, 'Are we playing *Upstairs, Downstairs*?' I said.

'Just it's different from the States,' Ed said, 'where posh is a lot more dissipated.'

'Well, there are Scottish poshes and posh boys who pretend not to be posh,' Teddy said.

'Who you can always tell are posh,' Ed said, 'because they don't say an.' He made his mouth donkey-ish: '*Can I get a oat flat white?*'

'Are you saying it's a good thing?' I asked. 'To be able to tell? I don't get the point of it—' And why were they asking me? It was the way they were all smiling too. From the safety of the right side of it.

'My daughter seems to have stolen your sense of humour!' Teddy said.

'Nimble pickpocket hands. No, I donated it,' I said. 'I wanted to give her a good chance in life. Told her she would need all the help she can get.'

They liked that.

'See, now,' Teddy said. 'That's why what's happening right now is interesting. Suddenly, politics is where it's blurry, and I find that fascinating.' His ginger concoction was a thing of the past. He opened a new bottle of wine, and spun it so we could see. It was an '82, their 'second wine', he said, but a corker.

'Not sure cork is what you want,' I said, but I sniffed the wine he poured. It smelled religious. It tasted like sucking on a garnet.

'Christ, I'm a bore!' Teddy said. Even in January his cheeks and brow had a glow to them; I remembered their basement sunbed. 'But there's something moving about drinking time, don't you think?' He swirled the red of it in circles. 'But politics, yes. It does all blur. These rich, rich socialists. Just begging to be taxed. Flog me harder, Daddy! And then *miners'* families voting for hardline right.'

'There aren't any miners in this country anymore,' I said.

'But sons and daughters of. Grandsons and granddaughters! It's where it gets shaken. Say what you will, the coalition *is* diverse in terms of class, is it not?'

None of us said anything.

'All of this mess,' he continued, 'and it *has* been a mess, I'm the first to admit it, it's a chance to get out of the *entrenchment*. And we can laugh about dividing up accents into bento boxes *but—*'

'You've become very emphatic, darling,' the wife said, at the same time as I said: 'Weren't you saying earlier that your daughter might have to move schools because even though it's private, her teacher sounded like she was on *Eastenders*—'

'Perhaps a joke, perhaps not!' Teddy said. 'Her being alive is none the less my main priority. Even if she sounds like an extra from *Pygmalion*. Oh come on,' he said, 'it's a joke. I know I *look like* and *sound like* a braying boring bastard – and don't get me wrong, I am one, but

259

I am radical and refreshing about some things.' He rolled his eyes with 'refreshing'.

'Is the word radical or . . . radicalised,' the wife said.

'Cue Ed making his favourite eco-fascist joke, I'm sure,' Teddy said. 'But laugh all you will. Nothing we are doing on the climate is even close to enough. Not even close.'

'But it's okay,' I said, 'because you have a fridge that talks to you.'

'A fridge with air that doesn't get recirculated so food stays fresher for longer! A fridge that tells me what food needs to be eaten.'

'. . . that you ignore—' his wife added.

'And that cost a million pounds that could be spent elsewhere,' I completed.

It was all said nicely. The soft pocks of ping-pong played over a table. He poured the last of the wine into my glass, a kind of displacement thing because I could see he wanted it. We were edging towards the end of the night – if I was going to make my move I needed to do it now.

'Ed said you came back for – what did you say again, Ed?' We passed the baton between us of who had said cometh. 'It's SPAD-ish stuff, right?' Ed said eventually. 'But higher up of course,' he added.

'Not exactly,' Teddy said. 'I'm helping out across the board. As, well, *the entire world knows*, the new gov is weak on the policy side of things. They're weak on . . . the general competence side of things. They're lacking adults. And these would be tough times even for a party that had a track record with governing. But Michaela is trying—'

Michaela. 'Do you work with her closely?' I asked him.

'Not in an everyday way. Perhaps because she vaguely trusts me.'

'Do you like her?' Ed slotted in.

Teddy spun his glass again. 'Well enough,' he said. 'She's a blunt tool; I think the appeal will swiftly wear off and we'll need someone a bit more . . .' He never finished the sentence. 'But, you know, for now it's—' He chewed for a word. 'She's not afraid to make unpopular decisions.'

'Like wrenching us out of human rights conventions—' I said. 'Not that I minded,' I half joked. 'Our stock projections rocketed.'

Teddy smiled: *see?*

'But wait, how does it work though?' I said. 'Your ...' what was the word he'd used? 'eco-fascism, alongside all your climate deniers who say we just need to suck up the North Sea with a straw—'

'All my climate deniers,' he said faux-fondly. 'Well, a coalition is a coalition! Don't forget all the crunchy mamas who don't want 5G towers. They're very *green*. And a little secret about our gas and oil in the North Sea?' He segued into a fake whisper: 'There isn't an awful lot left ...' He lifted the bottle to pour it again; a single drop. 'Getting the straw out is red meat for some of the base, but the facts speak for themselves: the business case is back. The Finns have the cheapest energy in Europe and it's ninety-five percent renewable. And more than anything it's *theirs*. They're not schlepping it in from some war-zone which could turn off the tap at any moment—'

'See?' Ed said. 'A veritable tree-hugger—'

'Oh, it's not about tree-hugging, and it's *certainly* not about climate finance and global targets and international-multilateral-sitting-for-hours-in-conferences bullshit. Excuse the technical term, but *fuck* the other countries—'

'Teddy, drink water—'

'Yes, yes. I know. But listen. Denialism tends to run out of steam a bit when people die in heatstrokes in October. And no one *adores* a flood. Fundamentally this is a national security question. And *that* angle the base can get behind – shore up defences, sovereignty, self-reliance. They *love* all the protect the land stuff—'

'See, he hasn't thought about any of this at all,' his wife said drily.

'So what's the plan then?' I asked.

'A lot. Striking while the iron is hot. That's where she's amenable, Michaela. Guided the right way she's ready to go for it with policy. Major infrastructure. Big-scale defence and energy security. Investing in ourselves. Our own stuff,' he raised a finger, 'that no other fucker can touch. Not ... wasting valuable time and energy scrambling around to protect the rights of – sorry to be blunt but – minor portions of the population.' The way he said minor: it became even smaller. 'When it comes to slimming down the burden ...' His gesticulations grew bigger and softer then, the shape of euphemism. 'Sure some of it's unfashionable. But bold is the only way. This is end-game stuff. I mean, it's all very well me stockpiling cash here—'

'Teddy—' his wife said.

And so his tone lightened: 'Oh, and should all that fail, we're buying a *very* sweet little place far north in the Highlands too. Stick out the invaders *Skyfall*-style.' He put his arms up like he was holding a rifle. 'What's that Albert Finney line in the Bond? *Welcome to Scotland.*'

'Teddy, honestly,' his wife said again.

'I'm just saying, perhaps if you play your cards right, I'll send you the co-ordinates ...'

25

I asked Ed how they'd become friends as we waited for a car. 'I mean I get why you stayed at the house, but . . . ' It was minus degrees that night and the cold broke on our cheeks.

'I don't know. He's always been supportive of me.'

Back in New York, Ed told me, Teddy had facilitated a fund for artists, writers; he was on the board. 'They didn't give out a lot, just a couple of thousand dollars here and there. And I don't think Teddy actually said *words* in my favour, but he'd always send me deadlines, stuff like that.'

'Ah,' I said, 'a mercenary friendship. My favourite.'

'Not like that. Anything I got I'd have gotten by myself,' he said, and it hit like a beam: the clean confidence of a man. 'But yeah.'

'I trust you,' I said, burying my hands into my coat sleeves.

Ed made his finger a worm and let it burrow into me, until it started to tickle. 'Come on, if you want to be puritanical about it,' he said, 'we're all bent over various barrels . . .'

'Okay Ed. Don't get too excited.'

When the car pulled up, it was enormous. It had huge, puffy seats that reclined a little in the back.

'—Like an American cinema!' Ed said. 'I'm adjusting worryingly well to your lifestyle. Anyway, Teddy's only *kind of* a Bond villain. Don't you think it's interesting? To spend time with people not like us? It's a kind of different privilege,' he said while reclining his seat to the max.

'What he was saying about the government having to intervene though. Force people's hand. Make people make *immense sacrifices.*' I did Teddy's voice. 'He was enjoying it so much he might as well have been touching himself—'

'Elle.'

'But it's true! All the climate stuff, it just felt a way of wrangling a moral imperative into his corner. Anyway,' I said. 'I will admit the pannacotta was delicious.'

'You met the kid, right?'

'Yeah, she's cute. But it's exactly that. Everything he was saying was so – "as a father of daughters".'

Teddy had said the moment when it had landed for him was when his wife was pregnant with their daughter. As her belly grew, the feeling grew inside him too: he'd destroy worlds if he had to, to protect her.

'And "as a father of daughters" is dumb because it's repeated,' Ed said, 'but don't you think it happens? You hold a little shrimp in your arms and your hormones are fucking surging – don't you think it does change you? I don't know. Isn't it important to have people who say things, who push the needle?'

'It's the same with people who push the needle being racist, or saying people like you and me should be conditioned out of it, or sterilised or—'

'So we only let it happen in that direction?' he said.

The needle made me think of the wheel of fortune, spinning every which way. Where would it settle?

'You know the one he's mainly meant to chaperone?' Ed said as we got out of the car. 'I thought he'd mention it tonight. Miriam Hartley, who he says is about to take over Business and Trade—'

'Seriously?' I said. 'The whole "it was a different time when I posted those messages" one? Who then took back the apology?'

'He doesn't deny she's an idiot. I think the words were "she's an unlocked door".'

'To where?'

'To parliament. Anyway,' he said, his key in the lock of my door. 'What did you steal in the end?'

The morning brought with it the beginning of a shift. Ed leaped out of bed, before me even. He got up in a single movement, a cowboy heave-ho, then slipped a T-shirt over his head.

'What are you doing?'

'New year, new me,' he said.

I looked at my phone. 'It's the twentieth.'

'It was interesting seeing Teddy who you hated,' he said as he made toast. Six slices of toast, not an exaggeration. I'd forgotten toast was a breakfast 'til he moved in.

'I didn't *hate* him.'

'It's just – I realised it's important to remember other bits of my life. Do things outside of us.'

'Not outside of us, Ed! Not the big wide world—'

'No but I'm serious!' he said. 'I do wonder, a bit, if that's why I've been stuck with my work.'

'Thanks,' I said, but he didn't hear it – it chimed with the toaster ejecting two more slices.

26

Daniel was due back from Bali any day now. Adnan, when he came in to empty my bin, gave me a heads up. 'Bossman's here,' he said. 'His energy . . . Bad as the smell.'

In fact, he was frantic. 'You're back!' I said, when he came to my door.

'Course I'm back,' he said. 'Got a serious shit on our doorstep this time. One of those shits they put in a bag that's on fucking fire—'

A flinch, a pinch in various points inside me. 'What is it?'

'Activist investor. A big deal one. Marshall fucking Landry of all people. Fucking sniffing around to do a massive fucking short.'

'How do you short a start-up pre-IPO?'

'If there's a way to make money, people will find it. It's something to do with credit default swaps? I don't know the exact mechanisms but it's fucked for a million reasons. We're *fucked* if it happens.' He took a drag of his vape and offered it to me, the mouthpiece wet. 'You know how bad this is?'

'I think so,' I said. But I didn't really. Not yet.

'If they flag stuff and make it public, the FCA are going to have to look daggers at the bid for IPO. You know, fucking deep dive. It'll two-prong us. Kill the engine and make us fail the MOT.'

As Ed often said, my entire work was acronyms. 'SSR – Short Selling Regulation,' Daniel said after that. 'Write it down. Not fake write it down, actually get a pen.' This is what one of Daniel's many unofficial advisors had said that we needed. 'Get this and I won't need my SSRI,' he said. 'My anxiety medication.'

'I got it.'

'I know the cabinet's shuffling like a deck of poker cards, but you've had time now. No more excuses. Don't even talk to me about Silly Sally or any of those idiots.'

'Apparently it's changing to Miriam Hartley—' I said. I blessed Ed for mentioning that the night before.

'I don't care about her. We need to go straight to the *top*. Big guns. Fucking *canons*. Other countries have it. EU, fuck 'em, forgive my French, but they're good on this. Pitch it as – we're behind, it's hurting industry—'

'Okay,' I said.

'We'll look at it in the War Room – Legal will need to pull their finger out – but a lot of it's going to fall on your weird little policy lot. We need the regulation stat.'

My weird little policy lot. 'We can sponsor a research paper,' I said. 'Do it through the IEA. Make it fast. Frame up the debate in the way that's conducive—'

Daniel looked at me like I'd said something obscene about one of his children. 'Stat means *yesterday*,' he said. 'Not some "results in fifty years" fucking *research* route. We could lose all of it—'

'Okay-okay-alright. I'll think of something.'

'There's one thing that could give us leverage though.' He handed me a piece of lined paper ripped from a small notebook. It was slightly damp. 'What?' he said. 'It was in my pocket when I went to the gym – listen, careful with this 'cos it's big,' he said. 'Check out who else is on the short seller's radar ...'

I looked at the bit of paper in my hand. It was a list of companies.

27

I was so distracted after Daniel left, that I bumped into Luisa in a full body slam as I made my way to the bathroom. She was plaiting her hair as she walked.

'I always imagine what he's saying when he's in there,' she said.

'Who?' I said. My stomach was churning.

'Mr Tuluminati,' she said. 'Daniel. In your office. I write the dialogue in my head. It's like fanfic—'

'What was this one?' I tried to say, tried not to look as fazed as I felt.

'E2L,' she said.

I couldn't understand anything. 'Is that a coding thing?'

'No,' she said. 'Romance novels. Enemies to lovers.'

Teddy came into my mind. I needed to speak to Teddy.

28

That evening I read everything I could find about Marshall Landry. He had an outfit called S&S Research. Sling and Stone: some kind of heavy-handed David and Goliath reference. His latest win had been a fintech thing called Avery, which he'd caught selling proprietary technology it hadn't actually developed yet. Marshall had spotted the plot hole, dug around for evidence, and within two months and one report, had exterminated their credibility. I'd read about the collapse but I hadn't realised he was behind it. Almost overnight, Avery's three billion market cap had all but shrunk to zero.

I didn't need my spreadsheet abacus to tell me how bad this could get. Daniel's 'we could lose everything' played in my head on a loop: he'd looked hollow behind the eyes when he said it. Gravity started to slip away again. 'Ed?' I said. I went into the kitchen to be close to him.

'Yes—'

His too-small laptop. How his face came together. Even his name. What was it about him that felt like safety to me?

'So it could all amount to nothing?' he said, after I'd talked him through.

'Worst case, yeah.' A shard inside me. I turned it against him in-stead. 'Is that a deal breaker for you?'

'Course not, I'm just trying to get it clear what you're saying. What are your options?' he said after that. 'Do you want me to do a pros and cons list with you?'

'And then what? Eeny, meeny, miney, moe?'

'Listen, you're the one who can do words and numbers,' he said. 'Anything I know about the economy is from *podcasts*.' He'd made soup and when he lifted the lid it made so much steam he coughed. 'So do the opposite of what I say but – you know what I'm going to say, right?'

'No,' I said. Except I hoped I knew.

'Your new friend from last week—' he said. 'I can ask him. If you want. Would you want to talk to him? I won't pass on *all* the things you said—'

'Are you sure? I don't want to threaten your own . . .'

'What?'

'A few thousand here and there.'

'Oh, he won't do it if he doesn't stand to benefit.'

'And you don't mind?'

He looked at me. 'See?' he said. 'Not just a house husband. A house husband with a well-kept address book.' He pressed his face into mine. 'I give you my blessing,' he said. Then he leaned back and touched my forehead.

'What's that?'

'I'm atoning you in advance for your sins.'

I messaged Teddy the next day, and he said I should call.

'Speaking on company time,' he said when he picked up the phone. 'How thrilling.'

Nothing I said – though I didn't say much – seemed to surprise him. Perhaps Ed had prepped him. Perhaps he'd looked me up. But it seemed he was expecting the call, and we arranged to meet as quickly as he could.

29

'Very *Slow Horses*,' Teddy said about their offices. 'Cheapest real estate per square metre in Westminster, but I can enjoy a little bit of rough and tumble.' He sent a younger man out for coffees. 'Shall we get right to it?' That clean smell again. 'Nice of you to take a break from the IPO roadshow.'

'The travelling circus,' I said.

'Go on then, show me your tricks.'

And so I said my spiel, tempered with a little irony. 'As you know – as the script goes – Gigr is a unicorn, one of Britain's very few . . .'

'Ah yes,' he said. 'An endangered species—'

'Well precisely. And we came close. The Zero Left Behind Bill would have been difficult to manoeuvre around, with our model.'

'More than difficult I'm sure. So some might say you already owe us . . .'

I looked at him. Remembered what he'd said at dinner. 'They're weak on the general competence side of things.' A week later, and it was 'us' already.

'In many ways that was incidental—' I said.

'Of course, but. I've read outside the press kit too. Gigr "news"

273

isn't the most sightly. As you can imagine, we get a lot of letters. It wouldn't be hard to re-launch. Those deaths at Christmas etcetera. Public support was very much behind the ZLB ...'

'Until everyone in the country needed a job. Our polls say the tide had very much turned—'

'Well, *your* polls would.'

'Our accuracy beats YouGov by fifty percent less margin of error ...'

'Do you want a prize?' he said, but he smiled. His chair had a swivel element to it, that gave him the illusion of fluidity and flexibility. Mine was static, and had an unstuffed seat I sank into.

'S&S Research ...' I said.

Teddy nodded. 'Marshall Landry?' he said. 'The short seller? I used to know Marshall.'

'And? Did you like him?'

'Thinks he's smarter than he is. But if that isn't a very male affliction ... I thought the position on Avery was ballsy. I'll give him that.'

'We don't know what his angle on us will be yet, but it's undeniable now that he's got the snipers out. He's been interviewing some of our former employees, hunting for disgruntled people on message boards. Apparently, he even did a call out on the radio.'

'What did I say? Johnny big bollock. Poor you. When he cranks it up, it's going to get crunchy – Marshall has a bunch of biz journalists in his pocket. The Landry playbook is not for the faint-hearted.'

'As someone prepping for climate breakdown, some of his other targets may move you a little more,' I said. He looked up. 'We have reason to believe that the other companies in the firing line are GBE, SWF and Nucleus.'

This was the list of names on the damp and crumpled piece of paper Daniel had given me. They were known, variously, as the Holy Trinity, and the Crown Jewels. GBE was Great British Energy, SWF was Southern Wind Farms and Nucleus was a project Teddy had specifically mentioned: a bid to rejuvenate former mining towns with small modular reactors.

Our own stuff – I'd let it play in my head – *that no other fucker can touch.*

'Ah,' he said. His face clenched a little. 'There's the rub.'

'And as you know—' I started.

'Aside from that minor business of ensuring our autonomy, the major investments of choice for the country's biggest pension funds—'

I finished the sentence: 'Pension funds reckoning with a drastically ageing population.'

He breathed out in a way that made a point of it. 'We'll have to go out doing a little cheer the next time they announce life expectancy in Britain has plummeted – but yes,' he said, 'I get it. It will be impossible for the country to operate if those funds collapse.'

I'd spent two days preparing for the meeting. I'd written phrases I might say on Post-it notes. There was another one, one I wouldn't say, but that I held in my head like a rudder. The IPO rides on this. And so much rides on that. My parents' house. My house. The price list I'd downloaded from the cancer clinic in Rotterdam. The waiting list I'd put my mum on.

'We think he's building multiple positions on British companies meant to capitalise on the current instability,' I said. 'We think it's likely there'll be a supplementary position on the currency too, to catch any shockwave. Our internal researchers are looking at all possibilities. But what it comes down to is this. All our major allies have better laws on this.'

'On what exactly?'

'On controlling activist short sellers bringing down any business that aims high before they can even go public.'

'Tall Poppy Syndrome,' Teddy said. He said it for me.

'Exactly, and in this climate, it sends the wrong message. At Gigr, we now employ one in six adults in the country. And one in four teenagers in our apprentice programme—'

'Life's a blast, isn't it?' Teddy said.

'Sorry?'

'One evening you're having dinner with someone, you know, spunky and sparky, and then days later you get to see them in work mode. It's impressive. Thank you, Caius.'

The young man had come back with our coffees.

'I need more time,' Teddy said. And when Caius left, he added: 'The soundproofing in this place is horrific. Listen. Besides all this, I'm not uninterested in the Gigr model.'

'What about it?'

'The economics of it. What do you pay, net, per hour?'

I looked at him.

'Come on,' he said. 'You're the one asking for a favour.'

'There are different ways of calculating that. There are benefits and other things – tips—'

'But what does it cost *you* per hour, these people's time?'

I weighed up whether to tell him. How much would I gain? How much would I lose? I rolled the dice. 'It ranges between five-twenty and six-ten,' I said. He hadn't expected me to answer.

'Pounds per hour? Staggering,' he said. He shook his head. 'And your apprenticeship scheme?'

'Twenty percent less.'

He laughed then. 'Do you want to know a fun little fact?' he said. 'Current government procurement procedures enforce a minimum "thriving wage" of twenty-one pounds an hour for any official con-tractees. The sheer waste! The sheer number of things we are unable to do. A hangover from cowing to public pressure, but it's not uncom-plicated to unpick ...' As if the word had made him think of it, he used a nail to get something out of his teeth. 'How flexible are they?'

276

'On price? That's the bottom limit. We've tested it to death. No pun intended. Anything under five slaughters retention and recruitment.' The thing is, the mood in the room had picked up, so of course I was enjoying it. I'd finally caught a current. I didn't mention any of what Daniel had called 'the intersections' – the greater leeway we had with various socio-economic or racial factors. 'We start them just over seven ... Once they're in, we can bring it down a bit.' It had become so normal, saying these things.

'And how flexible is the labour itself?' Teddy said. He had a pen poised to take notes, but I was sure he hadn't written anything down yet.

'For the specialist things – if you're going to HCA—'

'Sorry?'

'Health care assist, or, you know, substitute teach, or do construction, we run day-long mega-trainings. Paid,' I said. 'Aren't we lovely? Then it's just stuff like DBS checks, a lot of it's legal.'

Teddy was nodding.

'With the more technical stuff,' I said, 'there will always be skilled supervisors. But beyond that, with a lot of things, it's feet in boots.'

'I mean of course, on our side, we can't afford to do the vital work we need to do. There's the scandal. The flood alleviation project in Newham for example,' he clenched his teeth, 'the numbers are just silly. Plucked from the air it feels like. Anything public, it's like a wedding, they triple it and add three extra zeros. Of course we can't do it.' He looked at his watch; the first time his concentration faltered.

'I have to go too,' I said, wanting to match him.

He had that politicians' thing where he said my name a couple more times than was necessary. His eye contact was perfectly judged too, attentive, but it never felt like being pinned to a butterfly board. 'I don't like that phrase about scratching backs,' he said. 'It always makes me think of flaky skin.' He did a little comic grimace. 'But I don't know ... Perhaps we'll be each other's holy grail.'

He walked me to the door. 'Young Caius isn't back yet, is he?' I said.

'His walks take quite a while,' Teddy said. 'I wonder if he's cruising or something. If so, he has my full support.' He shook my hand.

'How do you deal with it?' I said, then looked at him. 'The other dissonance ...'

'What?'

'The bigots in your party.'

'Bigots. Such a funny word. I just ...' his mouth shrugged, 'find it largely un-sensible. I say let them blow on their sad little trumpets. Better out than in, perhaps. It's all so petty—'

'The changes to birth certificates isn't petty. Same-sex parents being taken off.'

'The furore about that is a *little* overblown. It's civil law, not criminal law. And we're not going to enforce it – people here aren't religious enough! Listen, I'm obviously not chomping at the bit to section trans people – too expensive to be honest! – but it's all ... energy, and that's useful.'

'Great,' I said.

'It can be redirected! If you find people's *passions*,' he laughed, 'you can lead them where you need to.'

He looked at me: how much could I be led?

'I wouldn't worry too much,' he went on. 'Most of it's just bog-standard backlash. The mainstream gets as far as boys in nail varnish and then it gets concerned about sperm count. I don't mean to sound *progressive*, god forbid. But most *normal* gay people will probably be okay. One thing I always think about homosexuality is that a white man can be gay. They can't really be any of the other ones.'

'What do you mean "other ones"?'

'Think of Ireland,' he said. 'They got gay marriage before they got abortion. Because a white man might need to marry another one, but he himself will never need an abortion. A white man will never be a black woman. A white-*ish* man could arrive on a boat, but then he's not *really* white. Not to them. But a white man can be gay, and often is. So. In time, over time, it will probably always not be *too* terrible.'

'Easy to say when it doesn't directly affect you,' I said, but lightly. Teddy opened the door for me, and we both looked down as if we might shake hands for a second time. We didn't, but he smiled.

'It doesn't exactly affect you at the moment either,' he said.

30

Teddy's office wasn't far from our Soho hubs, so I asked Cal from my team to meet me there. He was our self-described 'one man band' content producer, and I always expected him to turn up with a Dick Van Dyke drum backpack set up.

I should say: all the eye-watering valuations of Gigr were principally about two things. The first was profit: from year two onwards, we had defied all rules of other service industry start-ups and started to print money – no matter what we did we couldn't find enough marketing buy to sink it back into the business – but it was also, of course, a data play. 'It's either a data play or the Scottish play,' Daniel had said once, approximating a phrase correctly for once. 'It will either end in money, or in murder and madness.' It was our penetration – across all industries, and across such a sheer volume of people – that made us incomparable. For legal reasons, we avoided being an employer, but to put it into scale, even if they only worked a single shift a month, we currently 'connected with' more people in Britain than the entirety of the public sector put together.

I jotted down notes from the meeting with Teddy as I walked.

'Your surveys ...' he'd said. This was another thing that had come up. 'You said better than YouGov. I get it's the pure volume of people you have access to, but why is the response rate so good?'

'It's a pop-up when they do their timesheets,' I'd told him. 'They don't get paid otherwise.'

'Horrific,' he'd said, but with a smile. 'A unicorn with a very sharp horn.'

Cal was trying to vape subtly in a corner of the hub. Anyone from HQ, who could wear their own clothes rather than the Gigr get-up, was highly visible, and his camera didn't help. The social team didn't want to pay for content anymore, so we were launching a competition called 'Into the Gigrverse' where workers were encouraged to share authentic yet positive photos of their daily lives that we could re-use. I was dropping by a workshop showing people how to take good photos on their iPhone.

'They all have fucking Samsung,' Cal said when I arrived. 'And look, there's already a parody account.' He showed me a blurry photo of a Gigr delivery guy standing in front of his bike with both tyres slashed. 'God it's so grim,' he said, looking at his phone. 'Swear the internet used to be funny. All the comments here are just pleas for medical help.' He pressed the home button so the screen went dark. 'Want one, by the way?' He nudged a white bottle in my direction.

Speaking of surveys, we had discovered from one six months earlier that based on average consumption of food, and average expenditure of energy while working (we got all their step counts and cardiovascular activity through the app), the average driver was only getting 1080 calories a day.

'That's about right for a bony four-year-old,' our MD said, when the results came through.

'Well no wonder they're falling apart!' Daniel had said with one of those manic grins that meant I almost knew his teeth individually. 'We have to bulk them up!'

We'd enlisted a white label company that did meal replacement smoothies and patented a compound – adding caffeine – we called GigrFuel, though it was informally known as Gaggr.

The issue was, even though it was disgusting – at first sweetness hit you, but it left a coating in your mouth, not unlike silt – we found people were taking bottles home to their families.

'Fuck that,' Daniel had said in the meeting where someone told him. 'Make them drink them on site!'

'With what?' I asked. 'A funnel?'

'Use your imagination!' he'd said. 'Crack the seals, give them out open, pour it into glasses!' The Botox he'd had in his armpits was failing – dark islands appeared whenever he lifted his arms. 'We're doing it so they have fuel in the tank for *us*. Don't let them spunk it all away.'

Which meant we had a new rule where no food could be taken out of the hub. 'Look, it's already open,' Cal said, showing me the broken seal, and waving the open bottle in my direction. 'The temptation never ceases . . .'

People came into the room, and I listened as Cal told them what we wanted from the photos. Intimacy, conviviality, teamwork, fun.

When I looked at my phone, I already had a message from Teddy.

Great to chat.

Will get the short seller enquiry in discussion . . .

2 things in my head. Just a fun one.

Your surveys . . .

I have a few questions I'd like to slip in.

Perhaps a little test-the-waters collab?

It was sent with an app that deleted the message from both accounts once read.

31

It lasted beyond his cowboy heave-ho out of bed, Ed's rediscovered lightness. I saw it mostly in private moments. Whenever he waited for the kettle to boil, his hand would tap a beat on the wood. Normally, it was an impatient three-note trumpet, far too fast. Now, he'd gone all jazzy.

He started going to the local library which was eternally being threatened with being turned into luxury flats. And when we woke up, like that first morning, he didn't lie there anymore like bed was the only place on earth that was warm. He sprung out, our bedcover like the cover of a book, and went straight to socks and boxers and moisturiser with sunscreen and being ready for the day.

'Don't worry,' he said, 'it won't last forever.'

'What?'

'The happiness,' he said, happily. 'I'm just in a good ... I was about to say groove. I won't say groove. But I'm writing.' He was about to pause, then didn't. 'I don't think it's good, but it's words at least, and some of them are real ones.'

I asked if it was the same project he'd made a start on before, and he said no, yes, no, his trademark internal shuffle: he'd changed it. I asked what it was about, and he said he wasn't ready to talk about it yet. That it could lose energy if it left his body in another way. *'Left my body,'* he repeated, 'but you know what I mean. It's fragile at the beginning. By the way,' he said. And showed me his phone: *Guess who I had in my hot seat?*

It was a message from Teddy, who'd also sent a picture of my name in the visitor sign-in.

V. Impressive!

Tempted to ask Michaela to bring back bigamy . . . . . .

'Sorry, I should have mentioned,' I said. 'I went straight to a funder mixer after – also, thank you.'

'I don't mind! Speaking of seeing friends behind each other's backs, I'm going to head to Sean's thing tomorrow—'

'What thing?'

'Don't worry. You don't have to come. I know you hate him.'

'You think I hate everyone.'

'It's just I've been figuring I should stay in touch with – look, it's not like I lived in all-male communes before, but there was a certain rhythm to my life. Rhythm's not the word – collectiveness, maybe? – but it definitely was how my first book was written.' I wondered if he'd practised how to say it. It was the way one word led to the next, like he was moving through rosary beads.

'Isn't it a Wednesday?' I said. 'I thought Sean's gatherings were normally on a Friday . . .'

'I get the impression it's become kind of an everyday thing. Different day, different stragglers. You know what it's like at the moment. *Vive la résistance* or whatever.'

32

The following evening, my mum called me at 9.05 p.m. exactly. I tried to see through her too. All her calculations: I'd have had my dinner late, European, at 8 p.m., and by 9 p.m. I'd be free. (I hadn't had dinner, and I was still at the office, irritated before I even picked up.)

In all the rain, their house had flooded again, and I'd Gigr-ed a man to come and help lift sandbags. 'His main technique seemed to be kicking dirty water up the walls,' she said, and out of frustration, I rated him 1 star on the call. 'And your father must have messed up the forms, because the monthly charges have gone up again.' *Your father*, she always said, as if he were my responsibility.

'What do you mean gone up again?'

'For a sinking fund. Ironically. There's a new management company.'

I asked her to send me the documents, so I could look into it.

'And is Ed . . . ?' she said.

'Why the meaningful pause?' She did it every time – a long-distance scalpel. 'He's still alive . . .'

'Yes,' she set her trap, 'but is he with you?'

*

Was he with me? I had not been with him. Days rolled by at the office without punctuation. I looked at the clock on my laptop. It would probably be elevenish by the time I could make it to Notting Hill.

I flicked to Sean's account. He tended to livestream everything with his own name and birthday as a handle to a degree which very often made me think: how haven't you been fired?

First up was six short videos of Goran.

I liked Goran. Unlike Sean who loved to say cunty, but hated the idea of cunt, I'd once had a long conversation with Goran about his first girlfriend. I always remembered how he said it, maybe it was his accent because it was a simple thing he said, but it was the way he said he was crazy about her. Crazy, crazy, crazy, he kept on saying, shaking his head like she was still in it.

'Sean, you are an idiot,' he said now, the camera about an inch from his cheek. He had that Slavic way of saying things flatly. With the light up above us, his cap made shade under his eyes.

I had a sudden pang of wishing I were there. At first I never knew if Goran liked me. He didn't give it away too soon, the opposite. I'd look to see if he'd reacted to something I'd said but he'd pretty much always be rolling a cigarette. Patrician was the word that came to me the first time I met him. His height, his poise, the way he could make a muscular body feel light. But then he would burst into laughter sometimes, this explosive thing that wouldn't stop until tears were streaming down his face. He'd try to stop them with one finger at first, as if it were a button he could press, then it would be three fingers on each eye, and then he would give up entirely.

He pushed Sean's phone out of his face, and Sean followed the camera *Blair Witch*-style through to what he often called The Friday Room, his bedroom. It was a big room with a balcony. There were loads of people in there. Remembering now, my urge is to describe it in some Grecian way, reclined bodies, mouths receiving grapes.

A couple of guys were on their knees sideways next to a stool, lines of white against the wood, and a five-pound note rolled up which seemed noticeably blue. 'Say hiii,' you could hear Sean's voice saying, and all but one person ignored him.

Music was playing, two songs at the same time, mismatched. Anyway, then I spotted Ed. Hello Ed, I thought. He was sitting, leaning back against the wall and smoking a little rollie, Leo in *Romeo + Juliet* style, his finger and thumb like a circle above it. I noticed a hand on Ed's shoulder; another man was massaging it.

I screenshotted the video and sent it to him.

CAUGHT IN THE ACT:
CELEB WRITER SPOTTED
Who's your new friend?

I scrolled round the screenshot the same way I'd done with the invitation to his book launch. Weird the delay, because at first I didn't feel any jealousy. Not at first. And then it started to come. It was the way the man massaging Ed's shoulder seemed to be staring at his skin. It was my scrolling in until I saw baggy, blurry pixels I could interpret in any way under the sun. It was the way my message said seen, but there wasn't a reply. And it was the way that reminded me of the first time.

When I got home from the office, Ed still hadn't replied. Sean hadn't posted again either, but I screenshotted another old one and zoomed in and in and in on that too.

I sat in our kitchen for a while. I poured a glass of water that I didn't drink, I poured a glass of wine that I did. Then another glass. Then I finished the bottle. I went to bed.

I slept on and off for a time until I woke up to clattering. The sounds made their way into my dream and then I realised that they were downstairs and happening in real life.

I heard a shush. It was Ed's voice. Whoever he was with – I think it was one person, a male voice kept getting louder, and then it would sink back down again. The beginning of a song started.

My heart bounced like a tightly bound trampoline in my chest. I wished I didn't have an imagination. I wished I had cameras downstairs.

I should go down, I should say something. I was also – what is that inclination? For the bad thing to happen? For the weight of rightness to be on your side?

At some point later, the clattering made its way upstairs.

33

In the morning, I woke up to silence.

On the corridor, the door to the study was open a crack. I stood by it. I couldn't see through the gap by the hinge but I could hear a whistly snore. Someone, at least, was alive.

Downstairs, Ed had vaguely tried to clear up. The glasses were by the edge of the sink. I wanted it to be worse than it was.

I felt like I had a head cold. Jetlag. The time awake in the middle of the night had felt like crossing time zones. I dreaded Ed coming down, and I was desperate for it.

Eventually, two sets of footsteps headed down the stairs, like a kind of stretched-out elephant.

I only saw him briefly, but the plus one wasn't the shoulder massager, it was Sean. He popped his head into the kitchen, barely looked at me, said 'Bye kiss kiss' into his hand or fingers and then sprinkled it at me and left.

'Good morning,' Ed said. I expected him not to look at me, but he looked right at me, and it was me who looked away. 'Hey, I'm sorry for the noise. I was trying to be quiet but Sean was loud, and he kept saying it was okay, he was your friend too – he was quite drunk.'

'Drunk,' I said. I thought about all the things I'd seen, or pieced together, in the room.

'Yeah.'

'Just drunk.'

'Yes.'

'So it's Sean fault?'

'I'm not blaming Sean. I'm just trying to explain and apologise. It was a stupid, messy night.'

'You were in Sean's house. Why did you bring him all the way across London to my house? My house where I was sleeping.'

'We'd gone to a club. Here was closer.'

'And you couldn't wait?'

'Sorry? Couldn't wait for what?' His face. It pulled back. 'We were around the corner. It seemed like a good idea. It was a stupid idea.'

'I heard you coming up the stairs.'

'What's that supposed to mean? There are two sofas in that room. He has a boyfriend.'

'What difference does that make?' I had started. I couldn't stop. 'The way he called you a prodigy before. I bet you love that.'

'No I don't—'

'Last night. At Sean's. Did you tell anyone about me?'

'Tell them what?'

'Just did you?'

His shoulders had been stiff, primed for combat, but for a brief second they faltered. 'What do you want me to do? They won't understand—'

'They won't understand? Are they ...' What was a word that was acceptable?

'If I say it quickly. If I don't go into it. And anyway, it didn't come up. But it wasn't like Peter denying Jesus – and I did say to Sean we'd been hanging out.'

'Hanging out ... Ed, we are *living in my home.*' Something burned in me. I leaned towards it. It was like falling down a hill and gathering speed. 'In all of Sean's videos, you were being so different,' I said. 'Physically.'

'And what does that mean?' He took a step back. 'All this is *you*, Elle. The way *you* see me. The things *you* layer on top. Believe it or not, wherever I am, I'm me.'

'I just don't get why you do the whole nice boy skit and then you're just, like—'

'Just like what?' His whole face changed then. 'What are you talking about?' I'd never seen him angry before. It was quieter than I expected, but bigger. 'Sorry, but how are they incompatible? Going to a nightclub and "being nice"?'

Sharpness, hardness, they surged back. 'I have these things in my head, Ed, and they're called eyes—' I thought about one of the zoomed-in screenshots. 'There was all this,' I looked for the word, 'paraphernalia around.'

'Paraphernalia? Sorry I'm lost here—'

'There was a needle, right there on the table.'

'What needle?' He turned around for a second like he'd be able to see back into the past. 'Oh. *Oh.* That was some dosage thing – for G. To make it safe.'

'And that's normal on a Wednesday?'

'Elle, I was drinking beer. Is that okay with you? You're not my mother.'

'I know I'm not your mother.' I was tripping and there was nothing underfoot. 'It's just so predictable.'

Ed's shoulders. The expanse of them. 'I am, or you are?' he said.

291

'You do realise when you're angry you're scary,' I said. 'You're a man. You fill a room.' I don't even know if I meant that.

'What about if when I'm angry you're too small?' he said.

'What the fuck does that mean?'

'To fight back,' he said. 'It goes both ways.'

34

All morning at work, I fantasised about everyone leaving due to a bomb scare and putting my head down on my desk to rest. I could imagine the cool flatness against my cheek and the beauty of pressure, the way it would give the sharp heavy hammock of pain in my sinus a bit of relief.

Flo texted at lunch:

you're sure you saw a needle?

That bit was a false alarm
He said it was a dosage thing for GHB
I called it GBH and he looked
at me like I was so straight

Finally lol
and just to check
it's different when you come here
and theres bottles everywhere?

It's your house!
You choose for that to happen
also this is dangerous

Drinking is fucking dangerous!

Also I've seen you take a 'bump' of coke
the height of Mount Snowden, Elle

Luisa came back from lunch with a coffee for me. 'Corretto,' she said. 'Not to be confused with Cornetto.'

I took a sip.

'Brandy,' she said, 'I think? The Greek restaurant around the corner has an Italian owner. He pronounces Brandy "brendy".'

'It certainly strips the old sinuses,' I said.

'You look like you've had a rough week,' she said, halfway out of the door, but changing her mind and leaning back into the room.

'Glad I'm projecting it from my face.'

'You *look* great. But I'm not sure you've done any work.'

I looked at her. No one else at the office ever spoke to me like that.

'No I like it!' she said. 'I'm into it. I just came back from lunch and it's four p.m.' She looked around. 'Your office is like a fortress,' she said. I tried to keep a draught stopper at the foot of the door that made it impossible to get in from the outside. 'It always makes me want to cross the threshold.'

'How many correttos did you have?' I asked her.

'Oh, a few.'

I found myself looking at her like an animal in a zoo. 'You're very . . .' I stretched for a word, 'brazen.'

'But also diplomatic. Didn't I bring an apple for my teacher?'

I don't know what it was about that, but a shot accidentally ran through my body. Not a shot. An aerial being flicked.

'Very healthy,' I said. 'Okay, I should get on.'

She did an exaggerated double wink. I felt a laugh rising in my throat, but coughed it down.

'Hey, afterwards,' she said, 'a few of us might?'

'What?'

'Found an anti-capitalist communist party. If you want to join?
Burn things down from the inside.'

'That's my joke,' I said, but she was already shutting the door.

I had so much work to do I stayed long after everyone else had left.
The silence was pierced by a knock on my door.

'You're still here, good,' Daniel said.

'On the short seller front—' I started. I'd had another call with
Teddy by then. Ed had done that at least. 'I do have a good lead now,
a solid one—'

'Good,' he said again. 'Good. Just one more mini mission for you
then, my Daniel's Angel, if you chose to accept it. HR are saying we're
going to have a big retention issue.'

'Why?' I asked. 'Beyond the usual.' Currently at HQ, seven percent
of staff were signed off for stress-related reasons.

'After the protest ban malarky. Not with workers obviously but
with people-people in HQ. Because they're young and can afford to
they have morals ...' He rolled his eyes and wanted the same from
me. 'We should never have put the alert thing on the app. We should
have just handed in the names of anyone attending protests in secret.
Every single time I think this – serves me right for trying to "do the
right thing".' I looked for the irony in that bit too, but he was deadly
serious. 'Anyway, for the guys here, and the public, we have to do
something *nice* to boost morale.'

'Morale, not morals. Got it.'

'Use the infrastructure,' he said. 'Prove to them we're nice, and
that they're nice too. A hearts and minds thing. We don't want to be
a sin stock, we want to be a win stock. Smiles all round.' And he did
a nice big fake one.

I stayed at my desk and made a new to-do list, although I already
had thirty lists that were still undone by then. It had never been like

that before. It felt like falling through ice and new layers appearing instantly above me.

That was when I noticed the text from an unknown number.

We're at The Piper, the message said.

(This is luisa, hi)

35

I couldn't see them at first. But there were four people from work at the pub, including her. Two had their coats on, and I offered to buy a round to stop them from leaving.

At first I found it hard to look at Luisa. The message to a number I didn't know she had. I felt aware of my difference to the group. I don't know if it was age or professional superiority, but it seemed to manifest as height. A taller person dancing with short friends at a bar. The two people who originally had coats on tried to leave again, but then someone asked me about that day in the boardroom, and everyone sat back down.

'Oh,' I said, or 'Huh,' but I felt like all the air I'd had in my lungs had left me.

'Way to slaughter the mood,' Luisa said.

I realised everyone here was new. 'No, it's okay. Though we might want another drink—'

No one got up to get one. I had to say something, so I said something I'd said before. That moments like that feel unreal. It's like you're watching it all, including yourself, in the theatre. It can't feel real yet, so instead it's like you're being tested for how you react in the situation. Like you'd be given marks afterwards, and pass or fail.

'And what did you feel?' Luisa asked. 'Pass or fail?'

'I don't know what pass would have looked like. I imagine things going differently,' I said. 'His jacket catching on a door handle. Something that would have given us an extra second.'

'It's really horrible,' someone said, then shuffled in her purse.

Luisa's suggestion for shots was taken as a joke, and after the fake tug of war of 'would love to stay but it's late', everybody else left.

We had been sitting next to each other, squashed into the booth, and Luisa moved away from me when there was space. 'Just so I can see you,' she said. She used a tissue to mop up the ring marks of the people who had just left. 'No more balcony talk, promise.'

We got another drink and halfway through, it started to un-plait all the various things that were tight inside me. 'Do you do that a lot?' I asked her. 'The brendy coffee.'

'Not really,' she said. 'I acknowledge we're many drinks in, but that's not really my poison,' she said. 'It's like lighting a candle in a room, it kind of makes things prettier but—' she shrugged.

She told me a story about her family. A holiday in Florida that turned into a year because they never went home. A motel with an empty swimming pool. She was from a rich family, she said, a formerly rich family, but her parents had sold the family jewels. Not in a metaphorical way, she said, there were actual jewels. Or had been. A shadow passed across her face, then she recalibrated. 'I feel very awake,' she said.

I said I felt the same, but she said it was probably different. She had terrible insomnia. She probably only slept for two hours a night. Sometimes less.

'But you don't seem . . .' I started.

'Impaired? Whatever I'm doing seems to work,' she said. 'The

Margaret Thatcher of the zero-hours contract world. It's—' the 's'
dragged on, a kind of hiss. She was thinking, 'I go to places that are
always open.'

'Very Slytherin,' I said.

'Not my generation.'

I swerved away from that. 'Places that are always open like twenty-
four-hour garages?'

'Mmmhmm,' she nodded, 'I hang out in the freezer aisles. What's
your deal at home?' she said then, without missing a beat.

'What do you mean deal?' I looked at my drink on the table. 'It has
walls ... windows ... All the mod-cons.' I was wearing a suit, and all
of a sudden I could feel the label at the back of my neck.

'But do you live with someone?'

'I live with someone.' I was sure she knew this. A sudden tweak
to think of Ed. It all felt like playing chess. Side moves, diagonals,
defence.

'But do you have a curfew?' she said. I didn't say anything. 'Do you
want to come and see one of my aisles?'

It was tempting. What waited for me at home? Another argument?
Luisa took a Twix out of her bag and offered me half of it like she was
passing me a baton in a race.

That night, I said no. Or rather, I said 'rain check?'

She put her hand out, palm to the sky. 'Just checked,' she said.
'Seems clear to me.'

Our eyes caught until something happened in my belly.

'Another time,' I said.

'Do you want me to make you a little voucher?'

36

When I got home, there was a note waiting for me on the table. In a rush, I felt sure I knew what had happened. That he had left because of the fight. Or that he had somehow seen me with Luisa. But seen me do what? It felt like a magic trick. Bad magic – the cat out of the bag before the rabbit was even out of the hat.

I opened it.

Before you're terrified, it said, *I hand-washed your jumper.* There was an arrow on the note. It pointed to a jumper that was drying on a towel, carefully propped up on a series of chairs so it didn't get fold lines. *And your blue suit's at the dry cleaners. I'll pick it up tomorrow.*

I'm sorry Elle

Upstairs, he was still awake. His laptop on the duvet. 'I'm self-flagellating with work,' he said, 'and – look, I feel bad, because I feel bad, technically. Like chemically. But I don't feel bad because of what I did, because I didn't *do* anything.'

'Okay—'

'I sound like a grounded teenager, what I'm trying to say is, I promise, to you, I didn't. I'm sorry we argued. It just got my back up

300

because—' He shook his head. 'Look, two gay men can be alone in a room, you know. It's not like . . .' his head was still shaking, 'it's this carnal force and we're helpless in the face of it.' He looked up at me. I saw it differently then, the knot of hurt behind his anger. 'I get it didn't look great. But Sean and me, just never,' he said. He looked at his watch. 'You're back late.'

'Sean's just behind me,' I said. 'No – just work. Journalist dinner.' I'd thought about what to say in the car home. 'One of them wore earbuds the whole way through.'

'Yeesh,' Ed said. His face had the tilted expression of someone who wanted a bag of peas against their forehead.

'It looks like a bad one.'

'My friend once put it perfectly,' he said. 'After a wedding by the sea. The next morning he dived into the water and said there was a significant delay before he felt wet.' Ed held his head. 'It's like that.'

'Shall we test it out? I could get a bucket.'

'I misjudged some things,' he said. 'Out of practice, overexcited. It was ego too.' The pea face came back. 'Some of the boys there had read the book, and I wanted to *be that guy*, you know.'

Self-awareness. I thought about what Flo had always said. But it did help. It did help when people knew things about themselves, and said them out loud.

It had never happened to me with other partners before, but it happened then. It was different to the other fears, that it could happen immediately, to anyone. It was a suddenly solid, inescapable thing: one day, he would die. There was no getting away from it, one day he just would.

Maybe it did something to my eyes. Maybe it was just the truth when he said: 'Nothing happened with Sean, I promise. It's only you. You're the one I want.'

37

Weeks earlier, Ed had booked himself on a weekend away. A retreat, he called it, and it made me feel better, how normal it might be that retreating was part of it. That it might just be the book that made him sad sometimes, not me.

I asked if he could talk about it yet, and he said it had multiple strands. He talked for a moment about loneliness as an epidemic, particularly with gay men, and then he said something about race-play. 'Geopolitically, it's very interesting,' he said.

'Is it about that then?'

'In some ways,' he said, 'but not really. Listen, I don't have to go to this dumb self-organised thing—'

He reached to take my cup, and I saw a scratch on his arm. A long red cut. A ridge of dried white skin on either side. A flood again. A flood of images. The scratch on Bonnie's back. The man's hands on Ed's shoulders, Sean—

'The other self-flagellation,' Ed said.

I could barely say it: 'What?'

'I went to help your dad. Just before the party—'

'You did?'

'I guess it was another reason I was being defensive. I'd just spent the day shovelling shit.' He couldn't really look at me again, but more in his shy way.

'Why didn't you tell me?'

'I wanted it to be a surprise,' he said. 'When we'd finished.' I thought of my mum's call that night. *But is he with you?* I heard it differently now: she was checking that he'd got home.

'Jesus,' I said. I looked at him. 'Shovelling shit in suburbia . . .' I felt a change in my cheeks: them smiling. 'Has it come to this?'

'Yeah, and then, afterwards at Sean's, I wanted to feel, wait for it . . . *young again*,' he said. 'Still young. Speaking of which, your dad sent me a selfie.'

Ed took out his phone. It was a picture my dad had taken of the two of them. Ed and him. It was mostly the top of their heads.

Great bloke! my dad had written. *Thank you!* I'd never heard him say bloke before.

'Doesn't need me anymore,' I said. 'He has a new son now.'

'I like him. Let's send him one back—' Ed already had his phone up.

'Okay, but don't do the gay man angle,' I said.

'What's the gay man angle?'

'Ed, please. Jaw and shoulders first. You know, the hunker-down—'

He was laughing. He was Ed again.

'What!' I said. 'It's not good for women.'

38

At work, through the glass of my office wall I looked for the signs of the night before on Luisa but saw none. She was wearing the same long basketball shorts she'd worn to the dogs, low on her hips, and a tight black top with no sleeves. She did a salute when she saw me, which somehow looked cool rather than not cool. I began to mirror it, but stopped myself.

Ed had texted me: *Your dad put a crying with laughter face on our picture . . .*

That's a good thing, right?

Towards the end of the afternoon, Luisa came to my door. 'Last night,' she said. I was typing; I felt my forearms stiffen. 'You said you had a mission for me.'

'Oh, right.' I'd semi-forgotten I'd done that. It was the brief Daniel had given me to boost morale. '*Good* headlines, for once!' he'd shouted as he'd left.

'The surprise and delight,' Luisa said. 'The hearts and the minds.'

'The hearts and the minds,' I repeated.

I asked her if she wanted to bring her laptop in, but she said it would be better if we shared my screen. She had a tattoo of a dahlia on her upper arm, and it was so delicately and minutely done, I felt a quick flood of envy for the person who had gotten to look at her arm for so long.

'That voucher?' I said. It just came out of my mouth. I didn't want to specify a date, but I also didn't want to wait too long. Hearts, minds – mine were getting a little folded up. I thought of Ed en route to Wiltshire, or Shropshire or some kind of shire anyway.

'Point zero one pence cash value,' she replied.

'Right,' I said. I could leave it at that.

But 'What about tonight?' she said. 'After Daniel's weekly Kool-Aid drinks?'

39

'Okay so there's a group,' Luisa said, this was after Kool-Aid drinks had dispersed, 'to check where the night's happening.' She lit a cigarette, a hunger in each suck. She took drags longer than anyone I'd ever seen, the crackle, the pop. The tip burned like a tiny world.

'Where the "night's happening",' I said. 'Doesn't night happen everywhere?'

'So you kind of know where people are each night? I'm going to go back to reds,' she said, about the cigarette. She offered me one and I took it. 'They used to call them spiels, some old guys still do. To me it's just who's playing. I don't even play much,' she seemed to be talking to herself then, 'it's just interesting.'

'Your dad,' I said. I remembered our conversation at the dogs.

'Yeah, the gambling man. Perhaps we'll see him out and about.'

'Really?'

'Nah, he's in prison.'

'Shit.'

'Joking.'

'Oh—'

'He's dead.'

'Joking?'

'That time, no.'

The first one we went to I still see clearest in my mind. Perhaps because we went there twice or three times in the end. Perhaps because of all the unfolding shock of it.

'Kalooki,' Luisa said in the car. 'Ever played rummy? Some ban booze but this one's okay. Just remember you have to tip.'

I tried to find it on Google maps afterwards. I couldn't the first time. But I knew it was one of two corners. North London, Finsbury Park-ish. A pub that had been turned into flats. We went through a metal gate, then down metal steps into a basement.

Close to the door, someone was sleeping on a couch. When he woke up, he was a she, but mostly they were he's. Little else to unite them beyond that, because it really was, as they say, all walks of life. Baseball caps and flat caps. Black, white. Young, old. Happy-looking, deeply sad. Dehumidifiers ran in dark corners.

'Busy these days,' Luisa said.

'Recession, I guess,' I said.

'Not even. Gambling typically goes down. But not this lot. Hardcore. They really, you know, take off with each austerity.'

We found a table. Luisa told me I wasn't going to play, just sit next to her and share her cards. We were on bar stools, put to their lowest level. She rotated on hers, and our legs would knock. A guy at the table was wearing a proper respirator, pod filters on each side.

'He wears that 'cos of all the weed,' Luisa said to me. 'To keep a clear head. But I like it,' she took a deep breath, 'chills me out. Okay so,' she said, 'I could do this.' Under the table she pushed her leg into me so I'd stop looking around the room and concentrate on the cards, 'Or this.' She moved the cards around.

I found myself wondering if Ed knew about these places. The high-up TVs no one was watching. Football on one, a telenovela on another.

How we were almost the only women in the room. *Matching your all boys club with this one,* I wanted to text him. I collected things to tell him, but then: how would I say I'd been there?

There was something else he'd said, after he told me about helping my dad. 'I love this life with you, I do,' he'd said, 'but I don't want to pretend the old life didn't exist. Doesn't still exist. You know?'

'Hey,' Luisa nudged my arm, 'make a decision.' Her eyes flicked up at mine, 'it's your money.'

That was the other thing. When her card hadn't worked, I'd taken out £300. 'Big spender,' she'd said.

'Yeah?'

'No, not at all,' she laughed.

'I sign over all rights,' I said then at the table. I thought of Ed's fingers atoning me for my sins. I took another sip of my beer. I'd pulled the entire label off.

Luisa was wearing a thin dress, no bra. It was extraordinary to watch her. I don't mean the dress. Not just the dress. The boldness and knowingness of how she walked through the room, looked at tables, chose numbers. She looked like she'd known it all since she was a child. (I asked her; she said she hadn't.)

She knew people. They knew her. They kissed each other's cheeks. Occasionally, when we moved from one table to another, she'd tell me a story about the person we had just sat with and they were funny and brutal but never heartbreaking. A choice to stay above it. And the weirdest thing of all, to me, was that, with all these men, none of it was sexual. Friendly, yes, because that underpinned fairness, but their eyes moved through each other because the table was where the money was.

We won, and won again. And we lost a bit, but mostly we won, and eventually, as a new group of people at the table came and went, Luisa said it was time to call it. A thick stack of bills, each banknote rumpled by a thousand different pockets, came over towards the table at us. Luisa's eyes followed it. 'All yours,' she said. She stood up and I did too.

'I signed over my rights,' I said.

'Are you sure?'

I nodded.

'Put it in my pocket,' she said. There were two pockets on her dress. Both at hipbone level.

The path forks. The path is always forking. There is a version where I did not put the money in her pocket. In the version I chose though, I felt her hipbone through the material, smart and hard, and it sent a jolt through my body. But nothing else happened. She said thank you, she kissed my cheek. She said I should get an Uber, and she would take the bus. It was a remarkably well-behaved sequence.

'I can't let you do that,' I said, 'take the bus, I mean. As your—' I didn't say boss. 'When you're rich.'

But she said she wouldn't sleep anyway, so what was the difference?

As I travelled home, I thought about it. Shock was the right word. Shocked by the place, that it existed, in the middle of this decade's London. And shocked that I would feel shocked. Because how small, how trapped in set circuits, not to imagine that everything would exist in London. Shocked by the bone, her bone, and how it sent a spark through mine.

I played with it all in my mind like origami. I folded it back and forth until it sat right.

It was fun. It was living. It was life. The other life, the old life. But it was fine – nothing had happened.

40

The house was spotless when I got back.

Ed and his notes. He'd left another one on the pillow when he set off for the retreat.

Then my flick-book in the morning. A grip of fear that I'd crossed a line, relief that the scale of my crossing was minor. The doorbell rang.

'I remember you,' Flo said, faintly Chet Baker-ish, standing in the doorway. 'At some point, if you're not going to answer my texts, you do know I'm just going to turn up.' Taking off her coat, she did a smell test on her armpits and asked me if one of mine always smelled stronger too.

She followed me into the kitchen. A quick new fear I might have left poker chips or cash on the table – the word ephemera came to me – but all I could see was Ed's polishing job on the worktops. I ran my hand over them.

'Checking the cleaner didn't leave a touch of dust so you don't have to exterminate, sorry, terminate them?' Flo said.

'No—'

'Wait, are you actually being shifty?' she said. She took a step back. 'Bonnie? Are you there – *ere – ere*?' She called out in a fake, fading echo.

'Zero Bonnies.'

'What have you done with Ed though? Is he still kicking around in the doghouse?'

I told her he was on a self-imposed writing retreat.

She asked if I was over Seangate, and I said I'd been thinking about it. 'I've been thinking about society a lot, and how it organises things—' I said.

'At Gigr you mean? Oh my god, TP was on his *high horse* the other night. Walked *himself* to the restaurant to get our takeaway, like it was fucking *Selma*. Came back, and said, like he was so moved by his own actions he was going to cry, *I tipped them fifteen percent*.'

Just like Teddy had predicted, the Marshall Landry playbook was now in full swing. There was a constant drip-feed of bad Gigr news, all of which landed on my desk. This week's latest, picked up by all the last of the left-leaning papers was a whistleblower interview revealing how hard life was on the Gigr front-line. Our request rate was down nine percent which doesn't sound like a lot, but in a week that had rained solidly—

'Not Gigr,' I said, diverting back to my original point, which now seemed stupid.

At first I'd found it honourable that Ed had been so unfazed about Bonnie, I told her, but now something about it wasn't sitting right with me. 'Two gay men, there's a sanctity to it,' I said. 'It's the least likely to be interrupted.'

'What about glory holes?' she said.

'No Flo, I just mean, no straight man or woman is going to be like, I'll have a piece of that. We understand it's its own thing.'

'*You* don't.'

'I'm trying to say something serious. Meanwhile, if it's two girls, every Tom, Dick and Harry thinks they can join in. All those guys who are like, "Sure you can kiss another woman if you like. You'll never leave me and my penis."'

'Yeah,' she said. 'It's not cool.' Then laughed. 'Patriarchy? Ever heard of it? Not cool.'

'But d'you know what I mean? Society is so resistant to bisexual men, because why – after sampling the delights of a man – would anyone want to go back to a woman?'

'Isn't it quite chic to have a bisexual boyfriend at the moment? Aren't they in?' she said, hamming it up. 'In! Out! In! Out!' she said then, swaying back and forth. 'Make up your goddamn mind!' She looked at me, saw I wasn't enjoying it, and pulled her own reins. 'Sorry. But you're very . . . bee in your bonnet today.'

The truth was, I kept on seeing Luisa, and trying to find ways to worry about something else. 'It's just the hierarchy of it is fucked. The gay men are all up in the Pantheon, and somehow, no matter where, no matter when, lesbians are always at the bottom, with everyone throwing coins in the hat.'

I looked at my phone. Ed had texted from the place he was at. There was a lot of wisteria.

That doesn't look like Berghain to me, I wrote back.
The sex swings are all round the back
I miss you

Doubt it

I do! Come and check
'Well he still makes you smile a little,' Flo said. 'If that's Ed.'
'It's Ed.'
'Does this retreat thingy mean he's writing again?' Flo asked.
'Apparently,' I said. 'Genuinely no idea what about.'
'A *mystery* novel,' she said. 'Things are heating up!'
'Yeah,' I said. 'Who needs Gigr? Perhaps he'll be our big break.'

41

Hampshire for life, Ed said, multiple times, when he came back. 'Kidding. I mean there were literally the modern-day equivalents of "No dogs, no Blacks, no Irish" signs at the local pub, *but*—' he said.

'Wait, what were the signs?' I said at the same time as he said: 'But I do think I cracked something about the book.'

'Oh, one was *British Pubs for British People*,' he said. 'And the other was a pride flag, with the word pride, except they'd crossed out the "d" and the "e" and changed it to pri*vate*. Underlined. Very clever. Though nothing compared to my favourite classic from America. LGBT. Liberty, Guns, Beer, Trump.'

He gave me a hug. Then pushed back to look at me. It was hard to meet the way he was looking, and so I shut my eyes. 'You okay?' he said then. 'It's work, right?'

Early mornings, late nights, work was swallowing both of us.

'Hey,' Luisa said that next Monday. 'Can I?' She invited herself into my office. 'You paid for my coffee this morning,' she said when she sat down.

'I thought what happens in the wider Finsbury Park area stays there . . .' I said.

'I know. Finsbury fucking Park. Don't tell anyone I went anywhere *near* there.'

There was a moment of silence.

'So what are we going to do?' she asked me. I looked at her. 'To make the people love us, I mean.'

'The hearts and minds campaign,' I said. 'Well, I hope their love language is *gifts*.'

'Actually, I had an idea,' she said. 'As an orphan, I'm very empathetic.'

The brain is wider than the sky, but it also isn't. Something started ticking inside me.

My abacus was back, but it wasn't just numbers now – it was balancing out things that made a small crush fair. My still-hovering, occasional question mark about Sean. The way that even when we were together, I could see Ed was in another place sometimes: in the world of the book rather than the world with me. Then, on the other side, all the things he'd done right, and the fact I loved him, I did love him. Both sides piling up until I stopped counting.

Everything with Luisa felt elected, like an activity. I allowed it to make my stomach flip. Nothing happened in real life, but I would find her, in the places I could find her, and watch for the moments when she was online. Just seeing it was enough to imagine a dart going back and forth between us. The word 'typing' took on an almost monstrous quality. Like a false memory, but a false future. I wanted to see it.

When days spat me out from one meeting to the next, it made it better when my eyes had something to follow when she went to the kitchen. I could look forward to silences because I had a place in my head to go to. I'd meet her there and make things happen. Interesting, the way I'd look for fuel. At first only big things, obvious firewood, and then I went further and further, to the smallest moments, and I could make anything burn.

It was okay though, because I knew exactly where the line was. Not a line, an electric fence. I felt the crackle as I thought of things that would barrel into the border. If I were to let the things I thought about leave my body. So few words would do it. 'I can't stop thinking about you.' 'You're in my head.' 'I want you.' A classic crush, a rush to test it, to let the tripwire catch.

42

Teddy had gone concerningly quiet. And every time I'd see Daniel in the corridor he'd bark 'update?' in a way that sounded increasingly like a threat.

I asked Ed to text Teddy, subtly, to remind him of our existence – *DON'T IGNORE MY GIRLFRIEND!!!!!* Ed typed into the message box until I grabbed his phone out of his hand – and then, finally, Teddy sent through the questions he wanted to ask Gigr workers in a survey. His 'test the waters' collaboration.

The attachment came through when Luisa was at my desk. 'Those are eye-wateringly boring,' she said, reading over my shoulder. 'We'll send half the workforce to sleep. Who is this guy?' I kept it vague. She reached over me to use the mouse and looked at his email.

Luisa's idea for the hearts and minds campaign was good, and we were refining the plan. The report had just come out about how many kids in the UK were technically starving – comparable to somewhere like Guatemala that year, that was what the papers had grabbed onto anyway – and the plan was to use the Gigr fleet to deliver food to community centres during the holidays. A few different restaurant partners had agreed to donate food in return for promotions, and the drivers we'd run the idea by genuinely seemed to be enthused. 'He actually looked ... happy?' Luisa said after we left the meeting. 'I'm in shock.'

Daniel had signed it off – huge PR coup, he'd said, then he rubbed his thumb into his fingers: *money* – and it was planned for the end of term and the beginning of the half-term holiday. All we had left to do was nail down the messaging.

'Your email confidant is calling,' Luisa said, pointing at my phone.

I asked her for a minute, and she went out onto the balcony attached to my office.

'The questions come through?' Teddy said, when I picked up. 'We're good to roll?'

'All good,' I said.

'Sorry for silence. You know how it is—' I heard him tap his teeth together a couple of times. 'Actually, is now a good time?'

'Sure.' I still couldn't bear the balcony wrapping around the office. The thought of anyone on it.

'I have a larger thing I'd like to do a little off record,' Teddy said. 'The big Newham project I mentioned. The one with the wedding prices. I want to run an alternative costing.' There was something about the way he spoke that made me think he had his feet up on a chair, or the table.

'Okay ...' I said.

'An alternative costing with you. Gigr. With your structures. I want to make a case for a few changes.'

He told me he needed to liaise with someone who knew all the different industries Gigr covered so he could identify any gaps in capacity.

'Sure,' I said. Who would that be? I was painfully aware of Luisa standing on the other side of the glass behind me. Was she too close? Could she hear? Would she fall? 'Sure,' I said again. I coughed to make my voice more certain.

'Am I allowed back in now?' she said when I put my phone back on my desk. She had rolled up her shorts. 'Weirdly hot day out there,' she said. And she left them rolled up, a tattoo I'd never seen before pulling my eye up her inner thigh.

43

The safe and easy crush hit a stumbling block the day Teddy's survey was meant to be rolled out. Like Luisa had said, the questions were endless – what vehicle do you have? how frequently do you drive? how much meat do you eat? – and because it was longer than usual, it required a few tweaks to the app to get it to load correctly onto the system.

In our team meeting, Luisa looked even more bored than usual. 'Government pawns at the ready,' she said, when I'd finished briefing.

'Sorry?' I said.

'I just mean: anything for our overlords. This is a government request, right?' she said. The room chilled. Even just that morning, we'd lost someone who said recent company decisions didn't align with their values, and Daniel had issued a blanket ban on writing them a reference. I remembered Luisa seeing Teddy's email address. But then she said, 'You told me the other night.' It was the word night. It suggested an intimacy between us. 'Sorry, I didn't know it was a state secret,' she said.

The meeting dwindled. The team scuffed their way out unhappy. I told Luisa to stay behind.

Our conversation was short. I asked her what she thought she was doing. If that was in any way appropriate. She knew the pressure I was under, the balance we had to strike. I think I expected her to fight back, but shame seemed to swallow her. She looked down, went red. And she stayed that way all afternoon, head down, until the righteousness I'd felt had tipped into pity. Because that was the thing: what would I have done if someone else had said it?

Ed was the only one I could talk to. At home, over a paper manuscript, he had some kind of elaborate maté set up. He pulled a meal out of the oven. 'It's been there a while. Not against you,' he said. 'I know you're busy.'

'Printed,' I said, looking down at the table, 'exciting—'

'Or the opposite,' he said, 'it's terrible.' He stood up and put it underneath him, before sitting back down on it, like a booster seat. He looked at me, could see something was wrong. 'Short seller stuff? I've been reading a book about it, trying to understand—'

'Really?' I said. Standing in the kitchen, I almost wanted to cry. It spread out in all directions, how moving it was, someone caring enough to do that.

'Well, the only "really" is that I *really* can't understand.'

'It's okay. It's not that.'

Which way did it take me? It felt dangerous to bring her into the room with us, but it de-barbed it too – if we could talk about her, then what was there to talk about? I told him what had happened. A young, junior direct report was constantly trying to push the limits. That I'd told her off. 'She's sweet,' I said. 'Sweet-ish. Likeable in other ways. Probably very insecure.'

He listened. He nodded when I needed him to. 'I'd say, don't play along when she pushes your buttons,' he said. 'You're her boss.

Be an adult. It's like with a teenager. They need a steady presence. Something they can trust not to move.'

'Have you been talking to my dad again? How to harangue Elle into parenting?'

'Course,' he said. 'Been dutifully cutting every condom.' His T-shirt was stretched out of shape. I could see his day on him, the way he'd put his forearms inside the material and turn it into a hammock when he was thinking about things.

'But really though, do I be a boss bitch and stay hard? Or like ... what? Her bravado's so *there* in the room ...'

'Personally, I think you can apologise for being harsh. Be clear, and explain again. But be nice, be human.'

'*Me?*' I said.

'I've seen it,' he said, 'at least once or twice.'

'Shall we swap jobs?' I asked him. 'You're better than me with people.'

'Well you could definitely do mine,' he said. 'You're the only one of us whose words have made money—'

'Says the cult writer ...'

'Cult of approximately two—'

'Who'd commit joint suicide if they found out you were living with me though.'

Sometimes I wished he'd met the other me. I tried to say something along those lines, but it probably came out wrong. How I was less of a cosmic storm of stress before the man jumped. 'And before you met me,' he said. It sat with us in the room.

Ed said he was going to say something annoying and I was going to think: *shut up and die*, but he was going to say it anyway. 'When I was at school,' he said, 'there was a boy in my class who was so stressed about exams he'd actually pick off his entire nails.'

'Did it work?' I said. 'Should I try it?'

'No but we had this teacher who was so great. He'd make us all go outside at night.'

'At night?' I said. Then I remembered he went to boarding school.

'He'd make us look up at the stars and ask us how far away they were. He knew all the distances, these crazy millions-of-miles-away numbers.' Ed's head was tipped back as he said this. 'He'd remind us that each star likely had planets around it, just like ours did. Do you think it matters how you do in *exams*? he'd say. I remember the way he said exams, like it didn't deserve to be on his tongue.'

'Three million pounds and the only way of keeping my mum alive isn't quite exams,' I said.

'Right, I know. But the perspective bit. There's all the point in the world, but also no point in the world at the same time. And surely you know that if anyone on earth can do it, you can,' he said. He toyed with one of the buttons on my shirt like he'd never seen one before. 'I mean you shouldn't! For the soul of the nation. But you can. And then we'll be free,' he said. 'You'll be free.'

And so I sent Luisa an email. I'd never emailed her directly before, but I didn't want there to be a chain above it. All the different ways we'd already crossed the line.

Clear the air? I wrote.

I asked her to come to my office, and said it more calmly this time: I told her I was sorry that I'd overreacted, but in the work context there had to be a line. 'I get it,' she said.

'But really Luisa,' I said.

'No, I do. Line drawn,' she said.

Afterwards we went for a cigarette. 'The clearest of all air,' she said, when we got outside. 'You're right. I know you're right by the way. It just reminded me of this teacher at school.'

I thought about Ed yesterday. His story about the stars. 'An apple for my teacher,' I said.

'She was always so nice to me, and I obviously cared about what she thought and occasionally she'd just be like—' she made the sound of a guillotine coming down through the air. 'Kill me stone dead.' I nodded. 'Don't worry,' she said. 'I still liked her.'

'Are you going to Finsbury Park again tonight?' I asked her. The cigarette felt like it was blooming in my brain.

'I'm working all night, manually doing your survey shit. I'm the only one on the team who's any good on the back end,' she said. 'Wahey,' she added, deadpan.

'Do you want a hand?'

'Are you trying to make sure I don't commit corporate sabotage?'

'I could help,' I said. *You're her boss. Just be a steady presence.* I thought of Ed writing his novel. Flo writing her PhD. 'I don't have anywhere else to be.'

44

I ordered food for us on the company card around 9 p.m. I tipped the driver 100%, the least I could do.

Luisa was scanning all the drinks in the mega-fridge. 'This kombucha's zero point five percent alcohol,' she said. 'If we chug the whole fridge worth we could get a mild buzz.'

It had been another rough day. I told her I had a better suggestion. About a year ago, we'd sold the rights to a love story between two Gigr workers who'd met on a sequence of shifts at a restaurant chain. The chain wanted to use it in an advert, and after the shoot, their brand manager had given me an expensive bottle of aged mezcal. I poured some into two espresso cups.

Luisa peered into hers. 'You were saying you sold their love story...'

'Well, we got sixty percent of the fee. And yeah, uh, after the ad, potentially *as* a result of it, one of the two was deported—'

'Fuck,' she said, almost spluttering, then taking a sip and letting her eye dip. 'I can't wait for the podcast.'

The mezcal felt like it tucked my throat under a warm blanket. We talked about other things. It felt like it was easy again, and I was relieved it was okay, relieved I had put it to bed, relieved I had spoken to Ed. She tapped away at her laptop which had the E, T, A and L all rubbed away. 'Done,' she said. 'Finally. Hope we're getting something good out of it.'

'We're keeping our jobs,' I said.

'Aren't we lucky?'

'About the other day again,' I started. I paused. 'I know you're always rude. I like it. I can like it. It's just in front of colleagues—'

'I know. There's a line.'

'Right,' I said.

'That was dangerous, by the way.'

'What?'

'Way to make it appealing.' She looked like she was really thinking about it. It was only our third espresso cup, not a lot, but I looked at the bottle: 110 proof. 'I think I wanted you to tell me to stop.' I didn't say anything. She was thinking again. 'I don't know. I think sometimes I want you to say, that's enough now.'

I could have done that, then. Said stop it, said enough now. 'That management course really didn't pay off,' I said, reaching for the bottle, 'if my authority is that easily challenged and I'm drinking mezcal with a subordinate.'

Authority, subordinate. It set something in motion.

'I had a dream about you,' Luisa said. 'The other night.'

'I don't think that's—' I kept the bottle closed. My hand on the cap.

'Just let me tell you. It's a dream. Who cares? But maybe it explains something.'

'Honestly it's not—' But I couldn't commit to any of my sentences.

We were sitting on the floor for some reason, as if that made working after hours somehow more palatable. She was leaning against my desk, and she adjusted her back against it. The distance between us felt like it was made of risk. 'Let me tell you, and get it off my chest, and you don't have to say anything, and we can pretend it never happened. And I'll just walk away.'

When I swallowed, it caught in my throat. Breathe. *The panic might come in waves. Remember waves pass, remember to breathe in between them.*

'It was just there.' She pointed at the photocopier. 'I know. Not very imaginative. I was copying something—'

'I've never seen you copy a thing. Why do we even have a photocopier—' Nowhere safe to land.

'I was copying something. I was leaning over it.' This wasn't happening. 'And I felt something against me.'

'Luisa, stop—'

'Just your belt.'

'I don't wear a belt.'

'I felt you against me.'

'Stop it, what's wrong with you? '

'The world is ending,' she said. 'Isn't that what everyone's always saying? What does it matter?' She took the bottle out of my hand and filled up our glasses. 'You pushed me into the machine at first—'

Really though: what was happening? Was I just inventing the words and layering them upon a very normal scene? Maybe this was madness—

'And you see this—' she stood up without a hand on the floor, her body lifted like a snake, and she walked over to the machine and touched the corner. 'It was pressed into me,' she said.

Don't fucking say it. But then I heard it come out of my mouth, like it was operating outside of my control. 'Where did it press?'

'Against the top of my – yeah.'

Maybe she had a problem? But I had a problem too. It was right in front of me. She didn't say anything. I didn't say anything.

'You know no one likes hearing about other people's dreams,' I said. I shut my eyes. A childish thought: if I couldn't see it, it wasn't real.

'Anyway,' she said, and her tone turned so casual, the story of a journey on a bus. 'You put your hand inside my trousers, never undoing a single button, and you fucked me.' All air had left the room. 'I woke up coming,' she said, and that was when she walked closer to me again. 'I've never come like that.'

In your sleep? I wanted to know. Or that hard? 'We're not having this conversation,' I said.

But a drumbeat had started in between my legs when she said, 'What are you going to do about it?'

If I opened my eyes, I barely looked at her. 'Not here,' was all I managed to say.

45

I can't pretend, then. I can't pretend there wasn't a set of decisions, a journey. A journey I could have stopped at any point. I can't pretend there weren't messages I could have seen and used as a way to stop.

We sat separate in the car still. 'Your house,' I'd said, back at the office.

'What are you going to do to me when we get there?' she said.

I didn't say anything.

'Say something,' she said eventually. She shifted in her seat. 'I'm scared now.' I thought of all the times I'd said that to Ed, and he had said it to me. Except I didn't let the thought come whole, I pushed it away before it fully arrived.

'Do you want to be scared?' I said.

'Maybe.'

I tried not to see everything in her house. The Billy bookshelves that must have been there since they moved in. The student-ness of it all. Posters on the wall, in clip frames or none at all. The blanket over a shared sofa. A short, battered surfboard in the corner.

'No one will see,' she said, about her flatmates.

Her room had fairy lights in it. I shut my eyes to that too. When her door shut behind us, I pushed her into it.

'Enough being nice,' I said. 'Is this what you want? Who do you think you are?' This was the game.

'No one,' she said.

'To speak to me like that.'

'No one,' she said again.

'Face the wall,' I told her.

'Not too loud,' she said, but I pressed her face into the wall so she was the one who was quiet. This was the game. 'How do you want this to go?'

'I don't know,' she said. 'I've never done this before.' Was this the game?

'Do you think how you behaved today was okay?' I said.

'No,' she replied.

Her body in front of me. The stretched-out violin of her back. The finest hairs at the nape of her neck. Tiny tattoos each in their own orbit. I pushed her onto the bed, one knee up, and the other leg out.

'Please,' she said.

'Please what?'

'You know what.'

'Is this what you want?' I said, but her face was buried in the pillow.

46

My arms felt like I'd been climbing a wall afterwards. The blood in my veins seemed to run both up and down, these impossible back-and-forth sprints.

Then, a shrinking. How do you take it back? How do you collect all the things from air, and pull them back into your body?

'I should go,' I said.

And what then? Do you continue the game? Do you say sorry? I thought she might want to keep on playing, the way she wasn't moving still, because I'd asked her to do that, said she wasn't allowed to flinch.

'Are you okay?' I said.

I could see her nodding, I think she was nodding, in her tangle in the sheets. Then it was still the game? She wanted me to say, answer me with a yes or a no? 'Are you really okay?' I said.

She took a breath then rolled onto her back. 'Totally,' she said. A strand of her hair was caught in her mouth and she unhooked it, then rubbed her eye.

'And we're cool?' I said. I can't really describe the fear, how it opened like a faucet. How gross it was to feel it.

'Fuck off,' she said. 'You want to fuck me like that and get away with it?'

The flicker was a fire, was a feeling I should have been used to by then: everything is over now.

'Kid-ding,' she said, a downward slide on the kid. 'You're going to get a rave on your 360 review.' She laughed then, this stored-up thing. 'You do realise I'm going to be really badly behaved at work now.'

I wanted it to stop. In that blaze of a moment, I wanted to be able to fuck her – her specifically, whatever mad alignment of the planets and cells she was – every single day for the rest of my life.

It wasn't the alcohol from the night before that made me vomit as I turned the corner after leaving her house. I wanted to take everything back so much I needed space inside me. Or what I had grabbed from the air – I wanted it to be outside of me.

A group of teenage boys swerved away from me fast enough it looked like they had skateboards underfoot. They were talking to each other despite all three having earbuds in. They looked back.

'That's dutty, nah,' one said. 'Old bird too. Go home, fam.'

47

I did go home. Ed was refilling a bowl of cereal when I walked into the kitchen. His favourite mix of three types, certain English foods still having a certain novelty after years in New York. The outline of him, I looked at him and thought: *you don't know.*

'You look like you've seen a ghost,' he said.

I had, in a sense. I watched him eat like the first night I'd met him, these deep dives with an outsized spoon.

'Work again,' I said. My heart was stumbling in my chest. It felt like forward rolls. 'Daniel. And trying to keep Teddy sweet with this survey thing. I'm so sorry, it was an all-nighter.'

'Hey,' he started, and in that second, I wondered if I should say it all. That if I poured out the cup now it couldn't get any deeper. This was as small as it would ever be. He reached for me. 'Jesus,' he said. He sniffed near my head. Was it perfume? Did she even wear a perfume? 'Daniel really roped the booze in,' he said. 'There's also bacon. Shall I get the grill on?' He kissed my temple. 'Hey,' he said again, and I did think: *say it.* 'I'm sorry I've been such a hermit crab.'

Ed's outline. The sun still directly on us, but soft, like through a window, when I stood near him.

The hug I gave him then felt desperate. The speed of it, the tightness. Terror. Gratitude.

48

It was March. The date for the IPO was set for early May. The board-room was now a full-time War Room. We'd have 8 a.m. regroups before the external parties came in, and Daniel seemed to have lost all control of his volume, so I was grateful for the new sealant strips around the glass doors to make it soundproof when he would shout things like, 'Elle, remind me, when are we feeding the street urchins?' A whole wall was dedicated to Marshall Landry, and it looked like a detective's murder board. Investigators and journalists we thought might be digging around, the status of the Short Seller Regulation. My name underlined four times with dry marker on that bit.

At home, though I was barely at home, Ed and I started to move around each other differently. It had been so balletic, dipping under stirring arms in the kitchen, slipping around him as he brushed his teeth; now it could feel like a different dance. My training from child-hood hypochondria crept back: what I was doing to my relationship with Ed, I pushed it to one side. Wait. It would have to wait.

Sometimes it crossed my mind, when he fell asleep in the study and spent the night there, was he just biding his time until he finished his book? Because he was at a crunch point too. These shared deadlines that hovered over us: Gigr's IPO, and his cut-off point to send the book to his agent – they had been set for the same week.

Whatever it was, all through the start of spring, as light came back, we coasted.

'You're here but you're somewhere else,' Flo said. The same feeling I could have about Ed when he stood up from the world of his manuscript so we could talk.

We'd met in Green Park, since it was close to work and not far from her library. It was one of those first evenings of spring proper, and Daniel, in one of his random compulsions, had made the decision to shut the office early at 6 p.m. All around us, there were crowds of daffodils. I watched the reverence most people felt, and then others – a student with a hiking backpack, a suited man – who walked through them like grass, and sat down as if there was nothing that set a flower apart.

'I'm not somewhere else,' I said. 'I wish I were somewhere else.'

'Harsh,' she said. She looked at me. '*Are* you okay though?'

What had happened with Luisa. I'd never had a real secret from Flo before. I felt a fish swim around inside me whenever I thought about it. Another chance – but 'Totally fine,' I said. 'Period, maybe.'

'How's your husband?'

'He's not my husband.' The fish got sucked into a whirlpool.

'Your *partner* then. Keep it cryptic.'

'We've barely seen each other. My work, his book. It's been,' how to say it? It felt unfair to say anything bad about him, 'a bit stiff.'

'Stiff can be a good thing.'

'Not this one so much.'

'Is the milk okay?' Ed had asked me just that morning. 'Can you check the date?'

'It's today,' I'd said.

'Well that's what I mean.'

'It's Best Before, Ed, not Rotten On.' Except I'd made it sharp rather than funny.

Back in the park, 'Limerence is such a bitch,' Flo said. 'Always runs out when you need her the most.'

But it wasn't even that. His magic still worked. His magic could still work.

Confidence. I kept on thinking about how the same word could mean such distinct things.

Luisa's. She was the kind of person who could walk onto a plane without a ticket or a passport. This way of pushing repercussions again and again right to the edge, like a penny machine.

Ed's was so much calmer. Ed, eddy, a clearing in spinning water. I knew the provenance of some of his confidence – it was built in him from birth, it had been paid for, it was both those things and also something that had simply come when the wheel of who we become was spun. It could have been horrible, perhaps it should have been, but he'd shared that confidence with me. At the moment I had lost mine. I'd tried to explain this to Flo before. 'Oh god,' she'd said. 'Does he put you on his chest and make you do skin contact?' 'No,' I'd said. 'So basique!' she'd replied. 'I bet it's like that *Man and Baby* poster.'

It was true though, I would hold his forearm sometimes. That hadn't changed. I'd feel the soft rock of his pulse, always slower than mine, always solid. Other heartbeats I'd heard in bed I'd hated, I was sure I'd hear them stop. But with Ed, sometimes, particularly when I came back late, I'd look for his in the night, find it on his wrist or neck, on his back, and it would tick like a clock, sure and steady, and I'd try to let it take mine into sureness with it.

'What is it then?' she said. 'Your sad face. Is he emasculated by you being the big boss?'

'Not even, he actually listens when I tell him about work stuff.'

'Wow,' she said, her eyes wide. 'I would, but I always feel so dirty afterwards.'

'He just understands people. In some fundamental way.' I told her that a few days ago, I'd had a directors' meeting and I couldn't make myself walk into the room. My legs had frozen, in a way that felt like a sci-fi syndrome, but I just thought of Ed reading a book on the sofa and – 'I don't know. I felt okay again. Safe.'

'A straitjacket,' she said, then, realising the double entendre, 'ba da boom.'

'Yeah,' I said. 'A padded room.'

It was a strange spring. It would be burning hot, and windy at the same time, and then suddenly it would rain. Wild enough and quick enough for sudden pours to flood the keyboards of alfresco laptops. Roads would fill like pools. A few days earlier, hailstones had fallen the size of ice cubes and, briefly, golf balls. And yet that day was purely boiling.

'Shall we?' Flo said. We started walking. 'If it's this hot, this soon, I keep on thinking of all the excess deaths.'

'Always with excess deaths.'

'It's my conspiracy theory side. But yeah, over thirty degrees, cardiac incidents shoot up.' She told me that every time she saw a picture online of someone smiling she presumed they'd died. 'All these tribute posts designed to go viral. It's so weird.' She paused briefly to gather her thoughts. 'How do you put it into words? It's like – the superficial elements are all as they've always been. People drink rosé with ice on a Friday night in a pub and wear nice earrings or whatever. We all still pay our little subscriptions, and you can probably go to Superdrug and get the lipstick you need, and then right under the surface, it's just fucked. The national debt helpline service closed down. *Because it was in debt.* It's like—' she mimed her brain exploding. 'What are the rest of us meant to do?'

337

She was right. The houses I looked at started to change. Before, I'd mostly looked at normal sites, but with all the mortgage defaults a whole new category had popped up. Auction sites, reformulated for millennial eyes. Infinite scroll that would deliver one, two, three reasons to buy, and every day there were more and more of them. Normal houses, nice houses, the last ten years of interior design trends in set little slideshows.

'I always imagined being garrotted on a bus,' Flo said. It wrenched me back to the conversation.

'What?'

'When I was seventeen, I used to work in an Italian deli and they had this wire thing to cut hard cheeses. That's what I imagined. Someone doing that to me from behind on a bus. I'd forgotten about it for a while but it's back now. Everything's just *off*,' she said. 'People pushing into trains before anyone's got out. People ignoring zebra crossings. Also, whenever I type the year, I write 2927. And I swear it feels like that, doesn't it?'

49

The unravelling was happening everywhere. Work was like a shrink wrap around everything. Constant pressure, constantly getting tighter.

I'd handed over Teddy's request that we provide an alternative costing for the Newham project to a colleague called Jason who looked too young to be called Jason.

How's it going with the Teddy guy? I asked him.

Alright! I mean, he has kind of
creepy eyes but don't they all
He's getting me to do an alternative
site bid too. Out of my depth frankly

Site where?

West London.
Kew / Fulham

Right
Ok
Do you have everything you need?

Yeah, but like

339

I can't do flood mapping???
So I've got the AI working overtime lol
I mean that's what you want right?
We want the contract?

After our directors' meeting, Daniel told me that some of the 'young-ies in the office' were still furious about the so-called Trafalgar Ten: a group of workers who'd been fired for protesting on their day off.

'Youngies,' I repeated. 'We don't employ anyone actually underage, do we?'

'Who've you been talking to?' he said, straightening his back suddenly. 'Only joking, got you there. Anyway, they're organising a walkout in *protest*. In fucking *solidarity*.' He did that Italian thing with his hands – *va' fa Napoli*. 'Anyway I'm not too worried. They've organised it for their *lunch break*,' he said. He waited for me to laugh. 'But nevertheless the one who's running it ... We're going to.' He ran his finger over his throat.

I suddenly thought of Luisa, all her jokes about her exposé. Her trade union. I froze.

'HR are on it,' he said. 'Just wanted to give you a heads up.'

I went to see Luisa at her desk. Unsurprisingly she was in the kitchen, perched on the worktop, eating beetroot humous with a breadstick. I opened a cupboard next to her like I was reaching for a cup. 'Daniel just told me about a strike thing,' I said, quietly. 'The walk-out. That's not you, is it?'

'Oh the one at lunchtime?' she said. 'No, that's Lani from creative.'

'Okay good. Can you skip it? You know I'm counting on electric minds like yours at the moment.' I shut the cupboard I was look-ing in and opened another. 'And Daniel will have the neck of any ringleaders.'

'Are you making me collude with the fascists again?' she said.

'Lu—'

'If he's scared of Lani he's got more issues than I thought.'

'Seriously though.'

'Do I mind missing spending an hour with a bunch of blonde chicks with 2:1s? I'll cope,' she said.

I'd found the cup I wanted and held it in my hands. 'Thank you,' I said. I looked at her finally. 'For being good.'

She tensed her belly like she'd been shot. 'Hey,' she said. 'See you later?'

I would often pay when we went out, but never a huge amount, because she would win. And there was often nothing else to spend money on when we were there in the places she took us to. One of her favourite spots had this strange offer of three whenever we arrived: beer, baked potato, or strawberry ice cream. The beer was served warm, kept in a cupboard not a fridge.

There were TVs everywhere, showing sport. There were bottles of water everywhere, the huge ones you turn upside down to use in a fountain. They were always half gambling dens, half storage units. Cigarettes sold by the carton. Tropical sodas, laundry detergent, nappies. Plug-in oil radiators, gathering like gangs of redundant robots.

There were other places where they offered you everything. Fried shrimp, I remember, in a cone, and fizzy wine, though that wasn't cold either. Who knew? A broken-up, buried Nevada scattered across, and underneath, London.

I watched her. It was fun to watch her. When my eyes were locked on her I managed not to think about anything else. She explained how games worked to me – slow and pronounced and right into my ear at first – and then she wouldn't have time. She would always bring the money back to me, and she'd want me to say 'good', or at least that's what I ended up saying.

One night, a man walked in and people cheered. His first son had been born the previous night and so he'd left early, but now he was back again. 'Healthy,' he said. 'Robert. Bobby.' People came to him with money, and not small amounts.

'Do you ever worry?' I asked her.

'I count cards,' she told me, though most of the time, cards were not what we were playing. 'As we know better than anyone,' she said after that, 'these days, everyone has to do a second job.' She ate the last of her baked potato. 'Or you'll have to tell my boss to give me more money ...'

That particular night, she was wearing a red dress that was incredibly tight. Sometimes when I was with her, it was hard to breathe, like I was brushing too close up against a fantasy. Who did the other gamblers think I was, this woman, no longer young, watching it all like a show I didn't realise I was part of?

The truth was: they didn't think of me at all. I'd give Luisa a fifty. She'd put her hand in my pocket for a second one. She'd turn it into 300 at a table I didn't understand, partially because I was standing just behind her, and she'd lean back into me occasionally and ask if how she was playing was okay.

When I think about it now, it is a blur with a few solid, sharp images. Her strawberry ice cream melting, forgotten. At some point in the night, one of us taking the other's hand to go somewhere quiet, and in a rush and spin, her asking me to leave the money where she could see it, or in her mouth sometimes, between her teeth, which meant she couldn't make a sound.

Twenty-four. I'd never thought about a number so much. She had just turned twenty-four. I played with it too – would slight shifts make it better? Twenty-five? That somehow sounded even younger. Twenty-six would be good.

It would be better if she were twenty-seven or twenty-eight. But none of it was okay. In meetings, when I could see her hands above the table, I imagined them holding a bed frame and gripping it until her fingers went white. When her hands were under a table, I imagined one, then two, of her fingers pushing into herself, and her looking straight at me. It wasn't good.

'You don't want me to have a personality,' she'd said to me. We were in an old man pub a few roads away from work that no one else went to. They somehow still had pints for under a fiver, even if it always tasted like the keg was running out. Next to us, students with mullets played Settlers of Catan.

'I can see it,' she said. 'You hope it isn't there.' She opened her packet of crisps to a silver carpet on the table even if she was the only one eating them. She tried to kiss me and I put my hand on her knee to stop her.

''Cos of work, or 'cos someone will hit us?' she said.

'Just attention,' I said. 'And you know that's not true. I like the way you are. I've told you I like it when you're rude. When you're funny.'

'But just that. Just then. 'Cos what if you liked fucking me, and liked me too.'

'I do like you.'

'Liked me-liked me though.' She looked down at the table and so I looked at it too. There was a constellation of stars in her lip print on her glass. 'Because then you might have to worry about whether I liked *you*.'

Curious creature. Of course I worried about that. When I went to the bar, the bartender swirled the pint glass to create a whirlpool as the slow and tinny draught poured in. I worried about so many things I would rarely get to the end of one worry before a new one started. Of course I worried about whether she liked me. I worried that she saw her own future in my body. In a skin that 'held stories' as a product on my bathroom shelf had told me. Sometimes it was part of the reason I made her look away. Pushed her face into the mattress. Kept her body down with my hand wide open. Or made her turn back and look at herself, and asked her if she could see it, see where she was going red.

I worried about being caught. I worried that I didn't worry enough about being caught. By Ed. By work. I worried about the part of my brain that kept on saying: you need to do this so you can function. So you can work. As if it were just a performance sharpener, like Daniel's endless nootropics or hot yoga, or the wine I could sink like water. I worried about all of it, I worried about everything, and then each time it happened, a moment came where I didn't worry about a single thing at all, and everything went purely, shining white.

It was her littleness, I think, that got me. The feeling of return to it, again, after Ed. I could wrap my arms around her differently. I could pick her up. She stood too close. She held my eyes until a coin flipped in my stomach. Is it because it's wrong, that the body does that? Or is it because it's right? Two stories at the same time.

Sometimes in gambling places she'd pull me into the bathroom with her and pull my hand into her underwear, and she'd be so wet it was like dipping my finger in paint. And occasionally, it can't have been more than three times, and not for whole nights, we would go to hotels. I would find them last minute, as we were ready to leave, using an app on my phone that kept the name secret until you said yes.

I can still see it now, the way her skin took sheet marks. Her legs open as I went down on her. Like wings. Like she was flying a plane into my mouth. When her back was flat on the bed, the scoop between her underwear lifted by her hips and her belly looked like a letter box.

The few times we stayed in a bed 'til morning, I would wake up early if we had been drinking, my heart beating heavy in the pillow, no Ed to calm me down, and I would notice she would run in her sleep. If I held her as she moved, held her tight enough to feel it, but light enough to let the movement happen, I would think of those simulators. The van-like things that moved from side-to-side to reflect what was on screen. I would hold her and wonder where she was going, and who she was with.

At work sometimes, on days that were bad, I'd call her in for a meeting and ask her questions in a voice that was my normal voice, my face my normal face. Have you made yourself come this morning? How does your cunt feel right now? Do you think it needs help? Does it need my help? She'd answer the questions, and then I'd send her away.

When I thought about what we'd done or things we'd said, my torso would be struck by sheet lightning, a full sky of it. I'd play the sentences and make the lightning come.

I'd think of our eyes hooking into each other like metal, the way her breath would catch if I turned her body round without warning, or took her cheek between my thumb and finger and felt how thin the skin was between inside and outside.

For a while, she was everywhere. She was there at my desk. She was there in my bed. She was there when I was with Ed. She was there when he took me to see a bad play and it was better to shut my eyes. She was there in those moments before I fell asleep, and when I woke up. The place where Ed had been. The place we all know there is. Laced through my mind, like a trap.

50

'Can I ask you a question?' Ed said when I came home on time one evening. Contributing to the new distance between us, each question he asked me, unsure of what it might lead to, made me want to disappear.

But it was dinner he was suggesting. One of Ed's friends from school was in town for work, and he thought it would be good to invite Flo. They could be good together, he'd said.

'What shall I tell her to bring?' I asked him.

'Nothing much,' he said. 'Foie gras, lobster, Beluga caviar? Only joking. Just a starter, main and dessert.'

Whenever it was normal between us, however briefly, there could be a small glow of hope, the tiny brightness that comes from sucking on a cigarette. Then a series of things in Luisa's mouth blitzed into my mind: the same cigarette, a straw poking out of a can, my fingers. I'd never understood it before – life in a split screen – but here I was suddenly living it.

'Don't look at me!' Flo said that evening when she walked in. 'These trousers are too tight. A camel toe to go with my camel coat. Oh, hello,' she said when she saw Ed's friend, the 'he' high and 'lo' low.

The friend – Brad – was American. He'd done a sixth-form year abroad at Ed's school in Surrey and that was how they'd met. Flo loved that: 'Ed and Brad,' she said, 'it's like a show!' Brad was staying at the Premier Inn in King's Cross. He was from the Midwest and he spoke like the world was a mystery he was unpacking slowly.

Ed cooked and it was like a light was back on in him too. He felt more reachable, right there in front of me, awake and moving, rather than just at night, when I touched his back to check both of us were still real.

Before the others turned up, he kissed me then looked at me then kissed me again. 'I'm so sorry it's been hard,' he'd said, though I knew somewhere in the mix of him feeling better was Campari. 'I know it shouldn't be like this so soon—'

'It's my work,' I said.

'And my book. I can't tell you how much my mood relies on how I feel about whether it will work or not. It's like I've outsourced everything to it, you know? May fifth,' he said then. Both of our deadlines. 'And then we sort it all out.' Ed's changing eyes shot through with green. Those threads of it, the way a palm leaf splits and spreads. 'Go back to the beginning.'

'Not the *very* beginning . . .' I said.

'No, the second one,' he said. I looked at him and in that moment, I wanted that so much.

Brad had very bad hair, but was handsome, and he was funny rather than annoying about England. 'I was expecting 1930s Germany but really it's like 1890s Russia,' he said, 'queues for cabbage.'

'That must be so nice!' Flo said.

'Cabbage?' Brad looked at her like a kid who'd just done his first ollie on a skateboard.

'To have a sense of history!' she said. 'Like what happened when. The dark ages! The mini ice age!'

'She's obsessed with this,' I said. 'Eternally worried that "no one's printed off Wikipedia yet" and thinks we should do it.'

'Well we should!' Brad said. 'Also the booze here! Six p.m. Friday at the Premier Inn, it's like a bomb's gone off. Platform 9¾ into random walls . . .'

Ed served us in his waiter way. He always served me first. When he sat back down, I reached for his leg under the table and his thumb stroked my finger. The meal he'd made was delicious, and he seemed soft and quiet and happier. I looked at his belt next to me, and thought about taking it off later. And as if reading my mind, he said he was going to the bathroom.

There was something sweet about Flo and Brad too, they also made their own show. She was saying he reminded her perfectly of a kind of dog, an Afghan hound – it was the centre parting – and they were look-ing up breeds, holding the phone next to Brad's face and his hair she'd restyled when the music from the speaker changed, became a voice.

At first I wondered again if it was madness – so often, recently, I'd put my finger in my ear just to check a sound I'd heard wasn't in my head – and then I thought it was an advert. Then I realised it was Ed. Not Ed's voice – it was a different voice – but it was Ed playing it, a voice note, in the bathroom, and it was playing now to the room through Bluetooth speakers.

At the table, the conversation went silent. Then, when Ed played the message a second time – it started 'Hey you,' a you that stretched – Flo tried to talk again. 'My god, I need water,' she said, and she opened her mouth, tongue out, as if we'd be able to see her throat was dry.

Brad looked at his phone, tried his hardest too. 'Marx was the first person to bring Afghan hounds from Afghanistan,' he said. 'And apparently Picasso had one too – called Kabul.'

Ed came back down, and the music was back on again, and he kissed my head not realising that I'd turned to stone.

51

After they'd left, Ed started putting things in the dishwasher, water in pots to soak, and looked so proud of himself. He changed the music to a podcast, something about corporate espionage now. 'That was nice,' he said, or at least started to say, because: 'You do realise what happened?' I said at the same time.

'Sorry, what? Flo and Brad?'

'Your little voice note.' Anger was easier to show than pain, because of course it was. But something else was in the mix too: the desire for him to have done something wrong so it wasn't just me.

'What are you talking about?'

'Ed, he sounded like a caricature.'

'What do you mean?'

'So gay. Almost joke gay.'

'Brad? Brad's not gay—'

'Not Brad. When you went to the bathroom. The speaker. I didn't know that's what you were into.'

'Oh,' he said. 'Oh – no, that's not – I'm not into him.' He shook his head.

'You played it twice. He was saying he was thinking of you. In his ridiculous voice.'

'Sorry, his what?'

'You said you were into guy-guys. So I'm just interested. Because this was such a fucking performance.' It rushed out: a horrible impression.

'Just because you're angry can you stop being so—'

'I'm just saying I didn't know you were into guys like that.'

'Can you hear yourself?' he said. There was silence. 'I don't do this to you,' he said after that. 'I've never done this to you.'

'Ed, you're not some victim here. He said he was thinking about your dick!'

'Look, of course that would have been shit to hear—'

I pushed past him, and went to the fridge and pulled out another bottle of wine.

'Stop it, Elle—' he said.

'What?'

'Stop drinking,' he said, 'everybody's gone. Also, it's not my fault what someone said to me. You didn't hear me say something to him. You can read our messages.'

'I don't want to read your messages,' I said. I felt my face contort. 'I could have plotted all this out on day one. I didn't have to live it.'

'Neither of us *have* to live it. You've barely been here. I'm basically your housekeeper. Fuck,' he said. 'I'm so tired.' It was late but he didn't mean tired in that moment. 'I'm so tired,' he said again.

I thought it might happen then.

'The whole point of this was that we made each other happy,' he said. 'Like something about it madly worked. The first time you saw me, we saw each other and there was total freedom. Or I thought there would be. But then – I don't know – we fell in these traps and it turned out they were deep, and right by our feet. And it's even harder because we never thought we'd be in them.'

'Sounds like you have a whole speech prepared,' I said.

'I'm saying it for you too. Isn't it hard for you? And recently, you started looking at me in a different way, or I saw it, and all I could feel was the weight of my past.'

'The weight of your past? Fucking violins.'

'I'm serious. It had never been a weight before. It's not a weight.' He looked at me. 'I know you like to . . . *see through everything*. But you also see the wrong things. You have these ideas about me and they're wrong too. And it makes me feel crazy. And like the most trapped I've felt as a person is with you.'

'I don't think that's true.' But even then, I didn't sound like I believed it. Each time I took a breath it caught in my chest.

'When did you start hating me?' he said. The question hung in the air and it pulled us so close to losing each other that fear arrived for both of us. 'Actually, don't answer that. I'm just—'

'I know,' I said. 'You're tired.'

He picked up the Bluetooth speaker, the podcast still running quietly now we were both silent, and put it back in its place. 'Look, whatever. Space will be good. I'll be out of your hair soon anyway,' he said.

'What?'

'Vermont,' he said. 'The residency. Remember?'

PART III

1

Ed had been offered the residency in Vermont the week he moved in, but back then, it seemed far enough in the future for me to presume it would always stay that way.

'I really don't want to argue,' he said in the morning. 'I'm sorry you heard it, but he's someone I knew a million years ago and he got in touch out of the blue. I hadn't seen him since my twenties. I still haven't.' He'd finished the last of the washing-up. He'd slept on the sofa in the study. He dried his hands, then looked at his fingertips: prune-like. 'Like I said, I'm away so soon, let's just—'

'I hadn't realised.'

It's true, there is calm after a storm. The kitchen seemed an entirely different place from where we'd been shouting. The words I'd said sat so wrong there in the morning.

'You knew,' Ed said. 'Or you did know. We went for that dinner about it.'

'It's just. Time.'

'Yeah – it flies.'

*

The residency was in a tiny rural town, and was a mix of artists and writers, which was better he said. He would go to New York for a week before and a week afterwards, if that was still okay.

'As you said yourself, I'm not your mum, Ed. It's weird when you ask me permission for things. What am I going to say? New York, haram.'

'I just want to catch up with friends. Old life.' He shrugged. He really did look so tired. 'I feel funny about it. When you've been in a place for so long, and it was such a concentration of time. It's like you stand in a room with yourself again. And your old self judges your new self.'

It was exactly what I'd felt each time I'd gone back to Lisbon. I knew what he meant. Still, 'What about your new self?' was what I said.

The night before he left, as I watched him pack, I felt a sense of panic with each item he placed in the suitcase, as if each one were a brick on the side of the scales of away from me. They stuttered back, surging rushes of old feelings, and I was so desperate for it not to be bad, that of course it went mostly wrong. A stiffness again, a stoniness, not even the worst we'd had but still, the feeling of the first time Ed had come and sat at this table, like we were in a bad play.

'What time will you arrive in New York?'

'I have to check my ticket, but I think about five p.m.?'

'That's not too bad.'

'Yes, it's not too bad in this direction.'

Still, when he left, we held hands. Both hands, like kids in a playground. Briefly I imagined his plane crashing, and I wanted to say everything I hadn't said, but didn't.

'Do you want to think about it while you're away?' I said.

'Let's not do this now. Let's just—' He let it melt. 'Like I said, space is good. It will be good for you too.'

I felt a concentration of love for him. It rushed round my body. It rushed in my ears, surround sound. And then when the taxi disappeared and I went back inside, I felt suddenly, stupidly, pointlessly, angry.

There's no feeling like someone else pulling away. The desperation in the reach; the way you become the worst of yourself. I wondered how many times both of us were in bed, bodies close so we couldn't see each other, and said something again and again in our head that never left our mouth. I wanted to know all the things he wanted to say, and I didn't.

After he'd gone, I opened the fridge door, and shut it again, played a kind of rock-a-bye baby with it, back and forth. Eggs, cheese, radish tops. The tourmaline dregs of a bottle of rosé. My eyes flashed at the clock.

In the same way that the residency had seemed in a future that would stay there, his return date felt impossibly far too. I'd stumble towards it like a kid learning to walk to a parent, the parent ever edging back.

I didn't want to bother Flo. Or I wanted to, but couldn't. Her PhD deadline was creeping up.

The last time I'd gone to her house, her shoulders had looked like picked bones, and I'd told her she had to eat. I sent her a cheese delivery after that. Cookies another time. I'd send her motivating emojis. I'd ask her word counts, and when she'd reply, I'd machine-gun more flowers or faces or random items that were all one colour and amassed, like a lost game of Tetris. Another closeness had dissolved.

As if detecting an absence that needed to be filled, a message from Luisa. It said *'boss'*. I pushed my phone away.

There was an image I'd seen somewhere, of a blanket held up, immaculately woven but full of holes. I had seen it and thought *that is my life.*

When I reached for my phone again, she had sent nothing more. It would be easy not to reply.

I pulled out the stopper of the rosé to see if it was still good.

What, I wrote back.

Come see me?

Why

How do you unpick it, the things we are told are attractive, and so come to be, and the things that actually are? Why would it be thigh-high socks? Two of her fingers slipped under the band.

I started to feel the organs in my chest working a little bit harder than they should. My heart, my lungs.

I can't, I said.

I'm sure, she wrote back.

You want me in private?

or you want me out?

2

I tried to remember things I'd done as a teenager to make the time pass. I could just sleep.

Through security

A text from Ed.

Good time.

In good time? Or he was having good time? I put my phone on silent.

When I woke, or perhaps before I'd fully woken up, some in-between space, I imagined Ed on the plane. I thought about how, the one time we'd flown together, he folded the aluminium top of a plane meal. How he'd warmed up my patty of butter, making a quick grill of his palms, because his had pulled apart his bread. I thought of how he would read as he cooked, a book to the side of the hob, instead of watching something. I thought of the veins in his hands, standing to attention.

I lifted myself out of bed, and something else lifted inside me too. This break. Ed being away for a while. If I did things right, if I did everything right, it could be a new start. If I could keep Teddy happy and the short seller at bay. If I could pull off the hearts and minds thing and get the public and the team back on side. If Gigr could go public in May, and do it well, and I could finally get some money ... It could be a new start. No, would. It would be a new start. It had to be.

And so that was why I would see Luisa. To tell her it was over. To tell her I'd had a breakdown. We could go for coffee, maybe. Just coffee, normal coffee, nothing more. That would set a new tone. I felt hope. The second wind that comes from a second chance. It filled a sail in my chest.

3

The coffee shop was incredibly loud, as if they'd put boom mics around all the mechanics of the machines. The clangs, the hisses.

Hope had shifted into my stomach feeling at sea. The coffee they were brewing that day was called Black Death. Why did people want things like that? I kept my eye on the door, but Luisa must have slipped in, or been a ghost to start with, because she appeared behind me, and said boo into my ear.

'Hi,' I said. Were my hands shaking? I pushed my fingers into the side of my neck. 'How ya doing?'

'Ya?' she said. 'Like *Hey Ya*?'

'Sorry. How are you?'

She was wearing a silk skirt, thin, just below knee-length, but with a front of leg split to the just-too-high on the thigh. She pushed her hair behind her ear and it immediately came free again. She reached over and took a sip of my coffee.

'Watch out,' I said, 'it's the plague.'

'Well, let's not let that stop us,' she said. 'A real life Saturday,' she said, 'hot,' and she rose up out of her chair to kiss me.

'Stop,' I said. Which wasn't the word I meant to start with, but it

361

came again, and too soon. 'I can't do this. It has to stop. Just ... stop.'
I was shaking my head.

'Me, stop? You're the one who—'

'No—'

'You asked me here.'

'I am saying *I* have to stop. This has to. But I have to. It's all got—'
My hands were definitely shaking. I accidentally looked at them a
second too long.

'A nice little case of delirium tremens?' she said.

'Please stop,' I said again. At least I said please this time. 'I think
you're – I do think you're amazing.'

'So amazing you made me come to the worst café in Soho to make
me feel like shit.'

'It's not you—'

Eyes don't really roll. They just show you they hate you. 'Well spare
me that. And stop looking over my head. No one's going to see.'

'I'm not looking over your head.'

'See. Your impeccable management skills.' She sucked her finger as
if a cuticle was bleeding.

'I'm sorry.' The coffee did taste – not like death, but of decomposi-
tion. 'My mum is ill.'

'So sorry to hear that. Do you need to go and fuck her instead?'

'Lu—'

'I know she's ill. You've told me before.'

When had I told her?

'It's just. That stuff.' She moved her hands as if that stuff was a
box she was holding, all our stuff. 'It's fun. It's fun and hot and feels
good, until someone just ... Are you just going to bail? 'Cos then it
just feels—'

'It was hot and fun. It was so hot and fun. You're amazing.'

'Stop saying I'm amazing.'

362

'But you are.' I shouldn't but I did: 'Star employee,' I said.

She laughed then, and I saw there were also tears in her eyes. 'Yeah,' she nodded. I could see it, the sway, hard then soft. 'You'll regret it.'

We were laughing, then we weren't. She saw the fear on my face. An undignified fear. An undignified question too: 'Regret it how?' I said.

'Nice. Classy.' She nodded in a way that said *obviously*. 'Scared I'll go to the boss.'

'That's not what I meant.'

'Do you want me to sign a napkin? "Your secret is safe with me"?'

'It's not my secret,' I said. 'Our secret.'

'Oh fuck off. It's your secret.'

'I'm not – like … some …'

'Gross guy in a bad suit? I bet they have fucking expensive suits. Good suits. You're …' she shook her head. 'It's even worse for you to say that.'

'Can I get you anything?' I asked her. My Black Death, with its collapsed foam. The empty space in front of her.

'That's a good idea,' she said. 'I'll get a three-course meal, shall I? Let's really settle in.' She looked at me.

'You could have takeaway something?' I said. I felt empty too. Like everything I had had been poured.

'You think you're strong,' she said. 'Strong to do this. But I know you. You just pretend. You're weak.' She put a hand on the table and stood up. 'And I know you,' she said. 'You'll call me.'

~

In New York, it had snowed. Ridiculous, miraculous, that somewhere so dirty could look so clean. If Paris made postcards of itself, New York was like watching a TV that was flicking between ten shows at once. Ten decades too.

In a restaurant, when they had first talked about the city – not last night, or the nights before it, because by then it had started to go so badly wrong – Elle had told Ed that the first time she went to New York, it was as an adult, and she had been disturbed by the jump between recognition and not knowing anything.

'It's, like, Broadway!' she'd said. 'How can you not know where you are on Broadway? You know you're on Broadway. It's Broadway!' It was at the start of things and she'd been a different person, or at least he'd seen one.

'It's a long street,' he'd said.

'I looked demented that whole trip.'

'How old were you? Twenty-four?'

He was intrigued by her young. Hats? Shyness? Anger?

'The whole time I was there,' she said, 'I was applying dark purple glittery eyeshadow to my eyebrows. I thought it was brown, then I saw the photos. I looked like Boy George, and not in a good way.'

'Is there a good way?'

'Are you kidding? He shaped his own face with black paint.'

'Did you like it? Do you like it? New York, I mean.'

Him in New York, but with her. He conjugates it. A different life. It would be Brooklyn, he guesses. He imagines a one-bed, not a studio, a dog. A dog! He likes it. He feels sick.

Snow has tippex-ed all the window ledges and the topsides of trees. As he walks, he says his New York words. Bodega. Stoop. Alternate side parking. Nutcracker. Looks at signs that say: *Buckle up in the Apple. It's the law!* Looks into traffic-stopped cars to see a copse of Little Trees air conditioners – all pink – and a diamanté-covered steering wheel. Gets used again to how far back his head has to tip to see the tops of buildings.

He notices people smiling. Or, he notices the people that are smiling. He is glad to be away. It is a club to be happy.

'What's your plan there?' she'd asked him, the night before he left, those days where the weight had caught up with them.

'Rollerblading in Central Park. Lycra. I don't know. Like I said, see friends, art.'

She'd nodded. 'Will you see old boyfriends?' He'd watched her face, the quiet force of trying to say it neutrally.

'What do you think the lycra is for?' he tried. 'I might. I mean I hope. If that's okay.'

'I hope you're not bad at blading. That would be very embarrassing.'

If he had come earlier, before the new distance, before the fight, the fights, he could have felt safe. Max, for example, who had often been so dangerous, who he's meeting now for lunch, would have been destung. His silver rings. The way they made these bars of light across his hands. The back of his neck. The fold in his septum. Other flashes too: the way his cock could look like a forearm turned up to the sun, the soft, close way his body emanated heat in the early morning. Yes, before the fight, it would have been easier.

Max is late. Max takes Ed's head in his hands from behind to say hi. Max is half builder today – he's wearing electrician's trousers, a sleeve for screwdrivers at the front, like a sporran.

'Not a bun, Ed,' Max says about Ed's hair. 'Impossible to keep my hands off that thing.' He squeezes an imaginary ball. 'Hello,' he says then, 'it's been a long time.'

The waiter comes, barely a second after he sits down.

'I'll do a soda water,' Max says.

'Do what to it?' Ed replies.

'Don't worry – I'm still fun.' The space Max takes up, legs wide.

They'd only slept together twice, maybe three times. A single summer. But a strong, gentle thing they both knew could have gone somewhere. Reading in the morning, back-to-back, the same book, and Max's hand reaching over to touch Ed's temples. Max's head, heavy as a bowling ball, in Ed's lap while he took a nap, his muscles off-guard, kid-like, as he slept.

'Maybe later,' Max points to Ed's beer. 'Special occasion.'

'You're fucking enormous,' Ed says. 'Have you moved into the gym?'

'Times are tough this side of thirty-five! But layers too. Got a kind of onion thing going on.'

'Very Carol Ann Duffy,' Ed says.

Max squeezes the lemon slice into his water. 'Speaking of writers, I liked the book.'

'You don't have to say that.'

'No, I did!' It's easier, at first, to keep it surface level. 'There are pages that are a little sticky.'

'Fuck off—'

'Are you writing another? Asking for a friend.' Max looks down at his hand, then laughs.

'Seriously, not you too. It's not like that—'

Max looks at Ed properly then. 'I know. I thought it was beautiful. I read it twice if you must know. It meant a lot to me.' He pauses. 'Remember that book we were both reading that summer?'

Ed remembers. Max had read pages to him, he'd read pages back to Max. Ed remembers the way Max licked a finger to turn the page, like a preacher, a teacher. He remembers Max's glasses.

'Your book knocked that off the top spot,' Max says. 'Really. So, for a serious reader, another?'

'I've been struggling,' Ed says.

'I bet you're having to do a lot of research.' Max looks at him. 'No? Oh, come on. Terrible time to have a boyfriend.'

The choice – the choice not to say it – is a door that feels golden.

'Not a boyfriend, no. It's been funny—' He stops. Why is it, he thinks, so painful to have changed? 'A girl actually. A woman.'

Max laughs. Then: 'Oh shit, you're serious. No way—'

'I'm serious.'

'Fuck.' He's tipping back on his chair, a seesaw away from Ed. 'I just wouldn't have ... guessed.'

'Don't, like, *press* at that.'

He's chewing on the lemon rind now. 'How's that then?'

'Don't say it like "well that's a country I don't want to go to".'

'Stop telling me how I'm allowed to say things.'

Max does get a beer in the end. 'Taking the news hard,' he says, affecting a vibrating hand, but Ed can also see a sadness.

'You can take it easy,' Ed says. 'I think it's ending.' Even said in the most fleeting way, it knocks Ed sideways. A heavy pendulum, another hit on the way back. 'But not because of that. Not just that. Because it's got all fucked up.'

He talks about her. The way her mind felt acrobatic to him, or that it moved in these ways that made sense to him. How it felt so much less strange, and also more strange, than he ever could have guessed.

The little shocks of joy they gave him, the tiny noises she made in the night. And then, in a different direction, the sounds she would make when she had nightmares. Something animal, somewhere outside of normal octaves. And how, when it came, it would take him with both hands.

He never says her name. Privacy maybe, or no – he feels like it would summon her.

'So you're a straight-up straight white man now,' Max says. 'Putting the Ed in edgy.'

'The enemy,' Ed says. 'Yeah, she hates me.'

Another beer. Accompanied by a pickleback, mostly as a joke, the red freckles in the brine sticking in Ed's throat.

'It is weird to fall in a love that is not what you want,' he says. The sentence feels awkward, oddly archaic, but after all this time, it's still the only way it makes sense to say it.

~

4

I didn't call Luisa. I managed not to call her. Whenever I wasn't at work, I refreshed the internet until time passed. I forwarded articles I hadn't finished yet to Flo, who surely didn't finish them either. I went to a class at a gym near work that made me feel like my lungs had been scrubbed with sandpaper.

The days ticked down to the IPO. Luisa's eyes stayed locked on her laptop. She was rude in the way she'd always been rude, just with less of a punchline. She meandered less. She arrived late and left early.

It must have been a Tuesday, because we were just finishing our team meeting when Daniel pushed through the crowd. My team had grown again and the room was groaning. There were people in the doorway. He waited until most of them had left.

'It's fucking close to the line now,' he said. 'Do we have it locked down with our friends in high places? Low places.'

'Yeah, we rolled the contact's survey out a couple of weeks ago.' Daniel loved it when I called Teddy 'the contact'. 'And Jason is working on the bigger collaboration too. And then we're going to work out a road map for going forward.'

'The Short Selling Regulation though? Properly done and dusted?

I want Marshall eaten alive like one of those Andes plane crash people—'

'Underway,' I said.

'*Cannibalism*—' he specified.

There was a rap on the glass.

'Hey yo,' a guy from the design team, who had adopted elements of a Californian accent, stood in the door. 'Oh sorry,' he said, when he saw Daniel. 'Just you,' he said this to me. 'You left your phone on the coffee thing and it's going crazy.' He handed it to me.

Then, like a papyrus scroll unfurling, all these missed calls poured, a waterfall, unstoppable, down my screen. Missed Call: Mum, Missed Call: Mum, Missed Call: Mum, Missed Call: Mum, Missed Call: Mum, Missed Call: Mum, Missed Call: Mum, Missed Call: Mum, Missed Call: Mum, Missed Call: Mum, Missed Call: Mum. It went on and on. There must have been twenty, thirty.

'Sorry, I have to – sorry,' I said. I pushed out of my office and went to the boardroom, empty, always empty, since no one ever wanted to book it.

The horror then. The edges gone off everything.

It wasn't the worst of the worst things. But still, this is what horror feels like. Nothing is solid anymore. You can pass through tables. There are no doors or windows. You have no skin or bones. There is no wood under your feet, no earth. There is nothing.

When I think of the call, how quickly she picked up when I finally managed to make myself press the button, when I think of how her voice was, no breath in it and how it pierced me still, it's horror again, it's Dad, it's Dad, she said, horror everywhere, it comes back. All sides go, all floors, all ceilings, nothing to lean on, everything to lose, it's Dad.

5

I went straight to the hospital where they were. He was not dead, though I kept saying 'is he okay', and she kept saying 'I don't know', and both of us were saying it so fast that we were basically saying it at the same time.

When I got there, I saw her at the end of an impossibly long corridor. She looked folded, melted, small as a parcel in the corner of the waiting room.

'I thought I'd be calmer,' she said, after I'd hugged her, my arms feeling like I was caging a bird whose wings were beating, 'but it's the thought of everything. Everything going.'

He had been waiting for the bus, she told me, and he dropped to one knee, his hand on the red seat. It was almost religious-looking, like he was praying, the person who helped him said. There in the bed his tongue sat differently. Not that he spoke. His eyes were a light blue that looked like the end of something. I looked at him and I was an infant again. I fit on his forearm.

'He's in the safest place he could be after a stroke,' a nurse said, nicely, but she was standing in front of a sign on the wall about hospital-acquired meningitis. 'What we prescribe to families,' she said, 'is sleep.'

'I'll come,' I said to my mum, when they told us visiting hours were over. 'I'll come home with you.' I tried to take her hand but it was slack.

'I can't risk it,' she said. I looked at her, but she was looking at the band of her watch. 'Risk being upset.'

'Mum . . .'

'Just sometimes you don't help.'

'Okay,' I said, 'okay.' All I could do was nod.

Out front of the hospital, waiting for a car, she said, 'I hope Ed can look after you. He knows?' She looked down the street like he might suddenly appear.

'Will you be alright?' I asked her.

'What choice is there?'

There on the street, after I'd opened the door for her, I was so conscious of the way she had to bend her body to get in, that I couldn't move my thumbs in the right way to tell him. He'd arrived at the residency in Vermont ten days or so before. A few hours earlier, he'd sent me some photos of the first open studio night, and just one line of text: *second to last is made of DOG HAIR, can you believe it?*

Images sprinted into my head, a horrible mix. I tipped my head away, but they were too quick for me to dodge them. And that was when I got a message from Luisa, the first in weeks.

Sorry but

Tell me this isn't us

She sent the link to an article too: *THAT'S RICH! AS SHORTAGES LOOM, WHILE YOU CUT BACK, IMMIGRANTS AND 'POOREST' SUPERCHARGE CONSUMPTION, SURVEY FINDS*

I clicked on the link. I scanned it once, twice. The first section was about old, gas-guzzling cars causing a new London smog, the next was about meat consumption and number of offspring, under a subhead that read 'Over-Feeders & Over-Breeders'. There were graphs, pie charts, and I recognised the percentages, and the questions they had come from. Number for number, it was all the data we'd collected with Teddy's lifestyle survey.

'You're disgusting,' I said out loud, but it wasn't even about Teddy, it was about me. A man in a suit pulled an AirPod out of his ear and said, in a very friendly way, 'Sorry, what?'

I saw a bar. Lamps like small moons in a row above table seats. I went inside.

Outside the rain turned the last of the late afternoon dark. It felt better to have the outside match the inside. I got a drink. I got drinks. I read the article again, saw how many times it had been shared. I looked at the one picture I'd taken of my dad in the hospital and not even him, just his hand. I thought of Luisa. I thought of Ed. You're an idiot, I thought again, for the millionth time. Of course that was what you were supposed to do. That was the race or the plan or whatever it was, that was the whole point of all of it. To find someone else to park your love with before your parents died. How had I kept doing everything so wrong?

Every time I got a drink, I got a different one. I thought of a sailor changing tack. Trying to catch wind. Instead I caught an eye. A man, not tall, not short, just every way normal, walked past once, then another time. Picpoul now. Pick pool. My brain kept folding things up.

He came in, then disappeared to get his own drink. He didn't talk to me at first. Just watched the rain too. 'Saw you were alone,' he said eventually.

'That's a terrifying opener,' I said back. But there was something gentle about his eyes, or his voice more, because I hadn't seen his eyes yet.

'Like me,' he said. 'I'm alone. That's all I'm saying.'

'I'm a lesbian.' Muscle memory in situations like this; my mouth just did it.

'Ellesbia. That's a nice name. Is that Italian?' A half-laugh at his own joke. 'That's alright. Doesn't bother me. It's cool even. I rate that.'

'What do you rate it out of ten?'

'Eleven.' He lightly bounced his pint against the wood of the windowsill. 'You're not happy.'

'Yeah. Bad day.' I told him I was leaving anyway.

He nodded. 'Pissing it down though. What's wrong with pissing it up?'

His jacket, sopping, was hanging up behind him. He was wearing contact lenses, and later, when I looked closely, I noticed the slight mismatch with the edge of his pupils. 'You want another? Personally, I'm in—' he put on an Irish accent for this part, '—recovery. But I'm taking a little break. A holiday. Uneventful so far.' He lifted a lip: a broken tooth. 'Charming,' he said. 'If you're into Dickens.' He looked at me. 'Go on,' he said, pointing at my drink. My drinks. The unpicked-up glasses, all different shapes, in front of me.

'It's alright,' I said.

''Cos, personally,' he said. 'I was thinking of topping myself after this. Genuinely. Yeah, no I know. Big news. Oh what no!' he laughed. 'Did I darken the ambiance? So it would be nice if you did. Want a drink. It's tradition to flash a bit of cash beforehand.'

I asked if he was joking.

'Not my *best* if it's a joke. Definitely told better. Just one beer. Actually, no – you know when you get married? You ever been married?'

Funny that it was no longer a weird question. And how quickly it had changed. To feel far too young to have been married, have children, and then suddenly too old for it not to have happened.

'People just get – *nice*,' he said. 'A kind of one-day-only thing, but people just get nice to you. Don't know how to explain it, just, yeah, well I've said it a million times now: nice.'

'Have you been married? Are you?'

'Easy, girl. Yeah, course. Most people do it at some point. But I was thinking, this could be like that. It could be special, right? Would you give me that? 'Cos one drink . . . it's a bit sad. A bit nothing. But three! Feels good. We could talk a bit. You might start to look a bit more relaxed. 'Cos – tell you what – I don't want to spend my last hours with someone depressed.'

It was hard to read. He could have had one beer. He could have had a thousand. 'I was that close,' he said when he came back. 'Fuck, this is good.' He sucked a long sip of his pint. 'I had my foot right over the ledge. Thought about it before but never that close. On the District line as well. So dirty! Embarrassing,' he said.

How do you play it? Does taking it seriously make it more serious? 'Why didn't you?' I said. 'I mean, I'm glad you didn't—'

'The emotion!' He laughed. 'I drop the big old s-bomb and you're molten lava. I do think the dirt came into it. Both trains. They were both so dirty. I kept thinking about the mix of it. Cheers again.'

'Cheers.'

'And I don't know. It's like – life's tough at the moment. It's dominoes. But it's made it a bit of a cliché, see. A bit *obvious*. And also it's what they want. Scrapping every bit of help that makes it possible. Get rid of muck like me.'

'Are you okay now?'

'Sure, yeah. Totally cured!'

'Do you want me to call someone for you? I can do that.'

'Call who?'

'I don't know, a service?'

'What service?' He laughed. 'Where do you think we are? I just want a nice moment. Relaxed. That's all. Just one. You also look like you could do with a time out.'

I told him my dad was ill. That I'd been at the hospital.

'Did you do that fast-track "see you faster if you fucking pay" thing? Fucking joke.'

'I love my dad,' I said, as if that answered the question.

'So for once, I'm glad it's alright for the well to do like you—'

'I'm not well to do. Really not.'

'Let me guess, your grandparents built the railways . . .'

'Well they did—'

'You know how to *fit in*, though. You're flexi with it.' His hand moved like a flame was coming out of his mouth. 'Whereas I'm stuck in the mud.'

'Everyone's stuck,' I said.

'Yeah but different mud. I was in construction,' he nodded. 'You know how tough that is?' He cracked his neck, and I heard two pops. 'Do you know how much it costs your body? The weight of it. The chemicals. A whole fucking dustbowl in your lungs. And in heat like this? Like it was last year? You watch this monster go up, and you feel yourself shrink. It's life-force,' he said. 'And you give it away for basically nothing.'

I thought about what my dad had said about my mum: she's disappearing. I thought about the work they had done their whole lives. I thought about my dad in the hospital bed and I sank again, a plane hitting an air pocket. There were other drinks. He got them, I got them.

'You alright with it?' he said. 'Being – what's the *correct way* to say it – liking girls, or whatever?'

'Yeah, course.' I shrugged, nodded, somewhere in between the two.

'Well you're young, but not that young. Some people must have been divs. And the divs are back, big time,' he said. 'And in *London*, no less. All those gay lads being beat up.'

I looked at his glass again. How many had he had by then? I wanted another drink, while his was still half full. Was I worse than him? I wanted to see the edge appear that made him different to me. Where was it?

But there was still a finger, or two, left in his glass when he said it was lovely to meet me, but that he was going to head. I asked where he was going.

'Into the night. It's not for you.'

I thought of what Luisa had said. Where the nights happen. 'Are you going to be okay though? Because of—'

Concern? Be honest: it wasn't concern. A long obsession, what it would be like to have a wild life.

'Kid, I'm good.'

'I think we're the same age,' I said.

He pulled a drink out of his bag, 'A little stomach liner,' he said. 'I lost my job for this – but fuck 'em, I'd already lost it.' He saw me looking at the bottle.

'Bet you use it for taxis,' he said. 'My old ganger flipped us onto that shit. Same work, my pay went down by fifty percent.' He did a thumbs up. 'Did my back in, and got sweet fuck all.'

The bottle said in block letters on the side: 'PROPERTY OF GIGR: OFF-SITE CONSUMPTION PROHIBITED.'

For a while by then, I would have dreams that I was on a bike and crashing. My face would hit the pavement, sometimes more than once, and my teeth would crack. I read the bottle and I felt like I was in one of those.

We were on the street by then. We'd had more shots at the bar. It was already blurry. That's the last thing I remember. I don't know when I sent it, but in the morning I found a message to Teddy with a link to the article saying *What the fuck?*

6

When I woke up, there was a shoulder in front of me. My eyes started to focus. Dark pillows. My pillows were not that colour. A spoon started to stir the base of my stomach. But then it came back, bit by bit, the rest of the night, these soft chapters, growing, shrinking. Mostly shrinking.

The room came into focus. I had been here before. Only once. I felt someone shift on the bed behind me.

'You made it through the night,' Luisa said. 'Overkill maybe, but I did set my alarm at some random times to check. Never ideal, is it? Waking up in the morning to someone dead next to you.'

I felt her hand on my neck, play-acting looking for a pulse to check. I did feel dead. I felt a sadness that was razor sharp and broadly thudding.

'The guy who brought you here—' she said.

The thudding sped up. I sat up and my head was in a vice. 'Was he – how was—' I was going to turn to her but I couldn't face it. 'Was he okay?'

'Well he had roughly one tooth. Definitely a wrong 'un in the conventional sense, but he was lovely. Kind to you. Sweet with me. Called me your missus.'

I shut my eyes again and imagined her face. How young she was. The stretched-aheadness of that. How could it be a good thing to be paired with me? Had I been sick? What had I said? I thought then of my dad.

'My dad,' I said. 'He had a stroke and then I just—'

'Wanted to walk off the earth? Not even walk. Skyrocket.' I could tell her laugh was only to try and make me feel less bad. 'Is your dad okay?'

'I want to go home,' I said. I could barely get the word out. When I said home I wasn't thinking of my own home, I was thinking of somewhere long ago, somewhere safe, a drawing, a film, a sensation of being warm, childhood. She put her hand on my back, then tried to turn me towards her.

'There's something there,' she said. At first I thought she meant something on my body, but, 'Here, I mean. This. Beyond both being as bad as each other. Don't you think? Us in this dumb bed.'

It came into my head, what Ed had said the first night he moved in: *Us in bed. Way more pretend.* It was so quiet in her room I heard a bird outside.

'You don't give yourself a chance to like me,' she went on, the thing she had said before. 'You want it to be simple. A cut in half thing. But I think—'

I turned to her. 'I know I got things wrong. You're right to say I was wrong. But I—' This tiny movement in her face – hope. 'It's not an excuse. But it's my dad. It's so many things. I need to stop. It has to stop.'

It wasn't just tears in my eyes, I was crying. And that's when the hammering on the door – the hammering on the door, and the pounding of the doorbell, and the shouting, sounds that all in one filled the bedroom – started.

'Fuck,' Luisa said. Her hand left my body. She sat up. Soft to stiff. 'Just ignore it. Just ignore it and they'll go away.'

What had happened last night? What had I done?

'What? Who?' I said. 'They're going to break the door down—'

'Don't shout—' She reached her hand to cover my mouth.

'What the fuck, Lu?'

'I told you, shut up.'

'The police.' I scrambled for my phone, but it was dead. I reached for hers, the other square of black on the bed. As I pressed the second nine, she snatched it back.

'I said no.' All softness was gone. The high fist on the door had changed to a low kick. 'It's okay. The door is good,' she said, to herself more than anything. Then: 'They're not allowed to break the locks.'

'What do you mean "allowed"?'

'They've just got to try. And they'll go.'

'Who the fuck are *they*?'

'Stop fucking shouting,' she said.

But it wasn't me who was shouting, it was them. 'There's nowhere you can run, you little cunt,' the voice at the door said. 'We'll be back in an hour.' And then the slam, a final kick and the unmistakable catapult flick of the same mouth spitting onto the door.

I was still sitting on the bed. She was standing. How shallowly we were breathing made our bodies move.

'See? It's okay,' she said finally, moving her hands like she was settling a duvet. 'That wasn't too bad.'

'Are you joking? Can you just give me your phone and let me call the police?'

She looked at me, eyes stone. 'Why? What's it got to do with the police?'

'Some fucking giant was just threatening to kick your door down and he said he's coming back. That's what it's got to do with—' The splitting pain in my head.

'So? They have a right to come. I do owe them money. I do. So I just need to sort it. It's on me to sort it. And I can. I always have.'

'Fuck,' I said.

'Don't look at me like that. You know. You've come with me. You've seen it.'

'I didn't know.'

'How did you not know? Do you think it's an after-school club?' She was shaking her head.

'No—' I started.

'If you couldn't understand it might be a *little* complicated, then it's wilful blindness.'

'How much do you owe them?' I said.

'What's this low-down disappointed adult voice? Just speak normally.'

'Fine,' I said, louder now. 'How much do you owe them?'

'Don't say it like that either. How dare you – don't judge me. When you ... when you ...' She let me see it then. All of it in her eyes, like her pupils were mirrors. It bounced off her into me: look at yourself. 'And what was it you were saying before? It has to stop. You wanted to leave. So just go.'

'I'm not going to leave you like this. Back in an hour, they said. Fuck—'

'Unlikely. I'm hardly the only person on the list. It's just part of it. There's a structure. You don't understand.'

'I understand it's not a good situation. But if someone is battering your door down, you call the police.'

'What fucking world do you live in?' She banged her fingers onto her own head. 'Do you understand anything?'

She was breathing normally again now. And this new thing came over her. I watched it settle. Optimism, cool. It all felt madly misplaced. She went to a box on her dresser, and started counting some cash inside it. An actual money box. It seemed absurd to me. The pinned-up posters on her wall. How was I in this child's bedroom?

'How much do you need?' Again, without consulting my brain, my mouth just said it.

'I don't want your money.'

'Just tell me.'

'It sounds like a lot, but it's not real. When you play they're made-up numbers.'

I thought about how I'd always said it with Gigr. That same thing. It was toy money, made-up numbers. 'If I give you the money,' I said, 'then it's real. It's real to me even if it isn't real to you.'

'I don't want it.'

'Just take it,' I said.

I told her it could never happen again. I meant it both ways.

As I walked to the bank, I wondered if parts of my face had collapsed, particularly around the eyes. I moved my jaw, felt if one side felt different to the other. Maybe I was still drunk. There was a branch of my bank not far from her house, and by the stupid luck, whether good luck or bad luck, I still had my wallet.

I took the money for Luisa from the account where I was saving my house deposit. It was a special account designed for that, so when I asked to withdraw fifteen thousand of it, the man at the counter said 'congratulations!' He was incredibly thin and somehow his suit was still too tight.

I wondered for a short, dreadful second if they had a button they pressed and team members would come out of their offices with party poppers and do a dance. No one danced. 'Exciting!' he said again. 'Cash isn't typical, so just a few questions to check you aren't being scammed.'

I walked back to her flat trying to look normal, failing to, convinced that everyone who passed knew what was in my bag.

Just after I had given Luisa the money, and she had put it in a tote bag, the tote handles bound around it like that made it safer, Luisa's flatmate walked into the room, headphones on inside the house. 'Cool,' she said. 'How do you know Lu?' she asked me.

'We met on the street,' Luisa said.

In Vermont, Ed's colder than he's ever been. Whenever he comes in from outside, his jacket stays icy to the touch for at least ten minutes. In the cafeteria, which smells of tomato sauce kept at room temperature and hardening at the edges, it's all anyone can talk about. Not in an English way, but in the way that comes with the thrill of danger. Polar vortex, bomb cyclone, wind chill. Today at lunch, he'd sat with an incredibly tall Irish girl who'd put so much pasta on her plate she had to carry it with two hands.

The sensation of being in a film re-emerges, a sensation surely only a younger man should feel. In the cold, in America – he's laughing now – but he's developed a cowboy stance. Cowboy, caveman, iceman. At the same time light and heavy on his feet. He's taken to hooking his thumb into his belt loop.

They try to keep it mixed at the residency. Ten-odd writers and artists from each decade. Ten in their twenties, ten in their thirties, forties, fifties. His studio neighbour breathes through his mouth, and each time he bends over to reach for a dropped pen, the sound of the breathing pushes harder through the walls. He is thirty but looks older, the round Hockney glasses, the waistcoat which he puts on after meals and says is his corset. The kind of hair that picks up static, a mug of gin, no ice, by his laptop after lunch, but then his poems! Quiet, devastating, the comedy of him disappearing. He reads a poem about a boy he'd known at school, who hangs himself in the final lines, and there are tears running down Ed's face.

It is an extraordinary privilege to be brought together with people like this. He thinks of marbles knocking into each other, the fresh clean shock of the hit, and how in any other world these marbles would never meet.

Everyone is surprising. He knew this but it's easy to forget it.

He thinks of the other big surprise of his life, alive now with worry.

What did – what does – he love about her? If anyone were to ask him, he would say it didn't feel like a choice. But that's not what people want to hear. People want exact ingredients.

When they first met, after he had left her house in the morning, and did not come back or call, he couldn't stop wondering what she would think of things. Not of him, not at first, but just things in the world. Things he saw, things he heard. Like everything went through two filters. What do I think, what would she think?

Why? That was the question that had burrowed into him when he first met her. He still doesn't know. But in many ways, it is as simple as: he saw her and, as he'd tried to tell Max, she made sense to him. It is as simple as: he wanted to tell her things. It is as simple as: he knew all of it touched her too even if she couldn't say it, or found ways to make it light. It is as simple as: he just did.

It had been madness, happiness like that. It felt like encountering a new species sometimes. Something James Cameron would make, *Avatar 4*. When he went down on her, he would see things. He'd shut his eyes and everything would kaleidoscope: the backs of butterfly wings? Or pyramids? Building blocks. Always symmetrical, dancing.

He thinks of her split open. That's not the right way to say it. But it's so strange it's all inside her. He'd said this once and knew it was ridiculous. 'Dear Diary, today I saw a vagina,' he'd said after that. But it is different. Like space, or being underwater. And how hard

388

she could get too, new edges, firm as the walls of a cardboard box. A tightening that picked him up off his seat.

How to understand then, the moment that had come however many months later, when it felt like she was starting to disappear and the question entered his mind: Do I feel anything? If I never saw you again, would I feel anything? Moments – short moments at first – where he can't summon anything.

It feels like ice around his torso. Move and he'll crack it. But when he moves, it clings.

Surely it's just the fear of the thing happening, he tells himself at first. That it could. Contemplation. It had plagued him since he was a kid, until he realised your brain is designed to deliver images that shock you. It doesn't mean they're real. It doesn't mean you want them to happen. Just because he's contemplated not loving her, it doesn't necessarily mean it's true.

He'd never cared too much for alcohol, but more than before, before he left for America, it helped. It was easier to pick himself up when he wasn't as close to the floor. Think of a coin. His book; Elle. And what it would mean if either of them – both of them – failed.

Now in Vermont, he can't work out if he's in the best place to be, or the worst. All of possibility is here. And yet, in the face of it, a frown has set in. Not old frowns, ones he'd wanted to have, because he wanted to show that thinking was happening. The 'stress' of his twenties now feels ridiculous. He hadn't realised how much he'd wanted the stress then. As if it meant purpose. As if it meant weight. Confusion too – it had felt fun to unpick. To bring to a dinner with a friend, to set out on a table.

But now it was real. And it wasn't the made-up lines he'd imagined – boys or girls, New York or London, what he'd do, who he'd be, who he'd become, all those choices. It was as small as a single person. As big as a single person.

The moment that comes in everyone's life – is this going to be the person I choose? Is this the life I choose?

Because you take it seriously, he tells himself. *Because you take it seriously.*

But it's unbearable. How does anyone do it?

They don't think, he tells himself, *they don't think.*

With Elle, it wasn't like anything else on earth with anyone else on earth. Maybe that was part of it, but only a tiny part of it, these words that would come to him. That it was a grand love, a big love, something epic, something once in a lifetime. He knows himself: of course he's sensitive to words like that. But it wasn't just the story of it all. It was her voice, her hands. The way he saw her work out things to say she'd never told anyone before. The way she opened up before she closed. No, it wasn't just words. At first, it was like the concept of light itself had changed.

He thinks and thinks. A constant back-and-forth battle in his head. And there she always is. It's like someone hammering on a piano, pleasurable, but in a repeated chord, far too many notes.

He looks at himself as if it were with her sharpest eyes. When he locks or unlocks a door. When he does up his fleece all the way. When he packs his rucksack, tightly ordered, comfort in the jigsaw of it. 'Army boy,' he hears her say.

~

7

When my phone came back to life, somewhere, at first hidden, between offers and reminders and promotional crap that would forever stack up bolded and unopened in my personal email, I had a long message from Ed.

I clicked. Saw the length. Clicked away. Clicked back. Again, I had the recurring sensation that it would be it – the end, a goodbye, my chest felt suddenly tight – but it wasn't. Instead, there was a gentle, reflective happiness floating off the page, which in some ways felt even worse.

Dear Elle, he wrote.

I'm supposed to be working but I keep watching this bright red cardinal. He's in this tree with bare branches, and he can fly directly skyward – vertical, straight up like a lift – and I keep thinking he's a flame. Some kind of burning bush thing. There are two of them, and now they're taking turns at spinning a bird feeder.

I wanted to write properly. I'm sorry it's late.

The email was long. It said something about a poet he'd met, and how tears had been closer than they had been in years, but not in a bad way. About the space he'd had to try and work things out. It ended like this: *In moments, I feel happy, and so I feel love, or whatever it is you and Flo always say. Anyway, I'm thinking of you.*

He was happy. He was working. He was happy. The shame I felt was almost worse than an ending.

I found myself walking straight to the room he used as his study. Was it that I wanted to feel close to him? I don't know. But I sat in his seat. There was a scab of something crusty on my suit trousers, the trousers I'd worn yesterday for a full day of work, and then to the hospital. The trousers I'd worn to the bar, the trousers Luisa must have taken off for me. I tried to scratch whatever it was off. I tried to focus. His notes. His pens in their neat row made me think of a suspension bridge. I ran my fingers over them like steps.

There were pins holding pictures – one of Ed as a kid, a window between his front teeth, matchstick arms and a concave chest – and handwritten sentences on a corkboard. 'If in doubt, CUT.' 'Make it like a FILM.' Also a note, in his own writing, which said 'I hate you, Ed.'

His handwriting looked totally illegible from far away, but up close it was easy to read. There were held dots, where the ink had run, that felt like watching him think.

I sat down at the desk, and my shoe hit something. I thought at first it was a footrest, something ergonomic – his back always ached – but then my foot slid. Loose-leaf paper, a stack of it. His manuscript.

I told myself I would read one page. Just one at random. I wanted to feel close to him. It had all started to feel a little invented. 'I miss you's sent because that was what was said, not because we felt it. I reached forward and picked up a pile.

Leonard. Interesting. That was the character's name. This one's anyway. Ed hadn't told me anything about the book, but I found myself smiling. The narrative voice was different to what I'd read before – third person, and what time period were we in?

Leonard stood on weathered steps of the city bus, his hand gripping the overhead railing as the vehicle jolted forward.

I flicked forward a few pages, and the tone changed, so did the tense. I flicked back to check. The new section seemed to be in the present day. Someone called Leo now. He was looking at a man's back in utmost detail – the dips and divots he'd expect, and then new ones that appear when the man moves. Ed's handwriting was all over the text – a thin biro now, changing from blue to red to black.

Push it harder, he'd written, harder underlined. He'd changed the press to slam. *Pleasure must come through!* He'd circled that.

My eyes ran down the page. There were three men, maybe, no, four. Because it's a different man most of them are fucking and he's on his knees now. *Free now, but also freedom as trap?* Ed had written. Then he'd crossed out his own note and written: *This doesn't even make sense. Tone down. Shock factor shit.*

I skipped forward again, a hop, skip and jump.

Now we were with Leonard again. Leonard, Leo. Okay. I started to get it.

Leonard's on St James's Square on a cold day. He's wearing a red scarf and the wind blows the scarf into his mouth – it catches as his teeth chatter. Undeterred by the chill, he has a sandwich packed – corned beef on white bread – which he'll enjoy on a bench.

Another man walks past Leonard, unhurried. I'm paraphrasing, all this is paraphrasing, but it's something about how the man reaches the closest corner of the park, then circles back. Why? Leonard thinks. Surely there were other benches that were free on a day like today. Leonard rearranges his body closer to the armrest of the bench, and tries to focus on his sandwich – the pink of the beef, the yellow flash of the piccalilli, the safety of the bread – when the man says hello. Eyelashes with a splash of white that make Leonard think of moonlight.

Get ready, I said to myself.

But then Leonard goes home. And this is where we meet Vivian.

Need to make clear she's not bad, Ed had written in his biro.

I read on. It wasn't just one thing. There were so many things. How the softness of her body reminds Leonard of fruit. How he imagines his hand sinking through, like skin breaking on a peach.

Leonard steels himself and they have sex. He is grateful – again, all this is paraphrasing – that she hasn't had sex with other men so doesn't recognise his softening penis. And how it all blurs together, the man in the park, the redness of his scarf, and how he gets hard again, a miracle, thinking of him.

On the margins Ed's biro scrawl: *Next scene should redeem her. She's nice / fine, he just can't make himself feel anything?*

Back in the text itself, Leonard rests his head on Vivian's body – a sweetness, but wrong, daffodils left too long in water.

In my house. I kept on thinking: you wrote this in my house.

Sobriety crashed over me.

Sobriety. I had just given Luisa £15,000.

Sobriety. It wasn't my worst fears that had come true, because I hadn't known how low to go.

Sobriety. My father was slack in a hospital bed, unable to speak or move, and I had drunk enough to die before him.

Sentences from the scene kept knocking into me as I made my way downstairs. Ed's comments on the side. *Breathes through his mouth?*

My phone was alight on the table.

I had six missed calls from Flo. I must have told her about my dad. But I looked at our messages and I hadn't said anything.

I tried to call back but no answer. I texted. I took a shower – let the soap on my hands check for bruises, cuts, things that would tell me something I didn't want to know – then, finally, after two more calls, a reply.

Will you come over

8

When I got there, Flo's house was spotless. When I hugged her at the door, I could smell lemon, and I was about to say 'all this for me?', when I could hear something, and I didn't understand at first, but then I could feel her moving and it must have been tears that were shaking her body. 'Hey,' I said, 'are you okay?' I also thought: *why now*.

The movement stopped. It started again. It stopped. 'I'm fine,' she said. 'I'm okay.' She pushed away from me.

I peered behind her into the kitchen. 'It's like . . . gleaming in there. Did you kill someone?'

'Please don't. I shouldn't have asked you to come.'

'Wait. *Did* you kill someone?'

'No, course I didn't fucking kill anyone.' Tears in her eyes again. 'Stop being—'

'Me? I'm not being anything. And I need you not to be . . . like this. You have no idea what I've been through these past two days.'

And then she screamed. Or cried out. A sound I'd never heard her make before. She fell back onto the sofa, then was silent.

'Hey, look at me,' I said, 'why are you being like this?'

'Finish that sentence. Being like this *to you*. What about me?'

'I know the PhD is hard.'

'It's not any of that. You know you can ask questions?'

I was standing, she was sitting. All of it felt wrong. 'Look, my dad had a stroke, and I've been by his bedside constantly.' It felt like the truth when I said it. The self-righteousness felt like heat.

'Fuck, is he okay?' she said. 'I love your dad.'

'I think he'll be alright. And then Ed—'

'Please not Ed right now,' she said. 'I like Ed. He's fine.'

'His book . . .' How even to say it? 'I read some and it's basically about how disgusting I am.'

'Can you tell me another time?' she said. 'Things don't just happen to you.' She went somewhere else in her body.

'What?' I said. I reached for her.

'Nothing.'

'What?' I said again.

'Miles,' she said, 'he brought a friend over last night.'

'Miles is?'

'I don't know why I called him that. TP. I don't know why I called him that either.' She started looking around the sofa for something.

'He brought a friend over . . .' I repeated.

'They'd been drinking. But it was fun at first. I think it was. I've been working so hard, I haven't drunk more than maybe a beer in forever, and I hadn't seen him in ages. Anyway, they brought whisky. And sambuca or grappa, some clear shit they'd already opened. Like children. And weed. Also like children.'

My stomach started to feel hollow. 'Can you tell me what you're telling me?'

'I don't know,' she said. 'I don't even know. You want me to say something I don't know. But *I* don't know it—' She was touching her chest each time she said 'I'.

'Okay,' I said.

'They wanted to watch a film, and Miles kept on saying how fun I was, that the only place he had fun was with me. The friend fell asleep. And then I did. And then I woke up – it's just gross.' She wiped her eyes with the back of her arm. 'Miles was – I didn't want him to touch me with the friend right there, passed out. I told him to fuck off. He wouldn't and I pushed him and he hit me. I hit him back and then he hit me again and they sounded so different.'

She was young again. It all stripped back. But not even twenty, from when I first knew her. She was twelve. 'Please can I sit next to you?' I said.

'It wasn't what I wanted.'

I took her hand, and it was so hot, and I looked at her and I was so desperate to stroke her hair. Her tears, too, were such a different temperature that they left paths of red, like faint burns.

'Then suddenly, now I said no, he's saying I'd always been trying to trap him. That it was my plan all along. And how stupid I was—'

'You're not stupid. You're not stupid.' She let me come closer to her then, and I put my arms around her. 'You're going to report it? You have to report it.'

'I don't have *time*. I have no time. I don't have time for this even. To see you. Don't have time to be upset, let alone have a fucking row of his friends sit across from a table and – they'd find a way to make me fail—' She turned just as a fresh beam of light cut through the window, and as my eyes adjusted to the new light, I saw there was a bruise on her cheek. 'I need to finish my work,' she said.

I felt her bruise on my own body then, pain come to the surface. Ink spreading. Everything turning dark. She sat up, like the bones in her body worked again now she'd said it. 'Maybe Ed can shame him in the "literary community"' she said. 'Another way in which Miles is embarrassing. Claims he wrote a first novel that was "well received".'

'Flo—'

'I do have the power of Google. I know a vanity press when I see one. The publisher's name is his *own* fucking initials.'

I told her I'd help her with anything. I'd cook for her. I'd read her work for her. I'd stay with her. I'd take her to the doctor. I'd take her on holiday if she liked. I'd buy her clothes.

'What's wrong with my clothes?' she said.

'I just mean I'll do anything,' I told her. Our outlines on the sofa. The years between us. Our legs interlaced like the game children play with their hands. The fingers that make the church, that make the steeple, that make the people.

9

That TP had been so much worse could have made my feelings about Ed start to melt. Instead they melded.

I texted him as I turned the corner away from Flo's road.

Fucking fantastic book, Ed

Barely any wait:

Sorry what? he wrote back.

> *Did it add to the thrill*
> *to write it in my house?*

Are you going through my things?

> *Since you love a cliché,*
> *I'd leave your stuff in the road*
> *but I don't want to touch it.*

He called me and called me again, my phone squirming around like a dying bird on the table.

> *My dad nearly died and nothing*
> *But I found your shit writing and now*
> *you're terrified I'll burn it*

What? Your dad nearly died?

He tried to call another time, then sent a voice note. I thought of the other one, that had played through the speaker. In my memory, Ed kept saying my name, the way a teacher does, like saying it would bring me back to myself. *We're supposed to be in a relationship, Elle. Elle, pick up the phone.*

I went to the hospital. As I got there, I got a text from Ed saying *Please tell me what's happening. I'm changing my flight and coming back.* My mum gave me a tight hug, which may have meant sorry in some language. I didn't want her X-ray vision on me, so I kept my eyes locked on my dad's and said, 'how's the patient?' and other things that were safe. His mouth made the shapes of starting to speak but he couldn't get much further than that. He looked like he was tasting something. His lips were cracked and I went to the hospital shop to get Vaseline.

'It's like a third world country now,' my mum said when I came back.

'Mum—'

'No, not like that. Not because of . . .' She looked around. 'Just in lots of places all over the world, poorer places, the family is part of how the hospital works. They bring the food. Help the nurses change bedpans.'

When the woman who was next to my dad spoke to the nurse it was like her mouth was full of marbles. I looked at him. His body. A body. Any body like that.

My mum took pictures of the drip so she could tell him what medicines he'd had. A couple of beds away, someone with dementia or delirium was shouting, creating a chain reaction with the bed opposite.

He looked so calm. I thought about how you're only really allowed to look at people's faces – really stare at them without the other person looking away – when you're falling in love, or when someone is sleeping or dying. I kissed the back of his hand.

'I don't know what they do,' my mum said, 'the people who don't have anyone.' The way she said it suggested both her and me, in the future.

'It's not their fault,' I said quickly. 'Not the nurses'.' The cost of being overheard saying something critical. And they all looked so tired. I wondered what they were having to do outside of this; what they were doing for Gigr, for me.

'No one's saying it's their fault. Just the reality. Surreal,' she said, 'changing nappies just like you had. When we came in, the ambulance kept saying it was like Baghdad. But it was more like Broadmoor. Bedlam. Mentally ill people all on one side with a security guard.'

I looked at his wrist, at the coloured band that said Priority. 'It looks like he's going to a festival.'

I went to get a hot chocolate from the vending machine. Too sweet, too hot. I texted Luisa.

What's happening now
are you ok?

I don't know what I expected. A formal thank you? A speech? A terrible reason to be proud of myself?

When I got back to the ward, there was a puddle of water next to the bed. His IV wasn't connected to the cannula, and the liquid was dripping directly onto the floor.

I looked at my phone, but the only message that had come in was one from Teddy.

Teddy. Shit. I opened it.

He'd ignored my what the fuck about how he'd used the survey. *Listen,* he'd written.

Your feeding the kids skit next week –
that needs to be knocked on the head.

What? I wrote now.
You're joking
it's one day and some cameras

401

Non negotiable I'm afraid.

Directive from the top.

Wrong kind of attention.

I stepped out into the corridor of the hospital and tried to call him.

Can we at least speak?

Nothing to talk about.

Hungry kids = bad optics for the gov

Whats more important?

Killing the short sale or doling out some happy meals?

End it

Later that evening I got a message from Ed saying he was heading to the airport.

One small wash of relief put its cool hand against my cheek. Now it was over I would never have to tell him what I'd done.

10

Sometime the next morning, Ed texted to say he'd landed. Then he texted to say he was in a car. The surfaces in the kitchen were dirty. I didn't want to clean them for him. I kept on seeing Flo's bruise bloom dark.

Every time I took a deep breath, it caught in my solar plexus, at the back of my throat, and in other places I didn't know my heart would be. It felt all broken up, a jigsaw puzzle with all the pieces slightly separate.

And then his key in the lock. His bag in the hallway. The thud then rattle of the wheels of his suitcase. He said my name, then called it. He came into the kitchen. All of it slowly.

'Hey,' he said, when finally I entered his line of vision. He waited for me to say something back. Both of us were silent for a moment. 'The whole way I've been trying to work out what to say. I don't know what to say. Your dad, why didn't you tell me about your dad? What happened? Is he okay?'

The day had arrived with a cold spell. Rain slapped at the windows. Ed's cheeks were rubbed with wind. He pulled off his jacket, his too-long, tangled scarf. I thought of the red one in his book.

'Good question,' I said. 'Yeah. I don't know. Why didn't I seek comfort from someone who finds me—'

'Elle—'

'What's the right word? You're the writer.'

'It's not you—'

'Repulsive?'

'It's not *you*.'

'I doubt there's any other woman you've been pushing into like overripe fruit.'

'Haven't you read a novel before? The whole point is they're made up.'

'When that reviewer said you didn't have any women in your last book, I don't think *this* is what they meant—' I looked at him and he looked back at me. That was the worst part of it too: all the ways he'd looked at me, tried to see me, understand me. His attentiveness, the things I'd said that he'd written down, was that why? 'It's not even good, Ed.'

'I'm not saying it's good! I know it's not good. But it's not you. And the stuff with your dad happened before that. Why didn't you tell me?'

'Well, I had a few things on my mind.' The guardrails on the hospital bed. The flash of glitter in the thick laminate flooring. All the out-of-time beeps. I willed my brain to push them into his. Then new images replaced them: The bar. Flashcards of drinks. Luisa in bed in the morning.

'I'd have come right away,' he said. 'That's what this is. What it's supposed to be. I want to help.'

'The way you're making your eyes tear up! The way you convince yourself. Do you even know you're acting? Are you aware?' It burned in my chest. Pure and correct. 'Or are you so fucking good at it, it's just pure instinct?'

'I'm not acting. I like your dad. I care about him.'

'You've met him three times.'

'I didn't do this, Elle. Not to him. Please – could we be soft? Or just not like.' He banged two fists together, his knuckles hitting like rocks. 'Please.'

Neither of us said anything for a moment. He'd cut his hair short. I saw it now he took his hat off. 'Samson,' I said.

He touched it. 'Yeah. Some girl with overzealous scissors.'

'Some girl.'

'Please. Let's not. Where is it by the way?'

'What?'

'The manuscript. I just mean. Did you do anything with it?' When I didn't answer, he said, 'Whatever, it doesn't matter.'

'Can I just say it, directly?' I said. 'What I presume is the case—'

'You're looking at me like I disgust you, Elle.'

'Oh, and is that hard for you? Can I just speak?'

'Yes.' After the cold, the blood must have been rushing back into his hands. He kept flexing them, the movement people do in films after they've punched someone.

'All this,' I said. 'All this with me. It was just a perfect opportunity. A free house—'

'No. And I've contributed—'

'A free story.'

'That's not—' He kept shaking his head.

'I'm just sorry the research was so arduous, and I'm sorry that it was me.' I hadn't meant to get so upset.

'Say what you like but none of that's right. It's not true.' He looked behind him. 'I need water.'

He came back with two cups, one for me too. He always made the tap spurt, and there were droplets all over the edge of the glass. 'Your phone's going mad on the table,' he said. 'I don't know if you need to check with your dad. Work.' He sounded like he was speaking from under a bus.

'Am I tiring you?' I said. 'Are you oppressed?'

'No,' he said. He put his glass down on the table and wiped his hands on his trousers. I wondered, not for the first time, what it felt like in his head. If he saw colours differently. How he processed the distance between us. If he felt regret, and if so, what for? He passed me my phone.

I had four missed calls. All of them were from Luisa. Then my phone lit up in my hand right there and then. She was calling again. He saw me look to the garden for somewhere to go.

'Are you going to just take it?' he said.

'It's my mum, I need to speak to her.'

I went to the upstairs bathroom. I shut the door, then pushed the bathmat against the line of light along the floor that came in from the corridor. I'd missed the call, but called back, tried once, twice, three times.

When Luisa answered the phone, the line was silent at first.

'Hi ... hello?' I tried. I was whispering. I said it again louder.

Finally there was a 'hi', a tiny thing.

'Are you okay? What's going on? Did you give them ...' I couldn't say the money on the phone. Why the fuck was I standing in my bathroom wanting to say 'the money' on the phone? 'Did they get it?'

The line was silent again.

'Lu, this isn't funny—'

I checked the door was locked.

'It's not enough,' she said.

'I gave you what you asked me for—'

But the line had gone dead.

11

When I went back downstairs to Ed, he said my mum had called. 'On my phone. She said yours was engaged.'

I looked at him.

'She said he's spoken a few words,' he went on. 'Drank some protein shake. Said we should visit. That he'd like that. Who were you speaking to?' He said them all without any variation in tone.

'Flo,' I said. I either said it too fast, or too slow. 'Something happened to her last night.'

'Look – can we just be honest?'

'Why would I lie about that?'

'I saw the name on your phone. I've seen it before. Just please. If it's all broken anyway, please just tell me the truth.'

And how did I see him? How did colours work in my brain? Did I see him with regret? And if so, which part?

'It's just a girl from work.' On cue, my phone lit up in my hand.

'We're having a conversation,' he said.

'She's in trouble,' I said, and I left the room.

She told me they'd been waiting round the corner from her house. She said one had grabbed her from behind with his forearm round her throat, and while she was struggling to breathe, the other had slapped her, and lifted up her legs. They made her go with them. No one was around.

She said that right now she was in one of the places that we'd been together. The ice cream one, she said, Finsbury Park. 'But it's daytime, so it's empty. I need more money,' she said. 'I don't want to do this but I have to. My battery's dying.'

'What's happening?' From the changes in the volume on the line, I could tell she was covering the microphone on the phone when she wasn't speaking. I could hear the gaps in between her fingers. 'Who are you with?'

'It doesn't matter,' she said, her mouth pressed against the phone. 'I need money. And you have it.' Her voice was breaking. 'And you owe me.' Her fingers over the phone again. There was definitely someone in the room with her, more than one person. 'Don't make me list it,' she said. 'Don't make me say it.'

'What do you need?' I said.

I looked up and saw Ed. He looked at me. I could tell him to leave, but it already felt too late.

'Just tell me,' I said.

She said a number. Then she made the number higher.

'I'll send a pin,' she said, and then she hung up again.

'Are you okay?' Ed said. He didn't look angry. It looked like it had fallen out of him. 'Can I help?' he said.

Anger came for me instead, a pointless spear. 'I don't need your help,' I said.

'Well someone needs yours ... Is it Flo?'

'Yes,' I said, then, '—no. No.'

12

How long Luisa texted, after sending the pin.
    And when I didn't reply right away,
    You made me go to bathroom at work, she said.

                                        I am coming

    and send you a picture of me
    with my fingers inside myself
    We were at work
    I put my phone on airplane mode, then knew it didn't change any-
thing. What could I say to any of it?

                                        I'm coming, I wrote again.

'She gambles,' I told Ed. This is what I said back in the kitchen. She
gambles, comfort in the clarity of that.
    'Online?' he said. Funny how he said it. Boldly. Like he wanted to
know something about it.
    'Maybe. I don't know. But in person too. There are all these places
in London,' I said, 'you would never know.'
    'But you know,' he said. It wasn't a question.
    'I did go with her.' I chose my tenses so carefully. 'Once or twice.'

'And now what, she's been kidnapped by some criminals or something?'
I looked at him. 'Yeah, I think that just about sums it up.'

'Jesus Christ. And it's money. Money she needs, she owes or something?' This tiny tattoo on his face, and how far away he was from all of this.

'Thirty k,' I said. 'I don't have it.' What was the point in lying now? 'I gave her what I have accessible.'

'And how much is that?'

'Ten,' I said. I might as well say it. 'Fifteen. I can get the rest at some point, but it's all tied up—'

'Why's it on you?' he said, and when he saw my face he said, 'And what the fuck do they even want? Cash in a bag? Like some bad 1970s BBC drama?'

'I don't know.'

'You need the police.'

'She does owe them money.'

'As far as I'm aware, I know things are a bit fucked at the moment, but you're still not allowed to kidnap people,' he said. I was standing up by then. I looked through to the hall. His bags were still in the doorway, a neat pile. 'How old is she?' he asked.

'It doesn't matter.'

'Just tell me how old she is.'

I said her age, and he did the maths. Luisa was his sister's age exactly. The age she would have been.

'Whatever you're doing,' he said, 'you're not going alone.'

'Here we go—'

'Look, please don't be an idiot. Honestly.' He was shaking his head. 'This has been happening for countless millennia. Big idiot men squaring up to big idiot men – and now's the time for it to stop? You hate everything about this – me being a man – so at least let it serve you one single purpose.'

410

'I don't hate it. I didn't hate it.'

'What's the address?' he said. He put his jacket back on.

I had to find it on Google Streetview. I knew it was on a corner. I knew there was a graveyard opposite.

'Oh, good,' Ed said. He took my phone. Zoomed in, scrolled around.

We drove through London. We were driven through London. Ed said 'mate' a lot to the driver when we got in, and I wanted to ask if he was practising, but apart from that we barely talked.

I looked at my phone and had one message from Luisa:

Please. Don't be too late.

On the way, I wrote back.

The hood of the car tilted up. The angle of the road. But it was the trees I recognised – the camouflage of hand-rubbed city bark. We were back on Camberwell Grove.

'Ed, no—' I said. The wasted time.

'Where did you think we were going?'

'First of all, it's too close. We've literally had meetings in my office. Second of all, he's a fucking lunatic—'

'What's your plan? Hit up a grocery store with a banana in your pocket? It will take weeks for me to access anything I have, but he told us about his fucking vault, didn't he? His 'cash basis' or whatever he called it. He'll do it for me. We can pay him back.'

'The last message I sent him basically said fuck off.'

'Well then say sorry. Say whatever you need to if you're really worried about this girl.'

'Got a next one,' the driver said, flicking his phone.

We didn't ring the doorbell. Ed sent a message. Eventually the door opened, the stained glass catching the light from inside in a wave. Teddy in a white shirt. 'Come in then,' he said. He avoided my eye, or I thought he did, perhaps because I was avoiding his. 'No time for tea, I imagine,' he said. We walked through to the kitchen. 'Ed filled me in a little bit by message. Frankly, the less I know the better.'

'It's just a debt,' I said. 'A debt that needs to be paid quickly.'

'The main question is how much,' he said. 'And what's in it for me?'

'I'll pay you back. All of it. I got a good equity model. When we go public, I'll—'

'And that's going well, is it?' Teddy said.

His daughter appeared in the doorway. Our eyes dropped to look at her.

'Bedtime, Daddy,' she said.

'Quiet, puppy,' he replied.

'She's just a kid in trouble,' Ed said. His eyes flashed towards the tiny daughter.

'Trouble of her own making. I don't care about all that. I care about what we've discussed.' He looked at me. 'Making it work.'

Teddy's daughter was at his calf now, assessing his knee for merit as a climbing frame. 'Baby, this is a time for adults,' he said. I watched him look at her and assess things too. Assess what she might be able to understand. Assess how long it would take to put her back to bed. Assess how quickly he could get this to be over. He took her onto his lap. 'Look, I'm sure some of your younger, more radical staff wouldn't be too jazzed about our allyship, but with the survey for example, we were quiet about the connection to Gigr and,' he shrugged, 'if it's true, it's true.'

'They were leading questions asked under false pretences,' I said. 'The world isn't falling apart because Gigr drivers eat burgers—'

'And so? What impact does it have? It's yesterday's news, digital chip paper now.'

'You wouldn't have done it if it didn't mean anything. It matters when there are food shortages. And people in parliament are floating ideas of one child policies like its 1980s China—'

'Well, what's wrong with putting pressure where it needs to be?'

'The right place is industry. You know that. And I don't get why we can't feed some kids?'

Ed put his hand on my shoulder. Teddy let out a laugh. 'It's all so … tiny,' he said. 'Look. Bigger picture!' He lightly bounced his daughter on his knee. 'In slightly more important news, it's all lined up. I got it signed off today. We can start to put the Short Seller Regulation into motion and make the climate temperate for you. And you need that, don't you?'

There was more I wanted to say but I swallowed it down, Ed's hand still on my shoulder.

'How else will you pay me back if you don't get your little payout?' Teddy said. 'But it all has to come together. The other business we've discussed. Your slightly strange colleague Jason. That's the thing that needs to happen. Our meeting with Daniel's in two weeks, correct? And afterwards, just the same: action.'

He was nodding. That politician's nod that induces it in other people.

'A lot of it is outside my control,' I said.

'But you'll push for it,' he said. There was no choice in the way he said it. 'It's a win for both of us.'

'Boring, Daddy,' his daughter said.

The cash was with the wine. 'Rather gauchely behind the champagne,' Teddy said. I looked at Ed, *a gauche approach* must have run through both of our heads. 'I wouldn't have gone for that touch personally. Would have whacked it with the plonk.'

It could have been comical. He turned a bottle and a door opened. There was a safe behind it, both a code and a thumbprint required. Inside, the money was in stacks. There were dollars in there. Swiss francs, Chinese yuan.

'Does it have something funny about it?' Ed said. 'The money I mean. Will blue dye explode or something?'

'No, it's just money,' Teddy said. 'Classic old good-for-some-things money.'

Ed had his backpack in his hand. He opened it up. 'Do I just take it?' I said.

'For now, let's keep it simple,' Teddy said. He took a cocktail napkin from a stack on the sideboard, and he wrote on it, a joke I presume. *U O me.* 'Big time,' he added.

All the way to Finsbury Park, a rucksack at our feet, Ed's ankle through the armhole even though the door was locked, Ed never asked what there was between us. Luisa and me.

'I mean, for now I don't want to know,' was all he said. 'Not because of what you said before. That I didn't care. That it counted less or something.' He put his window down even though it was freezing out. 'Truth be told, I can't bear it.' He put his hand out, like he could catch the air and bring it back into the car which was suddenly far too hot. 'So let's just crack on.'

'You've never said crack on before.'

'And I owe you, too,' he said.

'The napkin was ominous—' I started.

'But really though,' Ed said. 'I do know I do.'

13

The road was empty. All the streetlights seemed dimmer than normal. But this was the corner, definitely. I remembered the tiles on the outside wall, swirling Victorian, the type that look almost glazed, all chipped now.

'So it's here,' Ed said. 'And you're sure it's here?'

'Can you not be so nervous? I can feel it physically.'

'It's the bag,' he said. 'It feels like some sort of flashing siren on my back.'

I looked at my phone again. A picture came through from Luisa. It was of her hand, someone's hand anyway. There were two bloody welts on it. A circle on the back of her hand, a crushed fingernail.

It must have been midnight by then. I opened the gate, loose on its hinges, I remembered that too, and made my way down the basement stairs. I banged on the door. Ed was behind me.

'Fuck off,' a voice shouted back eventually. 'Not fucking on today.'

'I'm here for Luisa,' I said. My voice sounded far more normal than I felt.

Silence. I looked around. A few cheap-looking cameras covering different angles. I rang the doorbell again, held down the button, until a guy opened the door, smaller than I would have thought. A zipped hoody on, and bad long hair that looked too loose for his head.

'Where is she?' I said.

'Easy—' he said.

'She's a kid,' Ed said.

'Well, she looks fucking legal to me.' He had an enormous vape in his hand, one of the big ones with the battery packs. 'I was about to say: come in.'

We followed him into the room at the end of the corridor. It was a back office – the big room I'd been in before was to the left, but there was a huge bike chain looped through the door handles.

'Why have you got her locked up?' I said. 'She weighs about ten pounds.'

'I wish she *had* fucking ten pounds. Anyway, she's not in there,' he said. 'She's got her own private quarters. Phones,' he said. He had a bubble tea in his hand – a giant plastic cup of it. He took a suck.

'Why am I gonna give you my phone?' Ed said. The change in his voice. I thought of what he'd said about posh boys pretending not to be posh.

'Ed whatever, just hand it. Look, I just want to give you money,' I said to him. 'Money. Then I want to get her, and get out.'

He made us unlock our phones then put a cable into each one.

'What the fuck is that?' Ed said.

'Chill, man,' he said. 'Scanning for any outgoing calls we don't wanna see. Nice,' he said. He tapped away at a computer. 'Also take some of these for just in case, y'know.'

He flipped his computer screen around, and there were pictures Luisa had sent me on it. Pictures I was sure I'd deleted. 'And there was me thinking you was sisters,' he said.

Ed stood taller, swallowed.

'Yours is clean, bruv.' Ed's phone was thrown back to him. 'You gay or what?' He laughed.

'I'm not giving you anything 'til I've seen her,' I said.

He blew a smoke ring that seemed to swell and shrink like an octopus. 'So let's get it done then.'

He took us downstairs another floor, which meant we were two floors below ground. He peered in through safety glass and gave a knock on the door.

'Everybody decent?' he said.

Luisa was on one side of the room, on a chair. The two men were on the other. A TV was showing *The Crown* of all things, the sound blaring, but both men were on their phones, staring down, fixated, the way babies are. There was no rope. She wasn't gagged or anything. But I looked at her hands and one was bleeding.

It was dirty even in the dark. It smelled of over-used air.

'Hey—' Luisa said, she went to stand up, but one of the two men, both bald and brick shithouse set, said 'oi'. And she sat back down.

'They good?' one said. Same heads, two different accents. One English, one Portuguese maybe, or Brazilian. ''Cos who are you? I don't know you.'

'I just know Luisa,' I said.

'Know her well enough to buy,' the guy replied. 'I give tip. Don't give her more money after this. She's not good for it.'

'I just want to go,' Luisa said.

'It's thirty,' the English one said, 'and that's being kind. That's fucking generous, isn't it?' he said in Luisa's direction. 'Rounding down for old time's sake.'

Ed opened the bag, and I took out the stacks. It looked a lot smaller than you'd imagine. It wouldn't fill a bath. It would barely coat the bottom of a sink.

'We don't take fifties . . .' the long-haired guy with the vape said. I looked up. 'Look at your face!' he said. 'I'm kidding. His watermelon fog hit the rest of the air. He checked a few notes with a UV pen. He looked at serial numbers. 'It's good,' he said. He handed over the bag. 'Gotta be careful with the megafakes these days. Criminals everywhere you look.'

The bald men stayed in the basement. We went up the two flights of stairs. Vape guy first, then Ed, then Luisa, then me. My brain estimated how many steps to the door, maybe ten, we were so close, when Ed pushed the vape guy back into his office, and smacked the vape out the way, a proper backhand that made me think of table tennis, so he could put his hand over his mouth. He pushed him down on the desk.

'Make a scene and someone's going to end up dead,' Ed said. 'You've got your money – now fucking delete the pictures.'

Luisa looked at me, I shook my head. I thought very clearly, the way I had in that car with Bonnie, *we are going to die here.*

Ed let the guy sit up, and his hands moved at speed and force over the keyboard, soldiers running.

'Don't you like them?' he said, pictures back on the screen again. 'For prosterity.'

'Posterity,' Ed said. 'Fucking delete it.'

The man pressed delete. 'There you go, you cunt.'

'Empty the trash,' Ed said. 'Do it on Keybox too.'

'Look who's an expert. Worry about this one,' the man said.

'You got what you want and it's done,' Ed said. 'Just be decent. Let it fucking go, now,' and as he said that, he let go of the guy's top.

I went to the hall, checked the front door was still open, then called for them both to come.

'What the fuck was that?' I said to Ed, but I looked at him and this thick slice of love swelled back.

'Let's get out of here,' Ed said, and he walked ahead of us. 'Turn some corners, I don't know.'

We walked, we ran. I imagined the sound of feet behind us. The way my heart was beating didn't sound normal, it shook my whole body. Luisa wasn't wearing a coat. I gave her my jacket. She wasn't wearing shoes meant for outside. Her good hand held her bad hand. 'I think they would have done it,' she said.

'What?'

'Killed me. Maybe. Who is he?' Luisa said, pointing forward.

'He's Ed,' I said. 'He's—' I wanted to say it. Or I didn't want not to.

'Don't worry about it,' Ed said from up ahead.

14

Luisa didn't want to go back to her flat. Ed sat in the front, up with the driver. Luisa and I sat either side of the backseat, and we all looked out of different windows, each of us pushed to the furthest edges of the car. I said A&E would be good, but Luisa said she would go to hospital the next day, she couldn't take the wait now. 'Ice maybe,' she said, 'if we can find some.' Her voice was shot through with sadness.

It was our home we took her to, and Ed gave her a glass of orange juice when we got back like he could see she needed sugar. He brought her food too, even if she didn't eat it. She sat at the table, her back like a forward slash, and I watched him operate around her with a blankness of sexuality and a quietness and a tenderness and thought: *you would be a good father.*

I think I expected Ed to sleep in the study, but he came in with me. I was already in bed. I heard him take off his clothes. I tried to work out what each sound meant – his T-shirt, his socks, his feet touching back down on the floor.

'Thank you,' I said to him.

'Let's just sleep,' he said.

He held me in his arms from behind. He pressed his face against the back of my head. 'Your feet are cold,' he said. I pushed them into his legs. 'If I don't fall for a while, it's jet lag.'

15

When I went downstairs in the morning, I thought there was every chance that Luisa would have packed up her things and left in the night, but she was still fast asleep on the sofa, and I didn't want to wake her. She looked even younger when she slept. It's weird what comes into your mind. Once, on a teenage holiday with a friend's family, we'd been on a boat that was tossing and turning in the water, and my friend's younger sister was so terrified that she fell fast asleep. The way she slept – a sudden, unstoppable decision to leave – that was how Luisa slept too.

The formerly frozen peas were flopped on a plate by the sofa. Her hand was above the duvet, dried blood outlining each of her finger-nails. I wondered what the truth of her life was. Was this the first time it had happened? Would it be the last? What made her happy? Had she really ever liked me?

When she came to, she stayed silent on the sofa, like saying something, or getting up, would increase the volume of the interruption.

'You okay there?' Ed said to her. He came into the room freshly showered, his clothes on. 'I put towels for you on the radiator. Might be good to clean up the hand again, and see what we're dealing with.'

'I can make some tea,' I said. It was impossible not to replicate those patterns: two parents, a kid. Because that was the pattern that made most sense of the three of us. The things I found myself saying. Were you cold in the night? Would you like something to eat? An egg or something. Protein.

Sometime early that morning, Teddy sent contracts with a Gigr courier. *On brand*, he'd written on the outside of the envelope. The courier waited while I signed, so I barely had the chance to read it.

'I know he's a piece of work,' Ed said. 'But like I said, apocalypse game.'

The contract had a Post-it on it, saying *Promissory Note.*

'He just texted,' Ed said. 'Said there's a second envelope in there too.'

I'd just found it. On the front, another Post-it said *Figured this is something you might need.*

Ed flashed me his phone. *Added a freebie*, Teddy had said. *Not sure what the situation is with Elle's . . . friend, but an NDA if she needs one.*

'Wait, what was that he said after?'

'It was just a joke.'

I scrolled down, and it said *Epstein lite.*

I didn't want to ask Luisa to sign it. When she was ready to go, we left the flat together. I said that I would see her out. I had the paper in my hand, behind my back, but in the end, she said it all for me. 'I'll ask to change teams,' she said. 'What I said in the messages. I didn't mean it.'

'It was all true—'

'But I didn't mean it. I had to. But I promise I won't say anything.'

It wasn't fair. Of course it wasn't fair. Her begging me. And that's what it was. 'I won't say a word,' she said again. 'I promise. I promise forever.'

'Let's just – it's okay,' I said. 'It can all be over.'

She was wearing one of Ed's jumpers he'd given her to sleep in last night. She turned back and for one moment I thought she was going to kiss me, but she gave me a hug. Is there a world where that felt good, like somewhere along the line I had done something for her? It did not feel good. She had lost weight. I felt in that moment like I knew where each of her bones were under her clothes. I thought of a bird I had heard of once in France. A songbird, tiny, that rich people would eat whole, bones and all, under a dark cloth or napkin. To preserve the aromas they said, or to protect god's eyes from the sin of it.

I watched Luisa go. I stayed standing in the garden until she was out of sight, and then for a while after that. The mirage of it, the madness. How it would have been a miracle if it hadn't also been the worst thing. Why does it happen? The catch, the explosion. Nothing, then everything, and you would give it all, all of it, away.

Vertigo. I had stood at the edge of the balcony too, and I had also jumped.

16

Not long after Luisa left that morning, Ed left too.

'I think there are some things to sort out,' he said.

'That is—'

'An understatement, yes.'

He was going to stay with a friend. He'd taken his pinned-up notes down from above the desk and they were like a deck of cards in his hands. His bags from the residency never got unpacked, he just added new ones to them.

He'd come to see my dad with me if I needed that. If I wanted him to stay, he would. If I needed to borrow money, of course he could find it.

'You have a lot to deal with,' he said. 'I mean like Flo, work—'

I remembered how, for a while, I could look at him, look right through his pupils until it bounced back and hit the back of my chest. 'Yeah,' I said. 'Yes.' I looked at him and I was sure it would happen again if he looked back at me, but he looked away.

When the car arrived, he carried his bags two by two out of the house.

'In a rush?' I said. I wished so much that I could stop myself.

It felt like a cut when I realised. Crazy how it can all telescope out so far then shrink back to so small a unit of time, but when I looked at the date, I realised it was a year to the day since we'd first met.

'See you soon,' Ed said. He kissed the top of my head, right in the middle of it, and for a second, or maybe two, his arms made their world around me.

17

It was two weeks after that, that Daniel finally got to meet the contact. We met with Teddy at 70 Whitehall. We were brought up to a room on the second floor.

'Natural light,' Teddy said, hands out to welcome us. 'What I hear they call "windows". Hugely exciting.'

He shook Daniel's hand, and kissed me on each cheek more quickly than ever before. I thought about the last time I'd seen him.

'Straight to business, shall we?' he said. We sat round a table wide enough for people to say what they wanted. 'I thought it was important we meet. Face to face. As you know, we've put through the Short Selling Regulation on the basis that it's a prerogative of the current government to see UK business thrive.' He moved his neck from side to side, hard chiropractor clicks. 'We do not want to see you fail. And we certainly don't want anybody to be embarrassed.' He said it carefully: emphasis on *see you fail*, emphasis on *embarrassed*. 'And that's where the IPO is starting to look a little concerning . . .'

'We have it covered,' Daniel said. 'There are a few calls to make, to make sure things are double, *triple* solid, but we have the numbers.

Obviously I *understand* the worry—' His 'I'm hearing you' hands came out.

'I'm here with good news, actually,' Teddy said. 'I've floated some partial ideas with Elle, and we've been running numbers here and there. Listen, Daniel, speaking on behalf of the powers that be, we're interested in partnership. Coming on as one of the pillars. Making Gigr a success. A success for everyone.'

This is what Teddy wanted. The government would come in as a major silent partner. In return, they would get a white label Gigr platform, and unrestricted access to algorithm. All of it for free. 'Govtech is booming,' Teddy said, 'but we'll wrap this up in a way that gives us insulation. Never fun to have the public breathing down the back of your neck.' He smiled. 'What we're after is profit and procurement in a one-two punch. As you know, the weight of the public sector is wringing British taxpayers. But this model – your model – would give us something lighter. Something light enough to stay afloat.'

'Right.' Daniel swallowed.

'Teachers, nurses—' he said it like they were flotsam in the air, 'just nips and tucks, here and there, for now—'

'But we'll come to an arrangement? Financially, I mean.'

Teddy looked at him. 'It's a pretty good arrangement that you survive, isn't it?'

'That's—' Daniel said. 'I'm not being ungrateful. I mean, we can license you the technology. But our IP for our IPO? I have investors. I can't swing that. Look, the numbers aren't going to be a problem,' he said. But he didn't seem sure, even to me.

'Right,' Teddy said. 'Of course, of course.' He was nodding. 'And on our side, we don't read emails. Of course. But if we did read emails . . .' He left it in the air. 'There would be lots of things we would want to know, wouldn't there?'

I looked at Daniel. He stayed still, and then I watched him deflate.

'I'll keep it crystal,' Teddy said then. 'We know what Marshall had. Where the bodies are buried, shall we say. What he was going to use to sink you.'

Daniel nodded slowly. 'I see what you're saying,' he said.

'No need to rush into anything, of course. Take a minute, have a thought. Consult who you need to. But yes, the advice I typically give someone in your situation, is . . .' he said to Daniel, to both of us actually. He stopped and smiled. 'Don't be catastrophically stupid.'

Caius tapped an imaginary watch on his wrist. 'Oh, how's our dear friend Ed by the way?' Teddy said then, looking squarely at me. 'He came in the other day to help out. These writer types, eh? Amazing to see in action. Pen like a knife.' He did a samurai thing, and made a swish sound with his mouth.

Behind Teddy, two new people entered the room, one old, one young, both lawyers.

'*Après moi, le déluge,*' Teddy said. 'Or rather, just a few little bits of paperwork . . .'

18

The lawyers spoke to us for five minutes, then left a sea of papers on the table.

It wasn't just the IP for the IPO. It wasn't just using the platform to undercut the public sector. It wasn't just cancelling campaigns to feed kids, and stopping people protesting, and all the other ways we'd given them what they asked for.

One of their old demands surged back again. They presented it as an 'amnesty'. They wanted the names and addresses of anyone working on the platform who was suspected of being irregular.

'What do you mean by irregular?' I asked them.

'Illegal primarily,' the woman said. 'But there are other things we're looking for – expired paperwork, admin hold-ups, criminal records. People whose presence in this country isn't in the public interest.'

'So you can do what?' I said. 'Mass deportation?'

'That's not the language we use anymore,' she replied.

In return, they told us, not only would the IPO deal go ahead, but since we'd co-operated, they would refrain from imposing millions – and by millions, it was in the tens of millions – in fines and legal fees.

'Fines for what?' Daniel said. 'Technically, we don't employ anyone.'

'That's irrelevant as you're aware,' the lawyer said. 'The Immigration, Asylum and Nationality Act 2006 prohibits facilitating illegal working, regardless of contract type. The onus on verifying immigration status is on you. Names and addresses,' she said again.

'I hate it too,' Daniel said after they left to let us decide, 'you know I do. But there's appetite for it. There just is. Voracious. That *is* what the people want at the moment. To get,' he lowered his voice a token amount, 'a lot of these people out. We all know it – our Gigr guys who don't speak much English, the abuse they get these days—'

'We talked about that, Daniel. We were going to do something about that.'

'And that big backbencher guy – what's his name?'

'The one who literally says shoot them on sight?'

'But have you seen the polls? He's shooting *up*. Angling to maybe lead someday – who knows what will happen to the woman.' Daniel always called Michaela Liddle 'the woman'. 'I reckon they'll Kennedy that shit soon enough—'

That was the thing. It's not that he was excited, but I saw him do the calculations live.

'We either go ahead or we don't,' he said. 'And if we don't – look, don't isn't an option. We can take the hit. I think we can. The ones we'll lose are the most effective, those guys go for hours. It's, what,' he said, 'the fifteen percent of the base that do forty percent of shifts? But . . .' In his head, another run of maths, 'if we take over in the public sector, the numbers will work out – we can get the utilisation rate way up. And the thing is, we can do it now there's such high demand. We can fill it with legal Brits in a second,' he said.

'I'm not worried about filling it, Daniel. You know what happens, don't you? They turn up at their door. They arrest children.' Those immigration raid flyers I'd found in the takeaway: that advice felt ancient, utopian. These days they broke the door down right away.

'Yeah, but now, right now they're not actually killing them or anything. They're not actually shooting them. What was the thing that minister said the other day, that wanky Shakespeare thing? "We shall be called purgers not murderers". The Julius Caesar thing. We're just purging,' he said.

'So they work for you for years, for nothing, and then you help throw them into cages?'

He started to get angry then. 'What about *you*? *You* don't work for nothing. You work for a lot. What do you think I was paying you for? To be fucking hard-nosed,' he said. I watched him do it, put the puzzle together in a way that made sense. 'With ID cards coming in soon, their days are numbered anyway. It's just a nudge along,' he said. 'The last people who got here. Doesn't it make sense. If they're the first ones to leave?'

'You're American,' I said. He ignored me.

'Now things are tight. Maybe we just give them half,' he said, then, 'No.'

'Exactly, Daniel. Please. No.'

'No. Yeah. We need to give them everyone. Do as they say. Get it just done. Get them all together in one place maybe. Get their ICE thing to come. Just get it done.' His eyes flicked up at me, then away. 'The market cap is eight bil. This is big-boy talk. It's not cry me a river.'

'Daniel – fucking listen to yourself.'

'Don't swear at *me*,' he said. 'He's your friend, isn't he? Your *contact*. You fucking loved saying that, didn't you? It was you who brought me here.'

'If you sign that paper—' My voiced tripped, like someone skipping stones.

He took the pen. 'It seems like you've made your decision, and so I'll make mine.'

'I'll leave, Daniel.'

He looked at me. 'Oh *you'll* leave?' he said. He started laughing. 'You're already out. You've been in the War Room, haven't you? You knew it was the plan to pump and dump on the P&L. Lose a bunch of dead weight right before we float.' The way he looked at me. 'Did you think that you were invincible?' He started signing the papers. 'I'd say it's been a pleasure,' he said, 'but you've pretty much always been a bitch to me.'

19

I knew what would happen. I'd seen it many times before. Most often people lost all of their logins before they even knew they'd lost their job. But I refreshed my messages: I was still in for now.

There was a message from Jason.

Hey this isn't normal is it?

A PDF – 117 pages. Teddy's alternative costing project.

I can't read it all now, what exactly?

Their risk analysis

Screenshot?

This bit

He sent a zoomed-in version.

They want to take potential worker
deaths into account at something like 3–4%?

What?

Cos they're less trained
But they're ok with it? Just baking it into insurance?
Also, his case for West London is psycho.
Look

Another screenshot:

'Preserving the western edges of London has clear social, cultural, natural and human capital. In contrast, the Newham site has little merit in all aforementioned areas – if comparisons are to be made, it is a necessary casualty.'

TLDR: bunch of poor people in
Newham, let it sink

Have you already sent him
what he wanted? I wrote.

Yeah course
I just sent through everything

20

The thing was, I still had my key to the office.

As I said, all through the first days, all through the first crises, before I met Ed, it had given me comfort to get to the office before everyone else, as if time, for me alone, expanded. That next morning, I got there earlier than I ever had before.

My office. All of the things that had happened here. The photo-copier. Luisa.

She was the only person I could think of who would know how to do it. I wrote to her on the encrypted messenger we'd eventually used:

Can I ask you one last favour

Of course, she wrote back right away.

Can you help me with a login?

When I told her it was for the backend, she said I'd have no idea how to do it, and that she'd be there in fifteen minutes.

While I waited for her to arrive, I found myself walking to the boardroom. The handle of the door to the balcony had a keypad lock now and the code was 9999. I stood where I'd been standing when it happened, and I tried to make myself watch it from start to finish. I thought maybe it would be the best chance – and regardless, the last chance – I had to stop the single images, the jump-cuts, the close-ups. I tried to see the man who had jumped again, not just the headshot in his passport, but the whole him. His shoes, his body, his face. See him move. There had been something in his eyes that had been desperate. Maybe I should have guessed, but I couldn't have. I saw eyes like that so often in the people that worked for us.

We had sent – Daniel had insisted – an investigator to his funeral, and we'd received a transcript of the ceremony, as well as pictures from odd angles taken from a secret camera.

It wasn't just the man's son who worked for Gigr. It was his daughter, too, and his wife. And he had worked for us for a whole year as well, before he got sick. He was Iranian, had fought in the revolution. The family wanted the funeral to end in his own words. With the note he'd left. I'd read so many notes by then. *Throughout my years,* he'd written, *I have given my life for my children and my children's children. I will give the next life too.*

I heard a sound at the door. I turned and I saw her. She looked tired, beautiful.

'Shall we?' she said.

'You know that anti-capitalist communist party you always mentioned,' I said as we walked back to my desk.

'Hoped so,' she said. 'I thought you'd never ask.'

We sat side by side at my desk. I didn't tell her what had happened in the meeting. But I told her what we were doing, and she said 'cool', and then her fingers moved like water in a storm on the keyboard. 'And you're sure,' she said. 'Sure-sure.'

'Surest I'll ever be in my life.'

After we had done it, I asked her what she was going to do next.

'Go back to bed,' she said. She looked at the clock on the wall, it was still only 7 a.m. 'Not to be pessimistic, but I'm starting to have a *slight* suspicion I may have lost my job.'

'But after that?' I asked her. 'Your life.' It felt so big in my mouth – I wanted it to be big for her.

'Like a lot of people, I'm going to head home,' she said. 'Home-home. To my parents. Where I grew up.'

As I was leaving I saw Adnan coming out of the kitchen. 'Who employs you?' I asked him.

'Good morning—' he said.

'Is it us at Gigr, or an outside contractor thing?'

'It was another company, but it's you now.'

I didn't want Gigr to be 'you'. To be me. Not anymore. 'Are you legal here?' I said.

'What?'

'I don't care, but are you legal? Are your papers in order and everything?'

'I've applied but I'm waiting. Waiting five years now,' he said.

I told him what I knew, and I told him what we had done.

Who knew how easy it would be to reverse it. Who knew how many doors eventually would be burst through, how many mornings and lives split open. How many shoulders would be pulled out of sockets as the person called for their mother or their children.

But we had done what we could, too little, too late.

Luisa and I had gone through the database of Gigr contractors, and using the criteria Daniel had told me about several times by then, had changed hundreds of thousands of addresses. The people most at risk were easy to find, because they were the ones paid the least. And we changed all of their addresses to a single house: to Teddy's address, the tall, handsome building on Camberwell Grove.

~

It was six weeks after he carried his suitcases two-by-two out of my house, that Ed wrote to me and asked if I would like to go for a walk. Hard summer had come too early in May once again. Wriggling halos of heat haze on the pavement, and for the past two days, they'd closed schools because of the temperature.

As I walked to the place we had planned, I wondered what my body would do when I saw him. If it would act of its own accord and give something away. If I'd cry without wanting to. If I'd find it hard to speak.

It was a Saturday drenched in sunlight and the world seemed only to serve up people in groups: couples, families, friends. Barely anyone was alone on the street. The speed of this year, I'd noticed it more than ever before. The light staying open longer each evening – that's how I'd always thought of it – felt, rather than hope, like not enough had happened to deserve it. Rather than a beginning, more like the promise of an ending. Melancholic-aholic, Ed had said, but there was no pleasure in it anymore. I woke up earlier each morning. Early, early. So why did it all feel so late?

I did not cry when I saw him. I could still breathe. I took air deep into my chest. He was wearing a T-shirt I had sometimes borrowed. His trainers were snow-white new. His hair was shorter still. 'Necessity of the climate,' he said.

'The price we pay,' I replied. But I didn't want it to go wrong. 'You look nice,' I said after that.

'So do you,' he said. But it wasn't true. I had tried, because of course I had, but it was harder and harder to find my face in the mirror. I could see them now, my wrinkles, even in subtle reflections, the windows of buses, the screen of my phone. There came a moment everything was ten years ago, and soon it would be twenty. When I ran into people I hadn't seen for a while, I would say, it's Elle by the way, in case they didn't recognise me.

'You're still here,' I said. 'In London, I mean.'

'I'm actually a very realistic hologram.' He angled his body like I would be able to see it in the light. 'No but I'm glad I'm not in New York, that subway stuff is crazy.'

'It's horrible,' I said.

'It's good to see you—' he said too, or tried to. I felt in that moment like we were trapped in a bottle, an invisible wall around us, nowhere to go.

'Is it?' I tried to smile. 'I hate seeing myself. Walk or bench?'

'Walk, I think.'

We took the path in the shade. Around us, through the grass, desire lines left dusty arrows in a mess of directions. I asked him where he was living. He said he'd just signed for a place, and shifting into an excitement that felt more real, he showed me photos. Photos he'd taken himself, white walls, a stretched-arm photo of a crown mould-ing, carpets he said he was going to pull up. He held his phone in his hand so I couldn't scroll freely. He left it ambiguous whether he was renting or buying. Whether it was alone or with someone else. *Six weeks*, I thought. Who knows. Maybe.

'So you're sticking around,' I said, 'on this failing island?'

'It appears so. Front-row tickets for the apocalypse. Which, I admit, is no longer a game.'

He was right. Overwhelm. I had once been immune to it; now it came with the smallest thing. I had started to see a therapist, a real one. 'Maybe it's not that you're broken *now*,' she'd said. 'Maybe it's that you were broken before?'

'Well how can I break myself again?' I'd asked her. 'Bang my head against a wall in just the right place?' I was only half joking.

'How's your dad?' Ed asked me.

'My mum said you sent flowers.'

He nodded.

'They didn't *arrive*, obviously,' I said.

'Obviously.'

'But a neighbour dropped them round wilted a few days later.'

'You see,' he said. 'It's the thought that counts.'

'He's okay. I don't know if she's always that nice to him. It's hard to see it. But you know – oh—'

This is what my body did instead: a drop of blood fell from my nose and I caught it on my palm, and then others followed. 'It's dry air,' I said. But over the past six weeks, it had kept on happening.

It wasn't true that it was the first time I'd seen Ed since he left. I had seen him, but not spoken to him, his outline in the distance. An outline I knew from so far away.

'You didn't say hi at the funeral,' I said.

'I didn't know if you wanted me to.'

The blood spread in the tissue he had handed me, and his hand reached for my back.

It had happened four weeks ago. True again, true still, true as it had always been, that everything always happens all at once. In the early hours of a Saturday morning, on an anniversary of the day it happened at the Admiral Duncan, an explosion ripped through a bar both Ed and I had been to several times. Neither of us were there that night, but some friends of ours had been. Sean, Goran, Zay, AJ. Of the people we knew, Sean had survived, and Zay and AJ. Goran hadn't. It was how quickly it could happen, all of the minutes, and days, and words ahead, a whole life gone in a second.

The day after we heard the news, my mum called me. She so rarely called me. She asked where I was. I was so used to being defensive. 'I'm fine by the way,' I said.

'I'm in London,' she said. 'Your dad isn't well enough to come. But I wanted to.'

'To see me?' I asked.

'The protest,' she said. 'If you're going, and you want me with you, I'm there. Or I'm happy to go on my own.'

I said this to Ed in the park. 'What did you do?' he asked me.

We met, my mum and I, on a train platform and I'd never had a stronger sense that everyone, at least everyone who was there, was going in the same direction. Flags in pockets. Signs under arms. An old man, totally alone, with a walking stick. He'd written on a piece of paper, just a normal piece of paper, *never again*.

'We went together,' I said. Every time I'd looked over at her, I'd wanted to cry. 'She really shouted so loudly,' I said, this half-laugh, but really it was to stop me crying. 'You know Goran,' I said.

'I liked Goran so much.'

'He came here to—' and then I couldn't speak anymore.

'Escape things like this,' Ed said. 'I know.'

It was the stuff of horror films. Running from the monster into something even worse.

The peace of the park – the naps, the picnic blankets – was suddenly interrupted by dogs barking and their owners screaming, and it left adrenaline in the air.

'Teddy – do you still?' I said.

'Is your nose still bleeding?'

'I think it's stopping now.'

'Do I what?'

'See him—'

I knew the answer, but what I really wanted to know was, did Ed know what had happened? Since I left that day, I had not gone back. Was not allowed back, of course. I'm not sure about other doors, but my door they had come to. A team of five, black clothes and cameras on the lapels. They had taken my laptop safe, taken my phone, had sat me down at the table, and mummified me with NDAs. An ocean of papers. 'Sign everything, and it's over,' they said. Or was it 'Sign everything, or it's over?' Perhaps both.

What happened to you? Cal from my team texted me on my personal number a few days later, *they won't say anything at all about you! Like a desaparecido. Blink twice if they've taken you somewhere!* A day later he said *p.s if you get bored in exile, always a job for you, recruitment drive coming up ;)* He sent a picture of one of the butter-yellow Gigr worker outfits. I'd remembered the first presentation I'd seen of the brand on my induction day, the rationale for all the choices, like poetry analysis, but meaningless. On the Brand DNA slide, it had said, proudly, 'Yellow, in nature, is the sign of danger.'

'He was cagey about it, said it didn't quite work out,' Ed said.

'He and Daniel together are just – there isn't a word.'

'I know you have differences of opinion . . .'

'It's not opinion,' I said. 'It's not opinion what he wants to do. What he has done. Will do.'

'Everyone reads different things. I mean different papers. You know how it can be—'

'Please don't say echo chamber, Ed. Bless me with a gas chamber over that.'

I couldn't say the big stuff, but Ed had known about the hearts and minds plan to deliver food to schools and kids at home in the holidays, so I told him how Teddy's team specifically blocked it. 'They said it would highlight child poverty too much,' I said. 'Show the government in a bad light at a time when they needed *unity*.'

'There'd have been another reason.'

'Ed, he told me directly. That was the reason.'

'Let's not talk about him then—'

'You were working for him. You wrote for him. He told me.'

I saw it in Ed's jaw; it would be easy not to tell the truth. But he let the tension go. 'What's that word you always use about your work? Punch up. I punched up a speech. It was a favour. He's done me so many favours—'

'And who did the speech punch?'

'It didn't punch anyone, Elle. It was against the attacks.'

'Right.'

'And I don't know – for balance. You know with everything happening, he has this idea for a campaign. A kind of Public Service Announcement thing, it's not fleshed out yet, so I'm helping him.'

'Poster boy again?'

'No. I mean maybe, who knows. The idea the agency came up with was fucking dross. It was like "Jamie is a banker. Jamie makes the perfect roast potatoes. Oh, and he's also gay. It's hashtag okay to be gay." Embarrassing.' I hoped I wasn't imagining it: Ed looking embarrassed too. 'He wants to put together a group of advisors for things like this, you know, to curb some of the darker stuff that's happening. He wants "thinkers from different disciplines". I know it's wanky but at least he accepts they need help.'

'Please, Ed,' I said. I could feel the blood waiting, I was sure it would come again, 'please don't help him.' I'd never given a fuck about NDAs before but these ones – I couldn't risk it. Every penny you have, the man had said when I signed it, every penny your parents have, every penny you will ever have. And so I said the stuff everybody knew. 'It's so many things. The families being kicked out of London and shipped to the edge of the country as it's starting to sink.'

'If there's anything to help him with it's this though, right? You were at the funeral. You've seen the news.'

I had seen the news. It was the first time since the '90s that approval of gayness had dipped below fifty percent, a dive-bomb. Religion was on the rise, that was part of it too. To be expected: natural disasters and people looking up to the sky. 'Talk about a resurrection,' Flo had said, 'that fucker is back from the brink.'

'If people like you,' I said, 'people who are smart and kind, and I know you are, work with them, what hope do we have?'

'But you worked with him too,' he said. 'Look, I know it feels like it's from another time or place, but obviously it's needed. To me it's bigger. And sometimes, you ignore the smaller things for something bigger.'

'None of it's small though. The small things are massive.'

'I know,' he said. 'But so is who we love. What's the point in life but that? I don't know. People do good things and bad things. It doesn't make the good less good, or the bad less bad. It's always more complicated than you think.'

'I think I understand that things are complicated.'

The papers I had signed backtracked me out of a large proportion of my shares. I had got some money, a micro payout at a value way under even the strike price. And almost all of it I'd paid back to Teddy. I'd get a little more after the lock-up period, but two to three percent of what I'd hoped, and in the meantime, I was deep in credit card debt. I hadn't told my parents about losing my job yet, and the recruitment agency that had found me the Gigr work had long since shut down. Also, who knew the ways in which my name had been blacklisted?

Gigr would continue without me. Of course it would. And it would be even worse. Not that I had done anything close to enough to stop it. 'Anyway, I'm hardly a martyr,' I said.

'Have you seen her?' Ed said. 'The girl?' I tried to read how he was saying it. 'I think about her a lot. And hope she's okay.'

'Funny,' I said. 'Well, not funny. She had told me both her parents were dead. And, of course, they were not dead. Not rich she said, but they're paying for some treatment thing near their house. But no,' I said. 'I haven't seen her. Or rather, I saw her once. But not like that. Not at all.' I would give him that at least.

We were still walking. We must have walked for a mile by then, only stopping when my nose had bled. The grass in the distance looked bright green, perfect, and then each time, as we got close to the place we imagined we'd sit, it had welts of dust all through it.

'What will you do?' he asked me.

There were a million things I could have said. I felt old muscles start to work. 'Great time to be a funeral director,' I started. 'But no. I don't know. Just something better.'

'Unbelievable it was only a year,' he said then. The thing I had thought so many times since he had left too. 'Us,' he said. He said it like he'd been waiting to say it.

I thought of what I'd felt about Bonnie, that the architecture of that time seemed so much taller than the other building blocks around it. But what had happened with Ed, how it had blown everything open, then blown it apart – all of that, it towered.

I wondered if I could imagine sleeping with him. For a moment, after I dropped something in a bin, I walked ever so slightly behind him, so I could look at him without him seeing me. His forearms, I could imagine kissing them. The shield shape of his back, I could imagine holding it. But I didn't want him to turn around.

We did find a bench to sit on. The wood was new and there was a laminated note from the mother of the young man the bench was dedicated to. Ed took a picture of it, the link to a petition about the spiralling costs of student loans. Neither of us said anything for a moment.

'Strange what you end up thinking about . . .' I said.

'What?'

'The other day, I wondered if,' once I'd started I wished I'd stopped, 'I'd ever been pregnant. Not pregnant, it's not even pregnant at that stage, but if parts of us had touched inside me and started something, however brief. I just wondered. Not because I wanted it.'

'I don't know,' he said, 'a million things could have happened. I still don't understand any of it.'

'What I did?'

He didn't look at me.

'Not even. Us. Whenever I didn't understand it, and I didn't understand it a lot, I smelled the back of your neck, or the side of it, and it felt like peace. I don't know if that makes sense.'

It did make sense.

'Or if peace is the thing you're supposed to be looking for. But it was the answer to something, even if I didn't know what the question was. I'm talking in circles,' he said. 'The book's going to change – my book, I mean. It's already changed a lot,' he said then, 'it wasn't about you—'

Was it possible that that felt even worse?

'You have to write about whatever you want to write about,' I said.

'I know. But it's not what you know that you write about. It's not about what's happening often. Sometimes it's what you're scared of. What you're scared might happen. I don't know if you got to the acknowledgements?'

'I'm afraid it was the other bits I was focusing on—'

'I'm sorry if I'm frowning, I keep on getting this sharp pain – like all through here.' He touched his face. 'This curtain of it.' He held his hand there. 'I don't want the book to have a thesis because no book needs a thesis. But I wanted to show how real it is. Being gay I mean. Because it is real.'

'Of course it's real—'

'I mean you know it's real. But then it's just also: we want to make everything neat. But nothing's neat.' He took his hand away because it was shielding his eyes too and he wanted to see me. 'Anyway, the acknowledgements,' he said. 'It was mad to write them. Who knows if it will even be published. But it is – it is full of love for you. I wanted to acknowledge that it wasn't you. It was never you. But at the same time, I keep thinking about something you said once, and I think you're right. What's more happening than love?' he said.

I nodded.

'Love is the main story we all have,' he said. 'Love starting, love ending. Bending, breaking. However it happens.' His hand, open upwards on the bench, the way it was in the first taxi, when I'd held it. 'We tried,' he said then. 'Didn't we try?'

A year after that day in the park, certainly less than two – I'm trying to work out all the things that happened in between – Scotland voting again, sepia-toned skies, and the rain that came and came and came and wouldn't stop coming. In a closer way, I watched the world change by looking at what my neighbours on trains' screens said. Apps I hadn't seen before but the language lit up was violent. And in ways that felt like panic rising, the way I found that growing in me too.

Anyway, a year after that day in the park, Ed sent me a copy of the new book in the post. I was in the acknowledgements, and it's true it was full of love.

'Do you think one day we'll meet again and see each other through some window again and by some magic, all of the shit will have gone by then, and it could just be easy?' he'd said as we sat on the bench.

'I don't know. Maybe,' I said. 'If we keep the window between us.'

'We could be fifty, sixty,' he said. 'It could be nice. For an hour at least.'

'Soppy in your old age. Soppy already. I'm serious though. Is it easy for you to imagine that age? I have – I can have a feeling I won't make it.'

'You've always had that. I know you.' I didn't notice either of us moving, but the gap between us had got smaller. 'You forget I know you.'

He had known me. He knew me.

'Worried. You know I always saw, like—' He took a breath that caught at the back of his throat. He started again. 'One of the things I loved about you, is that I could see everyone you've been, and will be, in one place. That place being your face.' I didn't want him to look at my face, but there he was, and he looked, and he looked. 'All at once. Like I can see you as a child, and you now, and you as an old person, and all of it there,' he said. 'Here.'

The book he sent was a proof. It arrived in a plain envelope. It had a plain cover. Just the words of the title, and his name, smaller this time, against black. It was only the second time I opened it that I saw the dedication.

For Goran Takács, it said, *and the seventeen other boys who lost their lives that night.*

And for Elle, my only girl.

'You see me old?' I said to Ed that day in the park.

'I see you old,' he said. He nodded. 'I'll see you old.'

ACKNOWLEDGEMENTS

In this novel, Flo says that, contrary to certain truisms, it's not gratitude that makes you live longer, it's spite. I could not agree with this less. I started writing a version of this novel 8 years ago. It's a long time, and despite novel-writing being something you do largely and unavoidably by yourself, you never really do it alone.

Countless conversations with friends shaped *My Only Boy*. I loved talking to gay male friends, and friends of friends, some of whom had had an experience like this, or couldn't even begin to imagine one, and everything in between. Thank you for your transparency, openness, challenges and book recommendations.

This sounds wildly overblown, but I feel a sense of gratitude to every lesbian I have ever met, and also seen. I am grateful that I saw ways to be before I came out, and I am grateful, still and always, to see my own life reflected. It has been a great privilege to be part of close friendship groups with other queer women that have shaped the way I understand myself and who and how it is possible to be. Thank you to Nadja for being the most constant, and often founding, member of these groups. (Friendship is going to a prevailing theme here.)

I am grateful to my agent Karolina Sutton for both expansive and painstaking reading. I truly believe you care about this book, and that means a huge amount to me.

I am grateful to my editor Chris White, for his faithfulness, rigour and imagination. That faithfulness part is so important, and often rare, for a writer. Thank you to the whole team at Scribner UK, all the people working behind the scenes who leave their mark on a book and guide its journey into the world who we often never get to meet - copyeditors, sales teams, people working at the printers, people working in warehouses. Thank you to Annabel Robinson and her colleagues at FMCM for being such a tireless, thoughtful part of the team.

Thank you to the Society of Authors for their K Blundell grant, at a very crucial time.

I am grateful to Kayleigh Llewellyn, and every single person involved with *The Dream Lands* show, for changing my life. Even though, as a writer, self-doubt still sets in and runs deep, you've created a bright well of something good and still-unbelievable to me that I can return to forever. Kayleigh, continue to be at the epicentre of miracles.

I am so grateful to dear friends who read early drafts of this book, that hard, risky job, and who helped me in innumerable ways: Leah (I am so sorry you always have to go first), Leila, Ralph, Teo, Elle (I am sorry for stealing your name *and* your sister's name, which I didn't realise until you pointed it out), and Holly. Each of you changed the book for the better - thank you.

Leila, it is tradition to have you in the acknowledgements twice, and here it is again. Thank you for knowing a lot more about IPOs than I do. Thank you for so many things.

Thank you to other people who spoke to me who would prefer to remain nameless - I understand why, and I'm indebted.

Elle's father, in this novel, has a stroke. My own beloved father had a stroke too, years after I wrote those sections of the novel. (In my next book, rather than anything bad happening to the main character or their family members or the world around them, everyone is simply going to become very rich and very good looking, and the world will be at peace). It feels important to me to acknowledge that despite this one particular overlap, the parents in this book are not based on my own. I love you both so much, and I'm so grateful to you. Parts of me live in different places. Often I will shut my eyes, and imagine myself with you both in your garden in Ramsgate.

I am grateful to my mother-in-law Butch, for the bounty of support and kindness she has shown me. Every day we think about David, and we wish he were here.

There will be people I do not know I should thank yet. Books are made by booksellers, by librarians, by readers who find something that resonates with them and mention the title to a friend. I am thankful to whoever you are who is reading this. A book takes so much time, hours of it: I do not take that time for granted.

I am grateful beyond words for my family, Leah and Mara, and the friends who are like family - you are the poi